Dear Reader,

They say that people a[...] it's a small village on th[...] [...] mining town nestled in the mountains, or a whistle-stop along the Western plains, we all share the same hopes and dreams. We work, we play, we laugh, we cry—and, of course, we fall in love . . .

It is this universal experience that we at Jove Books have tried to capture in a heartwarming series of novels. We've asked our most gifted authors to write their own story of American romance, set in a town as distinct and vivid as the people who live there. Each writer chose a special time and place close to their hearts. They filled the towns with charming, unforgettable characters—then added that spark of romance. We think you'll find the combination absolutely delightful.

You might even recognize *your* town. Because true love lives in *every* town . . .

Welcome to *Our Town*.

Sincerely,

Leslie Gelbman
Editor-in-Chief

OUR·TOWN

CROSS ROADS

CAROL CARD OTTEN

JOVE BOOKS, NEW YORK

CROSS ROADS

A Jove Book / published by arrangement with
the author

PRINTING HISTORY
Jove edition / December 1996

The Putnam Berkley World Wide Web site address is
http://www.berkley.com/berkley

ISBN: 0-515-11985-7

A JOVE BOOK®
Jove Books are published by The Berkley Publishing Group,
200 Madison Avenue, New York, New York 10016.
JOVE and the "J" design are trademarks
belonging to Jove Publications, Inc.

PRINTED IN THE UNITED STATES OF AMERICA

10 9 8 7 6 5 4 3 2 1

This book is dedicated

to

My soul mate, Ruth Lynch,
whose little jingle inspired,
"I think I can, I think I can;"

My critique partner, Martha Kirkland,
who said,
"You certainly can;"

and

The love of my life, Ray,
who said,
"There was never any doubt."

THE VIOLET

"The violet in her green-wood bower,
Where birchen boughs with hazels mingle,
May boast itself the fairest flower
In glen, or copse, or forest dingle."

—SIR WALTER SCOTT

CROSS ROADS

Prologue

"It won't be long, I promise." Seth Thomas Rowe smiled affectionately at his younger brother, Jedwin.

The two young men stood beneath the shed at Union Station waiting for Seth's train to leave. Jed's freckled face mirrored the gloomy weather outside, and Seth could well understand the boy's unhappy expression. Leaving Jed behind wasn't going to be easy.

"But why can't I go?" Jed asked. "I won't be no trouble." He pinned his older brother with eyes the same mahogany color as his hair.

"We've been over this a dozen times, Jed." Seth jammed his hands into his pants pockets. "I have to go to Florida alone. I'll find us a place to live and then I'll send for you."

Tears pooled in the child's eyes. "You won't come back. Just like Father." Holding his small shoulders rigid, Jed turned away from Seth, adding with a whisper, "And Mother."

Seth moved behind his brother, placed his hands on the boy's narrow shoulders, and squeezed them gently. "I will come back. Or better yet, you'll come to me. Just as we planned."

At the moment, Seth would have given anything to have been able to tell his father what he thought about his cowardly way out of a bad situation. They had all suffered from his father's mistakes, but ten-year-old Jed had been the real victim of the family tragedy. Caught in the storm's surge, Jed had been uprooted by a rush of circumstances that had left his young world tottering. He'd lost everything: his parents, his home, and his security.

Leaving Jed today would be the most difficult thing Seth had ever done. But there were no alternatives. For eight months he had searched in New York City for a position, but no one was willing to hire a twenty-eight-year-old engineer with no experience. Especially when he was a rich man's son who had never worked a day in his life. Seth needed this job as overseeing engineer for the Pensacola & Atlantic Railroad, which was being built in Florida. His and Jed's future depended upon it.

"What am I supposed to do without you?" Jed's voice broke, and Seth knew he was fighting to hold back tears.

"You'll stay here with Aunt Cloe until I'm settled. Then you'll join me."

Aunt Cloe, their mother's sister, lived in Atlanta, Georgia, on a small income left to her by her late husband. Aunt Cloe had been kind enough to take them in when Seth had written her of their dire circumstances. The brothers had moved in with her before Thanksgiving. It was through Aunt Cloe's church that Seth had met Harriet Archibald while she was visiting friends in Atlanta. It was Harriet who had convinced her father to give Seth the job in Florida.

He dropped to his knees in front of Jed. Already the conductor had issued the last boarding call for his train, and Seth had to hurry.

"I want you to promise me you'll obey your aunt. I need your cooperation in this, squirt." He teased his sibling, hoping to lighten his mood. "Your *job* will be to stay here until I send for you."

Jed's chin fell. To better see into his brother's eyes, Seth lifted his face with one finger. Jed's downtrodden expression almost broke Seth's heart.

"It will only be for a month," Seth promised. "All that time, I'll be working as hard as I can to get us together again. Can I count on you, trooper?"

Jed's face grew even more glum. "You won't forget about me?" he asked weakly.

"I could never forget about you, Jed." He pulled the lad into his arms and hugged him. "We're family, and nothing can change that." He cuffed his brother on the chin.

"You'll write me?"

"Every day. And soon you will be heading south to join me."

A rush of steam from the train's engine clouded the air. A shrill whistle echoed beneath the covered structure, announcing the train's immediate departure. Seth jumped to his feet.

Aunt Cloe, who'd been standing discreetly away from her nephews, moved toward them. "Best you get going," she gently prodded Seth.

"Thanks for everything, Cloe. Some day I'll repay you." Seth hugged the older woman to him, wanting to say more but unable to find the words.

"My recompense is having two such fine-looking young men in attendance. You know, I'm the envy of all my friends." She tittered like a young girl.

Jed rolled his eyes heavenward before the brothers' gazes locked in understanding. They both loved their aunt, but sometimes her girlish antics seemed foolish to them.

Aunt Cloe shooed Seth toward the departing train. "Jedwin and I will be fine," she promised. "Won't we, dear?"

Her question demanded only one answer, which he heard Jed reluctantly give. "Yes, ma'am."

Seth hugged his brother one last time, then bounded toward the already moving train. From the step of the passenger coach he looked back at the two people on the platform and waved. Everything was going to be fine. It had to be. . . .

Chapter One

Viola Mae Smith stood just outside the General Store on Palafox Street, allowing the playful wind to tug at her hair. Her braid was proper, but too restrictive, and she felt a small but satisfying victory when she released the heavy plait. Above all things, Viola Mae believed a person ought to be free.

So much for her grannie's lessons on propriety. Not many people in the port town of Pensacola, Florida, thought much about Viola Mae, except when she did something less than proper. Like wearing her hair unbound. Then she could be sure some well-meaning soul would remind her of the error of her ways.

Viola Mae had long since stopped worrying about what people thought. Sometimes she did things deliberately, just to set tongues wagging. But today was far too beautiful to worry about appearances, or anything else for that matter.

Overhead, downy clouds floated in a crystal-blue sky. Viola Mae inhaled deeply of the early morning air, breathing in the briny scent off Pensacola Bay while enjoying the sun's warmth against her skin. Yesterday's rain was no more than a memory that lingered in the slightly humid air.

Pushing back her now-unruly locks from her face, Viola Mae caught a whiff of the shampoo she'd used last night. The scent of wild strawberry leaves and soap-bark chips still clung to her hair. She'd made the concoction herself, using her grannie's recipe.

Everything Viola Mae knew about herbs, whether it was

cosmetic, medicinal, or culinary, she'd learned from her grandmother. Her grannie had been dead well over two years now, and she still missed the wise old woman.

Stepping down from the planked sidewalk, she headed toward the Plaza Ferdinand. The latest edition of the *Pensacola Gazette* was tucked beneath one arm, and in her other hand she carried a warm, fragrant cinnamon roll wrapped in brown paper. Her mouth watered in anticipation of the sweet confection, but Viola Mae refused to sneak a bite until she was seated in her favorite spot beneath the shady oaks.

Finally she reached her destination. Plopping down upon a wooden bench, Viola Mae sighed with pleasure. Every week when she came into town to deliver her medicinal herbs and jellies to her friend Gracie for her to sell at the General Store, she treated herself to this respite. Viola Mae would buy the local news sheet and one of Gracie's homemade cinnamon rolls. Then, weather permitting, she would while away an hour or more before returning to her farm outside of town.

Viola Mae glanced across the square. This morning the plaza was empty except for several children who played in the gnarled trunks of the older trees. Their laughter floated in the morning air, mingling with the chatter of the fat brown squirrels that scratched among dried leaves and acorns. A mockingbird's loud *tchack* competed with the screech of gray and white gulls, as well as the other bird sounds issuing from within the overhead branches.

Removing the udeky cinnamon roll from its paper, Viola Mae placed both upon her lap. Then with two hands, she lifted the oversized bun to her mouth and took a bite.

"Yumm." She savored the sugary sweetness.

No matter how many times Viola Mae tried to duplicate Gracie's rolls, she couldn't. Hers never tasted as good, even when she followed her friend's recipe to the letter.

After Viola Mae had eaten the whole pastry, she licked her fingers clean before setting aside the empty wrapper and picking up the newspaper. Immediately her emotional feathers became as ruffled as the fat blue jays that bathed in the nearby fountain.

TRACKLAYING PROGRESSING ON SCHEDULE.

The headline glared at her from the printed sheet. Viola Mae scanned the article. It told about the grading and clearing of the woods taking place almost in her backyard.

For weeks now the sound of saws and men shouting and the blasting of the train whistles carrying supplies from the Pensacola port to the construction site had been enough to drive a sane person crazy. She wasn't the only one the noise drove to distraction. All the animal friends that she considered her charges had been chased from their homes because of the railroad's activities.

The beauty of the morning no longer held its appeal. She tossed the offending news article aside. Viola Mae was fed up with progress. Even Gracie's feathery-light roll no longer satisfied her, but instead felt like a heavy weight in her stomach.

Reminded of yesterday's discovery, she jumped up from the bench and stomped across the square toward the hitching post where she'd tethered her horse, Ginger. The memory bedeviled her thoughts as she mounted up.

Viola Mae had visited the small pond that bordered her property to gather some leaves from the cattails that grew beside the bank. She had promised her nearest neighbor, Earle Forbes, that she would repair his chair seats come fall. The leaves of the plant made good rush material, and she needed to gather them early for drying.

Cattails were an especially useful plant. In the spring, the plant's stems could be used for salads or boiled like asparagus. Viola Mae sometimes used its roots for flour or the starchy core of the roots as a potato substitute.

But yesterday the aquatic plants were no longer growing beside the bank. Only a few charred stalks remained. Someone had burned the cattails down to the water's surface.

From the debris scattered about, it appeared to Viola Mae that careless revelers had caused the destruction. She wasn't certain. One thing was sure, however; since the railroad crews' arrival, men and nature no longer existed in harmony.

This latest discovery had been the straw that broke the camel's back. Noise, plunder, and now wanton destruction. Viola Mae wanted the intruders out of her woods before they completely destroyed the natural habitat.

Something had to be done!

Needless to say, her letters of complaint to the railroad had achieved nothing. They hadn't even been acknowledged. Obviously Jay Arnold Archibald, the man who was in charge of the project, refused to take her grievances seriously. But she was serious, and if she hoped to rid her woods of the railroad and the two-legged varmints that came with it, it was time to take matters into her own hands.

Inside the Concord stagecoach, Seth Thomas Rowe shifted his position on the narrow seat. He'd been traveling for the last four days with five other passengers inside the small cramped compartment. He cursed his decision to take the train from Jacksonville, Florida, instead of the longer sea voyage around the peninsula. Especially when they had reached the town of Chattahoochee. There the tracks had ended, forcing everyone traveling further west to take the overland stage.

After days of grueling travel over washboard roads and through snake-infested swamps, Seth had begun to question his judgment about coming to Florida at all. But then he would remember his ten-year-old brother waiting for him in Atlanta, and knew he'd made the right decision. As soon as he found a place for them to live, he would send for the lad. Together they would make a home for themselves.

No wonder the railroad ended in Chattahoochee. As Seth stared through his window, he concluded it would be almost impossible to lay steel tracks through such wild undergrowth. Along the way, he saw evidence of deserted spurs, but most of the rails had been forgotten by everything except the rust that clung to them.

The coach's wheel dipped into a washout, and Seth was almost tossed into the lap of the burly man who sat across from him.

"Sorry."

"Watch it, bub," the stranger cautioned.

Not to be intimidated, Seth returned the stranger's look, demanding the advantage as he studied him.

The man's stained work shirt revealed arms as big around as sides of beef, and a manner that suggested a restrained bull. Not someone that Seth would choose to tangle with, but he suspected that in his new position with the railroad he would be supervising the same sort of man. Beneath Seth's outward calm, his stomach churned up more acid.

No one knew better than he how ill prepared he was for his new job. After graduating from Stevens Institute of Technology in Hoboken, New Jersey, Seth had fallen in with his peers, other rich men's sons like himself who'd never done a day's work in their lives. He had spent years and a large sum of money traveling abroad. Up until a little over a year ago, his biggest financial worry had been if he would receive his allowance on time.

Then his world had crashed in around him. His father's death had brought him home and thrust him into a situation he had been ill equipped to handle. The family fortune was gone. Seth was twenty-eight years old and had never held a job of any kind. The responsibility of supporting his mother and brother had fallen to him, the eldest son. Now there was only his brother Jed. Their mother had died of a broken spirit six months after her husband's death.

In his own way, Seth felt he wasn't much different from his father, making bad decisions, wasting money. But unlike his father, Seth had the courage to stick by his convictions and to learn from his mistakes. He would never forget about his younger brother's welfare. He would never take the easy way out of a bad situation. He would succeed. He had to. His and Jed's very survival depended upon it.

Seth knew he couldn't change the past. It was best to put it behind him and concentrate on the future. And now was as good a time as any to begin.

"This your first trip west?" Seth asked the gentleman seated next to him.

The traveler hooted, slapping his knee. "West?" His bony elbow jabbed into Seth's already travel-bruised ribs. "Sonny, this here ain't the West," he continued, "we're in Floridy— paradise."

"Paradise?" Seth humored the fellow with a smile.

What he had seen so far of this wild untamed land wasn't exactly his idea of paradise. But then again, he doubted that his traveling companion had ever seen the Greek Isles that formed stepping-stones across the Aegean Sea. Now that was paradise, not this bug-infested jungle.

"Where ya from, sonny?" The man's question brought Seth back to the present.

"New York City."

A pall settled over the occupants of the coach. All eyes focused on him, and Seth shifted uncomfortably.

"A damn Yankee?"

Before Seth could respond, the fellow beside him had inched as far away from him as was possible on the narrow seat.

"Reckon, mister, that's why ya don't know paradise when ya see it."

Seth ignored the caustic remark and the snort of one of the other passengers. It appeared that his companions were die-hard Southerners. And although the War had been over for more than fifteen years, to them he was still the enemy. So much for friendly conversation, he mused, lapsing again into his private thoughts.

When he had first set out on his journey, it had seemed like an adventure. He'd been impressed with the settlements they'd passed, thinking them quaint. But that was before his train ride had ended. The more Seth saw of the untamed, uncivilized land, the more respect he felt for the people who'd settled it—barring his present company, of course. Now that the miles receded slowly behind him and stretched indefinitely before him, Seth doubted his ability to adjust to such an alien place.

Up until a year ago, he had had his own manservant to attend to all his personal needs. His clothes were laundered and laid out for him each morning, his boots polished and waiting. Seth had taken menial tasks for granted, and now they sometimes posed a problem for a man born into prodigal habits. Now he had no one but himself to depend on. Plus he had the added responsibility of his younger brother.

When they reached the town of Milton, the other passengers departed. Seth breathed a sigh of relief, glad that their ominous presence was gone. Two other men joined him for the remainder of the trip to Pensacola, but instead of involving them in conversation, Seth chose to keep his own counsel.

Not long after sunrise, the coach boarded a ferry that carried its passengers across the Escambia River. Seth left the coach to stretch his legs. He scanned the junglelike riverbanks. A panther's screeching cry echoed through the dense woods. Seth shivered.

"Only wild beasts could feel at home in such an untamed place," he mumbled before returning to the coach.

Was he out of his mind to bring Jed to such a place? Not according to Harriet Archibald.

"You're going to love Pensacola," Harriet had said. "Society is slim there, but several of us still enjoy the finer things in life. We have our musicales."

Harriet was the daughter of one of the wealthiest men in the South, Jay Arnold Archibald. Surely not everyone in the frontier town attended tea parties and socials.

And what about Harriet Archibald?

The pampered brunette surfaced in his mind. It had been four months since he'd last seen her, but she had written him several letters after returning home. Seth knew Harriet had persuaded her father to hire him as overseeing engineer. His job would be to supervise the piecing together of the tracks for the Pensacola & Atlantic Railroad across the Florida Panhandle. If it hadn't been for Harriet, he wouldn't be here now. For good or ill, he was in her debt.

He recalled her last night in Atlanta. They had dined at the house of her father's friend who lived down the street from the Governor's mansion. Harriet was a houseguest there and had arranged for a quiet dinner, just the two of them. Afterwards, they had strolled in the large orangery on the estate. When she had put her arms around his neck and kissed him on the lips, the atmosphere, coupled with the wine Seth had drunk at supper, had made him not unwilling to accept her advances. Before he knew it, the conversation of marriage had come up.

He realized then that Harriet was in the market for a husband, and not a local swain. She wanted to leave Pensacola, see the world. Seth had tried to explain to her in a polite way that he wouldn't marry any woman until he was financially able to support a wife. She had pretended understanding, complimenting him on his gallantry, but Seth knew she had completely dismissed his goals.

Harriet was a beautiful and intelligent girl, but the last thing he wanted was a romantic relationship—especially a relationship with a woman of Harriet Archibald's expensive tastes. Besides, her father had made it clear that he didn't approve of his daughter's interest in a near-penniless Yankee. The last thing Seth wished to do was to offend the man who'd given him a chance to prove that he was capable of doing what he'd been educated to do.

The coach jerked to a shattering stop, yanking Seth from his thoughts. As the conveyance rocked to a level position, he braced himself with his feet and arms to keep from being tossed into the laps of the two men who sat opposite him. At least now, he thought with relief, he'd be free from the crazy driver who'd driven the stage at breakneck speeds across the countryside.

Someone outside unlocked the stage door. His two traveling companions left the coach before Seth moved to follow them. Pausing in the doorway, he glanced up and down the street, his spirits lifting somewhat. Even in the blinding sunlight, he could see that Pensacola appeared to be a thriving seaport town. People strolling the planked sidewalks looked no different from the ones he'd left behind in Atlanta and New York.

About to step down from the coach, he stopped dead still on the step. A verbal combat was taking place between the wild coach driver and a young woman sitting astride the biggest horse he'd ever seen. Seth forgot everything but the captivating woman. She rode astride, her lifted skirts revealing naked legs above the top of her boots. He wondered if the warmer climate contributed to the lack of decorum of the woman and to the enormous dimensions of the animal she rode. He was surprised by both, but the people passing on the street didn't seem overly concerned with either.

He quickly appraised the woman. She looked diminutive perched upon the huge horse. A playful wind lifted her silvery, unbound hair, swirling it around her face and shoulders like a hirsute mantle. She seemed unmindful of her appearance, but appeared very distressed over the condition of the team of horses that had pulled the coach.

This, in itself, surprised Seth. Most of the ladies he knew were concerned only with their own image. But then, what did he know about the inhabitants of this strange place?

Forcing his gaze away from the woman, Seth reminded himself he had more important things to do than admire the lady's naked knees or concern himself with the argument taking place a few feet away.

He was finally here. This town would be his and Jed's chance for a new beginning. With a feeling of anticipation, Seth stepped down into the street and walked toward the back of the coach to retrieve his luggage.

Chapter Two

Viola Mae had just mounted her horse and started out of town when the overland stage careened past her. Sand and pebbles exploded like a powder keg when the coach skidded to a halt in front of the depot. Her Percheron mare snorted and tossed her head in alarm as the dusty cloud settled around them.

"It's okay, Ginger. No need getting your mane in a ruffle." Viola Mae patted and soothed the frightened horse before transfering her attention to the vehicle. "Booger Butts. I should have known," she mumbled angrily upon recognizing the driver.

She reined in Ginger several feet away from the panting team and looked up at the weasel of a man sitting atop the driver's seat. Booger Butts had no regard for anything, be it human or beast. Not only had his explosive arrival scattered most of the town's pedestrians, but his poor horses looked as though they were ready to drop in their tracks.

Booger pushed his Stetson back from his brow. With a soiled bandanna he swiped grit and sweat from his face. Stuffing the large handkerchief back inside his leather vest pocket, he flashed her a smile revealing teeth that protruded like a beaver's.

"How you doing, Viola Mae?" he asked.

"I'd be a hang of a lot better if you hadn't tried to run me down with that crate you're pulling."

His eyes narrowed to slits. "Now, Viola, you know I ain't in the habit of running down purty ladies. I've goods and passengers to deliver, and I aim to be on schedule. Now if you'll excuse me . . ."

The driver swung down from the high seat to the ground. Without another glance in Viola Mae's direction, he sauntered toward the front of the team of horses, securing them to the hitching rail.

"You belong in jail, Booger Butts," Viola Mae yelled, following behind him on horseback. "Not only for reckless driving, but because you mistreat your animals." She nodded her head in the direction of his wrung-out team. "Look at them," she demanded, "their sides are blowing like a smithy's bellows."

Booger's gaze slid over her mount, an arrogant leer shaping his mouth. "Ain't dealing here with worn-out horseflesh, Viola Mae."

People passing on the planked walkway stopped to listen. Booger, who loved to be the center of attention, noticed that he had an audience, so he continued to parley with her.

"That old nag you call a horse, she ain't nothing but a useless bag of wind. But these horses"—he pointed toward his team—"they're bred for speed . . . endurance."

Viola Mae knew no animal could endure for long under the cruel conditions Booger practiced. Several months back, she'd been called to the livery to deliver an ointment for one such abused animal. Even now her heart ached for the horse whose hide had been cut into ribbons by Booger's whip.

"That mare of yours, she's worthless as cold snail turds," he badgered. His wisecrack made the crowd snicker.

Worthless indeed. Ginger had been a part of her family for as long as Viola Mae could remember. The Percheron was not only the best workhorse a body could own, but the mare served as transportation as well. Not to mention the horse's status as a family pet. It didn't matter to Viola Mae that the mare was no longer as active as she'd once been. But because Ginger had belonged to her grandmother, she was a living link to a loving past, and no one, especially the likes of Booger Butts, could insult her mare and get away with it.

Booger glanced back at the gathering crowd. "I'm tired and thirsty. Ready for a beer. My standing here jawing with you is wasting time."

Glaring at him from Ginger's back, she didn't move.

"Get on home, gal," he ordered. "Some of us in this town have work to do. And I've still got cargo to unload." He turned his back to her as the stock-tender walked toward him.

Viola Mae wasn't about to let Booger escape so easily. She intended to teach the worthless man a lesson. He'd find out real soon that Ginger wasn't worn-out horseflesh, or anything else he'd accused her of being. She urged her mount forward until the giant animal had overtaken the puny little man.

Standing nearly sixteen hands from the ground, the Percheron was an opponent to reckon with. Ginger's strong, well-proportioned body and thick legs made her a formidable foe. Her size and appearance were reminiscent of the massive European *destriers*.

With Ginger practically breathing down Booger's neck, Viola Mae gave her the lead. Ginger clamped her yellowed teeth into Booger's hat and lifted it from his head, leaving his bald pate shining like a china plate in the brilliant sunshine.

"Useless bag of wind," Viola Mae taunted from her lofty perch on Ginger's back, edging Booger against the wooden hitching rail. "You sure about that now?"

Booger wasn't a man to be intimidated. He swung around to face her. "Gim'me that hat, you dang no-good-for-nothing piece of meat." Turning and twisting, he tried to yank his hat from the horse's jaws. Each time he reached for the Stetson, Viola Mae would maneuver Ginger backward, keeping the hat just out of Booger's grasp.

More people paused to watch, their pleasure evident from their comments. Most knew the two protagonists by their first names, and cheers and shouts were heard for each side. They all seemed to be enjoying themselves.

Bedeviling the driver would undoubtedly be the highlight of Viola Mae's day. She couldn't remember when she'd enjoyed herself so much. As far as she was concerned, making Booger the center of her joke was far less punishment than he deserved for his treatment of defenseless animals. He was getting his comeuppance, and she was championing her mare.

Rumor had it that Booger Butts could be a dangerous son of a gun. And Viola Mae wasn't stupid. She knew that bullies like Booger always retaliated. Especially against women. But even if everything she'd heard about him was true, even if Booger did come to her farm later looking for trouble, she had her grannie's shotgun and she knew how to use it.

"Viola Mae Smith, what in the name of heaven are you doing to Mr. Butts' hat?"

Without even looking in the speaker's direction, Viola Mae recognized the voice. It was the same sugary sweet voice that had plagued her throughout most of her growing-up years. It belonged to Harriet Louise Archibald, her childhood nemesis.

"Frog guts," Viola Mae grumbled. Disgusted, she looked in Harriet's direction. Why in tarnation did *she* have to show up now? Just when the fun was beginning.

Viola Mae had entertained thoughts of encouraging Ginger to take a nip from the seat of Booger's pants, but with the arrival of Miss High-and-Mighty Harriet, Viola Mae's playfulness wavered. The Archibalds had a lot of influence in the small community of Pensacola, and Harriet, out of spite, might insist that Ginger be shot for being a menace to the public. It wasn't beyond Harriet to wield her power; she'd been exercising it over Viola Mae for years.

Viola Mae met the other girl's accusing stare. The days of Harriet's rule were over. Viola Mae was now a grown-up woman who believed in her own self-worth. No longer would she allow the spoiled rich girl to intimidate her.

Mockingly, Viola Mae said, "If you'd wear those spectacles Dr. Lines prescribed for you, instead of worrying about how you look in them, you'd see that *I'm* not doing anything to Mr. Butts' hat."

Harriet's quick intake of breath was audible. Her pretty expression soured. She would have retaliated if Booger hadn't tripped over his feet at that exact moment and landed on the seat of his pants, making the crowd roar with laughter. The sheriff, standing among the onlookers, separated himself from the others and stepped down into the street.

"Miss Harriet," he acknowledged, walking toward them before turning his full attention on Viola Mae.

"Howdy, Sheriff," Viola Mae greeted him, bestowing upon him her brightest smile. She'd spotted the sheriff earlier, standing among the others, enjoying the show as much as the next fellow.

"Miss Viola." Sheriff Breen stepped between the horse and Booger, grabbed Ginger's bit, and gently pushed her backward. He stroked the mare's snoot and winked at Viola Mae. "What do you say we give Booger back his hat?"

"I suggested she do just that, Sheriff Breen," Harriet interrupted. "But you know how hardheaded Viola Mae can be."

The sheriff's glance silenced Harriet. Her meddling foiled, she reluctantly moved away. Grumbling to herself, she stepped back upon the planked walkway.

Viola Mae liked Sheriff Breen. It was known throughout the area that the sheriff treated everyone with the same friendly respect that he demanded from others. A fairer man Viola Mae had never known. If he said it was time to end her little game, then she would.

"Certainly, Sheriff," she replied, giving Ginger a signal to release the prized hat. It plopped to the ground several feet away from the mare's hooves. Booger glared at Viola Mae.

Turning back toward the crowd, the sheriff called, "All right, folks, it's time to mosey on."

Watching the crowd disperse, Viola Mae bent toward the sheriff and whispered to him, "You going to arrest me, Sheriff?"

He turned, a big grin lighting up his ruddy face. "Not today, Miss Viola. But in the future I suggest you choose carefully who you bully. Not everyone enjoyed this little show as much as you and me."

She didn't respond. The sheriff was warning her about Booger, and she appreciated his concern. After releasing Ginger's bit, Sheriff Breen turned to help Booger back up on his feet.

Viola Mae swung Ginger around to leave. As she did so, the mare's big foot landed firmly in the middle of the Stetson, smashing it flatter than a griddle cake.

"Oops!" Although she hadn't meant to ruin Booger's hat, a part of her experienced satisfaction on seeing it leveled. Serves him right, she decided, steering Ginger away.

"Hellfire and damnation," Booger shouted behind her. "I'll kill that she-bitch." He lunged toward the mare and slapped Ginger hard on the hip.

The smacking blow surprised both rider and horse. Ginger bolted. A woman screamed. The remaining onlookers scattered like an army of disturbed ants.

Fear knotted Viola Mae's insides. Ginger galloped straight for the parked stage. She had to stop her before she crashed into the vehicle.

From where Seth stood behind the coach, he watched the whole confrontation between the girl and the driver. He laughed with the others when the girl, who was a superb horsewoman, encouraged her horse to remove Butts' hat from his head. Both woman and horse performed the trick as though they'd practiced it many times. It appeared to Seth she was enjoying needling the man.

Not that the driver didn't deserve it. The man was a jackass. His lack of respect for everything had been evident when Seth had first boarded the stage in Chattahoochee. He wondered if the young woman realized what a bad temper the driver had.

Seth pulled his fob watch from his pocket to check the time, but on hearing Booger's angry oaths, he looked back toward the scene. He saw the bad-tempered boor slap the mare's rump. Then all hell broke loose. The startled animal bolted, charging straight toward the parked stage where Seth stood.

While Seth watched, the rider locked her arms around the mare's neck and swung down from the animal's back. She used her weight to try to steer the horse out of harm's way.

Realizing that her efforts were in vain, Seth dashed toward horse and rider, waving his arms like a banshee. They bore down upon him as Seth groped for the bridle. His fingers latched around the leather strapping, and he hung on, expecting at any moment to be trampled beneath the giant hooves. Their combined weight caused the frightened horse to slow, but not before they'd been dragged several hundred feet down the street.

After what seemed like an eternity, the horse stopped. Seth's arms felt as though they'd been torn from their sockets, but he was too weak-kneed to relinquish his hold on the animal.

Heroics were not something Seth normally practiced. His knees were knocking so badly that he suspected the lady clinging to the other side of the animal's head could hear them.

The girl was the first to move. Ducking her head below the animal's throat, she brushed her hair away from her face with her free hand and smiled up at him.

"Howdy," was all she said.

Seth gazed into her face, unable to utter a word. Any discomfort he'd felt earlier disappeared. Hidden beneath the mass of silvery-blond curls was the face of an angel. With eyes the same blue color of the crystal marbles he'd coveted as a lad. And until this moment, he realized he hadn't thought about them for years. Seth tried to speak, but his mouth felt as if it were stuffed with cotton. She stared boldly at him from beneath layers of silky black lashes. Seth's breath tightened in his chest, but he dismissed his reaction as nothing more than delayed fright.

Her perfectly shaped lips drawled out the words. "You all right, mister?" Then, as though remembering her manners, she wiped her free hand on her dress before grabbing his hand. She pumped his arm up and down like the handle on a water pump and introduced herself.

"I'm Viola Mae Smith. And I'm real pleased to meet you." She smiled at him again. "Who might you be?"

"Seth Thomas Rowe," he croaked, sounding more like a frog than a man.

Her hand felt as small as a child's, warm and moist against his own. The horse's musky smell hung in the air between them, its large head separating them except for their still-locked fingers.

"This here's Ginger," Viola Mae offered, peering at him beneath the mare's throat.

She introduced the horse as though it understood protocol. Oddly enough, Seth responded to the introduction in the same way. "Glad to meet you, Ginger," he replied.

"Ginger and me wish to thank you. You saved her from near-disaster."

"Ah . . . it was nothing." He felt as tongue-tied as a schoolboy, but courtesy demanded he explain. "I couldn't stand by and see this magnificent animal injured." He noted Ginger's size. "Can't say I've ever seen a horse as large as this one."

"She's a Percheron," Viola Mae said. "My grannie said her lineage dates back to the fifteenth century. Can't you just see her carrying a noble knight into battle wearing five hundred pounds of armor?" The girl's beautiful blue eyes glowed with reverence as she touted her horse's history. "She's something special all right."

"Yes, she is at that." Suddenly Seth felt noble, confident. He surprised himself with his next witty comment. "Maybe I should have been more concerned with the fate of the coach."

She looked at him as though digesting his words. Then understanding lit her face. She chuckled. "Why, mister, you may have something there. I 'spect there wouldn't be nothing but splinters left if Ginger had hit it." Stroking the mare's head, she said, "Serve old Booger right, if he had to pay for it."

She laughed then. Her laughter surfaced from deep inside her chest, filling the sunny morning with its rich sound.

Seth watched the emotions play across her face, and soon he was laughing with her. Gladness filled his chest. His earlier doubts about coming to Pensacola floated away on the spirited breeze.

Viola Mae couldn't help ogling the fancy-looking man standing on the opposite side of Ginger. Although his fine tailored duds were a bit travel-worn, he was still the spiffiest-looking fellow she'd ever seen. But it was more than the stranger's clothes that fascinated Viola Mae; it was the way he wore them. His tall, lean, well-proportioned body would have looked good in a croaker sack . . . or nothing at all. This last image brought a rush of warmth to Viola Mae's face. *Lawsy sakes, girl, the sun is frying your thinker.* Her eyes focused on his, hoping he hadn't read her thoughts.

After a strained moment she mumbled, "The sea . . ."

"Excuse me?"

"Your eyes are the color of the sea," she explained frankly.

Viola Mae didn't believe in beating around the bush with her opinions; she believed in speaking the truth. "They're a little bit blue, a little bit green." Rounding Ginger's head, she stopped in front of him and raised up on her tiptoes in order to make a better assessment. "Course, that depends on how the light hits them."

Seth disengaged his fingers from hers and fumbled with his shirt collar, which suddenly felt as though it had shrunk several inches. If he didn't know better, he would believe he was blushing because of the heat burning his ears. It had been years since he'd blushed, but then it wasn't every day he met a woman who spoke so candidly.

"It's the humidity," Viola Mae informed him, noticing his discomfort. "Makes a body miserable until he gets used to it."

Seth pulled a limp handkerchief from his pocket and dabbed at his warm face. "I'm sure there are lots of things I'm going to have to get used to around here." *Outspoken ladies for one,* he thought.

"Seth. You've arrived."

In a cloud of magenta tulle, Harriet Archibold blustered toward them. "I couldn't believe it was you. You could have been killed, and I'd never forgive myself."

Harriet thrust between Seth and Viola Mae, jockeying for his attention. Brushing the dust and debris from his lapel, she cautioned him, "You should never have risked your life for that beast." Her pert little nose turned up in disgust as she eyed Ginger over her shoulder.

"It was the lady's—" Before he could finish, Harriet interrupted him.

"Viola Mae . . . a lady? Not hardly," she quipped.

Viola Mae noticed the slur on her character and wanted to kick the obstinate girl. Instead she only stared at the man, who would have had to be blind, deaf, and dumb not to have noticed Harriet's tactless remark.

Confident that Seth hadn't been harmed, Harriet turned angry brown eyes on Viola Mae. "See what you caused with your foolishness? If you hadn't been bullying poor Mr. Butts, this unfortunate incident wouldn't have happened."

Seth rallied to Viola Mae's defense. "I believe it was the driver who caused this mishap."

Harriet's mouth gaped open as she looked between the two. Before another comment could be made, the sheriff hustled to join them, practically dragging Booger with him.

"You haven't got the brains God gave a duck," Sheriff Breen accused him. "Someone could have been killed here because of your dang temper."

"Wait a damn minute, Sheriff. She's the one at fault." Booger pointed an accusing finger at Viola Mae. "Look at my hat. She ruined it." He held out the flattened disk that had once been a Stetson.

"A hat can be replaced, Booger. A life can't. You shouldn't have spooked that horse and you know it." He scowled.

"I don't give a *shiet* about her or her stupid horse. Whole town knows she's loony, living alone out there on that farm with nothing but animals for company."

"That's enough, Booger," the sheriff ordered. "There are ladies present who don't appreciate your foul mouth."

"She's gonna pay for my hat. One way or the other." Booger slammed the crushed felt against his thigh, his face mottled with anger.

"I'll see that you're reimbursed," the sheriff promised. "But I believe you owe Miss Viola an apology."

"Apologize? To her?" Booger shook his head in disbelief. "If anyone should apologize, it's her. Scatterbrained woman."

"I'm warning you." The sheriff placed a restraining hand on Booger's arm.

After a tense moment he conceded. "I'm sorry," he blurted out defensively. "Now if you'll excuse me, I've got work to do." He turned on his heel and stalked back toward the stage, mumbling to himself. "Damn loony woman."

"You all right, Miss Viola?" the sheriff asked her.

"Yes, thank you, sir. I'm sorry I goaded Booger. I was wrong, but he—"

"You certainly were, Viola Mae," Harriet lectured. "Seth could have been killed, and then what would you have to say about your foolishness?"

Viola Mae's mood shifted from amicable to belligerent. She'd had about enough of Harriet Archibald's opinion, and something else was annoying her as well. Harriet kept batting her weak eyes at the stranger, lighting up like a dang glow-worm whenever he looked or spoke to her. Although Viola Mae had vowed never to be jealous of Harriet Archibald again, the unbidden green-eyed monster clawed at her insides. She was tempted to yank Harriet's fancy bonnet right off her empty head.

"Now Miss Viola, Miss Harriet." Sheriff Breen's voice interrupted the charged silence. "We don't want to give this here stranger the wrong idea about our town."

Viola Mae knew he must have sensed the squall that hung threateningly over the crowd. Everyone within shouting distance of Pensacola knew of the ongoing feud between Harriet and her. The sheriff was trying to control the fury about to be unleashed among them. She heard him say as he extended his hand toward Seth, "I don't believe we've met, young fellow."

Seth grasped the sheriff's hand. "No, sir, we haven't. I'm Seth Thomas Rowe."

Viola Mae watched the exchange, then settled her gaze on Harriet, who interrupted again.

"Sheriff Breen, Daddy hired Seth to oversee the building of the railroad."

Harriet flapped her lids so fast, they reminded Viola Mae of a baby bird's wings the first time it was nudged from its nest. *No wonder she's near-blind.*

"He's an engineer. He's come all the way from New York." Smiling at Seth, Harriet stepped closer to him. "We're just so glad to have him in our town at last."

Harriet's gushing made Viola Mae sick, but then her peer

had always affected her that way. Because Harriet's father nearly owned the railroad—

Railroad. Viola Mae's gaze shot toward Seth's. She should have known anyone who looked as good as he did would have to be in cahoots with the devil.

Their eyes locked for several seconds before Viola Mae jerked hers away. Although he'd saved Ginger from disaster, he'd now become her enemy. Not only because he'd be working for the railroad, but because he was Harriet Archibald's friend as well.

"Glad to have you in our community, Mr. Rowe," the sheriff added. "I expect Viola Mae here is doubly grateful you arrived when you did, loving this horse the way she does." The sheriff winked at her. "A mighty heroic thing you did, son. Not only saved the horse, but Viola Mae as well."

"It was nothing, sir." Seth looked at Viola Mae, expecting her to grace him with a grateful smile. Instead her expression had changed from sunny to stormy, and she sent him a withering stare. Could this be the same girl who moments before had warmed him with her friendliness?

"Well, you're here now, and that's all that matters," Harriet chirped, threading her arm around Seth's. "I suggest we put this unfortunate event behind us and get you settled in. Sheriff, Viola Mae, if you'll excuse us." She attempted to usher Seth away, but he stopped her.

Turning toward Viola Mae, he asked, "Miss Smith, will you be all right?"

Viola Mae held the reins in her hands and was getting ready to mount Ginger. She'd stayed in town far too long already. Pausing only long enough to address him, she said, "I'll be fine, mister." Without another glance at anyone, Viola Mae swung up onto Ginger's back.

Seth unwound himself from Harriet's grasp and clasped Ginger's bit to steady the big animal.

Harriet watched him through narrowed eyes.

Viola Mae felt like telling her to put her glasses on so she wouldn't have to squint so much. Disgusted, Viola Mae looked away, her gaze connecting with Seth's. He smiled up at her, and she felt a rush of heat clear down to her toes. Unnerved by her reaction, Viola Mae wanted only to distance herself from the handsome stranger.

"I'm sorry that your horse was spooked," Seth offered.

Viola Mae couldn't reply, for she felt as though the cat had taken her tongue and run with it. The way he kept looking at her made her skin feel as prickly as a plucked goose.

His thick lashes swept upward. When his sea-green gaze slid over her naked calf from above her boot to her knee, Viola Mae fought the urge to cover her exposed leg. Suddenly she was acutely aware of the warm leather of the saddle pressed intimately against her most feminine parts. A strange occurrence, considering she rode astride every day of her life and had never felt such a stirring in her lower regions before.

As though her sudden discomfort had been revealed to him, Seth's cheeks plumped into a knowing grin. Viola Mae's face burned.

Although Viola Mae had made up her mind not to like the stranger after hearing he'd be working for the railroad, she knew that manners dictated that she thank him again before departing.

"I appreciate what you did for Ginger, Mr. Rowe. Thank you."

"Seth, really, must we make such an issue of this?" Harriet broke in, her cold sarcasm directed at Viola Mae. "She brought the whole incident on herself, acting without thinking of the consequences, as usual."

Harriet's last comment made Viola Mae see red. She'd had enough of her goading for one day, and enough of the handsome stranger looking at her like a hungry gator. Whipping Ginger around to leave, she watched over her shoulder as Harriet scampered behind Seth for protection.

Her posture militant, Viola Mae replied, "I'm sure, Harriet, if someone hit you on the ass, you'd bolt, too." With this parting remark, she spurred Ginger into a trot, and they headed out of town.

While Harriet fumed and belittled the woman who'd left them standing in a dust cloud, Seth had trouble controlling his laughter. Never in all his life had he met anyone quite like Viola Mae Smith. This town on the edge of nowhere was proving to be anything but dull. Especially if the silver-haired, outspoken girl was going to be around. He watched Viola Mae until she turned Ginger down a side street and disappeared. Already he was anticipating their next meeting.

"I swear she gets worse instead of better," Harriet complained. She brushed at the grainy sand embedded in the soft folds of her dress. "Just look at me. I'm a mess." Gripping her skirt, she shook it.

He knew she expected a compliment, and the gentleman in him would not allow him to disappoint her. "A pretty disarrangement."

His words brought the desired response. Harriet's fiddling stopped, and her expression changed from condemnation to approval. She beamed a smile at him, the annoying incident obviously forgotten.

"Do you really think so?" she asked.

"Prettier than a northern spring."

Harriet's brown eyes twinkled. "After your harsh winters, I expect they're quite lovely." He watched her cheeks dimple when she smiled up at him.

"Not as lovely as you," he answered honestly.

"I do believe you're trying to charm me, Mr. Rowe, but you just keep it up," she teased. Harriet linked her arm with his and steered him toward the parked coach, adding, "I hope you won't believe us all to be barbarians because of Viola Mae's actions."

"Certainly not." Seth patted her gloved hand. "Anything but."

Although the young woman's behavior had been unconventional, Seth wouldn't call it barbaric. In fact, he found her quite fascinating. Never in all his twenty-eight years had he met anyone like Viola Mae Smith.

As he and Harriet moved along the boarded walkway, Seth studied the array of shops lining Palafox Street. Everything from a ship's chandler to a confectioner's. When they passed a barbershop, he made a mental note of its location, planning to return later for a much-needed haircut.

He smiled down at the woman on his arm. "I'm sure I'll be very happy here."

"Oh, I hope so," Harriet cooed.

Although manners dictated that he not ask too many questions about the mysterious horsewoman lest he offend Harriet, his curiosity got the better of him. Hoping his interest wasn't too obvious, Seth inquired, "Does Miss Smith live in town?"

"Heavens, no," Harriet replied. "Town is much too civilized for Viola Mae's tastes. She prefers the company of animals over that of humans."

Nearing the parked coach, Seth saw that his luggage had been unloaded from the boot. He inspected its condition, pleased to see that it had arrived undamaged. This done, he continued his conversation.

"Miss Smith appears to hold that horse of hers in very high esteem. It is a most unusual animal. Can't say I've ever seen such a large horse."

"Pshaw! You'd think the dumb old thing had royal blood flowing through its veins the way Viola Mae carries on. As far as I'm concerned, a horse is a horse." Harriet wrinkled her nose in disgust. "They all stink."

Seth chuckled at Harriet's obvious aversion to the horse and its rider. After witnessing the earlier scene between the ladies, Seth had decided neither liked the other. And the reason was obvious. The two women were as different as night and day.

He studied the dark brunette beside him. Harriet was beautiful: immaculately dressed in the latest of fashions, every raven hair in place beneath her plumed straw hat. But in spite of the lovely woman on his arm, the rustic beauty kept intruding into his thoughts. Seth pictured her in the faded calico dress, sitting astride the giant dapple-gray horse, her silvery hair more reminiscent of a mop in its wild flyaway state. He would be lying to himself if he denied his interest in the girl called Viola Mae.

"Seth, did you hear me?" Harriet tugged on his sleeve, calling him back from his daydreams.

He'd been so preoccupied, he hadn't heard Harriet. Embarrassed, he apologized. "I'm sorry. I must be more tired than I realized."

"Of course you are," Harriet consoled him before repeating herself. "Daddy insists that you stay the night at our house. Tomorrow you can travel out to the railroad camp."

Damn! He'd been crowded in with strangers for the last week, traveling inside what seemed like an eight-by-five rocking box. It had been the promise of a hot bath, a good night's sleep in a real bed, and a bit of privacy that had kept him going throughout his long journey. Staying with the Archibalds, whom he hardly knew, wasn't exactly his idea of a relaxing night.

"Thank you, but I don't wish to impose. A hotel will be fine."

Harriet insisted. "Daddy said he had some business to discuss with you about the tracklaying. We both agreed it would be more convenient for everyone if you stayed with us."

Still unwilling to forfeit his night of privacy, Seth tried again. "I appreciate your offer, Harriet—"

"Indulge me, please?" Her dark eyes danced. "It has been months since I last saw you." She paused, then turning toward him, tapped a gloved finger against his lapel. "We have a lot of catching up to do."

Harriet's full lips formed into a perfect pout, and Seth's resistance faded. Pretty women had always been his weakness. He loved them, loved being around them, loved indulging them, and loved dallying with the ones that were willing. To Seth the opposite sex had always been a pleasurable diversion. Although he no longer had the means or the time to enjoy such pastimes, old habits were hard to break.

But after all this time he wanted to believe he'd grown impervious to a woman's charms, especially the charms of a woman of Harriet's background. But Harriet had intervened for him, helping him to get the job with her father's railroad when Seth knew there were many other engineers more qualified for the position. Accepting her invitation was the least he could do to show his gratitude. And, he reasoned, Harriet was the boss's daughter. If Mr. Archibald needed to discuss business with him, Seth could see the advantage of his staying in their home. His need for privacy would have to wait another night.

He threw his hands up in submission. "You win," he said, smiling.

"Wonderful." Harriet linked her arm with his again, and they began moving once more. "Wait until you taste Spacey's cooking. It's much better than any silly old hotel's food, and our guest room is certainly more comfortable."

After Harriet informed the baggage handler that she'd send someone to pick up Seth's trunk, she led her guest away from the depot.

"We'll walk. It's not far, and I'm sure after your long ride you could use the exercise."

He fell into step beside her. As they walked toward the Archibald's home, Seth listened to a running list of parties Harriet had planned in his honor. He didn't have the energy to tell her that he'd come to Pensacola to work, not socialize. Maybe, he decided, this was Harriet's way of making him feel welcome, so he pretended interest in the proposed guest list.

Until a year ago, he would have been delighted to meet Harriet's realm of friends and would have enjoyed attending the many functions she had planned. If fate and bad luck had not interfered, eventfully Seth would have settled down with a girl just like Harriet. Their marriage would have been the perfect match between two monied families.

Soon enough, Harriet would realize that he wasn't the rich, debonair young man she wanted him to be, but a near-penniless one who had to work for a living. A man also responsible for the care of his younger brother. Once Harriet realized those things, Seth knew she would tire of him and look elsewhere for someone who could keep her comfortably in the life to which she'd been born.

"We're here." Harriet paused in front of a large two-story house built in the Greek style.

A picket fence surrounded the impressive facade, its whitewashed brightness almost blinding in the sunlight. Harriet pushed open the gate and bade him follow her.

In New York Seth had lived with his family in a much

larger and much grander home than this one. His family's wealth had guaranteed him an invitation to the finest drawing rooms both in this country and abroad, yet Seth couldn't recall a time when he'd felt more uncomfortable, more out of place than he did right now. Following behind Harriet, he suddenly understood the reason for his uneasiness. Those halcyon days were gone forever.

Circumstances had forced Seth to be someone he didn't know how to be. He no longer belonged on the other side of this rich man's door, and he wasn't certain how a man standing on this side should act.

"Father," Harriet called from the entryway once they were inside. She closed the door behind them.

A hell of a situation to be in, Seth thought with worry as his eyes slowly adjusted to the dim interior. Soon Harriet's father strode toward them from the adjoining room.

"Mr. Archibald." Seth extended his hand. "It's good to see you again, sir."

For now, Seth would draw on all the training he'd had as a gentleman to get through this uncomfortable night. Later, when he was alone, he would focus on the man he must become.

Chapter Three

On the way out of town, Viola Mae turned Ginger up the road that ran by St. Michael's Cemetery. Normally she visited her grandmother's grave on Sundays, but today's incident in town had left her feeling unsettled, in need of solace. It wasn't so much her clash with Booger Butts that disturbed her as it was her encounter with Seth Rowe. With his sparkling eyes and pleasant smile, the stranger had made her insides feel like cream being churned into butter. A novel experience for Viola Mae Smith, who'd decided long ago not to be attracted to any man. But even her fascination with the stranger couldn't compare with the anger she'd felt when she'd learned that he would be in charge of building the Pensacola & Atlantic Railroad. Any friend of the railroad, or Harriet Archibald, was no friend of hers.

As horse and rider approached the wooded graveyard, a crow called from a nearby tree. Soon the overhead branches vibrated with life as a flock of raven-winged birds soared toward the sky, their noisy departure leaving the little woods in a hushed silence.

A minute later, Viola Mae pulled Ginger to a stop, dismounted, and left the mare munching on spring grass that grew at the road's edge.

She moved toward the Smith family plot, thinking today as always that the old cemetery reminded her of a natural cathedral. The mottled leaves and gnarled branches of the surrounding oaks formed its ceiling, their density broken only by flecks of sunlight that splashed gold across the shady, hallowed ground beneath.

All of Viola Mae's relations were buried in St. Michael's, or all the ones she knew of. She stopped near two graves: her grandfather's and, beside his, her grandmother's. Dropping to her knees between the two graves, Viola Mae rested her hands on each of the grassy mounds.

"Hope you won't mind the intrusion, but I needed to sit a spell," she announced. Because Viola Mae had never known the man buried beside her grannie, she directed her conversation toward the latter. "It's a right beautiful day," she said. "Just the way you like it. A warm day with a cool breeze."

The clematis vines that Viola Mae had planted between her grandparents' graves now twined around the double marble headstone, the shiny green leaves ruffling in the soft breeze. Soon the purple bell-shaped blossoms would open. Viola Mae had chosen the flowers because of their color, hoping that her grandparents would remember her when they saw the violet blooms hanging above their heads.

Last night's rain had left the ground damp. She inhaled deeply, savoring the fragrance of the moist earth. Beneath the shady bower, the ground would remain wet until the sun had risen well beyond its zenith. Sinking deeper against its coolness, Viola Mae felt her muscles relax.

"Didn't want you to be worried about our Ginger," she told her grannie. "She's just fine." Begrudgingly she added, "Thanks to that spiffy-looking Yankee who jumped in front of us."

Although Viola Mae doubted her grandparents had witnessed the earlier incident in town, she didn't believe in taking risks where her grannie was concerned. If by some remote chance the revered old woman was already an angel and could see everything her granddaughter did, she wanted to keep the record straight.

Viola Mae reiterated Sheriff Green's words. "Booger ain't got the brains God gave a duck." But in the hushed moments that followed, her statement roused a truth that she hadn't considered until now.

Regardless of Booger's lack of brains, Viola Mae had been the real troublemaker. She'd bullied Booger unmercifully, then ruined his hat, even though that part had been an accident. Because of her behavior, Booger had taken his anger out on Ginger. And because of her actions, Ginger could have been fatally injured.

Viola Mae shivered. "I acted foolishly," she admitted, hanging her head in shame. "Grannie, you always told me to think before I acted. I guess I'll never learn. . . ."

To her own ears, her rebuke sounded like her late grandmother's. Viola Mae brushed several strands of wayward hair from her face, the bothersome locks reminding her of her hair's unbound state.

When her grannie was alive, the old woman had insisted that Viola Mae conduct herself like a proper young lady, especially on her visits to town. Her grandmother would turn over in her grave if she knew her granddaughter's hair hung as loose as a common hussy's.

"I know that ladies ain't supposed to wear their hair unbound in public and all. But you know me, sometimes my good sense turns to nonsense." Reaching inside her pocket, Viola Mae found her ribbon and quickly anchored her hair in place.

Today it seemed she couldn't do anything right. Maybe that was why God had seen fit to route her by St. Michael's in the middle of the week, so as to remind her of the error of her ways. This revelation prompted her to continue with her confession.

"Now don't get me wrong. I am grateful that there Rowe fellow saved Ginger." She recalled the incident in all its clarity, including her fizzy reaction to his nearness. "But, Grannie, he plans to work for the railroad, and I ain't so sure he's as nice as I first pictured."

There was more to Viola Mae's disdain of Seth Rowe than his connection with the railroad and Harriet Archibald. Never in all her young years had she met a man who made her feel both hot and cold at the same time. By confessing the stranger's effect on her to her grandmother, wouldn't she be admitting it to herself as well? At the moment, she wasn't willing to do either.

Again his likeness appeared inside her head, his sea-green eyes taunting her. Just thinking about him caused her to experience a rush of heat, and suddenly the cool, damp ground felt sultry beneath her worn calico dress. Her limbs felt clammy. Unable to contend with her feelings a moment longer, Viola Mae jumped up from the grass.

"I best be going, Grannie," she insisted, brushing at the back of her skirt. "But I'll be seeing you, as usual, on Sunday." Viola Mae backed away from the two graves, then turned and darted to where Ginger waited.

Normally her visits with her grandmother left her feeling refreshed, but not so today. Never could she recall such a need to escape. Not only from St. Michael's, but from her own puzzling sensations as well.

She swung onto Ginger's back and jerked the mare into motion. Soon she'd be back on her farm, and she could put the morning's events completely from her mind. But no matter how hard she tried, her fancies kept rushing to Seth Rowe.

So what if he had saved Ginger. That didn't make her indebted to him for the rest of her life, did it? Although Viola Mae did believe that one good deed deserved another, she needed to keep things in prospective. Seth Rowe worked for the railroad, and that made him her enemy. It didn't matter that she found herself drawn to him, liking him in spite of herself. Her land and heritage were being threatened by the railroad's proximity. She had already witnessed the destruction firsthand when she'd visited the pond yesterday.

"Are you dense, girl? You have to look out for your own."

She made her decision.

Viola Mae would proceed with her plan to rid her woods of the railroad, and the troublesome Yankee as well. As far as she was concerned, Mr. Rowe's soon-to-be closeness was about as welcome as a polecat at a camp meeting. Only difference was, she reasoned, the dandy smelled a heck of a lot better.

Dear Jed,

At long last I've arrived in Florida. This town is really something, and unlike anything you or I have ever seen. Although Pensacola is a busy seaport and as civilized as New York City and Atlanta, it sits on the edge of an almost untamed wilderness. A jungle might be a more apt description.

The Archibalds have been very kind to me, welcoming me into their home upon my arrival. I stayed with them one night before installing myself in the railroad camp several miles outside of town. For now, my home is a canvas tent, and the camp is no place for a lad such as you. When the tracklaying is completed here, we will finish the railroad bridge across the bay. At that time I'll be close enough to town to establish a residence. Miss Archibald has offered her assistance in locating a place for me to live. Just think, if all goes as planned, you'll be in Pensacola in time to start school in the fall. I'm sure that thought makes you eager to join me. Ha!

I'm really enjoying my job and the men I'm working with, but the weather here takes some getting used to. Although it is only May, it is very hot and humid . . . and with mosquitoes as large as horseflies.

I trust you are taking good care of Aunt Cloe and have settled into the household as I knew you would. Keep the faith, little brother. Remember we are working, each in our own way, so that we can be together again soon.

Your brother,
Seth

Seth folded the letter and placed both pencil and paper inside his shirt pocket. He would send it by the next post to Atlanta. His letter was long overdue, but he had been so busy since his arrival at the railroad site that he hadn't had the time, or the energy, to scratch out a note until now.

Everything about his new environment required all his concentration, including the simple act of getting to know his men. Men who resented his being an outsider, and a Yankee outsider as well. To some of them, the North's victory was still an issue.

Seth lay on a small rise about a mile away from camp. Most of his men had been unable to work yesterday and today because of a strange malady that had overtaken them after eating jars of blackberry preserves found in the woods not far from the campsite.

Because Seth couldn't tolerate blackberries in any form or shape, he'd passed up the treat. Today he was equally glad that he had. All the men who'd eaten the preserves were paying with bellyaches for their gluttony. The outhouses and the surrounding woods had been getting plenty of use for the past forty-eight hours.

He chuckled to himself, recalling the condition of the men he'd left behind. Nothing was as uncomfortable as a cramping stomach. He felt sorry for his charges but wouldn't change places with any of them.

All in all, Seth liked the responsibility of his new position, but he also knew he had a tough job ahead of him. Winning his men's approval was at the top of his list. Most of the laborers were Southerners, some local, some from Mississippi and Alabama, plus a few Irishmen who'd come to work for the steady wages paid by the railroad. But having to answer to a wet-behind-the-ears Yankee engineer wasn't exactly what they'd bargained for. Seth knew the salary and the three square meals a day provided by the railroad was what had kept his workers from abandoning their positions as soon as they'd learned that he was to be in charge.

On Seth's journey from Jacksonville to Pensacola he'd seen the poverty that existed throughout the area. Because of the isolation of the settlements along the stage route, there were not many jobs to be had. Men went elsewhere for work, most of them leaving their families behind. With the completion of the railroad tracks, all that would change—especially with the lumber industry starting to boom in the area.

It felt good to be a part of progress. Seth took pride in his work, overseeing the linking of tracks across the panhandle. But his being a Yankee had posed some problems with a few men he supervised. If it weren't for his foreman, Riley, Seth might have had an all-out rebellion on his hands. Only yesterday, Riley had saved him from his own hanging.

One of his workers had accused "the damn Yankee" of trying to poison his crew with the tainted fruit. The bully of a man, not unlike the one Seth had encountered on the stagecoach, had convinced the other laborers of his guilt and nearly incited his lynching. Only the foreman's interference and Seth's ability to out-wrestle the troublemaker had saved his hide. Afterwards, Seth had fired the man, issuing a warning to stay away from the railroad camp or face being arrested by Sheriff Breen.

This morning, when he'd found the streambed almost dry, Seth had suspected the disgruntled worker. Last night when everyone had retired to their tents, there had been a steady flow of water in the stream. Not so this morning. Whoever had tampered with the water supply also had to know that the creek was the camp's only water source.

If it wasn't the fired worker trying to get even with Seth, then who was it? The incident with the tainted preserves still raised questions in his mind. Had the same person been responsible for both acts? Maybe it was a conspiracy among all the workers, their covert way of getting rid of the Yankee railroad boss. If that were the case, Seth wouldn't go down without a fight. That was why he'd taken it upon himself to investigate the water problem. He couldn't trust anyone but himself.

Leaving camp early, Seth had followed the creek shoal until the area around it had become impassable. Hills and wide gullies had forced him to hike away from the stream. Thank God he knew how to read a compass. He had left instructions with Riley, advising him that if he hadn't returned by nightfall to send out a search party. They'd both had a good laugh, but only Seth knew the truth behind his orders. He was a tenderfoot and didn't fancy being lost in the woods overnight, or ending up as dinner for some wild animal.

"Hellfire and damnation." He swatted at the swarming mosquitoes that buzzed around his head. Instead of being eaten alive by a wild animal, he was facing a swarm of the blasted insects. The little vampires were about to milk his jugular of another pint of blood.

Since his arrival at the campsite, Seth had been bitten so much, he'd swear his veins were as dry as the streambed. His face and neck were covered with angry welts—welts he had scratched until most were raw and swollen. Shaving was nearly impossible, and so he hadn't shaved, hoping that his whiskers would hinder the attacking armies. But even the thick stubble had failed to keep the mosquitoes from declaring a private war on his blood supply.

Inside his knapsack he found a small packet of salt. Riley had shown him how to make a paste with water to apply to the bites. The salty remedy burned like hell, but he preferred the fiery pain to the annoying itching. He might look ridiculous with gobs of white goo dotting his face and neck, but his appearance was the least of his problems. Seth had other more pressing things to worry about. Like getting railroad ties in place for the iron rails that Archibald said would be delivered next week.

Thirty minutes before, Seth had arrived at the steep rise where he now lay. The closer he'd come to the water source, the louder it had become. He could hear the water gurgling, its low, even sounds echoing off the rocks and trees. After he'd rested, then eaten a few bites of hardtack, he'd penned the letter to Jed. Now he was ready to begin his search again.

Returning his salt supply to his pack, he pulled out field glasses and scanned the surrounding woods. Below him the ground sloped downward, the undergrowth all but disappearing, giving him an almost clear view of the forest floor. Longleaf yellow pines studded the slope. Beyond the tall trees a streak of light flashed against what could be water. Seth studied the spot that looked like quicksilver. If indeed someone had interfered with the camp's water, Seth wanted to know how many people were involved before he made his presence known.

Sunlight sliced through the grove of tall trees, painting their scaly bark an orange brown. Drooping green needles flexed to life as a warm wind whistled through the pine corridors. Overhead, squirrels darted among the branches and a woodpecker hammered the trunk of a tree. Seth dropped the ends of his binoculars to the pool's edge, following the water's flow along the streambed for several hundred feet.

"Aha." There was the crux of his problem. Seth laughed aloud, his laughter echoing off the nearby pines. He'd found his culprit, or the lodge of the animal.

He sprang to his feet. Although he was an inexperienced beginner in this wild frontier, Seth recognized a beaver dam when he saw one. As an engineering student at Steven's Institute of Technology in New Jersey, he'd studied extensively the beaver's skill. Unlike any other animal, the beaver had the ability to fell trees and build dams to control the water's current in his home. This had fascinated Seth. Eager to get a firsthand look at the structure, he headed down the slope toward the stream.

The rise was steeper than he first suspected, making his descent difficult. His boots slipped on the slick pine needles still damp from last night's dew. He steadied himself by gripping the trees he passed.

"Nuts!" he shouted when his feet slipped from beneath him. Landing on the seat of his pants, Seth skidded downhill before tumbling to a stop mere inches from the pool's edge. He lay on his back, unmoving, waiting for his breathing to return to normal. Then he wiggled his toes, fingers, and limbs to make certain he'd broken nothing. Satisfied that he was still in one piece, he relaxed. *The last thing I need is a broken bone*.

Overhead, a wind stirred the needled branches. Across the pool underbrush shuddered. The bell-like sound of laughter singsonged its way through the pine trunks, warning Seth that he might not be alone.

He jerked up on his elbows and stared toward the spot from which the sound came. A branch snapped, causing his nerves to become as taut as a bowstring. Who besides himself would be in the woods? After sighting the beaver's dam, he'd ruled out the man he had fired yesterday. But now he wasn't so sure. Maybe the man was lying in wait for him. Hellfire. The crazy worker could kill him, throw him in a ravine, and who would be the wiser?

Maybe he'd only imagined the laughter he thought he'd heard. Unfamiliar with the woods, he felt isolated. Before now, Seth hadn't considered himself a coward; even now the impression didn't thrill him. Drawing rooms he could handle, but the wilderness?

His gaze shot to the underbrush, where again he detected

movement. Frozen, he pondered his next move. Without a weapon, he was completely defenseless, and he cursed his stupidity for leaving camp unarmed. A wiser man would have brought a gun, and next time he would, too.

Next time. If there was a next time. Indecision knotted Seth's stomach. Could he outrun whatever it was? He was about to try when two squirrels darted from behind a decaying log, shattering the tense silence.

Seth expelled his breath through his teeth. "Squirrels." His earlier spineless behavior mocked him. Thank heavens no one else had witnessed his cowardly display. Standing, he brushed the debris from his pants and shirt and peered down into the gurgling spring. Damn, it felt good to be in control again.

Suddenly an odor reached up to choke him. "Pshaw!" It smelled like rotten eggs.

When he had first arrived in Florida, he'd been introduced to sulfur water and quickly developed an aversion to it. He'd been told that underground springs like this one abounded throughout the state, feeding artesian wells and local swimming holes. Most Pensacolians claimed there was no finer water anywhere, but to Seth the water was almost intolerable. Especially when it was heated for bathing.

He shrugged. "Beggars can't be choosers," he said aloud.

He was thirsty. His trek through the woods and the rising humidity had left his throat parched. Squatting down at the spring's edge, he scooped up a handful of the ice-cold liquid, bringing it to his lips. He swallowed, refusing to breathe until the fetid substance went down. Still holding his breath, Seth doused his face and neck and glanced across the stream.

He couldn't shake the feeling that he was being watched. Shadows darkened the opposite bank where the undergrowth grew thicker, more dense. Someone or something could be concealed in the tangled brush.

City fool. There is nothing out here but the wildlife and you. Dismissing his apprehension as ludicrous, he turned and headed toward the beaver barricade. After he'd unclogged the stream, maybe he would return to the spring for a much needed bath.

Already he could feel the curative powers of the icy water.

It would numb the incessant itching that had begun immediately after he'd washed away the salt paste. Seth controlled the need to scratch, determined to abide the annoying discomfort, no matter what.

He followed the creek bed downstream, stopping several feet away from the beavers' lodge. The barrier would have to be removed to allow the water to flow again. Scanning the area for a sign of the big-toothed rodents, he wondered if the animals would become aggressive if cornered. His beaver research hadn't embraced the animal's temperament.

Seth moved cautiously toward the dam, stomping his feet to warn the beavers of his approach. He bent and picked up a loose branch, planning to use it as a weapon if the need arose.

"Right, old man—charge a beaver with a weapon that he could shred into kindling in a matter of minutes." Still, he found the club bolstered his flagging courage.

Something about the site wasn't right. Seth looked at the lodge, and the ground surrounding it. There were no animal prints, and no evidence of wood shavings anywhere along the bank. A beaver required two things in order to build his lodge: water at least five feet deep, plus plenty of softwood trees nearby for building and food. No willows, alders, or birch trees grew near the shallow water. Only mile-high pines, reaching toward the sky.

"Hot damn. I'm right."

Closer inspection revealed that a beaver hadn't built the dam. No mud cemented the barricade together. Instead, the wood was stacked into a neat wall. Seth waded across the stream. Beside the water's edge footprints marked the ground. Human prints, shoeless, which even he could identify.

After closer inspection of the prints, Seth ruled out the man he'd fired yesterday. The imprints were much too small to have been made by the giant of a man he recalled.

But who, then? Seth squatted down and scooped up the wet sand. Glancing around the woods, he pondered the facts. First the blackberry preserves and now the dammed-up stream.

The hairs on the back of his neck prickled. Something

lurked behind him; he could feel its presence. His fingers inched toward the piece of wood he'd dropped earlier, closing around it. If the unknown thing planned to do him harm, Seth was determined to come out the victor.

His pulse rate rose, and his breathing quickened. He spun around and dived at the blur of fabric behind him, knocking it to the ground. Fingers jabbed at his eyes, feet kicked his shins, but soon he'd pinned his attacker beneath him. Several winded moments passed before Seth realized he'd tackled a woman. The silvery-blond hair concealing her face was a dead giveaway as to her identity.

Viola Mae Smith pushed up on her elbows, trying to slither from beneath him. Her movement flattened her rounded breasts against his chest and allowed him to settle himself more comfortably between her spread thighs. Seth held her with his weight, refusing to free his prize.

"Get off me, you big lummox," she ordered him. Her cornflower-blue eyes launched daggers at him as she squirmed to get free.

A gentleman would have immediately done the lady's bidding, but proper behavior was the last thing on Seth's mind. He was a man, she was a woman, and they were locked in an embrace that would have put Adam and Eve to shame. Birds sang, water gurgled, and Viola Mae smelled like Eden itself . . . a mixture of evergreens and wild violets. Paradise, Seth acknowledged, and one he wasn't about to quit. Besides, he was curious about the girl, and had been since their first meeting.

The harder Viola Mae struggled to free herself, the more evident it became that the Yankee wasn't going to release her. Having grown up an oddity in the small town of Pensacola, Viola Mae had learned early to defend herself both physically and emotionally. She had always considered herself a match for any critter she might encounter, but this one seemed more apt than most at squashing the breath from her lungs. She would have jabbed him with her knee, but his weight and long muscular legs had leveled her best defense. So instead, Viola Mae lay in explosive submission beneath his powerful hulk.

If she hadn't been so dang nosy, she wouldn't be in this predicament. When Viola Mae had first spied the Yankee walking in the woods, she'd never suspected that he was on a mission. She'd followed him, curious as to why he wasn't in the same throes of agony as the rest of the railroad workers. Her doctored preserves had disabled most of the men in camp, but for the life of her, Viola Mae couldn't understand why Seth Rowe wasn't suffering a gut-wrenching bellyache.

As far as she could tell, his biggest problem had been staying upright on his feet. She saw him slide down the needle-coated ridge. It was so funny that her laughter had almost given her presence away. Then he'd really surprised her when he'd headed downstream directly toward her recently constructed barricade.

The last thing Viola Mae had wanted was to cast suspicion on herself. Her dam had been meant to look like a natural barrier, built by a beaver, if it were discovered. And then she'd decided that a city fellow like the fancy Mr. Rowe wouldn't recognize a beaver if it bit him on the behind, much less a beaver dam. But the longer she'd watched him, the more uneasy Viola Mae had become. His investigation of the dam and his unvoiced conclusions had at last gotten the better of her. That was why she had decided to get closer, and why he'd caught her off guard. And why she was now his prisoner.

"What do you know about this beaver dam?" Seth asked her. His sea-green gaze slid over her face, warming her like the sun on a summer day.

"Beaver?" she scoffed. Her grannie had always told her the best defense was a strong offense, so she retorted, "Anyone with a lick of sense knows that no beaver builds his lodge in shallow water. Goes to show you that a big city fellow like yourself don't know nothing."

Viola Mae's implication that he was ignorant about such things rankled Seth. Although he wasn't an expert woodsman, he knew about beavers, barring their temperament.

Seth rolled off her, the thrill of his catch forgotten with her insult. They sat side by side, glaring at one another. Breaking the silence, he cocked his head to the side and said, "Maybe you know how this blockade got here, if you're so sure a beaver didn't build it.''

"Me? Why would I know?''

The words sounded guilty, even to Viola Mae. She could have kicked herself. Did he suspect that she had something to do with the dam's construction? If so, she needed to delude him.

"Curiosity brought me here,'' she quickly explained, smoothing the hair back from her face. The tangled mane fell forward again when she jerked her head toward the stream-bed. "I noticed the water wasn't flowing this morning when I went to the creek to get water. Thought I'd see why.''

Her explanation sounded logical, and he accepted it as that. He wanted to accept it, for again her rustic beauty enthralled him.

"You live around here?'' Seth asked her. He searched the surrounding woods, recalling that Harriet had said Viola Mae lived on a farm outside of town. But he'd never dreamed it would be in the same area as the railroad camp.

"Back a piece,'' she answered, not willing to reveal the whereabouts.

Viola Mae's gaze scanned his face, then lowered to where the button locked his shirt closed. It was then that Seth recalled the many bites that covered his face and neck. Having always prided himself on his good looks and meticulous grooming, he stuttered an explanation. "The mosquitoes like me.''

"I'll say.'' Amusement lit up Viola Mae's face, masking out what he'd noted earlier as concern. "Looks to me like they were as persistent as a starving bedbug.''

"Worse,'' he answered, hating the way he looked. "The itching is driving me crazy.''

"Tried salt?''

Seth nodded his head.

She watched him, offering her next suggestion. "How about moonshine?''

"You mean liquor?''

There was plenty of the local brew around the camp, although there was a rule about its misuse. It was odd that Riley or someone else hadn't mentioned it as a curative. It would certainly be easier to apply to his welts than the gooey paste made from salt and water. His spirits lifting, Seth asked, "You just dab it on the bites?"

Viola Mae's mouth dropped open. She stared at him speechless, before jumping to her feet. *Dab it on the bites? The man is as crazy as a beetle bug,* she thought.

Seth noted she wore the same faded calico dress that she'd worn the first day he'd met her . . . but minus her boots. His gaze locked on her naked feet, which, if he'd wanted to, he could have reached out and touched. Her bare toes were almost buried in the soft sand, and the sugar-fine granules dusted her shapely ankles.

Desire ripped through him like a bullet. Where Seth came from, women never went without their stockings and shoes except in the privacy of their bedrooms. Now he understood why. Fighting his heated reaction, he too jumped up.

"You really are a strange one," she told him, backing away.

Her statement puzzled him. "Strange—what do you mean?" he demanded.

"The whiskey." Viola Mae looked disgusted as she turned to leave. "You ain't supposed to dab it on your bites, you're supposed to drink it. Even Booger Butts, who's dumber than dirt, knows that. I guarantee, if you guzzle enough of it, it'll numb you senseless."

"You mean . . ." Seth would have said more, but Viola Mae had all but disappeared into the thick brush on the ridge.

"Wait," he shouted. Only silence answered him.

Viola Mae's logic astounded him. "It'll numb you senseless," he quoted aloud.

Seth had been that way a few times in his life, and knew the advantages of being that drunk. He also knew the disadvantages the next morning, and decided he'd stick with the saltwater paste.

Seth shook his head in astonishment, searching the woods for a trace of Viola Mae. But she was nowhere in sight.

Like the forest nymphs of Greek mythology, he thought, a female spirit who dwells in the woods, living beneath leaves.

She certainly had managed to cast a spell on him. Seth was still puzzled over his body's reaction to her bare toes. Never had he met another female who affected him the way Viola Mae Smith did.

He wanted to find her, to get to know her, although his better judgment warned him against such notions. But maybe after he'd cleared the stream he'd go in search of her farm. He needed a friend, he reasoned. Someone like Viola Mae could teach him how to survive in this wild place.

Besides, Seth's logical side dictated that if there were criminals in the area, a woman living alone needed to be warned of possibly impending danger. His illogical side dictated that he look beneath every leaf until he found Viola Mae's hiding place, regardless of the risks.

Chapter Four

"Won't."

"Will, too." Jedwin Rowe insisted, lying on his belly beside his one and only Atlanta friend.

Benjamin Hartley was a year younger than Jed's ten years, but the boys had become constant companions after their first meeting, not only because of the proximity of their houses, but also because there were no other boys their age in the neighborhood.

"Believe me. Adults lie," Ben insisted.

Jed shot him an angry glance, and would have punched him for calling his brother a liar, but thought better of it. Yesterday the rain had stopped, and today the sun shone so brightly that it warmed the spring grass where the two boys lay. Also, this morning the long-awaited letter had arrived from his brother Seth. As far as Jed was concerned, it was too perfect a day to risk being sent to his room by his Aunt Cloe because of a tussle between friends. So instead of punching Ben, Jed defended his brother.

"Not all adults lie. Especially not Seth."

"Betcha." Ben seemed determined to not let the argument die.

"You're just jealous because I'll be leaving this boring town, and you won't."

"Ain't jealous. Besides, who wants to go to a mosquito-infested swamp and live in a tent?"

"Me, that's who."

Jed wished now that he hadn't read Seth's letter to his

friend. Especially since Ben seemed determined to take the joy out of his earlier pleasure.

The door to the back of the house swung open, then banged shut. From behind a hedge of gardenia bushes where the boys lay, they watched a pair of booted feet move toward the clothesline.

"It's just Tilly," Jed informed Ben. The boys' earlier argument was forgotten while they watched Aunt Cloe's maid hang out Monday's wash. After her task was completed, Tilly returned to the house.

Taking the lead, Jed slid on his belly beneath the waxy green leaves of the gardenia bushes. The torrid, moist scent of the newly opened blooms absorbed the air above their heads, the sweetness wrapped around them.

"Yuk!" Benjamin exclaimed. Until his gaze followed the younger boy's, Jed wasn't certain what had brought on his friend's response.

"Right," Jed said, agreeing with Ben for the first time today. On the clothesline, his Aunt Cloe's bloomers flapped in the wind like pale flags. Disgusted, Jed showed the size by stretching his arms as wide as they would spread. "They're this big."

Giving in to laughter, Benjamin responded. "Dummy. That's why they have drawstrings."

"Hers don't." Jed would have revealed the conversation he'd heard earlier between his Aunt Cloe and Tilly about the absence of drawstrings, but Ben calling him a dummy angered him.

"I've got sisters, remember," Ben said. "I know all about undergarments."

Angrier now, Jed replied, "You don't know slop."

"Do so."

"Don't."

Jedwin had all he could take of Benjamin's quarrelsome attitude. In spite of the beautiful day, and in spite of Seth's recent letter, Jed's patience was worn thin. Though he had resolved not to spoil his afternoon by fighting, Jed could not resist boxing Benjamin on the ear. Soon the two boys were locked in combat. Together they rolled over and over the grassy carpet until bony, flapping limbs tangled with Aunt Cloe's freshly laundered drawers, yanking them to the ground.

In a tangle of lye-scented muslin, the wrestlers tumbled across the lawn. Suddenly both boys were jerked to their feet by their shirt collars. While Tilly restrained Benjamin, Aunt Cloe restrained Jed.

"Stop it this minute," his aunt ordered. "Gentlemen shouldn't act like jackanapes." She gave Jed a sharp jerk and untangled her grass-stained drawers from around his body. "You should be ashamed of yourselves."

"It's his fault," Jed yelled.

"Ain't neither," Ben replied, dodging Jed's attempted blow.

"Tilly was going to offer you some of her homemade cookies, but under the circumstances, you don't deserve them."

Jed met his aunt's gaze with a defiant one that quickly turned to disappointment with her remark about the cookies. The boys exchanged warning glares.

"Jedwin Rowe. You, young man, will spend some time in your room contemplating your ungentlemanly behavior. Benjamin Hartley, you go home. I'll talk to your mother later."

Leading Jed by the car toward the house, Aunt Cloe continued her admonishments. But already Jed had stopped listening. More than ever, he longed to distance himself from this household of old ladies, spinsters who knew nothing of the character of young boys. A little tussle was good for the soul. He knew even his older brother, Seth, had enjoyed a few fights.

"To your room, young man," Aunt Cloe ordered. "When you're able to conduct yourself properly, you may come down and apologize to poor Tilly for making her redo the laundry."

Belligerently Jed stomped away from his aunt.

Some friend Ben turned out to be. Because of him, Jed would miss a snack of Tilly's cookies and would have to stay holed up in his room like a trapped rabbit.

Once inside his bedroom, Jed flopped down on the flower-sprinkled print of the window seat. His eyes scanned the room. Everywhere he looked were lace and women's gew-gaws.

A house for a sissy!

No place for a man. Ever since his brother's departure, Jed had contemplated following him. Not that living with Aunt Cloe and Tilly was all bad, but they were old maids without any idea how to treat a boy of ten. He recalled the words of Seth's letter. *If all goes as planned, you'll be in Pensacola in time to start school in the fall.* To Jed, fall seemed like a million years away. This last thought coupled with the recent episode involving his aunt's bloomers had Jed convinced that he couldn't stay there a day longer than it took for him to plan his escape.

Initially Seth would be angry at Jed for disobeying him and causing his aunt undue worry. But once he arrived in Pensacola, Jed knew his brother wouldn't send him back to Atlanta.

Why, then, shouldn't he strike out on his own? How hard could it be to journey to Florida anyway? *I could just leave Aunt Cloe a note, and she won't worry about me.*

Before the sun had been above the horizon for more than an hour, Viola Mae had milked the cow, gathered eggs from the henhouse, and checked the herbs growing in the patch of yard on the sunniest side of the cabin.

It had been two days since she had encountered the Yankee by her so-called beaver dam. And it had been two long nights since their encounter and she hadn't had a good night's sleep. No matter how hard she tried to push the Yankee rascal out of her mind, she couldn't. Mr. Seth Thomas Rowe kept flaring up in her thoughts like an unwanted rash, and was about as welcome as a bad case of poison oak.

With her early-morning chores completed, Viola Mae dragged herself into the cabin for breakfast. At the dry sink in the kitchen, she splashed cold water from the pitcher onto her face, put the coffee on to boil, then dropped down in the closest chair. Mustard, the house cat whose coat resembled the color of the herb that was her namesake, took Viola Mae's flattened lap as an invitation for her to nap. The oversized cat leaped onto Viola Mae's thighs, rolled herself into an indistinguishable ball of fur, and soon dropped off to sleep.

Eyeing the cat with envy, Viola Mae thought, *I wish I could be you right now. No roaming Toms disturbing your feline dreams.*

Inside the cabin, the cat's lusty snore joined the quiet ticking of the mantel clock. Shadows and sunshine stealing past the windows looked like puzzle pieces where they mottled the rough-hewn floor. Viola Mae drew in a deep sigh. Lemon wax from yesterday's cleaning still scented the air, reminding her of her most recent burst of energy. Like a house-a-fire, she'd cleaned the whole cabin, hoping to dispel her unwanted guest from her thoughts. She believed that that same spurt of energy was what had her feeling all tuckered out today.

"Mustard, I feel like a bar of soap after a Saturday night bath."

Wearily Viola Mae glanced at the top of the kitchen table where several pieces of board lay. She had placed them there last night, intending to make "No Trespassing" signs to post around her property. Needless to say, since the railroad crew's arrival, she found more and more of her land infringed upon each day.

Nothing she'd done so far to rid her land of the railroad seemed to be working. Although she knew the tainted preserves had shackled the railroaders to their camp, making them unable to work, the effect would last only a couple of days. The image of the men's discomfort made Viola Mae smile. They had certainly kept the privies busy.

But the damming up of the camp's water source had been an effort in futility. Thanks to the citified engineer, her beaver dam had been discovered before it could cause the workers any major problems.

How could a greenhorn like Seth Rowe, a friend of snooty-hooty Harriet Archibald, know about beavers? The only experience with the animal that Harriet and her friends had was with the pelts that came molded into the latest fashions. This thought sickened Viola Mae. Such decadence was nothing more than a heartless act of destruction. As for the Yankee—

as far as she could tell, the only thing he was good for was feasting your eyes upon. A delight to look at, mosquito bites and all.

Disgusted with the way her thoughts were headed, she stood up, dumping the golden ball of fur onto the floor as she did so. The coffee was ready, and she needed a cup of fortification if she was to make it through the rest of the day. Viola Mae took a bite from last night's hoe cake and flopped down again at the kitchen table. Although her grannie had reminded her many times that ladies didn't dunk, the mannerless act gave her added pleasure this morning. The sugary taste of the coffee and milk mixed with the corn bread as it slipped past her tongue was like a balm to her restless soul.

Viola Mae deliberated. If she didn't get a response to the letters of protest she'd written to the backers of the railroad soon, she would have to reach into her bag of tricks for more mischievous stunts to stall the railroad's progress. It wasn't fair. A body didn't stand a chance to have her opinions aired unless she was rich like the Archibalds.

Her breakfast finished, she took up a brush and paint and went to work lettering her warnings. She would stake the signs near the boundaries of her land.

"Top of the morning to ye, laddie."

Seth nodded a sleepy thank-you to Riley when the Irishman thrust a cup of coffee into his hands. Walking to a pine log in front of the cooking fire, Seth dropped down on the dead tree, trying to shake the sleep from his mind.

He had never been a morning person. It took two cups of the thick, black brew and a good half hour before the cobwebs unraveled inside his head. For that reason, Seth made it a point to rise an hour before the other camp workers so that his mind would be clear and ready for thinking when the day finally began.

At the fire, Tater, the camp cook, was already stirring up a giant batch of pancakes, getting ready to feed the huge appetites of the railroad workers when they rolled out of their tents.

In spite of the early hour, Seth found he enjoyed this time

of the day, the hour right after daybreak, more than any other. Mornings dawned softly in the camp, bringing with them a tapestry of brilliant colors that would soon roll back to reveal a clear sky.

Afternoons brought in the fat-bellied clouds that hung close to the horizon, bulging with humidity. The nights could be so still and thick with heat that one's own breath felt cool in comparison. Florida, he thought. The fickle siren could be both enchanting and offensive in her primitive beauty.

Seth glanced toward the busy cook. He was a wiry little man who, when he spoke, boasted of having cooked for the Confederate troops during the War. He was a man of few words, especially to one he considered the enemy. Tater's vocabulary consisted of grunts of either approval or disapproval, but God help the man who uttered a complaint against his cooking. Seth had heard about but never witnessed the cook's temper, and he didn't care to. It appeared the others in camp didn't wish to be on the receiving end of his fury either, because no one ever complained about the meals he served.

No need to. It was the celebrated opinion of everyone in camp that their cook was the best to be had. Seth was amazed at the culinary dishes that Tater could prepare on an open fire. Just the thought of food made Seth's mouth juice up for the lighter-than-air pancakes, the golden, fluffy eggs, and the pork sausage and bacon whose scent already was more seductive than a Saturday night whore. Seth's stomach rumbled with hunger as Riley took a seat beside him on the log.

"No more trouble with the water supply?" he asked, taking a big swallow of coffee.

"Neh, laddie," his foreman replied. "Ye took care of that just fine. Ye're still convinced it wasn't the work of the big-toothed rodent?"

"Positive." Seth wrapped his fingers around the tin cup. Its warmth felt good against his blistered palms. "I'm sure of it, especially because of the dysentery the men experienced after eating the mysterious blackberry preserves. I'd wager my next paycheck that it was the mischief of the man we fired the day before."

Riley shook his carrot-colored head in denial. "It might be, but the lad didn't seem to have the wherewithal to come up with such a scheme. And where would he be a-gettin' them preserves? Remember, I ate them, too, suffered with the worst of 'em because of me own gluttony." He licked his lips in memory. "Best damn preserves this ol' Irish tongue ever tasted."

Seth chuckled. "So he knows a good cook."

"Or a good murderer. We all 'bout died, we near did." Soon they were both laughing at the folly that had beset the camp.

Riley returned to the fire to refill their cups, and Seth sighed with pleasure. It still amazed him how much he enjoyed his new position as engineer. For a man who had never worked a day in his life, he felt pleased with his accomplishments.

Already he and Riley had become friends. Their friendship had sprouted and taken root in spite of their dissimilar backgrounds. There was no common ground between the son of a banker and the son of a potato farmer from Ireland, but each of them recognized in the other the misfortune of being considered an outsider. Just as the Irish weren't accepted in this country, Seth had not been accepted by his men, who were mostly Southerners. But he was determined to change that.

Riley returned with the coffee, and excused himself to make a trip to the latrine before the rest of the camp roused themselves from sleep.

Seth watched him go, then took a whiff of the aromatic brew cupped in his hands. Tater certainly boiled a fine cup of coffee. Best Seth ever recalled having. With only the one cup under his belt, his head had already begun to clear, and he was anxious to get to the tracks and begin again the back-breaking but rewarding task of laying railroad ties.

Looking toward the stand of long-leaf pines on the opposite side of the clearing, Seth glimpsed a flash of brilliant red color. Immediately he recognized the male cardinal whose feathers resembled fiery flames against the subdued green needles. He listened to the bird's clear slurred whistle that lowered in pitch as he sang. *What-cheer cheer cheer.* Seth raised his cup in confirmation—*what cheer* it was to be alive on such a fine, spring day.

Seth continued to listen. The woods were charged with sound. The early-morning coolness that now cloaked the woods would soon disappear. A white-winged butterfly fluttered several feet away. His gaze riveted on its silvery-blond color, which reminded him of the country girl who had teased his idle musings for the last two days.

In fact, Viola Mae Smith hadn't been far from Seth's thoughts since their first meeting. He'd been too busy to seek out her hiding place as he had promised himself he would do, but that didn't mean he'd dismissed her from his mind. She haunted him. She and her damn naked feet, her slim ankles coated in the sugary white sand of the stream. Even as he tromped through the woods, he kept constantly alert, hoping that he would stumble again on the forest sprite who Harriet had said preferred the company of animals over that of humans.

"Morning, Mr. Rowe."

Seth was jerked from his musings as the first of the workers began to tumble out of their tents and wind their way through the woods to the outhouses.

"Good morning." He returned several men's greetings, wishing they would call him by his first name as he'd suggested. But most still thought of him as the Yankee invader, still refused to use the less formal salutation. At least, they weren't calling him Mr. Seth, a respectful Southern greeting that he'd heard often since his arrival.

As the others filed out of their tents and went in various directions, Seth realized that no bugle call was needed to rally this group from their beds. The scent of Tater's breakfast about to be served was enough to rouse even the heaviest sleeper. Seth picked up his tin plate and joined Riley and the others already forming a line for food.

An hour later, Seth stood in the timber-cleared roadbed. It was his crew's responsibility to lay track eastward from Pensacola, hooking up with the bridge-builders already spanning Escambia Bay. The railroad bridge would link with the other tracks being built toward Milton and the Blackwater River.

Because of his position as engineer, Seth had taken over the duties of leveling each tie. Tracklaying was a joint venture of everyone employed. If they were to meet the projected schedule, there was no room for sloths or troublemakers like the worthless man Seth had fired several days before—the same man he suspected of having had something to do with the tainted fruit and the blocked water supply.

Again Riley's friendship had proved to be invaluable. His goodwill, coupled with the experience he had brought with him from having worked on the Transcontinental Railroad, was an unexpected stroke of luck. Although Seth had his engineering books, Riley had firsthand experience, which had saved Seth countless hours of searching through bookish material that he soon learned was outdated. Both he and Riley knew that the Irishman was the better man for Seth's job. But again, that knowledge didn't affect the respect they held for each other. They were a team with a job to do and they dedicated themselves to that end.

It was Riley who had instigated the efficient system of railroad construction he had learned from Jack and Dan Casement when he'd worked with them in 1866. And so far, except for minor delays, tracklaying was progressing almost on schedule.

Seth had finished leveling a row of ties when a noise caught his attention. He looked toward the sound and saw a carriage approaching. The vehicle was barely visible in the cloud of dust that horse and wheels kicked up. It moved toward Seth along the length of the roadbed.

It was not unusual for a group of locals from town to ride out to the site to check on the railroad's progress. Most of the time the workers ignored the curious spectators, continuing with their backbreaking work while the revelers drank sarsaparilla and picnicked in the shade of the towering pines. In his other life, Seth would have probably been in the picnicking party, but all that had changed. More interested in the present than the past, he turned back to the task of making certain the next rails were the proper distance apart.

Instead of heading for the cool shade beneath the trees, the carriage rolled to a stop several hundred feet from where Seth

and his men worked. Immediately he recognized his visitor—
Harriet Archibald.

"Hello!" she called, waving a virginal-white hankie in
Seth's direction. With the sound of the lyrical voice singling
out one of the laborers, all activity up and down the line came
to a standstill. All eyes focused on the feminine apparition in
vanilla lace now standing in the shiny, black dogcart with the
vermillion stripes.

Seth wasn't certain if it was the stoppage of work or Harriet's presence that annoyed him the most. But he did know
that he wouldn't allow his charges to stand around making
spectacles of themselves by staring at the boss's daughter.
And he was too much of a gentleman to allow Harriet to be
the object of crude men's ogling.

"Break for lunch," Seth shouted, wiping the inside of his
shirt collar with the bandanna tied around his neck. It was
almost noon. As a man, he knew that a woman, especially
one as fetching as Harriet Archibald in her spring confection,
would demand more of the men's attention than a spike and
hammer. Under the circumstances, Seth decided to allow his
men's hungry bellies to override their lewd minds. With the
mention of food, it wasn't long before the workers abandoned
their positions and disappeared into the woods leading back
to the campsite.

Walking to the cart where Harriet waited, Seth caught the
horse's bridle. "Miss Archibald, what brings you out this
way?" From beneath the wide-brimmed hat he had recently
purchased to protect his head and neck from the merciless
sun, he squinted up at her where she stood posed in the cart.

She smiled down at him. "Why, Seth Rowe, do look at
you. Aren't you the dashing cowboy?"

Harriet's hot gaze slithered over his new bib pullover shirt
and lingered on the front of his copper-riveted Levi's. In that
moment, Seth realized that coyness wasn't one of Harriet's
traits. She was anything but shy; in fact, she was downright
brazen. Although Seth was a man with considerable experience with women, he still felt the hotness of her gaze as it
slid back over his chest before locking with his eyes.

Her lips turned up in challenge. At that moment, Seth decided that Harriet Archibald was as dangerous as a keg of dynamite.

She motioned him to her side. "Please help me out of this old buggy."

Seth hesitated, searching for an excuse not to get within range of her explosive power.

"Miss Harriet, I've been working all morning in the heat and dust. I certainly don't want to soil your pretty frock."

"Pooh. This old rag? If that should happen, Spacey will have it sparkling clean in no time."

Spacey, Seth recalled, was the Archibalds' black servant. She lived with father and daughter, cooking, cleaning, and doing whatever else the young miss of the house demanded. And those demands were many, he'd learned during his overnight stay in the Archibald house.

"Well . . ."

Reluctantly Seth led the horse over to a nearby oak tree, where he looped the reins around a limb before presenting his hand to assist her. Somewhere between the hand-joining and Harriet's descent to the ground, she lost her balance. Soon she was sliding down his body like a skater gliding across an icy pond. Seth shivered in spite of himself. His reaction seemed to please her. Once her feet touched solid ground, Seth untangled himself from her clinging grasp.

"Forgive me," he apologized, putting distance between them. "My present state must be offensive to a lady." He swabbed the sweat from his brow.

"Nonsense," she teased, "I'm sure it's only the humidity. You'll soon get used to it. But do let us find some shade." Flicking open her lace parasol, Harriet led the way, stopping beneath the tree's dense shadows.

"Now," she said, turning back to face him, "this is so much better." After a moment of strained quiet, Harriet asked, "Aren't you glad to see me?"

Hell, no, I'm not glad to see you. Instead of speaking his thoughts, he smiled and replied, "Of course I'm happy to see you. But I'm still curious as to what brings you out here on such a miserably hot day."

"Papa sent me. He told me to be sure and invite you to

church services this Sunday. Afterwards, the ladies of the church are serving lunch across from the parish in Seville Square.''

The last thing Seth wanted to do was put on a suit and attend church services. Especially in this heat. He had intended to relax this weekend, perhaps familiarize himself with the maps and charts of the railroad's path that he hadn't had a chance to study.

He tried to appear apologetic as he offered his excuse. ''Harriet, please convey my apologies to your father, but I feel I need to stay—''

''Nonsense. Papa is planning on you being there. Many of the railroad's important backers will be present. Colonel Chipley himself has promised an appearance.''

Great. Just what he needed. Another Confederate veteran to stare daggers through his enemy hide.

''Papa says it's important that you be there. After all, you are the engineer hired to oversee their interests.''

Harriet stepped closer and patted his chest with her lace-gloved hand. ''You will be there, won't you?'' Her dark eyes searched his face, daring him to refuse.

How could he? She was his boss's daughter, and if *Papa* wanted him present at the church and luncheon, Seth would have to accept the invitation.

He smiled blandly and replied, ''Yes, I'll be there.''

Excitement lit her face. ''That's wonderful,'' she exclaimed. ''There are so many people I want you to meet. And, of course, Papa's friends, too.''

''Now, my pretty miss, it's time for you to leave so I can get back to work.'' Already Seth could hear some of the men tromping back through the woods toward the tracks.

Harriet, having accomplished what she set out to do, was easily persuaded to return to the waiting buggy. Assisting her back into the carriage, he watched as she urged the mare into motion.

''Sunday, then,'' she called over her shoulder, and waved at the men merging from the edge of the woods when she trotted past.

''Sunday,'' Seth confirmed as the dogcart disappeared in a

distant cloud of dust. Thanks to her untimely visit, it would be dinnertime before he got a chance to eat. Hell. After this most recent development, his appetite had vanished along with Harriet anyway.

Chapter Five

With her "No Trespassing" signs hung, Viola Mae had decided to check on the railroad camp. It had been several days since the men had ingested her slicked up fruit. She figured by now they were all fit, weaker perhaps, but again able to put in a full day's work. In the thick underbrush, close by but not too near the campsite, Viola Mae watched Harriet's arrival.

The minute the chariot pulled to a stop beside the tracks, Viola Mae recognized the vehicle by its shiny black color and the reddish-orange stripes streaking its sides. The painted cart had always reminded Viola Mae of the beautifully marked garter snake that made its home in the woods and fields of Florida.

Viola Mae studied the fancy wagon. Although she wasn't one to covet something that belonged to another, as a young girl growing up she had longed for a ride in Harriet's two-wheeled wagon. Often she had watched from afar while Harriet and her friends sported around town and to the seashore in the fancy little rig.

Of course, Viola Mae knew that an invitation to ride would never be issued by Harriet. The girls were too different. Harriet was rich and lived with her father in a big house in town, while Viola Mae lived without a father on a dirt farm in the neighboring woods. Their lives intermingled only because of the closeness of the community they lived in and the school they both attended. But this knowledge hadn't kept Viola Mae from desiring a ride in Harriet's cart, or entertaining the idea of what it would feel like to race at breakneck speeds across the ground in such a fine vehicle.

Shoving the unwelcome memory aside, she studied Harriet poised like a princess in her ready-made clothes. Although Viola Mae wouldn't be caught dead in such feminine trappings, she admitted begrudgingly that Harriet presented quite a fetching image, if the men gaping at her were any indication.

Apparently the new railroad boss must have realized that the men weren't interested in working anymore because he shouted for them to take a lunch break. Viola Mae slunk deeper into the shadows to keep from being discovered as the workers left the roadbed. When the sound of their voices and stomping feet diminished into the distance, she took up her post again.

As she watched she decided that Harriet Archibald should be on the stage. Her ability to play the defenseless heroine made Viola Mae's breakfast of coffee and hoe cake threaten to make a reappearance.

At that moment, nothing would have pleased her more than to drive the last of her sign-hanging nails into Harriet's scheming hide. But since such an act wasn't possible, Viola Mae took out her frustration on the nearest tree. She whopped the hammer against the trunk. The loud thud echoed throughout the woods and caused a flurry among the escaping critters. Seconds later, she regretted her actions when she felt Seth's attention center on the brush where she stood hidden. She didn't dare breathe or move, for fear of being discovered, but Harriet wasn't about to be ignored. At that precise moment, Miss Priss demanded that Seth help her down from the carriage.

"Slippery as an eel," Viola Mae whispered, and gasped when she watched Harriet pretend to lose her balance, then slide down the muscled length of Seth Rowe's body. Not that he seemed to mind, or think that Harriet's behavior was unladylike. Viola Mae noticed that he seemed to be enjoying himself.

"The weasel."

An image of that same powerful length pinning her to the

ground by the streambed surfaced in Viola Mae's memory. The same image that lately had popped in and out of her head at will.

It appeared that the Yankee engineer had more on his mind than just bedding the new railroad track. And if Harriet Archibald wanted to be the one to scratch his itch, then so be it. Her old grannie had warned her in no uncertain terms about the consequences of itch-scratching, using her own daughter as an example. Viola Mae wanted no part of such behavior.

Disgusted, she whirled away from the lovers and started for home. But distance didn't erase from her thoughts the two people locked together. A thrill walked up her spine. Why, after years of promising herself that no man would ever get into her bloomers, was she wondering how it would feel to have the new railroad boss try?

"Merciful heavens," she said aloud. "Enough of these cracked-brained thoughts."

In truth, the sooner she could rid her woods of the likes of Seth Rowe and everyone else connected with the railroad, the sooner her life could return to normal.

Determined to fling away her restlessness, Viola Mae began to run. Soon all thoughts of the handsome Yankee disappeared as she flew through the woods like a golden eagle. Her next plan to rid herself of the railroaders had already begun to hatch in her mind.

Sunday morning dawned with an orange-yellow sky that rivaled a fiery opal, in Viola Mae's opinion. She paused in the brushing of her wet hair to savor the moment. Inhaling deeply of the early-morning breeze, she recognized the familiar scents: the bay's briny water, the beach's warming sands, the surrounding evergreens, and last but not least, the newly opened magnolias that grew on the giant tree beside the house.

She watched the early-morning gold fade to periwinkle, and the sunlight ease the diffused shadows in the yard into distinct and recognizable shapes. Barefooted and clad only in her nightgown, Viola Mae dropped down on the porch stairs and continued the task of brushing the knots from her waist-length hair.

Every Sunday morning before church, she went through the same routine. The ritual had carried over from her youth and her grandmother's insistence that her hair be washed and bound like a proper lady's before they set out for church.

Most days, Viola Mae attended to her ablutions without thinking. She'd learned long ago that she was a creature of habit, rising at the same time every day, retiring at the same time every night. Not unlike the roosters that crowed at sunup, or Rosemary the cow, who expected to be milked by first light. Just as she never questioned the biological occurrences of the farm animals, Viola Mae never questioned her own habits.

Until now.

This morning was different. She felt different, fidgety and restless—unwilling to accept the mundane sameness of her daily routine. Could it be that last night's dreams of the new railroad boss, both singularly and entwined with Harriet Archibald, were the reasons for her anxiety? Why did his image insist on bedeviling her every thought? She had no time for such fantasies, or more importantly, she didn't believe in them.

Viola Mae dropped her head into her hands. As she combed her fingers through her hair, they tangled in the springy ringlets that had begun to dry around her face.

Today was no different from any other Sunday, her rational self insisted. She would dress in her same Sunday-go-to-meeting clothes, then hitch Ginger to the farm wagon and head for town. When she arrived at Christ Church, she would meet her friend Gracie. They would sit together during the service, then attend the covered-dish luncheon together. Afterwards, on her way home, she would visit her grandmother's grave. If today was no different than any other, why then did she feel so out of sorts? She stood up, wearied by her frustration. She said a silent prayer that Seth Rowe wouldn't be in attendance at the function.

An hour later, Viola Mae was on her way to town, wearing one of the two good dresses she owned. She'd chosen the blue one, a lightweight cotton, over the brown one, wondering as she did so if it was her blue mood that had influenced her choice, or if it was because the preacher's son had commented on how the color made her cornflower-blue eyes sparkle. Not that she was interested in the preacher's son. He was so homely, the tide wouldn't take him out, but he was a man. And the only male who'd shown any interest in Viola Mae as a woman.

Dressed and ready to go, she had stood in front of the vanity mirror examining her reflection. No matter how hard she tried to look the part of a lady, which wasn't very often, she always looked as though she had thrown her clothes in the air and then run under them. Today was no exception.

She was a dwarf, too short for the fitted bodices, vertical panniers, and bustled skirts that were in fashion. As for the high collars and narrow sleeves that appeared elegant on those blessed with height, the sophistication was totally lost on someone so small.

Her straw hat was the only article of clothing that she believed reflected her true persona: a straw poke bonnet whose color reminded her of hay. The cluster of field flowers fastened to the hat's brim embraced her love of nature.

When Viola Mae rolled into town, the streets surrounding Seville Square were packed with wagons of every shape and size. Adults and children, dressed in their Sunday best, milled around the entrance of Christ Church in animated conversation.

Some one hundred years before the United States had acquired Pensacola from the Spanish, the town was predominantly Catholic. In 1832, Episcopalians, Methodists, and Presbyterians had united to build a house of worship. Christ Church was one of the oldest churches in Florida and a pillar of the community.

Viola Mae saw a group of children playing chase with a dog that darted among the worshippers, while anxious mothers tried to intercept and still keep their cheerful dispositions. Several ladies waved, and Viola Mae returned their greetings. She spotted Gracie Marle standing on the church steps talking with the preacher's son. Their gazes locked, and Gracie's sent a silent message that said, *Rescue me*.

Biting back a smile, Viola Mae negotiated Ginger past the throngs of people and turned up a side street. The earlier babble diminished to a distant echo as she searched for a place to park the wagon. Beneath a big tree that provided adequate shade, she found her spot. When she jumped down from the wagon seat, her walking boots pinched her toes, reminding her of how much she hated wearing shoes. She much preferred going barefooted or wearing her old, worn riding boots. But on Sundays she adhered to the standards her grandmother had taught her, and that included dressing like a lady for church.

No one set such rigid standards of dress for Jesus, she grumbled to herself when she stepped in a hole and felt a sharp pain radiate through her ankle. In the few renderings she'd seen of him with his disciples, they all wore sandals and had their long hair unbound. But, of course, Jesus was a man, and no such allowances were made for the women of the world.

Her mind's ramblings made her acutely aware of a hairpin that felt as though it were digging a well in her scalp. She, too, preferred wearing her hair unbound—free. And it seemed her hair agreed with her. Before the day was finished it would spit out the pins she had so carefully secured earlier. With a little luck and much intervention from the Holy Spirit, she hoped, it would stay in place throughout the long afternoon.

By the time she reached the door of the church, she was in no better frame of mind than when she'd awakened this morning. Gracie's greeting didn't improve her disposition.

"That time of month, huh?" Gracie whispered as they slipped inside the sanctuary door.

"How did you know—" Her friend's knowing glance and her own easy admission made them both break into laughter. All eyes of the seated congregation focused on the late and noisy twosome as they shuffled down the aisle to the only seats that were still empty, at the front of the chapel.

Although Gracie was ten years older than Viola Mae, she was her closest friend. Gracie and her husband had moved to

Pensacola from Virginia five years earlier. Not long after they arrived, they'd purchased the General Store. Soon after that, Gracie's young husband had contracted yellow fever and died.

It was Viola Mae, along with her grannie, who had seen Gracie through those difficult months following his death. A friendship had blossomed among the three women. So instead of returning to her family in Virginia, Gracie had chosen to remain in Pensacola. A natural businesswoman, she made the best cinnamon rolls in the world, and Viola Mae thanked her lucky stars every day for her friendship.

Three years later, when her old grannie had died, it was Gracie who had given Viola Mae support. As far as Viola Mae was concerned, her friend was as comfortable as an old shoe, barring the ones that were pinching her toes at the moment. Gracie's outspokenness complimented Viola Mae's unaffected nature, and both women could barely tolerate the vain Miss Archibald.

Right after they had taken their places in the front pew, the preacher stood up behind the dais. His hands raised towards the heavens, he invited the congregation to stand and sing the opening hymn.

While the preacher's wife pumped away in the corner on the organ, the congregation waited for her flourish of a refrain to be finished before they would dare open their mouths in song.

From the back of the church, the inner doors burst open, and a gush of activity made its way up the aisle. All faces turned toward the latecomer as she flounced toward the front of the church.

The music stopped as the preacher spoke. "Miss Archibald," the Reverend Hunt intoned, "we're so glad that you could join us this morning."

Although no invitation was needed, he still motioned with the bible he held in his hand. "Please, child, do come forward." He paused, and his flock snickered good-naturedly. "Because of the lateness of the hour, I believe you and your party will have to sit in the front row."

"I'm sorry, Reverend," Harriet apologized, "but we were

detained.'' She chattered endlessly as she led her guest up the aisle toward the front of the church.

"You know my special bread that everyone in town adores. Instead of rising like it should, it fell as if it had a bad case of the dropsy, leaving me no choice but to begin again. I was knee-deep in flour when I realized the lateness of the hour.''

Viola Mae and Gracie exchanged glances. Anyone who had been forced to eat Harriet Archibald's bread knew it would gag a maggot. She was the worst cook in Pensacola, and the whole town knew it.

"No need for an apology,'' the reverend said again. "Since this is God's house, I'm sure you're forgiven for your tardiness. Who knows better than Our Lord about bread?'' The preacher smiled at his cleverness, and the congregation chuckled. "Please do find your seat so we may begin.''

Everyone had to wait until Harriet and her guest had taken their places in the pew before the minister began again.

"Let us get on with the business of feeding our souls, so that we can feed our stomachs with the wonderful spread I'm sure all you ladies have prepared for us.''

A murmur of approval rolled throughout the congregation.

Everybody but Viola Mae seemed unconcerned by Harriet's tardy entrance. She looked around Gracie's stout form to let Harriet know how much she disapproved of her behavior, but when she did, Viola Mae wanted to sink beneath the hand-hewn flooring where three Episcopalian ministers of an earlier time were buried, for her eyes locked on the devil himself.

Seth Rowe looked little better than a flimflam man up to his usual deceptive nonsense in his short gray frock coat, silvery blue vest, gray silk tie, and boldly checked trousers.

"Miss Smith.'' He bowed his head slightly in her direction.

Viola Mae only nodded her reply because his glance had taken her breath away.

From beneath shaggy brows, his sea-green eyes stared into the depths of her soul, or so Viola Mae thought as she felt his piercing gaze make her face bleed with scarlet color. Ducking behind Gracie to escape his overwhelming presence, she used her hymnal as a shield, while only able to mouth the familiar words of the song.

For once in her life, she was thankful for her dwarfed height and Harriet's stalwart determination not to allow Seth to look anywhere beyond her immediate vision.

"Heavens to Betsy, Viola Mae. What's ailing you?"

Not stopping to explain, Viola Mae dragged Gracie along behind her, away from the emptying church. She wasted no time in leaving. Before the last words of the benediction had slipped from the reverend's mouth, the two women had quit the service by a side door.

Gracie dug her high-heeled boots into the dirt. "I'll not go another step unless you tell me." The maneuver did no good, for Viola Mae kept beating a path away from the building.

"Why the big rush?"

"Gotta get my picnicking vittles," Viola Mae said. "You gotta help me tote them."

"We have to run because you're so hungry?"

"You could say that," Viola Mae mumbled.

Craving a peek at someone, both night and day, was no different from a hungry man craving food. What if she took a big bite of the handsome Yankee and chewed him up real fine before swallowing him? Would her yearning be sated?

"Okay, okay. I'll come," Gracie called behind her. "Not that I've any choice in the matter. But land sakes, slow down."

"I'm not hurrying," Viola Mae said, although she continued to hurry along the road.

"You could have fooled me."

Viola Mae glanced back over her shoulder. Gracie looked as though she'd been running a footrace. In this heat, too. Taking a deep breath, Viola Mae stopped and released her friend's hand.

"Oh, Gracie, I'm sorry. It's just that, well, lately I've been out of sorts."

The older girl pulled a hankie from beneath her cuff and mopped her brow. "Tell me something I haven't noticed."

Viola Mae ignored the remark and pointed to where she

had left the wagon. "Over there." Walking slowly now, they headed toward the buckboard. When they reached it, Viola Mae climbed in and bent to lift a basket from beneath the seat.

Behind her, Gracie asked, "That's it?"

Viola Mae straightened and looked from the basket to her friend. "What do you mean, that's it?"

"The way you talked, I expected a feast. Not one tiny basket."

Viola Mae covered her mouth to stifle a nervous giggle. Her piddling little dish probably did seem like nothing, especially after she'd insisted that Gracie help her carry it. The whole situation, from the time she had left the church and raced down the street pulling Gracie behind her, was absurd. Taking a rough breath, Viola Mae dropped down upon the wagon seat. A sob rose in her throat. Soon she was blinking back tears.

"Now I'm really worried," Gracie said. Seeing her friend's distress, she pulled herself up into the wagon. "Move over." She plopped down beside Viola Mae and draped her arm around her shoulders. "You want to tell me about it?"

Viola Mae gulped. "Ain't nothing to tell."

Tears were a luxury that she seldom allowed herself. Long ago she had learned that to ooze with such emotions only opened herself to hurt, making her more vulnerable.

She had grown up an oddity in the small Pensacola community because her mother had abandoned her and she'd had no father to speak of. Her orphaned state had made her an object of ridicule. Early on, Viola Mae had learned to fight back, not only with her fists, but with her cunning. She had never, ever, allowed anyone to see her cry. But now she was blubbering like a fool.

Burying her nose in Gracie's hankie, she honked like a goose. "It must be my monthlies," she said.

"Could be," Gracie replied, "or it could be that fancy Yankee that's eating at your craw."

Viola Mae nearly choked on her tears. "Don't be ridiculous. Ain't nobody eating at nothing that belongs to me, especially that Yankee."

"But you would like him to."

Viola Mae's face burned with heat as she jabbed her friend with her elbow. "Gracie Marle, you've been reading too many of those dime novels."

"I saw the look that passed between you two in church."

"You saw nothing of the sort. Besides, Harriet wasn't about to let that fella see beyond her upturned nose."

"Maybe. But he darn near broke his neck trying to see around her to the other side of me."

Viola Mae sat back surprised. "Do you think so? Really?"

"Aha! I was right." Gracie pounded her feet against the floor of the wagon. "I believe that Yankee has struck your fancy, girl."

Viola Mae leveled a disgusted look at her. "If you keep this up, the only thing around here that's gonna get struck is you. Besides, I ain't wanting no part of such nonsense."

"Nonsense or not, we don't always have a say when the love bug bites."

"Love bug?"

Viola Mae stared off into the distance, pondering Gracie's remark. Since she had never been bitten before by the mysterious bug, she had no way of knowing if she was indeed suffering from its bite.

A festive chatter from where the picnic was getting underway floated toward them on a warm breeze. Ginger chomped away on the spring grass and swished away a fly with her tail. Several moments passed before Gracie bent forward and looked into Viola Mae's face. "Well? Have you been bitten?"

Viola Mae blinked her eyes. Lately she had been out of sorts: unable to sleep, daydreaming, bored with the repetition of her days. If what Gracie suggested was true, it would explain the strange disorders she'd been suffering. And if it was true, Viola Mae wanted no part of it.

She jumped up from the wagon seat and thrust her basket of food into Gracie's hands. "I reckon that settles it. I ain't attending no picnic. I need to get home to see to the chickens."

"Home? Chickens?" Gracie gaped at her. "What does

home and chickens have to do with anything?''

"The hens. They weren't none too happy about me cooking up ol' Joy Pye for them dumplings you're aholding.''

"Viola Mae Smith. I don't believe this.'' Gracie stood and faced her in the wagon. "Never in all the years I've known you have I seen you back away from a conflict. If indeed that Yankee fellow is diddling in your brain, and you don't want him to, the only way you're going to be rid of him is to confront the situation.''

"Oh, no. I ain't confronting no one but them chickens.''

Gracie glowered at her. "Only chicken I see around here is you.'' Disgusted, she turned to climb down from the wagon.

No one called Viola Mae a coward and got away with it. No one, she realized suddenly, but her dear friend Gracie.

Viola Mae watched her drop to the ground and swing around to pick up the basket of food. Was what Gracie said true? Was she running away? Before Gracie turned to leave, Viola Mae stopped her.

"Just supposing what you said is true. And just supposing that bug did take a nibble out of my hide. There ain't no way I can go to that picnic and face that varmint without getting as flustered as a long-tailed cat in a roomful of rocking chairs.''

Gracie placed the basket back upon the seat and shook her finger at Viola Mae. "You can, and you will. If you sneak away now, don't you think he'll suspect it was because you wanted to avoid him? It's not likely that he didn't notice your full-blown color when he greeted you in church. And the way we left before the benediction was over, I bet he already suspects something.''

"Oh, no.'' Viola Mae pressed her hands to her cheeks. "What am I going to do?''

"You're going to go to that picnic and you're going to enjoy yourself. If he gets within an inch of you, you can hide behind a tree for all I care. But no matter what, we're going and we're going to enjoy ourselves just like we planned to.''

"I ain't so sure that's a good idea.''

"It's our only idea. Now come on before those folks gobble up all that wonderful food and you and I have nothing but old Joe Pye's remains to feast on.''

Reluctantly Viola Mae climbed down from the wagon.

"It's only for a couple of hours," Gracie assured her.

The two women linked arms, squared their shoulders in determination, and walked back toward the square.

Chapter Six

It was a gathering unlike any Seth had attended before. As soon as the service ended, the congregation had formed into work groups. From a storage shed behind the building the men had collected makeshift tables that consisted of sawhorses and large pieces of board, carrying them to the square across from the church. Ladies and children alike retrieved the homemade delicacies from their parked wagons or the preacher's rectory, where they had deposited them earlier.

Tablecloths from the finest linen to common homespun now decorated the crude tables. Spread on the ground beneath the towering oaks, blankets formed a pattern of squares that resembled a giant chessboard. From where Seth stood in a circle of men, it looked as if everyone in town, regardless of whether they attended church or not, had shown up for the entertainment.

Harriet had been called away to help set out the food as soon as they had joined her father and the group of men who were responsible for bringing the railroad to Pensacola. Seth still didn't feel comfortable in the senior Archibald's company, and he had breathed a sigh of relief when Archibald, too, had been summoned elsewhere. So far, the gathering of the railroad barons had seemed amicable, their attitudes friendly. Not what he had expected, especially considering his background.

Among the group was Colonel Chipley. Seth had learned about him from Harriet. He was the driving force responsible for bringing the railroad to the panhandle. An officer who had fought for the South during the War, he had survived combat and gunshot wounds and had been a prisoner of war in Ohio.

Harriet also told him that the colonel's name had been linked with Ku Kluxers in a carpetbag murder case in Georgia. Not that this last piece of gossip interested Seth. His own family had skeletons that he didn't wish dug up. Besides, past was past, and he was more interested in the future.

"You from Atlanta?"

Seth turned toward the stately gentleman standing beside him. "No, sir, I'm originally from New York State," he replied, speaking into the man's ear trumpet. "But I have an aunt who makes her home in Atlanta. I've been visiting with her for the last few months."

"Don't you remember, Bard?" the man on the old gent's right yelled at him. "Miss Harriet met this young pup while visiting Atlanta this past Christmas. They attended the same party."

"Hardy? Yep, he appears hardy all right," the old relic replied, looking Seth up and down, "but then Miss Harriet always did like the sturdy fellows."

"Not hardy, Bard, party."

Others in the gathering looked as though they were having a hard time controlling their amusement as the older man continued to entertain.

"Fine party. You agree, Mr. Crow?" The distinguished geezer's eyes settled on Seth.

Seth nodded his head and smiled. "A lovely party."

"Name's Rowe, not Crow," the old man's helpful friend corrected.

"Eh, what's that you say?"

"Rowe. His name is Rowe."

"Roe?" The old gentleman shook his head in puzzlement. "Never could eat those damn fish eggs."

The colonel cleared his throat. "If you'll excuse us, gentlemen, Mr. Rowe and I have some things we need to discuss."

"Nice meeting you, gentlemen." Seth turned and fell into step beside the colonel as he walked away from the group.

"It's nice to meet a man who still respects his elders,"

Chipley told him. "The youth today aren't as tolerant of age as they were in my day. Although old Bard can't hear it thunder anymore, he still has an astute mind. He's one of the railroad's staunchest supporters."

"Not unlike yourself." Seth's comment seemed to please the former military man.

"I like to consider myself a visionary, but I'm not impractical. Archibald repeated some of your comments about the poverty you noted on your trip here. I inspected every inch of the granted land along the one-hundred-and-sixty-one-mile route between here and Jacksonville, and like you, I saw people living like animals with no means of improving their lot." He shook his head in dismay.

"Let us hope that situation will change," he continued. "When our line is finished, the whole of Florida will prosper because of it. Timber and turpentine experts agree that the forest resources along the rail line are perfect for harvesting, and there will be jobs for everyone."

"I agree," Seth said.

"But let's talk about the present. I understand you've encountered a few problems at the site."

Seth was taken aback by his statement. He thought no one, except Riley and the men in his employ, knew of the tainted fruit and blocked water supply. Now it appeared someone in camp must be reporting directly to the board members, which wouldn't make his job any easier.

Chipley added, "The culprit is probably that man Riley told me you fired the other day. I've alerted Sheriff Breen to be on the lookout for the troublemaker. I assure you if anything else untoward happens, Breen will be the man who can get to the bottom of it."

"Do I have your support in conducting an investigation of my own?"

"By all means, handle it as you see fit. You're in charge." The colonel paused in mid-stride, the bright sun causing him to squint as he looked up at Seth. "Although Archibald wasn't too keen on hiring you, you being a Northerner and all, and of course because of Miss Harriet's interest in you. But I feel certain you're more than qualified for the position."

"Thank you, sir. I appreciate your vote of confidence and I'll do my best."

"I'm certain you will, son. Now if you'll excuse me, I'd best go find the missus. She hates it when I spend the whole time talking business instead of socializing."

Seth watched the colonel walk to where a group of ladies were gathered around the tables. Maybe coming today hadn't been such a bad idea after all, Seth thought.

After meeting the railroad backers, he didn't feel as pressured by his background as he had before. Business was business, no matter what part of the country a man came from. Unless, of course, he had a daughter of marriageable age who insisted on keeping company with a one-time enemy.

Not that Seth was interested in Harriet. Problems with Archibald were the last things Seth wanted. In truth, he wanted to win the older man's respect, knowing if he did so he would be guaranteed a good reference when the job was completed. He would like to have a recommendation that would allow him and Jed to go anywhere there was a need for an engineer.

Jed. He wondered how the squirt was faring in Atlanta with his aunt. By now his brother would have settled in with the ladies and probably made a few friends to play with in the neighborhood. Perhaps, when the time came for Jed to join him in Pensacola, the boy wouldn't want to leave, having established himself in his temporary home.

Suddenly Seth wanted his brother there—wanted the two of them to be a family. Seeing all these folksy people gathered together, enjoying such a fine day, he wanted Jed to share in the closeness of the small community—an experience that neither of them had ever had. Their former life had been connected with New York City's best families. Not like the majority of the people who attended today's picnic.

Uncertain where Harriet had gotten off to, and not really caring at the moment, Seth walked beneath a giant live oak tree. They didn't have trees like this where he came from. Once underneath the huge canopy, he noted that he was well hidden from the other picnickers. The lower limbs of the ancient tree dipped and curved just above the ground.

Walking over to one, Seth settled into its willowy bend.

How many before him had used the bough as a bench? How many Pensacola ladies had been courted, perhaps kissed, on this very spot?

Kissed. For some reason the word brought to his mind the image of the silver-haired Viola Mae. He wondered what kind of bee had gotten into her bonnet to make her rush from the church before the preacher had completed his benediction, before he'd been able to speak with her. Where was she now? He had looked for her while Harriet paraded him among her friends before they had joined her father and the other men.

Beneath the giant tree where Seth sat, the air felt cool. He inhaled deeply of the acorn-scented shade. A soft breeze sucked at the leaves above his head, teasing the beards of moss that attached themselves to the branches. *I could get used to this place with its primitive beauty and slow, easy pace.*

"Now, Willie, now!"

The voice of an excited female broke into Seth's musings. He jerked around toward the noise.

On the opposite side of the square, away from where the crowd had gathered, a woman riding a high-wheeler bicycle tottered from side to side above the big-spoked wheel. Seth vacated the limb where he'd been sitting as the cyclist wove a wobbly path in his direction.

"How am I doing, Willie?" the adventurous girl yelled to the boy in knickers who ran along behind her. The boy's reply was lost by the sound of the woman's bubbly laughter when she picked up speed on the flat grassy surface.

It took only a moment for Seth to recognize the rider. "Well, I'll be damned," he mumbled, jumping across the limb to watch the lady's progress.

"I love it, I love it," Viola Mae yelled above the wind.

She had her blue dress rucked above her knees, and Seth saw that her booted feet barely reached the pedals. She didn't seem to mind that her stocking-covered legs and ruffled petticoats were on exhibit to the world.

Above the birds' songs, he heard her musical laugh. Its sound pierced something deep within him that made a knot form beneath his breastbone. He was not a man given to great emotion, or so he had always believed, but Viola Mae's pluck delighted him.

Seth had tried riding a bike on his last trip to England. With a front wheel almost as tall as a man and a tiny back wheel, keeping one's balance took practice. He had never mastered the machine, but it was apparent that Viola Mae had conquered the two-wheeled beast. No longer did she weave like a snake across the ground.

"Amazing," he said to no one but himself. But then, everything about Viola Mae Smith amazed him.

He stood with his hands anchored on his hips, watching and smiling. Although she still wore the straw bonnet, the wind had loosened several long ringlets from her tightly wound chignon, and they waved like silver ribbons on the breeze.

"Hey, Willie," she called, "how do you stop this critter?"

When she looked back at the boy, her gaze touched lightly on Seth. Her brows wrinkled in a frown. Everything went wrong.

The big-wheeled machine began to sway, then listed to one side. Once the contraption canted there was no way Viola Mae could keep it balanced. She tried leaning away from its tilt, but her efforts were useless. The metal frame began a sudden involuntary drop toward the ground.

When Seth saw her falling, he began to run. He reached the bicycle as gravity thrust Viola Mae from atop the high seat. Intent on softening her fall, he grabbed for her, and they rolled across the spongy turf.

When they wound to a stop, Seth held her on top of him. Their eyes locked for an instant before she dropped her head to his chest. He felt her tremble in his arms.

"Are you hurt?" he asked.

When she lifted her face, he saw not the tears he expected, but a lovely, wide smile that warmed him from the inside out.

She struggled to stifle a chuckle, but it was useless. It was only a moment before her sense of humor took over and she burst into laughter. Her features became animated, inspiring him to join in her mirth. Their combined glee floated on the air above them.

When her straw hat dipped cockily over one brow, Seth righted it. Without relinquishing his hold on her, he wiped a smudge of dirt from the tip of her nose. His tender gesture solicited another round of laughs from the two entwined parties.

Damn, she was beautiful, he thought as he looked into her crystal-blue eyes. More so than he remembered. His gaze slid over her delicate face, her flushed and creamy complexion. As though he half expected her to escape, Seth tightened his arm around her back and continued to study her.

Her lips were full over even white teeth. Behind a strand of silvery hair, a purple stone twinkled in her delicately shaped earlobe. He reached out to touch the stone, feeling an overwhelming desire to press his lips to the private place behind her ear.

"They belonged to my grannie," Viola Mae informed him when he fingered the small jewel. "Her birthing stone. And a gift from my grandpappy. Grannie liked the color so much, I reckon that's why she named me what she did."

"They're beautiful. Like you."

"Ah, mister, I ain't beautiful." She ducked her head as color blushed her cheeks, replacing her earlier healthy flush.

He was about to say that to him she was the most beautiful woman he'd ever had the pleasure of knowing when the sound of trampling footsteps brought him back to the moment.

"Miss Viola, are you okay?" the child asked. It was the same lad Seth had seen earlier, running behind the bicycle. His face was creased with worry, and his breath came in heated gasps as he bent over them.

"She's fine," Seth assured him.

Relieved, Willie answered, "Good, but I'm not gonna be if I've ruined my pa's bike. He'll skin me alive."

The boy's confession caused them both to remember themselves. Seth felt Viola Mae pull away from him, but before they could untangle petticoats from limbs, the ground around them vibrated with another's approach. The intruder stopped several inches away from where they sprawled.

"Viola Mae! What in heaven's name are you doing to poor

Mr. Rowe?'' Harriet's gaze darted suspiciously between Viola Mae and Seth.

Seth didn't care what Harriet thought of him, but he didn't like her implication that Viola Mae had manhandled him. He said, ''Harriet, I can explain—''

''No need for an explanation. I can see Viola Mae is up to her usual tomfoolery.''

Seth didn't miss the flare of temper that ignited in Viola Mae's blue eyes. He wondered briefly why he always seemed to be at odd ends when these two females confronted one another. Not wishing to make a bad situation any worse, he jumped to his feet to assist Viola Mae to hers.

But instead of taking his proffered hand, she stood unaided, then concentrated on shaking the debris from her skirt. She met Harriet's accusing stare without flinching. ''Although it ain't none of your business, I wasn't doing anything to the Yankee that he wasn't enjoying.''

Damn right, he thought.

Harriet looked as though she had a fish bone caught in her throat.

Wanting to smooth over the incident, Seth said, ''I merely saved her from being injured.''

''Injured?'' Harriet appeared puzzled as her gaze landed on the boy. ''What happened, Willie?'' she asked, looking from the downed bicycle to the now-cowering lad. ''You tell me right now, or I'll call your father over here—''

''Ain't nothing that concerns you or his father,'' Viola Mae interrupted. ''This here's between Willie and me.'' She put a reassuring hand on the younger boy's shoulder and steered him in the direction of the toppled bike.

''Seth,'' Harriet said, her expression begging him to interfere.

Instead of doing so, Seth told her, ''Let Miss Smith handle it.''

But Harriet wasn't about to let the subject drop. Suddenly understanding enlightened her features. ''You were riding that bicycle, weren't you, Viola Mae? No need to answer, it's just the kind of harebrained thing you would do. You fell, and Seth had to come to your rescue.''

Her deduction seemed to please her. ''And I thought—''
What she thought she kept to herself. Instead she said, ''I
swear, will you never learn to act like a lady?''

Ignoring Harriet's reprimand, Viola Mae and Willie bent
over the downed bike. After a thorough inspection to make
certain the machine wasn't broken, they righted it back upon
its wheels.

''Seems okay to me, Willie,'' Viola Mae told him.

The boy nodded his head in agreement.

''Our secret,'' she whispered in the lad's ear.

Willie gave her a smile before he pushed the big-wheeler
back in the direction from which he and Viola Mae had come.

Brushing her hands together, Viola Mae walked to where
Seth and Harriet stood.

Harriet quickly placed herself between them.

''I'll tell his father,'' she threatened, her face a glowing
mask of anger.

''You do, and I'll knock knots on your head faster than
you can rub them.''

''You'll do no such thing—''

''You'll see.''

With this threat, Viola Mae whipped around and walked
toward the picnickers who were lining up for the meal.

If she hadn't promised Gracie that she would stay for lunch
on the grounds, she would leave right now. She certainly had
no appetite. She had lost it along with her dignity. Angry with
herself, she wondered whatever had possessed her to carry on
so with the Yankee.

They're beautiful. Like you, he had said.

''Fool!'' *Seth Rowe ain't nothing but a smooth-talking
scoundrel. And at this very moment, he's probably saying the
same sweet things to Harriet Archibald.*

Curious to see if this were true, she glanced over her shoulder. Sure enough, Harriet was hanging all over the scamp.

Seeing the two of them walking with their arms looped
made her stomach feel queasy. Even the thrill of her very first
bicycle ride paled as she wondered how long it took to re-
cover from that pesky love bug's bite. No matter how soon,
it wouldn't be soon enough.

Chapter Seven

Seth overslept. He would have still been sleeping if the commotion outside his tent hadn't awakened him. He sat up slowly on the canvas cot and dropped his socked feet to the floor. With his elbows propped on his knees, he rubbed the sleep from his eyes.

"It's jest like I told you, Mr. Riley. Someone's filled them privies with sand."

Seth shook his head, trying to clear it. Surely he hadn't heard what he thought he heard. Riley's voice drifted to him.

"Tied on a good one, did you, laddie? Sometimes the drink will do that to ye. Makes the very ground rise up to meet ye when ye least expect it."

Inside the tent, Seth continued to listen. He had never heard the effects of drinking described quite like that, but Riley's comment did bring to mind a few occasions when he'd suffered such a fate.

"I ain't been drinking, suh. Never touch the stuff. But I swear, it's jest like I said. Filled up they be, and that ain't the worst of it."

Seth rubbed his burning eyes and wished he could go back to sleep. He shouldn't have done Harriet's bidding and joined her and her friends after the picnic yesterday. He should have ridden straight back to camp as he'd planned to do. But because Harriet had reminded him that it was because of her that he had his *silly old job,* Seth had conceded. Reluctantly he had stayed.

Soon the little gathering had turned into a full-fledged party, ending with a campfire on the beach that lasted until the early hours of the morning. Seth had returned to camp a few hours before daybreak, and now he was paying for his folly. He had a whole day of work stretching before him with only a couple hours of sleep behind him. And a problem that he was in no mood to deal with.

Sand in the privies. Pushing to his feet, he heard Riley try to calm the disgruntled worker.

"Perhaps, laddie, we best take a look together," the foreman said.

"We'll take a look, all right, but believe me, you ain't gonna believe your eyes. Every one of them holers have been filled with sand. But like I told you earlier, that ain't the worst of it. There's poison ivy a-growing out of every pot."

"Poison ivy. Are ye sure you haven't been in the sauce?"

"On my mammy's grave, I swear I ain't. I tell you, it's poison ivy. Believe me, suh, I knows poison ivy when I see it."

"Jesus H. Christ! Ye better get back down to the latrines now. Warn off the others until Mr. Rowe and I can get down there and have a look."

"Yessuh, I'll do that. Yessuh. I'm on my way."

After shoving his feet into his work boots, Seth threw back the mesh netting covering the opening of his tent and stepped outside. His and Riley's gazes locked.

"Ye heard, did you?" Riley asked.

"I heard," Seth replied. "We best get out there and check it out." The two men headed for the outlying woods.

A few minutes later, Seth stood with Riley among a group of men gathered in the latrine area of the camp. Five outhouses had been erected for the railroad crew's use. Beyond these, the stream provided a place where the men could bathe if they chose to do so. Seth had used the creek several times since his arrival, thinking only yesterday that the sulfur water didn't smell quite as bad as it had when he'd first arrived. He must be getting used to it.

Word of this latest skullduggery had spread through the camp like wildfire, and most of the men present had come to check it out for themselves.

Someone, probably the man Riley had spoken with earlier,

had propped open all the doors to the outhouses. And sure enough, the condition of the privies was just as the man had said. The seat holes had been filled to the rims with sand, and inside each round hole a bushy green-leafed plant with clusters of yellowish-white flowers sprouted from its middle.

"Now who do you suppose would do such a fool thing?" Seth asked Riley.

He shook his head. "Beats the devil out of me. Unless some of the men be having fun amongst themselves. Joking. I imagine we should question them." He turned away from Seth and asked the men who were talking and chuckling among themselves, "Anyone know anything about these shenanigans?"

"Ol' Pete here jest told us he heard poison ivy grows in waste places. 'Pears he heard right." This brought a loud guffaw from the others.

"Also 'pears to me we're being attacked from the inside out."

Seth recognized the man who'd spoken.

"How's that?" Riley asked.

"First them blackberries had us trotting for a day, now this. All I can say, we're lucky we weren't hit with doctored fruit and doctored outhouses at the same time."

The others chuckled in agreement, and Seth joined in their merriment. He could understand and appreciate the man's logic. "Then we would be at a dual disadvantage," he added.

Everyone laughed.

Encouraged by their response, Seth continued. "If it's like Lefty said, that someone is trying to harm the camp, we need to be on the lookout for anyone or anything out of the ordinary. People hanging around that we don't recognize— strangers."

"Ye blokes have any idea who could be behind these shenanigans?" the Irishman asked again.

"No," someone shouted. The others agreed.

Seth spoke again. "If you men can recall, I'd like to know the last time during the night that you used the outhouses and what their condition was. I hope to heaven none of you stumbled in here in the dark and exposed your backsides unknowingly to that devil weed.''

"That's all we be a-needing is a bunch of itchy arses," someone interrupted.

"It's not your asses I'm worried about," Seth said. "It's your family jewels." He smiled at the men's response.

There was a general cursing among the crowd. "We'll lynch any skunk who meddles with our gems."

"I hope it won't come to that. But in the meantime, I think we better get these things cleaned up and back into service."

Seth grabbed a shovel, and started shoveling out the extra sand, careful not to let the bush planted in the middle come in contact with his skin.

Most of the workers looked surprised that the boss would take on such a task. A look of admiration passed over Lefty's face. He grabbed a shovel and joined Seth in putting the houses right. Earlier, Seth had recognized Lefty's status among the men. He was well liked by all, and they listened to him. Soon the others had joined in the repairs without him ordering them to do so.

As Seth worked knee-deep in muck and waste, he realized just how far he'd come since his arrival in Florida. In New York he had never even emptied his own slop jar; others had been employed to perform the menial task. But those days had all but disappeared.

As Seth's muscles responded and warmed to the chore he had set for himself, surprisingly he couldn't imagine ever returning to that former life. It felt good to work with his hands. He wanted to learn more about the men working beside him. He wanted to win their respect. By not asking them to do something that he wouldn't do himself, he felt one step closer to that goal.

It was hot, humid, and still. The oppressive heat mocked Viola Mae's mood. It was the same temper that had accompanied her home from yesterday's picnic. She'd been in such a black mood when she had finally left Gracie at her house that she had skipped her weekly visit to her grandmother's grave.

Now as she rocked backward and forward in her grannie's

swing on the cabin porch, she wondered if her reluctance to
visit her grandmother at the graveyard had come from her
suspicion that the wise old woman could have witnessed her
unladylike behavior with the Yankee scoundrel. Whatever had
possessed her to roll around on the grass with the likes of
Seth Rowe, Viola Mae would never understand.

She hugged the feather pillow that she had brought with
her from her bed. When she squeezed it, it plumped wide
across its top, and for a moment she imagined a face concealed in the downy folds.

The soft light of the moon that washed the yard in tarnished
silver made the pillowcase appear human. The embroidered
blue flowers turned to sea-green eyes, and the trailing vines
transformed into familiar brows, nose, and lips.

Slowly Viola Mae lowered her head toward the pillow,
burying her nose and mouth in the linen's sunshiny smell.
Her heartbeat quickened, causing a thick, sweet liquid to
warm and seep from her most intimate place. In her mind's
eye the pillow became Seth's face, and she kissed it with all
the longings of a first love.

"Jumping Jehoshaphat!" Viola Mae slung the pillow
across the porch. "That dang good-for-nothing scallywag has
me drooling into my bed pillow." She jumped up and began
to pace.

Her violent movements shattered the night's stillness. Mustard, who'd been catnapping beneath the swing, dashed across
the yard and disappeared beneath the closest bush. Soapwort,
the hound dog, lumbered to his feet. He howled like a coyote
before reverting again into the pile of bones and fur that lived
beneath the front porch.

It was bad enough, Viola Mae thought, to have allowed
the scamp to manhandle her yesterday in the park. But tonight
her actions were far worse. Mooning over feather ticking. It
was humiliating that she should resort to such behavior.

Confused, she walked to the end of the porch where her
grannie's prized jasmine bush twined and climbed to create a
shady screen. Even in the moon's subdued light, the small,
white, waxy flowers stood out like stars against the shining,

dark-green foliage. Viola Mae inhaled deeply, allowing the flowers' light ambrosial scent to calm her.

She swung around and headed back toward the swing. Dropping onto the weathered frame, she pushed it lightly into movement, its familiar creak reminding her of all she had.

"I've so much to be thankful for," she told Mustard, who'd returned to the porch and leaped into her lap.

"I have you, this comfortable house, the land." She continued to stroke the cat's silky fur, while the slight movement of the swing cooled her heat-dampened skin. "And soon I'll be rid of the railroad and the unwanted railroad boss."

After she had filled the privies with sand last night, she had stayed clear of the camp. Filling them had not been an easy feat, but she knew it would be an even harder one to empty them. Adding the poison ivy had been a stroke of genius that had occurred to her when she passed several vines by the creek bed.

Without Ginger and the wagon, she would never have been able to transport the heavy bags of creek sand to their destination. But the trickiest part had been not to be discovered while she worked. She had waited until the hands of the clock reached the back side of midnight and she was certain that everyone in camp was asleep.

Earlier, her investigation had proved that most of the men were snoring off the effects of too much local brew on their days off. Even Seth's tent had been dark. Assuming that he, too, had returned from town gave her a moment of pleasure, until she recalled the way Harriet Archibald had hung on his arm throughout the rest of Sunday afternoon. In truth, it had been this act that had urged her to speed up her earlier plan to rid her land of the railroad.

Viola Mae leaned her head back against the swing chains and closed her eyes.

"I surely would have liked to have seen them fellas' faces when they discovered their holers with poison ivy growing as pretty as you please from the rims." She laughed and scratched Mustard behind the ears. "That would have been a sight too good to behold."

She stiffened on the swing, opening her eyes. Her senses

became alert. Standing and carrying Mustard, she walked to the edge of the porch. Beyond the trees, toward the site of the railroad camp, a bright orange light lit the sky above the treetops. No longer did the sweet scent of jasmine permeate the air. Instead she smelled smoke.

"Fire," she exclaimed, dropping the cat gently to his feet. Her stomach clinched into a knot before she whirled around and ran into the house.

As a child of the woods, Viola Mae knew ground and crown fires were slow-moving in the pinelands. But she also knew if a strong wind came up, fire could easily get out of control. The damage caused by wildfire could be disastrous, destroying the plants and trees that provided food and homes for the animals. She had to make certain that her woodland was not in any immediate danger. After she threw on her clothes, she sprinted out the door.

The forest was blanketed with an eerie red-amber glow, and the scent of scorched wood filled her nostrils. As she ran, her route carried her past fleeing animals, their instincts warning them to run. An armadillo with his stiff-legged jog passed her, and an opossum hissed and salivated, showing his disapproval at her for crossing his path.

"I'll not hinder your escape," Viola Mae told him, veering away from the frightened animal.

Cotton mice, gray squirrels, and a rabbit joined the opossum's plight, and Viola Mae continued on her own way.

At the edge of the cleared railroad bed, she stopped. Beyond the tracks, opposite from where she stood, she could see the edge of the woods were aflame. Men rushed like ants, beating back toothy flames that licked at the underbrush. Not far from the blazing bush, several stacks of railroad ties burned out of control.

No longer hesitating, Viola Mae left the woods and ran toward the fire. To keep the flames from spreading to the surrounding trees, every ounce of manpower would be needed. She dashed around the glowing ties to where the fire nipped at the ground cover. Most of the men worked shirtless, having abandoned their garments to dip them in water, before using them to beat down the flames. Their upper torsos were slick with perspiration. Orange and blue fire danced in reflections on their moist skin. Seth stood amidst the others.

"Get more water up here from the creek," he shouted at several men with buckets. "Keep soaking the ground between those ties and the woods. The ties are lost. We'll concentrate on the brush and hope the whole damn forest doesn't go up in flames."

The men obeyed, running toward the stream. Seth wiped his sweat on his arm before plunging his shirt back into the bucket of water. He appeared to be the one in charge, so Viola Mae hurried to his side as he straightened up.

Surprise creased his brow when he recognized her. But his surprise was quickly replaced by worry. "You'd best step away, Miss Smith. This is no place for a lady."

"I've come to help," she answered.

Her response seemed to amuse him. In a tone both courteous and patronizing, he told her, "With that skirt tail dragging, I believe you'll be more of a hindrance than a help."

"Don't you worry about me none, mister. I can hold my own."

Viola Mae swung around, turning her back to him. After a few moments, she'd shed her bloomers and pulled her skirt tail up between her legs, securing it in the waistband of her skirt. With her bloomers in hand, she spun around to face him.

Speechless, Seth's eyes raked from the tops of her boots to her bare knees that jutted from the bulbous slits of her skirt.

"Miss Smith, I assure you your help is not necessary." He looked uncomfortable as he glanced at the men to see if they were watching. Satisfied that they were not, he brought his gaze back to the bloomers now clutched in her hands. Instead of speaking the words, Seth croaked them. "Surely, you aren't—"

"What else might you suggest I use to beat out the flames?" Viola Mae responded. "Would you prefer I take off my shirtwaist like the rest of you?"

This last remark made his face turn redder than the embers glowing not far from their feet. "Certainly not, but—"

"Ain't nothing but my drawers." She shook them for effect.

She imagined that where the Yankee came from a woman wouldn't drop her drawers or tuck up her skirt. But since her old grannie had been stubbornly opposed to her granddaughter wearing men's trousers, she'd taught Viola Mae the skirt trick for working around the farm. Both women had employed it, but of course they had kept their bloomers on. Since this was an emergency, Viola Mae had decided her grandmother wouldn't mind her small indiscretion.

When Seth still seemed unable to speak or move, she shot him a challenging look and strode past him. Bending over, she dipped the undergarment into the water pail and hurried toward the others, who stood close to the burning underbrush. Bent on smothering the fire that threatened to destroy her woods, Viola Mae beat the flames with the soaking-wet fabric.

Advancing toward the assembled firefighters, Seth took his position next to Viola Mae. She glanced briefly in his direction, her face flushed and glowing from the scorching heat. She wiped the sweat from her brow, before beginning again on the backbreaking chore of snuffing out the flames.

It was daylight before the fire had burned itself out and the firefighters could see the destruction. It had cut a wide, ugly wound through the once-green undergrowth, scorching tree trunks and leaving the ground barren. A pall of smoke shrouded the charred and parched earth, casting a gloominess over the forest in the gray light of dawn.

Viola Mae looked at the destruction through burning, tearful eyes. Her throat felt parched, and she ached all over from the strain of the last few hours.

Unconsciously she massaged the small of her back. She felt heartsick. From where she stood, it appeared that most of the pines had sustained little damage, but the hardwoods growing among them were burnt completely back. Not only had dozens of wild animals lost their homes, but without the vegetation that held the soil in place, the land would be vulnerable to erosion.

Once the stormy season began, there would be heavy runoff

that would cause destruction to the forest floor. Not only would the burned-out area suffer, but the span where numerous trees had been removed to build the railroad bed would be ruined.

She looked around at the weary men. Their efforts had kept the fire from spreading and killing more of the forest. But Viola Mae also believed that if it weren't for the railroad, none of this would have happened. The crew had taken down the trees, and someone's carelessness had caused the fire. Was she the only one who could see the problem?

"You did a fine job, Miss Smith."

She jerked around to face the speaker.

"We appreciate your help," Seth acknowledged.

Her eyes raked over the railroad boss. He looked haggard beneath the ash that streaked his face. Soot covered his arms and chest and clung to his sweat-dampened hair. He deserved to be commended, Viola Mae thought, just as the others did who had fought so tirelessly to put out the fire.

A burly man with carrot coloring walked over to where they stood. "Any notions, lad, as to what might have caused this bit of a flare-up?" he asked Seth.

Seth cleared his throat. Turning from Viola Mae to the man, he said, "Excuse me. Miss Smith, this is Riley, my foreman. I don't believe the two of you have met."

Viola Mae extended her hand to the stranger while he looked at her as though seeing her for the first time. Courtesy demanded that she respond to the newcomer. Although she didn't feel like being neighborly, she managed an appropriate response.

"I'm pleased to meet you," she replied, shaking his hand.

The man winked, holding her hand in his big paw. "The pleasure be all mine, lass. I daresay, it would have been a more pleasing time than it be that I would choose to meet such a fine lass."

Seth glowered at their locked fingers. The foreman's response apparently hadn't set right with him. Viola Mae watched his stormy expression while he continued with his introduction.

"Miss Smith lives close by, but I'm not certain where. She saw the fire and volunteered to help."

Riley beamed down at Viola Mae. His smile was contagious, and in spite of her earlier reflective mood, she smiled back at him.

Encouraged by her reaction, Riley continued. "Perhaps, lassie, you would allow an old Irishman to escort ye back home."

Seth interrupted, scowling. "Perhaps the old Irishman should be more concerned with getting to the bottom of this latest mishap."

His vinegary remark surprised not only the Irishman, but Viola Mae as well. For the life of her, she couldn't imagine what had riled Seth to rudeness. Maybe he didn't like the man's lilting speech. To Viola Mae, his brogue was very appealing, and if he had not worked for the railroad, she might have encouraged his friendship. But because he did, she wanted no part of him.

Liking him or not liking him was immaterial. As soon as Seth's statement about "getting to the bottom of this latest mishap" was uttered, the Irishman colored visibly beneath his dirt-covered face and quickly became businesslike.

"Ye believe it be connected with the other problems we've faced?" Riley asked.

This time it was Viola Mae's turn to blush. She knew exactly what other problems they referred to. Tainted preserves and filling privies with dirt was one thing, but setting her beloved woods on fire was another thing entirely.

Without thinking, she responded, "I'd never—" Realizing what she had almost implied, she clamped her mouth shut.

Both men stared at her, their expressions questioning.

Will I never learn to keep my lips buttoned? Drawing again on her philosophy that a good offense is a strong defense, she blurted out, "It was carelessness."

"Carelessness?" Both men repeated the word at the same time.

"Yes, carelessness," Viola Mae echoed. "*Your* carelessness."

They watched her as though she had suddenly taken leave of her senses.

"Ah! Ahem!" she continued. "Your men burned those *cattails* clean down to the ground. And because of it, there ain't no rush material to recane Earle Forbes' chairs."

"Cattails?" Seth questioned, puzzled.

"Recane?" the Irishman asked.

"The leaves," she explained, "of the cattails." When both men continued to study her, she finished in a race of words. "When they're dried, they make good rush material."

"What do cattails and rush have to do with any of this?" Seth asked, indicating the burned and charred area with a sweep of his hand. He focused on her again.

"When folks mess with Mother Nature, this happens."

Her answer sounded dumb to her own ears, but Viola Mae was tired of being questioned. Besides, she had nearly admitted her part in tainting the fruit and filling the privies, something she didn't dare confess. It was time for her to be gone from this place and from the green-eyed monster of a Yankee who kept gaping at her.

She looked at both men. "I'd best be leaving," she said with more determination than she felt.

"Wait," Seth demanded.

Viola Mae glared at him.

"Please, let me see you home," he insisted on a kinder note. "It's the least I can do after all the help you offered us last night. Besides, I'm interested in learning more about those cattails."

"Ain't no need," she responded. "I found my way here without you and I can find my way back."

"But—"

"But nothing, mister. I've said about all I'm gonna say. It was carelessness on the part of your men that burned my cattails to the ground, and I'd be willing to bet it was that same carelessness that set those woods a-burning."

She turned to leave, but before she did so, Viola Mae called over her shoulder, "And since you seem so all-fired determined to hold an inquisition, I suggest you question your workers and leave me alone. I've had about all the questions I can take for one day.''

Seth watched Viola Mae walk away. Once again he had been taken aback by her spirit. While most women would have felt threatened by the blaze, Viola Mae had seemed fearless. She had worked like a man, determined not to be bested either by his opinions or the fire.

When she had arrived on the scene, he had assumed that she'd been awakened from sleep, because her hair still hung in a long braid down her back. Against the flames, the shorter ringlets surrounding her face had held the luster of a halo. Could his forest nymph be an angel in disguise—an immortal being attendant upon God? Whatever she was, she intrigued him. As she had from their first meeting.

What manner of woman defied all the conventions placed on other women, from riding astride a giant horse to riding a two-wheeled bike? Or stripping her drawers off in public?

He shook his head in disbelief and amusement. The little scrap of a girl had more mettle than most of the men he'd known. She had looked so small and delicate working beside the rough males, so unaffected by the raging inferno that could strike fear in a stronger man. Seth felt an overwhelming need to protect her, but he knew Miss Smith wouldn't take kindly to any heroics. This difference was another puzzle to Seth.

He'd known many women in his life, all much more sophisticated and cosmopolitan than Viola Mae. Perhaps, he decided, it was her innocence that charmed him.

He thought back to yesterday evening, and to Harriet Archibald and her circle of friends. Although they were nice enough, he'd realized after spending the entire evening in their company that they seemed shallow—selfish.

It was hard for Seth to imagine that less than a year ago he would have been in tune with them. But not so today. Today there were more important things to consider. He had his men's welfare to think about, as well as the slip of a girl who had insisted on working fearlessly beside them.

It was surprising even to him, but this was where he wanted to be.

Chapter Eight

After signing his name to the note, Jedwin Rowe went to get the money.

During the short time that Jed had spent in his Aunt Cloe's house, he had learned that his elderly aunt had a peculiar habit of hiding her money in odd places around the house instead of depositing it in the local bank. She had hidey-holes located between chair cushions, inside books, beneath furniture drawers, underneath chair bottoms, and in any other out-of-the-way place that an unknowing adult would never discover.

But to a curious boy of ten who spent more time on the floor with a book or with his advancing army of toy soldiers, the rather inconspicuous hiding places became immediately noticeable. After Jed figured out the money's significance, it became a game for him to seek out all the places where his Aunt Cloe might have hidden her cache.

Soon Jed knew every hiding place in the small house, and he also suspected that his elderly aunt had long forgotten their location. As she now forgot, with regularity, where she had placed her glasses when they were sitting on top of her head.

It was after he decided to head out for Florida in search of Seth that the idea to borrow from his aunt had formed in his mind. A loan, short-term only. Seth would pay it back once the two brothers were reunited. Although Jed didn't enjoy living with the two elderly spinsters, he loved his Aunt Cloe and would never do anything that he believed would make her worry.

With his aunt's money he purchased a ticket on the same train that would follow the path his brother Seth had taken to

Florida weeks before. Before his departure, Seth had purchased and marked a map for his younger brother, so that Jed would know the exact route he had taken to their new home. This same map had made Jed's planning relatively easy.

Pleading a bellyache this morning, he had not attended church with his Aunt Cloe and luncheon with her friends as he usually did. Tilly, who spent every Sunday morning working in her garden in back of the house, had been left in charge of the patient. After bringing Jed dried toast and milk, she had left him to sleep off his little discomfort. Five minutes later, he had slipped out the front door of his aunt's house and was on his way.

Dressed in his Sunday best, looking much the part of the little man he felt himself to be, Jed boarded the train for Jacksonville. As Atlanta faded into the distant Sunday morning, he felt a moment of homesickness for the two ladies he'd left behind. But soon the lure of open land and the sound of the wheels clicking against steel rails overrode his bout of melancholy. In a few days he would be with his brother Seth in their new home.

Seth shook his head in disbelief. "Kerosene. Are you certain, Riley?"

"Me and some of the other lads checked the area, especially where those ties were stacked. Whole bloody place reeked of fumes. Including an empty jug that didn't smell like good Irish whiskey."

"Damnation." Seth slammed his hand against a tree trunk and swung around to face the Irishman. "The iron rails arrived this morning, but without the ties they're useless."

"It appears we have us someone trying to hurt us. And he's turned mean." Riley scratched the sprinkling of coppery whiskers on his chin. "We can count ourselves lucky that no one was injured the other night. If they had been, we'd be looking for a murderer right now."

"Yes, we are lucky."

The image of Viola Mae helping to beat out the flames surfaced in Seth's mind. She could have been hurt as easily as anyone. It was a sobering thought. "What kind of man are we dealing with here?'' Seth asked. ''I believe I preferred his earlier tactics over this last one.''

''Me, too, laddie. I'm sorry to tell ye this—some of the crew are getting anxious. Seems they could deal with this fella's earlier foolishness, but now they be fearing some idiot might take a potshot at them while they work.''

''You're saying they're thinking about quitting.''

''I'm saying the thought may have crossed their minds.''

The two men looked at one another before Seth responded. ''I guess we better call the men together.''

At the meeting Seth took a count to see who wanted to stay and who wanted to go. Surprisingly, all but a few of the men said they were determined to see the work through to the end. Since the ordeal with the privies and later the fire, it seemed that a few of the workers had begun to respect Seth's authority. It was a step in the right direction, but one he wished could have been reached without the delays.

Seth decided that guards should be posted both day and night until the person who had set the fire could be flushed out. Also, he needed to ride into town to speak to Archibald and the sheriff about this latest mishap. The person responsible for setting the fire had become dangerous, and the sheriff needed to know. Tainted fruit and sand-filled privies weren't life-threatening, but fires sure could be.

Leaving Riley in charge until he returned, Seth headed to town, determined to check in the warehouses and mills to see if more railroad ties were available. In the meantime, the tracklaying was stalled.

Not much of a horseman, Seth had chosen one of the camp's nags for his personal transportation. He had ridden the old saddle horse, Clyde, to town and back on Sunday, and an instant friendship had formed between the two. Man and beast understood one another. Seth respected Clyde's twilight years, never pushing him beyond a slow walk. Equally, the old nag respected Seth's equestrian inexperience and never advanced beyond a sluggish gait.

In spite of Seth's problems at the site, he was enjoying his afternoon sojourn. Almost daily, he'd been adjusting to the heat and humidity of Florida. The mosquitoes, although still bothersome, did not attack him with the same vengeance they had used when he first arrived. Like his men, they, too, seemed to be getting used to him.

On Riley's suggestion, Seth was taking a different route to town. Although it was the longer way, the narrow wagon trail meandered beneath a thick canopy of oaks. Beneath the trees the air felt cool because of the wide spread of Spanish moss that filtered out the hot sun. A breeze tiptoed through the hanging vegetation, causing it to wave slightly as Seth passed.

The diversity of the land around Pensacola still amazed him. The Southern pinelands were not a one-of-a-kind forest, but a mixture of oaks, sweetgum, magnolias, sand hills, bogs, and bays. On the coast, blinding-white sand flirted with jewel-colored water before moving inland to become dense, brooding swamps and narrow rivers. It was a land unlike any Seth had known, but a land that appealed to all the senses.

As old Clyde clip-clopped along the packed-sand road, Seth listened to the active noise of the woods. Thrushes sang, chickadees chattered, and blackbirds squawked in the overhead branches. On the ground, wildlife flitted in and out of the thicket, rattling the underbrush with their movement.

Seth saw a woodrat scamper across the road in front of Clyde's hoofs. He understood the rodent's flight when a large king snake slithered past in pursuit of the little creature.

Although snakes weren't a favorite of Seth's, he knew the chocolate-brown fellow wasn't one of the dangerous species that made the pinelands their home. But old Clyde wasn't as knowledgeable. The frightened horse stepped around the reptile and jerked to a stop, nearly tossing Seth off his back.

"Giddy-up," Seth cajoled, regaining his balance and flapping his legs against the animal's sides. But Clyde refused to budge.

Recalling his youthful riding lessons, he pressed into the saddle with his backside and squeezed Clyde's girth by closing his legs against the animal's sides the way his childhood instructor had taught him. His efforts were useless, for Clyde still wouldn't move.

Disgusted with the animal, Seth dismounted. "Ornery old

cuss. I guess you'd prefer that I lead.'' He started down the road again with Clyde following behind him.

As Seth walked, he studied the surface of the road. A horse and rider had passed this way earlier because the tracks were still fresh. Halting, he squatted down to compare Clyde's hoofprints with the much bigger ones. Only one horse could make prints that large—Viola Mae's horse, Ginger.

He looked up and down the road, then peered into the thick growth of trees on each side of the lane. He knew she lived somewhere close to the railroad camp. Could it be in the vicinity of this road?

With thoughts of her, his heartbeat increased. Although there was no sign of a house, or barn, or anything remotely resembling a farm, he wanted to find Viola Mae's house, her hiding place. Seth had not seen her since the night of the fire. Now that he knew someone had intentionally set the railroad ties ablaze, he wondered if the same person would be above threatening a lone woman if he came upon her.

Booger Butts, the coach driver. Maybe he had set the fire.

Seth and everyone else in town had heard him threaten Viola Mae after Ginger had flattened his hat. Although it wasn't likely that the driver would take out his wrath on the railroad, he might if he was a friend of the man Seth had fired. Now that was plausible. Bullies made good buddies.

That long-ago day in town, Seth had interfered, saving Viola Mae from being injured. Was it possible the two bullies had joined forces to get back at both of them? The stage driver knew where Viola Mae lived. Perhaps he had set the fire, hoping to burn down the whole damn forest and Viola Mae's farm as well.

"Impossible," Seth told himself. "You're grasping at twigs."

But the more he thought about the scheme, the more believable it became in Seth's mind. That plausibility made finding Viola Mae and warning her about the setting of the fire the most important thing he had to do.

It was already mid-afternoon. By the time he arrived in town, it would be too late to contact Archibald. He had told Riley that he could be gone as long as two days, depending on Archibald's schedule. When he arrived in town, he would find a hotel and seek him out first thing in the morning. An hour or two delay wouldn't matter much one way or the other.

His decision made, he studied the giant hoofprints. He would follow them and maybe they would lead him to Viola Mae's farm.

Anxious now, Seth pursued the prints several hundred feet before the big horse turned off the main trail. The prints all but disappeared beneath the heavy ground cover of leaves and pine needles. Only because he was looking for the tracks was he able to pick out the deep impressions in the loamy soil. After a few more feet of tracking, the trail widened into a sandy path. Its surface was dimpled with the identifying marks.

By this time, Clyde's advancing years made him wheeze and blow with the effort of walking. Because Seth feared the old nag might suffer a heart attack and die, he left him tethered to a nearby tree and continued on his way.

Not long after leaving Clyde, Seth saw the first sign. Painted in bold, black letters, the words read: "Trespassers will be shot!" The word "shot" gave him pause, reminding him that the pistol he had started carrying after his episode with the beaver dam was still packed away in his saddlebag.

"Damnation. Won't I ever learn?"

He hoped whoever had posted the sign wouldn't shoot first and ask questions later. Convinced that no one in this day and time would be that uncivilized, Seth kept walking.

A hundred yards later, he came upon another sign: "Keep out. Intruders not welcome!" This time the sign painter hadn't mentioned shooting, which buoyed Seth's confidence.

He continued along the trail. He knew in his bones that he would find Viola Mae's farm soon. When the path widened into an open clearing, he was certain he'd found her. Especially when the sign posted on the split-rail fence read: "You're dead, mister."

Earlier, Viola Mae had been in the woods gathering the allium herb, looking for a certain species of the wild onion that was best harvested in May and June and made excellent vinegar pickles. Fascinated by all critters, she had been distracted by the king snake that had been chasing his next meal and had followed him to the road's edge. That was when she spied the Yankee.

Upon discovering Seth, she remembered she was still angry about the wildfire's destruction and her belief that it was set by one of the railroad workers.

Viola Mae had no intention of revealing her presence to the railroad boss. She was tired of this love-bug foolishness that Gracie spoke about and she was determined to put the handsome Yankee out of her mind. But instead of being on his way to town as Viola Mae had expected, he'd started following Ginger's horseshoe prints in the sand, and her curiosity had gotten the better of her. She dogged his trail. It was evident the Yankee couldn't read, or he was intentionally ignoring her signs. This insult made her grow angrier by the moment.

It was time she taught the railroad boss a lesson.

When Seth first entered the clearing and stood outside the split-rail fence, he took stock of the log cabin, built on cypress, standing in the middle of the yard. The structure appeared small by his standards, but it was well kept and sturdily built. It had a bucolic air about it. Just like its owner, Seth found it charming.

The house looked as though its interior consisted of one long room with wide porches extending around three sides. It was built of hand-hewn pine logs, and at the rear of the long gabled roof he could see the brickwork of a chimney. There were three center doors opening onto each of the side porches, and they were all open.

Beyond the house was a barn and beside it a smaller, similar structure that Seth supposed could be a smokehouse, or some other kind of building that was found on a farm.

It appeared as though no one was at home. From beneath the stoop, a sleepy old hound dog stared at him from soulful eyes. Some watchdog—not even a bark to warn his master of an intruder.

Should Seth walk right up to the front door and knock? He

didn't fancy getting shot, but surely Viola Mae wouldn't shoot him as her signs had suggested. Besides, Seth reasoned, once she recognized him and heard why he had come, she would appreciate his concern. He would tell her about the fire being started deliberately, and his suspicions about who he believed was behind the mischief, and then be on his way.

If that was all there was to it, then why did his feet remain rooted to the ground? Seth's earlier uneasiness at being shot gripped him again.

Maybe this wasn't Viola Mae's farm. Maybe it belonged to one of those Cracker homesteaders that Harriet and her friends were discussing on Sunday. The kind of people who shot first and asked questions later. How had they described them? Cantankerous loners—withdrawn, suspicious characters who were quick to anger.

If that had been true, he'd be dead right now. He had been standing in the same spot for the last five minutes. The tales he'd been told on Sunday were making him crazy. Surely if he wasn't wanted here, someone would have told him by now.

He eyed the sign warily. "You're dead, mister." Except for this warning and the two others he'd seen, nothing seemed out of the ordinary.

"Hell. I don't have all day to stand here and wonder if I'm going to be shot." Seth cupped his hands around his mouth and yelled, "Hello! Anybody home?"

Tha-wunk. The handle of Viola Mae's mattock hit the Yank dead center on the back of the head. His knees buckled, and he folded like the pleated bellows of an accordion before he hit the ground.

After hog-tieing him, she pulled a gunnysack over his head. Standing back, she inspected her handiwork. Lucky for her she'd had all her herb-hunting tools with her when she'd discovered the railroad boss tracking Ginger's hoofprints.

She used the mattock to dig up roots, but its wood handle had made a good solid club. After whacking him on the head, she had emptied the onions from the sack and used the rope that held the bag closed to tie him up with. So that he wouldn't recognize her, she had slipped the burlap over his head. Now her next problem was how to get her prisoner to the henhouse.

Viola Mae frantically searched the yard. On the clothesline she saw the sheets she'd washed that morning. Without hesitating, she ran toward them, yanked the muslin from the line, then hurried back to where the railroad boss lay. She would have to drag him.

Struggling to get the sheet beneath him, she grumbled, "He weighs more than a slaughtered hog." When Viola Mae had butchered the old sow last fall, Myrrh had weighed close to two hundred pounds. But she wasn't near as difficult to handle as the deadweight of the Yankee.

She pulled and tugged until Seth was finally centered on the sheet. She said a small prayer of thanks that he was still unconscious. Viola Mae wasn't certain she could deal with the smooth-talking fella, especially when he realized she was the cause of his fate.

If he ain't dead. "Oh, lordy, what if I killed him?" Her fingers poked and prodded his warm flesh, searching for a pulse. After she found the faint thud of a heartbeat in his chest, relief washed over her. But the intimate contact with the scoundrel made her realize how he affected her. Touching him with her fingers made her heart flutter. Considering all she knew about the Yankee—his position with the railroad and his friendship with Harriet Archibald—there was still something she liked about him. The idea that she might have injured him burdened her down with guilt.

At her feet, Seth groaned. She hadn't killed him, and his coming around spurred her back into action. She had a hostage, and maybe now the railroad would take her complaints seriously. The latest mishap with the fire could have been disastrous, she reminded herself, especially if the fire had gotten out of control.

Recent rains and early-morning dew had kept the whole forest from going up in flames. But what if Pensacola had been suffering a drought? What then? This careless disregard for the woods had to stop. With a strength Viola Mae didn't know she possessed, she dragged the Yankee across the yard and into the henhouse.

Seth came to slowly. Disoriented, he blinked several times, trying to adjust to the haze that clouded his vision. The back of his head throbbed, and he couldn't think right. To clear his head, he took a deep breath. The air he drew into his lungs smelled of jute, raw onions, and fertile soil. The roaring in his ears diminished to a murmur. He heard throaty, humming sounds he couldn't identify.

His mind raced. He searched for tangibles that would explain the ache in his head, the foreign smells filling his nostrils, the unfamiliar sounds, and the pale darkness clouding his vision.

I should get up.

Seth tried to push himself to a sitting position, but found his movement restricted. The simple act of sitting became a chore. Soon his efforts exhausted him, making his head explode with pain. He stilled, wishing he could awaken from his bad dream.

That was it, he reasoned. He was sleeping—dreaming. Not only was his mind asleep, but his limbs were asleep as well. That explained why he couldn't move. From his side he tried rolling to his stomach, and waited for the uncomfortable tingling that would accompany the rush of blood to his numbed limbs.

He waited. No cold needles pricked his arms or legs as he anticipated. Only fear thumped against his rib cage. Could his nightmare be real?

No. All he had to do was wait. He'd be patient, and the dregs of sleep would disappear. After a moment he tried to sit again, but he couldn't. His arms and legs wouldn't budge. He began to suspect that his limbs were constrained by something more than numbness.

Think, Seth, think. He willed himself to lie still, to concentrate on the events leading up to this moment. *Don't panic. Think!*

He had been on his way to town, using a new trail that Riley had told him about. He'd been walking Clyde. *Clyde.*

Where was his horse? And why had he been walking the animal instead of riding him?

Seth searched his memory. It had been daylight when he'd left camp—late afternoon when he started for town. But surely only an hour could have passed since then. He strained to see beyond the brown haze that covered his eyes. Not enough time had lapsed for it to be night. Unless he'd been unconscious.

Unconscious. That could explain his confusion. But what had led to this? *Think, fool, think!* Yes, now he remembered. He'd been following tracks that he believed were made by Viola Mae's horse. He had wanted to tell her about what he had learned about the fire. Seth recalled seeing the warning signs, then coming upon a farm. At the edge of the yard, he'd called out. That was the last thing he remembered.

Someone must have discovered him and hit him from behind. But why?

Seth cursed his stupidity. His earlier doubts at having been at the wrong farm resurfaced. It hadn't been Viola Mae's farm he'd happened upon. It must have been one of the Cracker settlers he'd been warned about who had attacked him. This explained everything. He was now some backwoodsman's prisoner.

Having regained his wits, Seth understood his immobility. They had bound his hands and feet. Removed his boots. Hogtied him. That was the reason he couldn't move.

He also knew now why he couldn't see. Whoever had hit him had covered his head with a gunnysack. His sweaty skin itched and burned because of the rough fabric. The pungent smell of the onions was almost overpowering. Seth's uneasiness returned—what the hell was he going to do now?

As always, she got into trouble for acting first and thinking later. And because of her haste, it looked as though she was stuck with her prisoner. After perching on her porch for the better part of the afternoon and staring at the henhouse, Viola Mae had worked herself into a quandary.

"This time you've really done it."

She jumped up. Wringing her hands, she began to pace the

stretch of porch. Her restlessness must have bothered Soapwort, because the old hound dog strayed from beneath the stoop and collapsed in the nearby bed of phlox. On most occasions, Viola Mae would have scolded him, ousting him from the flower bed immediately, but this evening she had other things on her mind.

"Sheriff Breen's gonna string me up by my toenails when he learns I kidnapped the railroad boss." She swung around and traipsed in the opposite direction. "Harriet Archibald will be standing there saying, 'Won't you ever learn, Viola Mae Smith?'"

Shivering, she rubbed her arms, then came to a complete stop. She didn't want to dwell on being hanged, but most of all she didn't want to think of Harriet standing there, gloating at her with that "I told you so" look on her face.

Then there was the railroad boss himself. She especially didn't fancy making him angry at her, but she hadn't decided why. After all, he worked for the railroad. And the way she figured it, it was the railroad that had gotten her into this mess in the first place.

Viola Mae flopped down on the steps, staring off into the distance. "There I go again, Grannie, blaming others for my own shortcomings."

Twilight had settled softly over the little farm. Above the treetops, the sky no longer burned with the fire of sunset, but was now cooled by the approaching dusk. Soon nightfall would cloak the land, and the stars would sparkle like scattered diamonds against blue-black velvet.

If nothing else seemed certain in Viola Mae's world tonight, her place here on the land that her grannie had left her did. It had been so for as long as she could remember.

Viola Mae sighed, breathing in the nighttime scents. Only moments before, a chorus of frog song had begun over by the creek, and fireflies floated on the thick, humid air.

Unbidden, her grandmother's words came to her. *It's the rhythm of the earth that controls all things. And if we don't take care of it, it won't take care of us.*

Wasn't that what she was trying to do? Take care of the earth—her land? Since no one but her seemed concerned about the destruction to the woods, what else could she do to get the railroad's attention?

She didn't mean the Yankee any harm. After all, she aimed to feed him, to make him as comfortable as possible. And once she got an audience with Mr. Jay Arnold Archibald, she'd let the rascal loose.

There. She felt better already. She would protect her land at all costs, even if it meant taking a hostage to do it. Her land was all she had left of her family. It was her heritage, and she didn't aim to lose it.

Feeling better again, Viola Mae returned to the henhouse and her prisoner. When she paused in the doorway of the shelter, she saw that Seth still lay where she had left him. Her muslin sheet, the one she'd used to drag him from the yard, she had spread beneath him on the sawdust and dirt floor to keep him off the ground.

She set the tray of food down outside the shack's only door and hung the lantern on a peg inside the entrance. The flames from the kerosene lantern washed the rough interior walls with a palomino glow and painted the eight White Plymouth Rock hens, nesting in straw-filled boxes, a tawny color. The chickens clucked their indignation at being invaded at such a late hour.

Normally Viola Mae would have crooned to the upset birds to calm them, but the presence of their overnight guest kept her silent. Until she was more certain about this hostage business, she didn't want her captive to recognize her.

Besides, she'd been feeling guilty ever since she had whacked him on the head. She knew her old grannie would never have approved of her behavior, and if the truth be known, Viola Mae wasn't too sure if she'd done the right thing either. At the time it seemed right, but now when she saw the man who had haunted her dreams both day and night hog-tied like an animal, she had doubts.

She hadn't considered how he would perform his personal business now that she had hobbled him. Viola Mae didn't dare free his hands or feet, because if she did, he would surely escape and probably knock her senseless in the process. After all, who knew better than she that a Yankee couldn't be trusted?

She had thought about using some of her sleeping herbs to sedate the prisoner—it would be a lot easier to attend to his personal needs if he was in a drugged state, much easier than helping him if he were wide awake. This thought unnerved her, and she pushed it to the back of her mind.

If she'd known that being a jailer was going to be so dang inconvenient, she might have thought twice before her decision to kidnap him.

But right now, first things first—the man had to eat. She didn't want him getting sickly and dying on her. Besides, Sheriff Breen wouldn't take too kindly to the man being murdered even if he was a no-good rascal.

Slowly she approached Seth. He lay unmoving on the sawdust floor, and she thought he was dozing. With one barefoot toe she poked him in the ribs. When he didn't move, she jabbed him again, this time a little harder. When he still didn't respond, Viola Mae pushed him, causing him to roll away from her, moaning as he did so.

The moment the lantern's glow had filled the rectangular shape that Seth had determined earlier was the only door to his prison, he decided to play possum. Whoever his jailer was, he either couldn't speak or had chosen not to, perhaps to conceal his identity. The silhouette paused to study him before approaching. It was obvious the stranger had come for a reason, when his third jab to Seth's ribs brought him to full attention. If roughing him up was the stranger's way of communicating, it appeared that Seth's earlier idea to play possum wasn't the best plan.

He tried to sit up, but it was impossible because of the way he was tied. Realizing this, his keeper grabbed him by the arms and soon had him on his knees. His captor placed a finger in the center of his chest indicating to Seth that he should sit back upon his haunches.

Once in this position, Seth felt lightheaded, unsteady as he fought to maintain his balance. He wasn't certain if his fuzziness was caused by the blow to his head or the covering over his face. He willed himself to stay upright, concerned about what his captor might do to him if he should waver. Seth had decided earlier that his survival depended on keeping a clear head and remaining calm.

When the body moved back toward the lantern light and the doorway, Seth thought he was leaving. He wondered if this latest punishment, remaining on his knees, was to be some latent torture dreamed up by his captor.

"Please, wait," he insisted, hoping to learn what was expected of him.

At the sound of his voice, the captor paused but said nothing. The fuzzy image began to move again, momentarily blocking out the light before disappearing through the opening. A few moments later, he stepped inside again and moved toward him, carrying a tray.

Seth smelled the food before the person carrying it reached his side. Its fragrance stood out distinctively from the other scents that in the past few hours had become a familiar part of his cell. He hoped the mask would be removed from his head now so he could eat. But Seth soon learned he wasn't to be granted that small pleasure.

The figure bent to place the tray beside him. He shrank away from the unknown form when it lifted its arm as though to strike him. Seth nearly lost his balance before the figure steadied him, and he realized the earlier movement was meant to check out the contours of his face that were hidden beneath the scratchy burlap. Fingers reached out to touch his brow, slide down his nose, and trace his lips.

Gently the hands slipped to the back of his head, playing over its shape from the top of his spine upward. When he felt fingers prod the sensitive area made by the blow, Seth realized the mystery person was checking out his injury.

He thought he heard a swift intake of breath at the discovery of a large bump on the back of his head. But the area was so sensitive that Seth wasn't certain if it had been his own startled breath or that of the one who held him captive. Seeming satisfied with the examination, the hands dropped back to their owner's side.

"Will I live?" Seth asked.

The only response was silence.

He waited for the jailer's next move, and watched when he kneeled in front of him. The person fumbled in a pocket for something. When he pulled out that something, a flash of silver caught the lantern's glow.

His captor held a knife.

"No," Seth shouted. Believing his death was imminent, he prayed it would be swift.

At his outburst, the figure hesitated, before reaching toward him again. This time when the fingers made contact with his face, the touch was oddly soft, caressing, and familiar.

"You're a woman," he accused.

All movement stopped with this outburst. Seth could feel the heat of the small hand that cupped his chin. He felt it tremble. Inside the confining space of his one-room prison, the air became charged with carnal tension.

So much so that a tremor of desire snaked through him. It was as though his body sensed an attraction to this unknown female while his mind remained in the dark as to her identity.

Unless—could it be Viola Mae? He strained to see through the scratchy mask that covered his head, but his efforts were futile. No, it couldn't be her, he reasoned. She had no grounds for holding him captive.

When he thought he couldn't stand any more of the sweet torture the woman's closeness evoked, or control his body's reaction, he felt the tiny fingers trace his lips again, feeling, exploring, urging them open.

He complied, uncertain what to expect, and was surprised when a rush of cool air seeped into the hot tunnel of his mouth. Now he understood the reason for the knife. His lips had been made accessible by the narrow slit she cut in the burlap fabric. For a moment, her fingertips rested against the opening before they jerked back as though his feverish breath had scorched them.

The spell was broken. Almost as though she were angry at her response, she began to shove food into his mouth. Automatically Seth chewed, the fare tasting flat on his palate. Soon she forced the vile sulfur water down his throat.

Gone was the lady's attentive gentleness, replaced by

severe indifference. Seth knew she crammed the food down his throat so that she could be done with the odious task and leave. Did she realize the effect her touch had on his body? For her not to have noticed, she would have had to be blinder than he was at the moment. Perhaps it was his evident discomfort that had made her wish to flee.

Whatever it was, he, too, was glad that she was going. He watched her pick up the tray and hurry toward the door. Lifting the lantern from the hook, she stepped outside, and he was once again in darkness.

Still on his knees, he wondered what kind of woman would take advantage of a man who was both blindfolded and tied up. She certainly couldn't have been a gentlewoman, but was probably one who sold her favors for coin. Loose women— they were everywhere, he supposed, even in the backwoods of Florida.

In his youth he had enjoyed a few wild escapades, but in the last years those types of relationships had lost their fascination for Seth. They had left him feeling empty, melancholy. And then with the business with his family, his responsibility to his mother and brother, and now just to Jed, he no longer had time to entertain the thoughts of being with any woman, frivolous or otherwise.

Seth slumped back to his side. Since the woman had left him, there was no need for him to remain on his knees. He had more immediate problems to worry about than a crazy woman who had fed his blood with fire with a mere touch. Although he imagined the worst about his lady jailer, Seth couldn't shake the feeling that there was something remotely familiar about her. Come tomorrow, he planned to find out what it was.

Chapter Nine

Seth spent a hellish night, sleeping fitfully. Every time he nodded off, he would be jerked awake by the constraints placed on his limbs when he moved.

The unfamiliar noises surrounding him haunted both his dreams and his wakefulness. One time during the long night, he decided he shared his quarters with a flock of pigeons. The low, murmuring sounds reminded him of the plump, fast-flying birds that populated a New York City park.

Outside, beyond the walls of his prison, he heard the sonorous, *hoo, hoo-hoo, HOO HOO* of an owl that had taken up a vigil in a nearby tree. His call had made Seth wonder *who* would knock him on the head, then hold him a prisoner. Why not go ahead and kill him and get it over with?

Mosquitoes attacked him with a vengeance, biting him through the thick fabric of his shirt. The burlap sack covering his face had kept the bloodsuckers away from his head and neck, but he had been pestered all night by their annoying drone and quest for his blood. Hell, if his captor didn't kill him, he'd probably die of yellow fever.

The only kindness shown him was in the softness of the ground where he lay. The filler beneath him conformed to the hard plains of his body, allowing him a modicum of comfort. It was only after the strong odor of onions faded that Seth realized his mattress was made of sawdust and wood shavings. He recognized the substance by its woody scent.

It was daylight before Seth identified the place where he was being held prisoner. He had finally dozed off again, but was snapped awake by the crow of a rooster.

"Chickens?"

Several other cocks soon joined in the early-morning chorus.

Seth had always heard that roosters crowed at first light, but in the city where he had spent most of his life, no one kept chickens in their yards. This was his first experience with the barnyard critters. And being as grumpy as an old bear, had he not been hobbled like an animal and had his pistol, he would have shot the domesticated bird.

"No wonder farmers get up with the chickens," he grumbled. "They have to—in self-defense."

With the cocks' announcement that it was daybreak, a flurry of activity began among the remaining flock. The hens clucked and scratched in their nests, and Seth assumed they were laying eggs.

And if they were laying eggs, that meant that someone would soon come to collect them.

With a basket hooked over her arm, Viola Mae started for the henhouse. After gathering the eggs, she would fry up a batch for the prisoner, along with some country ham. No one would say that she had tried starving the man to death when the time came for her to free him.

There was no doubt in her mind that she would be letting the railroad boss go, but only after Archibald offered to meet with her to negotiate the release of her prisoner. Initially he might not choose to negotiate, but once Harriet learned that Viola Mae had the Yankee in her custody, the girl would hound her father unmercifully until he bargained for Seth's return. Not because she didn't want Seth within a hundred yards of Viola Mae, but because she considered the Yankee her own personal property.

For some reason, this last thought didn't sit right with Viola Mae. What made Harriet believe that the Yankee belonged to her anyway? Was it because he was a good-looking son of a gun and when he spoke his gentlemanly manners could curl your toenails? That is, if you had a mind to allow it to happen. Not that Viola Mae did, but it annoyed her that Miss

Spoiled-Rich Harriet believed that she deserved the best that Pensacola had to offer in the way of a man.

The Yankee certainly wasn't the *best*. But, Viola Mae reluctantly admitted, he was dang near close.

It wasn't fair that Harriet Archibald always got the best of everything—the best part in the school play, the best-looking dress, the best and biggest house, and now the best-looking man in all of Pensacola.

Viola Mae wasn't the least bit interested in keeping the Yankee for herself. In fact, she'd spent the whole night wishing she didn't have him.

All these thoughts were running rampant through her mind when she paused in the doorway of the henhouse. Her prisoner lay on the floor where she had left him, his hands and feet still hobbled, his head still covered with the burlap.

She didn't speak, hoping that she would be able to complete her chore without Seth discovering that she was there. Seeing such a fine specimen of a man hog-tied like an animal, and by her own hands, made a fresh rush of guilt surface.

Stop acting like a dang sissy. You're doing what you must, and he deserves what he gets for taking that stupid job with the railroad.

Stepping inside and quietly working her way along the length of the building, she began gathering eggs.

Of all the chores on the farm, Viola Mae enjoyed egg gathering most of all. To her, it was almost a holy time, in the morning's sleepy light, while the air was fresh and almost cool, and when the confining space of the henhouse smelled of life.

The chickens began to cluck when she reached her hands beneath their warm feathers. She usually crooned to her charges as she went about her egg gathering, but this morning because of her prisoner she kept silent.

"I know you're there." Seth's deep voice cut through the sound of the chickens.

Viola May nearly jumped out of her skin, almost dropping the egg basket as well.

"Speak to me, please. Tell me why I am here. I don't understand."

Viola Mae froze. Maybe if she didn't move he would believe that he'd imagined her presence.

"How long do you plan to hold me here?" he asked.

He squirmed around on the wrinkled sheet as though he were trying to see her through the burlap fabric. To Viola Mae, it felt as though his sea-green eyes burned a hole right through the woven fabric.

"I'm sorry if I trespassed on your property. If you don't want me here, release me and I'll leave. You have no right to hold me."

Viola Mae turned to flee, not wanting to hear Seth's complaints. She would finish gathering the eggs later, after she fed him his breakfast.

"Ma'am," he said, his voice sounding angry, out of patience with her. "If you don't allow me to tend to my needs soon, I'm going to embarrass both of us."

His admission fed Viola Mae's earlier fears. She would have to do something that would allow the man his request. *But, oh, lordy, what was that something to be?* She couldn't think about it in his presence. Right now all she wanted to do was escape.

Cursing her prisoner for the trouble he was causing her, Viola Mae ran from the shed toward the house. She needed a clear head so she could think. She hoped she would come up with a solution to her problem while preparing his breakfast.

"Damn crazy woman." Not that Seth had had much experience with kidnappers, but he thought she should at least explain the reason he was being held against his will.

Surely she couldn't be holding him for money. If she was—it almost made him laugh. If years ago someone had taken him with the idea of acquiring cash, it would have made sense. Seth's father had been very well known in the financial world and had been a wealthy man. But that was long ago and far away. Not today. And not in the middle of a near-jungle where no one knew him to be anything other than a Yankee outsider.

No one Seth thought had any money. And he certainly

didn't. Only the Archibalds did, and he couldn't see Harriet's father willingly dishing out any money on his behalf. Judging from the impression he had of the older man, Archibald would be glad to see Seth gone—away from his daughter.

Seth figured the only way out of his present situation was to escape. But with him bound the way he was, the possibility of a getaway was damn near impossible. He couldn't even remove this abominable gunnysack from his head.

Helpless as a babe in the woods, he thought, chuckling at the thought. A babe in the woods was exactly what he was. Maybe he should request a diaper from his captor. The picture he'd conjured tickled his funny bone, but he dared not laugh because his bladder felt as though it might explode.

"God, man, you're going mad." He breathed an exasperated sigh. "What in the devil am I going to do?"

This is the kind of situation that my little brother would get into. The thought of Jed burst in so fast it took his breath away. He'd promised his brother that he would take care of him, that they would soon be together permanently.

Jed was depending on him. Except for Aunt Cloe, Seth was the only family his brother had. Not that his aunt wouldn't take good care of Jed, but she was elderly. Much too old to raise a ten-year-old boy.

His thoughts about Jed were comforting, like a magic charm, something that he could hold onto.

"By golly, I'm going to get out of this," he exclaimed. Somehow he would outwit his jailer, taking her by surprise.

"First I'm going to get this shroud off my head." Once he managed this, Seth knew he would have a better advantage. He wanted to see the person he was dealing with. Although he lacked experience in handling such matters, he damn sure had the wits to outsmart some backwoods hillbilly.

It had been a long time since Viola Mae had prepared a meal with so much enthusiasm. Thick slices of country ham sizzled in the skillet while she fried a half-dozen eggs, their yellows so golden they looked like suns. She boiled grits, and baked a batch of spoon biscuits that were so light she'd swear they had wings.

Her old grannie used to say, "Fertilize friendships—cultivate friends."

Not that she suspected for a moment that Mr. Seth Rowe would want to be her friend, especially if he ever learned that she was the one responsible for putting that lump on the back of his head. But, Viola Mae reasoned, if she fed him real proper, maybe he wouldn't be so apt to take out his bad temper on her during his prolonged visit.

Also, Viola Mae felt good because she'd arrived at a solution to her earlier problem. When she'd gone to the barn to do her morning milking of Rosemary, she'd discovered how to shackle her prisoner differently. On the wall of the barn she had spotted the three-foot-long chain manacle. Grannie had said that Grandpappy had used the chain to hobble a stud bull he'd brought from Houston to Pensacola on his sailing ship.

Viola Mae had never known the old bull—it had been a gift for her grandmother—but Grannie had told her the story of the bull countless times. The animal was so ornery and so worthless as a breeder that they finally had to butcher him for steaks.

If one could shackle a bull, why couldn't she shackle a man? Her plan was to anchor the chain into the wooden side of the henhouse by the big screw welded to one end. The iron bracelet on the other end she would fasten around Seth's ankle. This way he would be free to move about, but she would still keep his hands tied. When she supplied him with his own thunder bowl, he'd be able to see to his personal needs without her interference.

Pleased with the solution, she smiled. Already this whole business was getting easier.

When everything was cooked to perfection, Viola Mae poured sweet milk from the pitcher into a glass, spooned a big dollop of butter onto the biscuit plate, and filled a china cup full of freshly brewed coffee before setting everything on the tray. As an added treat for her guest, she dished out some of her prize-winning blackberry preserves. Checking one last time to make certain everything was perfect, she covered the tray with one of Grannie's fine linen napkins.

With the shackles thrown over her shoulder and her shotgun tucked under one arm, Viola Mae picked up the tray and headed out the door.

Already the sun was a golden orb in the crystal blue sky, and the heat of the morning beat down furiously on the top of her head.

''Whew! Today is gonna be as hot as a June bride in a feather bed,'' she told Mustard when she stepped down from the porch.

Not a hint of a breeze stirred the ring of trees surrounding the farm, confirming her prediction that the day was going to be a scorcher.

''It would be a fine time for a dip in the spring, but of course that ain't possible with our guest.'' The yellow cat flounced along beside Viola Mae when she rounded the corner of the cabin and walked toward the henhouse.

Several of the chickens were pecking at the feed she'd tossed outside the coop earlier. Beyond the rectangular door, the interior was in shadow, and Mustard disappeared inside before Viola Mae could enter.

The cat earned her keep on the farm. Not only was she a wonderful, loving pet, but also she was the best mouser around, keeping the various buildings on the property free of pesky little mice.

Taking a deep breath, uncertain of what to expect of her prisoner, she stepped into the dim interior. It took a moment for her eyes to adjust to the darkness, but when they did, she saw that Seth lay on his side where she had left him.

Viola Mae steadied the tray with one hand and propped the shotgun against the wall before placing the manacles across one of the nests. The chains rattled unmercifully, reminding her that it was a man she planned to shackle instead of an ornery old bull. She quickly pushed the disturbing thought aside and started toward him.

''You're back,'' he said accusingly when she stopped at the edge of the sheet.

The burlap bag still covered his head, but it lay in rumpled disorder. She would have to locate the slit she'd cut in the fabric last night and return the opening to his mouth so that she could feed him breakfast.

This meant that she would have to touch him again, feel the heat of his breath through the woven fabric, endure his closeness. Endure the ache in her heart when he pleaded for her to reveal her identity. Not an easy task since Viola Mae had spent the best part of the night doing exactly that, touching him and feeling him, in her dreams. When she'd awakened this morning, she'd been determined to put these fantasies from her mind and go about this whole business with indifference.

Easier said than done, she thought when she put the tray down beside her feet and kneeled beside him. She wanted Seth to rest on his knees as he had done the night before when she fed him. But to her horror, when she pulled on his shirt, trying to lift him to that position, the burlap bag fell away from his face, and she stared straight into his accusing eyes.

Shocked, Viola Mae sprang to her feet. Somehow, during the short interval when she had left him to prepare his breakfast, he'd managed to get the gunnysack off his head. Now she understood the reason for the jumbled mess of fabric. But the thing that galled her more than the bag's removal was that he'd been waiting for her, planning on shocking her by learning her identity.

Her chest felt as though someone had dealt her a swift kick to the breastbone. "How did you get that sack off your head?"

Seth didn't reply. He only stared at her, his sea-green gaze shooting daggers that went straight to her heart.

"Think you're right smart, don't you?" she berated.

Not knowing how to react, she inched backwards, clamping her fingers around the shotgun, and aimed it straight at Seth's chest.

"What other good-for-nothing, weaselly trick you got up your sleeves?"

Seth cursed under his breath. "All I want to know is why. I thought you and I were friends."

The look he sent her made the earlier darts he'd discharged

her way twist deeper into her heart. But Viola Mae wasn't about to allow the handsome rascal to get the upper hand. She had to remain immune to his charms.

"I ain't no friend of a Yankee. Especially one that hobnobs with the likes of Harriet Archibald and works for the railroad to boot."

"Since when did it become a crime to befriend a person or to do an honest day's work?" he asked.

Everything he said was true. It wasn't a crime to do either, but trespassing on folks' property sure was. And if he needed an explanation as to why she was holding him, he would have to make do with the one she was about to give him.

"Trespassing."

"Trespassing?" He shook his head as though trying to clear it. "Ah, yes, the signs. Am I wrong to assume that I should be dead right now?"

His tone was condescending, and Viola Mae was in no mood to be belittled. "Maybe you are dead, and this is all a nightmare. Or maybe if you're not dead yet you will be shortly."

He swallowed, and Viola Mae watched his Adam's apple bob up and down in his throat.

"People hang for murder," he said, "in case you don't know it. And murder *is* a crime."

She grinned, pressing the gun hard against his chest.

"Can't be hung if they can't find a body. Maybe I've got me a pit full of hungry gators just waiting for their next meal. They like city fellas."

Seth didn't like her reply. "You're as crazy as Booger Butts," he told her. "I should have let you and your damn horse scatter your brains all over that coach the first day I set eyes on you."

"Maybe. Maybe not," she responded calmly, although his remark left her feeling anything but calm.

It hurt more than Viola Mae cared to admit that he would wish her and Ginger such an end. But then, given the circumstances, she could well understand his anger. She brushed his words aside. They weren't exactly chewing the fat at a church social.

"I've brought you your breakfast." She looked at the tray at her feet, then back at Seth.

"Sorry, I seem to have lost my appetite. But I do have other needs." His green-eyed gaze locked on her. "Or have you already forgotten what those needs were?"

Viola Mae was glad it was dark inside the chicken coop so he couldn't see the rush of color that crept up her neck. *Hang, no, I haven't forgotten.*

"Ain't forgotten nothing, mister. But I believe you'll just have to cross your legs until I can make a few arrangements."

"Cross my legs?" Seth hooted. "That might work for a woman, but not for a man. In case you haven't noticed, our plumbing is a little different."

His statement flustered her, and she whipped quickly around, stomping to get the shackles she had left hanging on one of the nests. She could feel Seth watching her, and when she returned to his side with the heavy chain, he stabbed her with a piercing glare.

"You don't intend to use that on me?"

Viola Mae propped the shotgun against the wall behind her.

"Since you seem so all-fired interested in comparing your plumbing to mine, I figure you ain't no different than the ornery old bull we chained up before you."

"A bull." He looked from the large manacle back to her face. "You'd chain me like an animal?"

"I 'spect so," she said, enjoying his discomfort. Maybe if she could make the Yankee squirm, he'd be in a better frame of mind.

"And just like your predecessor, I'll butcher you up real good and sell your Yankee hide as New York strip."

"Steak? You've got to be kidding."

Of course, I'm kidding, she thought, *but if you believe it, that's fine, too.*

Viola Mae found a hammer she kept inside the shed, then moved behind where Seth lay. She squatted down and began pounding the heavy nail into the wooden wall.

With that chore completed, she secured the iron bracelet around his ankle. When the manacle was in place, she locked it.

Stepping in front of him again, she brushed her hands together to clean off the dust and said, "It seems you and that other old bull had the same size bones."

He glared at her. "I've never heard of such idiotic, barbaric, and savage treatment of another human being."

"Now ain't that why you Yanks fought the war? To civilize us heathens in the South?"

He ignored this remark and continued with his diatribe. She watched him. Best to let him blow off steam and get all his anger out.

"Don't you realize when I don't show up at the railroad camp this morning that Riley will come looking for me? He'll find Clyde where I—"

She nearly laughed at the expression on Seth's face when he almost let it slip about his horse, then stopped himself after he thought he might be giving away a clue that would help someone rescue him.

"He won't find Clyde unless he takes a notion to look in my barn. He might not even find my place. We're kinda off the usual trail."

"Your barn? How did Clyde get in your barn?"

"Why, I put him there. Right after I put you here."

"So. You knew I was trespassing all along. You followed me. I guess you were also the one who nearly knocked my brains out of my head."

"You could say that. But seems to me that you asked for it when you didn't heed my warnings."

"I wanted to see . . . I mean—what I mean—I wanted to warn you about the fire."

"Warn me? What do you mean?"

"That fire the other night was deliberately set. This, coupled with the other pranks we've been experiencing, makes me believe that someone is deliberately trying to stop the building of the railroad."

"Is that so? Now what kind of skunk would do such a thing?"

"I don't know, but when I find out I'm going to turn him over to Sheriff Breen and let the law deal with him."

She took a deep breath and adjusted the expression on her

face to one of indifference. Seth's last statement didn't set well with her. Sheriff Breen was not part of Viola Mae's plans. All she wanted was to meet with Archibald and the railroad's other backers. She wanted them to take her complaints about the careless disregard for the land seriously, and do something about it. She certainly didn't want to get the law involved.

Tired of dawdling, she asked Seth, "You want this breakfast I fixed you, or not?"

"Hell, no, I don't want it. I want you to let me go. I promise I'll walk out of here, and you'll never hear from me again. I won't come near your land, and I'll make sure my men don't either. If you let me go, I won't tell a soul about this encounter."

For reasons beyond Viola Mae's understanding, the thought of never laying eyes on the Yankee again left her feeling as if she had a big hole in her stomach.

"Can't do that, mister," she added, lifting the fancy napkin from over the tray of food.

"I can't believe you're going to keep me here against my will." His gaze pleaded with her.

Viola Mae felt as though it was not so much a plea for his freedom, as a plea for the friendship that they had both felt budding between them. It was Viola Mae who looked away first.

Retrieving her gun, she said, "I'm gonna untie your hands and I want you to clasp them in front of you. Then I'm going to retie them. If you try any foolishness, I'll blow you clean out of this shed."

She stepped behind him and unfastened his hands, careful to keep the barrel of the gun pressed against him.

"Clasp them in front of you," she ordered when Seth hesitated.

"I don't believe you could shoot me," he told her, his warm breath lifting a strand of hair from her forehead as she moved in front of him again and lashed his wrists together.

"Oh, I could do it, mister," she told him, pulling the knot tighter.

Seth's fingertips accidentally brushed against her breasts

when she jerked on the rope to tighten it, and Viola Mae jumped away from him. Her breath quickened, and she felt her nipples bud against the fabric of her dress. Seth stared boldly, assessing her body's reaction. Something intense had flared between them, and Viola Mae felt a tingling in the pit of her stomach.

For a brief moment, she forgot their circumstances and became lost in the depths of his green eyes. What she saw there—a spark of animal passion—frightened her more than if she'd seen hate and disgust for the person who held him prisoner.

Looking away, she cleared her throat and pretended not to be bothered by his nearness.

"It's up to you whether or not you wish to eat the breakfast I fixed you. About the other matter we discussed, I'll be providing you with a chamber pot."

After saying her piece, Viola Mae picked up the gun and turned to leave.

"Please," Seth pleaded, "tell me why you're doing this."

It was the hardest thing she'd ever done, having to meet his gaze again. But when she did, her answer came out breathlessly.

"Because I have to."

Having answered, Viola Mae ran from the shed.

Chapter Ten

"You what?"

Viola Mae repeated her statement. "I kidnapped the Yankee."

"Lawsy sakes, child, have you lost your mind?" Gracie stood behind her store counter, her hands propped on her aproned hips, scowling at Viola Mae. "You could go to jail. Keeping a person against his will is unlawful."

"Oh, I ain't planning on keeping him. I'm only borrowing him for a spell." Viola Mae had just polished off one of Gracie's cinnamon buns and now licked the sugary icing from her fingertips.

Gracie's voice dropped to a whisper when the door opened and a customer walked in. "Are you so desperate for a man that you had to steal one?" She motioned with her hand for Viola Mae not to respond until she had addressed the other woman.

"Miss Sophie. How are you today?" Gracie smiled at the hefty elderly lady. "That material you ordered hasn't come in yet, but you look around and if you need me for anything give a holler."

Sophie stepped inside the door, closed it, making the bell jangle, then dabbed at her forehead with a lace hankie. "Oh, I'm not fretting about material today," she said. "Too hot to be sewing anyway. I only came in to get out of the heat and get a drink. Can't remember another June as hot as this one. Not a breath of fresh air stirring."

The older woman looked at Viola Mae for the first time. "What brings you to town in the middle of the week?"

"Gracie's baking day," she answered as Gracie slammed the rag she'd been dusting with down on the counter. "I came in special to get one of her fresh cinnamon rolls." She smiled at Gracie, who shot her a look that said she wanted to strangle her. Now what could have her in such a temper? she wondered.

Was it because of the Yankee, or because she had encouraged a conversation with Miss Sophie? Everyone in town knew the matron had a tongue like a bell clapper, but Viola Mae figured the poor old dear was just lonely, which was why she talked so much. But she also had begun to question if she'd done the right thing in telling Gracie about her prisoner. The way Gracie kept staring at her made Viola Mae feel very uncomfortable.

She dragged her eyes away from her friend and asked, "Miss Sophie, you ever tried one of Gracie's wonderful confections?"

"Oh, no, dear. Sweets aren't particularly kind to my delicate digestive system." Miss Sophie looked at Gracie, who had just poured her her usual—a big glass of water—and placed it on the counter in front of her. She walked to where Gracie and Viola Mae stood and said, "But, Grace, if you happen to have a sample, I could bring myself to try a small pinch."

Her pinch turned out to be a whole slice as she rambled on about last Sunday's social after church, the delicious food she'd enjoyed, and how afterwards her constitution had suffered severely because of all the rich desserts.

"If you don't mind, I'll have another slice. Thank you." She took a big bite and chewed with relish. "Grace, I never knew you were such a good cook." Another half of roll disappeared before her mouth was clear enough to speak again.

"I must say that Harriet's new beau is a real gentleman." Sophie took particular enjoyment in licking the icing from her lips before she continued. "Even though he is a Yankee, he is a handsome one."

Viola Mae felt herself blush at the mention of the Yankee. She and Gracie exchanged conspiratorial looks.

"I guess if we must consort with the enemy, they might

as well be good-looking. Don't you agree, ladies?'' Sophie
asked.

When Miss Sophie's gnarled fingers reached for another
slice of cinnamon roll, both girls were ready to stuff the remainder down her throat to muffle her before she continued.
Hearing about Harriet's new beau, the one Viola Mae held
captive in her henhouse, wasn't exactly their favorite topic of
conversation. But Miss Sophie wasn't finished yet.

She drained the last drops of water from her glass and
banged it down upon the counter.

''Would you mind, Grace?'' She indicated she wanted
more water by tapping the glass. ''I can't understand why I'm
so thirsty—it must be the heat. Harriet tells me that her new
beau has a real future working for her father after the railroad
is completed. I understand his family is well turned out and
that he has spent numerous years living abroad. Imagine that.
Seems he's interested in showing the other side of the world
to Harriet. But of course that won't be until after his work
here is completed.''

Viola Mae wondered what else he was planning on showing Harriet. The way Miss Sophie was carrying on, it sounded
as though the two were planning on getting hitched. For some
reason, that didn't sit right with Viola Mae.

She wished now that she hadn't encouraged the older
woman in conversation. Besides, she decided, she had been
away from the farm far too long. She'd only come to town
to ask Gracie if she would deliver her note to Mr. Archibald,
requesting to meet with him at his convenience. She hadn't
meant to spend the whole day in town jawing. It was time to
go home and make sure Romeo hadn't escaped.

Suddenly Miss Sophie let out an earthshaking belch that
startled both girls. The older woman's hand slapped against
her big bosom, and she looked as though she might relinquish
the two-and-a-half slices she had just downed.

''Mercy. I told you ladies I shouldn't eat sweets. I should
never have let you talk me into having a taste.'' The matron
took another big gulp of water, and all three of them waited
for the next expulsion to occur.

On cue, the gas erupted, shattering the silence inside the

store and destroying what little dignity Miss Sophie had left.

"Ladies, you'll have to excuse me. I must get home." She turned and waddled to the door.

Viola Mae called out to the elderly woman, "Miss Sophie, will you be all right? Would you like me to see you home?"

Miss Sophie paused at the door and looked back at the two women. "I will be fine, won't I?" Not waiting for an answer, she continued. "But between the heat and your baking, Grace, I might well meet my Maker before my time." She stepped outside and slammed the door shut behind her.

"I guess she ain't wanting me to walk her home."

Gracie looked at Viola Mae. "Can you believe that old cow? Imagine blaming her bellyache on my cooking. If I ate as many of those slices as she did, I'd probably sound like I was going to explode, too."

"Ah, she doesn't mean you any harm. She's just a lonely old lady who fills up her emptiness with food."

"Need I remind you she didn't pay for any of those slices? Didn't even offer to. It's not like she can't afford it. Her late husband left her a fortune, plus that big house in North Hill."

"Grace Marle, I'm surprised at you. It's the first time since I've known you that you ain't lived up to your good name."

"Right now I'm not in the frame of mind to live up to my good*will*. Truthfully, I don't understand yours. What were you thinking when you used *your* will to hold a man against *his* will. Your *will* to win this thing with the railroad makes me certain that you *will* live to regret your actions."

Gracie paused only long enough to catch her breath. "Now tell me again about this idiotic, harebrained, scheme of yours."

"Whew! I ain't never heard so many different kinds of wills."

"Well, I hope you left one when the law finds out you've kidnapped Mr. Rowe. You might need one."

"It ain't as bad as it seems, I promise. I'm only borrowing him for a short time until you can deliver this here note to the Archibald house." Viola Mae reached inside her pocket and slammed a white envelope down on the counter.

"Hold on. I might be your best friend, but I'm not delivering any note to anyone."

"Gracie, you got to. I'm depending on you. Don't you understand? I want to be home before you deliver the note. It's the only way I can get it to Archibald and still have time to get back to the farm."

"You ever heard of posting a letter?"

"Can't do that. Everyone knows the postmaster's so nosy he reads everyone's mail by holding it up to the light. Don't want no one to know about this but me and the railroad."

"And what am I? You don't seem to be mincing words with me." Gracie picked up a couple of jars of preserves and placed them on the shelf behind the counter. "What does this here note say anyway?"

"It says I'm holding the railroad boss captive until Archibald is ready to listen and then agree to my terms about the destruction to the forest. There was a fire the other night, and if circumstances had been different, if we were suffering a drought or if a good strong wind had come up, the whole dang forest could have gone up in flames."

"Haven't heard about a fire. Of course, no one would unless it happened right here in town. Do you know what caused it?"

Viola Mae recalled Seth's words about the fire being set deliberately, but she wasn't ready to repeat them to Gracie. Viola Mae's earlier attempts at hindering the tracklaying were the only things Gracie knew about. Since her mischief hadn't stopped the railroad's progress, Viola Mae decided to keep the information to herself.

So instead she told her, "Someone's carelessness, I reckon. Just like them railroad fellas burned down my cattails by the creek. You remember, I told you about Earle Forbes' chairs."

"Honey, I know how you feel about those woods, like they belong to you. But other folks don't see it the same way you do."

"Well, they dang sure should—"

The front door opened again, the bell on the door announcing a new arrival. Mr. Whitehead, the town ancient, inched inside.

"Afternoon, ladies." He nodded and smiled his toothless smile in their direction. With a sluggish gait, he dragged his feet across the wood flooring until he reached the ladies. He looked at the tray of sweets on the counter.

"I thought I smelled them cinnamon rolls." He winked at Gracie. "Not much else works anymore, but I can smell them rolls a block away."

"You weren't a block away, Mr. Whitehead. You've been sitting on that bench across the street for the better part of the day."

"Heh haw," he laughed, slapping his bony thigh in his too-big trousers. "Saw me, did you? I knowed today was your baking day and I felt if'n I sat there long enough, I could get me a taste of your sugar cakes."

"You're lucky there's any left. Miss Sophie just about finished every last one of them."

"Sophronia? Naw, she wouldn't eat these. Her digestive system is much too delicate." He took the knife from the counter and sliced off a big hunk of one of the rolls. Stuffing a bite into his mouth, he began gumming it until it disappeared. When he was finished, he said, "If'n I was a little younger, I'd marry you for your cooking."

"And if you were a little younger, I might take you up on that, Mr. Whitehead."

Her response seemed to please him. He turned to Viola Mae. "Miss Violee, what brings you into town in the middle of the week?"

"Same as you Mr. Whitehead. I knew today was Gracie's baking day."

"Too hot to bake, ain't it, gal?" He looked back at Gracie, who had covered the remaining rolls with brown paper. Several flies had come in with Mr. Whitehead, and she swatted at them with the fly swatter.

"Yes, it's too hot. But unfortunately I don't have the luxury of sitting all day on that bench in the square like you do. Some of us have to work for a living."

"Well, now. I guess there are some advantages to getting up in years, ain't there, gal?" He chuckled before shuffling over to a chair beside the pickle barrel and dropping into it.

"I'm about to melt in this heat," he said. "It's so hot, I know we must be in for a storm."

"Your bones telling you that, Mr. Whitehead?" Gracie asked.

"My bones and other signs. Yesterday I see'd a black snake in a tree. A sure sign it'll be a blowing rain in three days."

Viola Mae thought about the black king snake she had trailed to the road's edge when she'd found Mr. Seth Rowe snooping after Ginger's hoofprints. Course, that particular reptile was on the ground and not in any tree.

"And the surest sign yet, beside this infernal heat, I dreamed about your cinnamon rolls last night, Gracie gal."

"You old fool. My cinnamon rolls wouldn't have anything to do with the weather if you dreamed about them or not." She picked up the hem of her apron and wiped her hands. "You dreamed about them because you knew today was my baking day."

"It's true, I tell you. Mark my words. If you dream of eating something, that means there will be bad weather."

"A little rain wouldn't hurt none of us," Viola Mae added. "It surely would cool things off a bit."

The old-timer nodded his head, agreeing, "It sure would do that, Miss Violee."

Viola Mae turned back to Gracie. "Well, I've visited long enough. I best be getting back to the farm."

"No. You mustn't leave yet. Not until we've had time to finish our discussion." Her eyes pleaded with Viola Mae not to go.

Ignoring her plea, Viola Mae replied, "Can't stay, Gracie. I've been gone too long already. Now if you'll just deliver my note this evening, like I told you, everything will turn out fine."

"But, Viola Mae, you can't—you mustn't—you have to let him go."

"Let who go?" Mr. Whitehead asked, jerking to attentiveness.

After he had settled into the chair, both women had assumed he would drift into a nap. They had seen him do it often enough in the past. But apparently not today.

Viola Mae answered him. "Ain't nothing but a stray old bull. He moseyed onto my land the other day, and Gracie was going to ask around to see if anyone knew who he might belong to."

"Bulls can be mean sons of guns. You best be careful, especially with a beast you don't know nothing about."

"Oh, I ain't worried about him. Me and old Rosemary put him in his place right quick. Tethered him with my grandpa's old shackles that I found hanging in the barn."

"Heh haw! I remember them shackles. Your grandpa sailed to Texas for that bull your grannie wanted. He brought Beatrice a stud cow for her heifers. In the end, they had to shoot the ornery old cuss. That bull, he made mighty fine steaks, though. Had one myself. Of course, that was when I had my teeth and could still chew."

"Well, if this one causes me any problems, I've done and told him he was gonna end up the same way."

Gracie mouthed the words *You didn't!*

"Did, too, and he will. Don't have much use for cantankerous males, be they human or beast."

Mr. Whitehead shook his bald head. "Sure glad you told me that, Miss Violee. Wouldn't want to get on your bad side."

Viola Mae moved toward the plate-glass window and looked up and down the street.

"Viola Mae, don't you dare leave this store."

"Gotta."

Before Gracie could stop her, she had sashayed to the door, opened it, and stepped outside. She waved at them as she passed by the front window.

"I won't do it, Viola Mae. It doesn't matter if you are my best friend," Gracie shouted at her.

"Ah, just do it, Gracie gal," Mr. Whitehead encouraged. "People might want to know if their bull is missing."

He ran fast, his muscles cramped, but he pushed on. Pitch-black darkness consumed him, and he lost all sense of direction. But he wouldn't stop. Seth had to get away. Jed was depending on him.

"I won't die, little brother." His promise came out in panted syllables. "I know you need me, Jed. I won't let you down."

Bullets from Viola Mae's gun winged off the trees, missing him by mere inches. Although he couldn't see them, he felt their deadly power as they split the air around him. The chain around his ankle cut into his bruised skin, hindering his pace by catching on the tangled brush he passed. Seth stumbled and fell, but forced himself to his feet again. He had to escape.

"Damn crazy woman," he said and gasped. "Why, Viola Mae, why? I thought we were friends." He envisioned the woman pursuing him. His silver-haired angel had fallen from goodness like the devils of hell.

Faster and faster Seth ran until his lungs felt as though they would explode. The ground grew steeper. He almost crawled to the summit before the land leveled out. He loped along, pulling the damnable chain behind him, aware of the danger behind him, oblivious to what lay ahead.

He lost his footing and plunged headlong into what seemed like a bottomless hole. Out of control, he spun toward the unknown, the black abyss swallowing him.

His chest hurt like hell. Had she shot him as she'd warned she would? Over and over again, a tattoo of pain throbbed against his rib cage, driving him mad and following him to certain death.

Seth jerked awake. It took a moment for his eyes to focus. No longer was he plunging through hell; instead he faced it in the eyes of the woman who stood above him, repeatedly drumming the end of her shotgun against his chest.

Seth tried to sit up, but Viola Mae kept him pinned where he lay with the butt of her gun. Reality set in. She wasn't chasing him. It had all been a dream.

Jed. Relief washed over him when he realized he still had a chance to see his brother again.

"Is it true you're getting hitched to Harriet Archibald?"

Seth shook his head to clear it. "Hitched?" The only hitch he knew about was the one chaining him to the wall.

"Answer me," Viola Mae demanded. "Are you?"

She'd asked him a question, but he couldn't recall what it had been. Still groggy, he asked her again. "Am I what?"

"Are you jumping the broom with Harriet Archibald?"

"Jumping the broom? What the hell does a broom have to do with any of this?" He looked around and added, "Except maybe to clean up the chicken—"

He caught himself before the word slipped out, but then questioned why he cared what he said in front of the lady. *Lady, ha!* She wasn't like any lady he'd ever known.

"If you're interested, I've had more important things to do today than muck out *Mr. Romeo's* chicken coop."

Her expression indicated she wasn't in the best frame of mind, but then he wasn't either. *Who the hell was Romeo? One of her damn chickens?*

After Viola Mae had left him the chamber pot, Seth had spent a good part of the day trying to escape. But his efforts had been futile. With his hands tied, he couldn't twist the iron screw from the thick four-by-four that she had secured it to that morning. Finally, as the day grew hotter and the stench of the chickens became stronger, he had fallen into a restless sleep, only to be awakened a few moments ago by Viola Mae.

"I've brought you your supper."

"Supper. In case you haven't noticed, I didn't eat my breakfast. It's not exactly my idea of a fine place to dine. Especially with those chickens clucking and pecking. If I ever get out of this—this coop, I promised myself I'll never again touch a piece of the wretched fowl."

"Wretched? Oh, I don't know about that. Although these accommodations probably ain't what a city boy like yourself is used to, I always kinda liked this old henhouse." Her eyes took on a dreamy look. "Especially early in the morning. I find it takes on a certain coziness."

"Coziness? You're crazier than I first suspected. And you're right, this is the first henhouse I've been in. And it's not to my liking."

"Is that so, Mr. Romeo?" Viola Mae's expression turned stubborn. "I understood that philanderers usually frequent houses of ill repute."

Suddenly her meaning sunk in. "You mean whore—" Again Seth found himself interrupting his own speech. "Surely you're not thinking what I think you're thinking."

"And what might that be, Mr. High-and-Mighty? Just 'cause you don't say the word don't mean they don't exist. There are plenty such places along the docks. The men from the ships visit those same places while they are in port. Course, no one is supposed to know about them. Not decent folks anyway." Her lips lifted in a tentative smile until she saw him staring at her.

Again Seth was amazed by Viola Mae's plain speaking. He would have had to have been blind not to notice the beginning of the smile on her lips. He wasn't certain what had amused her, but he suspected it was the incongruity of decent folks who pretended not to know of such places. Damn, he couldn't help but like her. He decided to tease her.

"So, I guess that makes you not decent. Since you know about such places, I mean."

Indignation replaced her earlier humor. She whipped the long silver mane of hair back from her face before she answered.

"I'm decent, all right, but I also believe in speaking the truth. Growing up on a farm, I know what goes on between animals, and I suspect it ain't much different than what goes on between folks."

"Is that so?" He raised his eyebrows inquiringly. "How much could a little speck of girl like yourself know about what goes on between a man and woman?"

"Plenty," she answered, daring him to question her further.

He watched her natural flush deepen to crimson. Without being aware of it, she had answered his question. She might know about animals, but she didn't have a clue about the pleasures of the flesh.

This woman was an enigma with her plain speaking and her unconventional ways. One moment she talked about a brothel like a man, and in the next moment she was blushing like a new bride. He wanted to dislike her, should dislike her, but he couldn't. Besides, he reasoned, maybe if he seemed amicable, she would tire of holding him prisoner and set him free. If she didn't, Riley would come looking for him since he knew the route Seth had taken to town.

In the meantime, he aimed to get to know her better. Besides, the free-spirited forest nymph intrigued him more than the woman standing at the opposite end of the shotgun. Seth believed the real Viola Mae lurked just beneath the tough veneer.

"I was hoping that we could become friends since I'm going to be detained here for a few days. I know you said no Yankee was a friend of yours, but maybe we could try being civil to one another. The best way to do that is for you to tell me about yourself, and I'll tell you about me."

"Don't know if I'm interested in knowing about the likes of you." She eyed him skeptically.

"But I am interested in learning about you. At least tell me what you meant when you asked me earlier if I was getting *hitched*?"

After a moment she responded matter-of-factly, "Hitched. Tie the knot. You know. Wedded up?"

"Me?" Seth shook his head vehemently. "No, I'm not getting hitched to any woman. If there was someone I wanted to wed—but there isn't—I'm in no position to support her."

"Now that ain't what I heard. I heard your family was right uppity. Enough so that you traveled all over Europe."

"Maybe my family once was, but no more," he explained, feeling the old bitterness creeping up on him. Seth pushed aside his resentful thoughts and finished answering her question. "Yes, I did travel abroad. Extensively."

"Harriet told Miss Sophie that you're planning on showing her that side of the world."

Miss Sophie was no one Seth recognized. Apparently she was an acquaintance of Harriet's. For the life of him, he didn't understand why Viola Mae would be concerned about such gossip, other than the fact that she didn't like Harriet. The two women's dislike for each other had been apparent at their first meeting when he had arrived in Pensacola.

To smooth things over, he said, "Harriet must have misconstrued my meaning. I merely suggested that she should travel to Europe and spend a season there. I never said I would accompany her."

After several contemplative moments Viola Mae responded, "Having known Harriet for most of my life, I know how she can twist the truth. She usually does it to suit herself. I can just see her jabbering at the women's circle, telling everyone that you're her intended."

"Intended? I should say not," Seth answered with deliberate purpose.

Gossip about Harriet and himself was the last thing he wanted circulating around town, especially knowing how Harriet's father felt about him. As far as his feelings for Harriet, he felt nothing but gratitude for her help in securing his job with the railroad. Seth had no intention of marrying Harriet, or any woman for that matter. Not for a long, long time.

He would have told Viola Mae that, too, if he wasn't trying to keep their conversation on an even keel. It seemed every time the subject of the railroad came up, or Harriet Archibald was mentioned, she become angry and unapproachable. Seth didn't want that to happen, not now anyway. He hoped to convince her to let him go.

"Now that I've answered your questions, maybe you'll answer some of mine," he said.

"Ain't no riddles about me that need answering. Besides, you've jawed enough. I suppose you should eat your dinner before it gets stone cold and tasteless."

"Oh, yes, dinner." He looked toward the two trays that sat side by side on the floor.

Seth hadn't eaten anything since last night, and he knew if he hoped to escape, if it came to that, he would need his strength. But recalling how she had shoveled the food down his throat the night before, nearly choking him in the process, he thought he would try another tactic. "If I promise not to try any foolish stuff, will you consent to untie my hands so that I can feed myself?"

Her eyes narrowed suspiciously. "What kind of fool you take me for, mister? You know I can't do that."

Conceding, he said, "Okay, if you won't untie my hands, will you please call me Seth?"

He knew his request had taken her completely by surprise when her luminous blue eyes widened. She studied him from behind heavy dark lashes that seemed to tangle constantly with her flyaway hair. She brushed back the errant strand and hooked it behind her ear. Her answer was a long time in coming, but Seth didn't mind; it gave him the opportunity to study her.

Viola Mae Smith was a natural beauty. There was nothing artificial or phony about the woman who stood in front of him. What you saw was what you got. She was no bigger than a marsh mosquito, and her bones were delicate, but she also had curves in all the right places. As she contemplated his last request, she stood unaffected in front of him with her toes peeking out from beneath the hem of her worn dress. At that moment, Seth knew it would be those damned bare feet that would be his undoing.

"All right, mister—I mean, Seth," she corrected. "Since you and me'll be stuck together for a few days until this business is settled, it would make it a lot more pleasant for us both if we ain't nipping at each other like dogs after a coon."

Viola Mae picked up a dinner tray and placed it on the sheet in front of him.

"And since you ain't too interested in feeding yourself, I'll be happy to oblige you."

She plopped down in front of him, opposite the tray of food, and sat cross-legged. Her bare toes peeked from beneath the hem of her skirt, and the thin material of her dress barely disguised what lay between the valley created by the breadth of her open knees. Or what his imagination created, he amended. He'd never sat across from a woman with such disregard for propriety, except maybe in a sporting house. But there was nothing remotely similar about those women and the one who faced him.

A hot rush of desire slammed through him. How in the hell was he supposed to swallow food with such a provocative woman sitting across from him? His throat felt like parchment when he tried to concentrate on what lay beneath the linen napkin on the tray instead of what lay beneath the flimsy garment of her skirt.

Seth's stomach rumbled with hunger as the smell of food drifted up to him. Viola Mae recited a litany of the food while he repeated it in his mind: black-eyed peas, mashed potatoes, corn pone, fried chicken.

"Fried chicken!"

Seth glanced nervously around the coop, expecting at any moment to be attacked by an avenging fowl. Then he felt ridiculous for entertaining such a thought. Not only could animals not reason, but chickens were some of the dumbest creatures alive.

"Now, don't you fret about ol' Joe Pye here," Viola Mae said, interrupting his thoughts. "He had long outlived his usefulness as a cock, so I figured I better cook him up before he got too tough and stringy for eating. Wrung his neck." She tucked the linen napkin into Seth's shirt collar, smoothing it down over his chest, before continuing her story. "I used most of his parts in those dumplings I took to the picnic on Sunday. This is the last of him."

"Wrung his neck?"

"How else did you expect me to kill him? Never did take to beheading chickens with an ax."

"Wringing their neck is better?" Seth asked.

"Oh, there is an art to it. You grab them by the head and give one swift jerk with your arm. It's over so fast, they don't even know they're dead. You put them down, and they'll run around for a few minutes before they actually keel over."

Seth's stomach rumbled again, but this time it wasn't with hunger. "If you don't mind, I'll think I'll leave the chicken," he said.

She looked at him long and hard, then took a bite of the drumstick. "Suit yourself," she told him, "but you don't know what you're missing. My fried chicken is delicious. I make it just like my grannie taught me."

To Seth this grannie character seemed a far safer topic to pursue than food, so he asked her, "Was this grannie your mother?"

Viola Mae loaded the spoon with potatoes and peas and

lifted it to Seth's mouth. "Ain't never heard no one call their mother by the name of Grannie." Viola Mae looked at him, her expression disbelieving. "She was just what I called her. She was my grandmother."

She dipped up another spoonful of food and looked as though she had more to say on the subject. "I reckon, though, now that you mention it, she was more like a mother to me than a grandmother."

Seth chewed the potatoes, the corn bread, and the black-eyed peas. It was all delicious. This was Seth's first experience with black-eyed peas, but he wasn't about to tell Viola Mae. He didn't want to hear about their origins, although he suspected they grew on vines like other peas. But knowing Viola Mae, he was almost certain she'd come up with some tidbit of information on how the peas got eyes.

While he ate, he delighted in watching her polish off the meat on the drumstick. As she did everything else, she ate without any inhibitions.

If the juicy meat dripped from the corners of her mouth, she captured it with her tongue. Also, she licked her greasy fingertips clean. If licking didn't remove enough of the residue, she reached across to the napkin she'd hung around Seth's neck and wiped her fingers against his chest. Her every move was unfeigned, and she was completely oblivious to how alluring she was.

Seth imagined how it would be to remove the greasy substance from her lips and fingertips with his own tongue. He had experienced flashes of desire before during their brief encounters, but those moments were nothing compared to the hunger that gnawed at his insides now. Maybe it was the mood of the isolated farm, knowing that he was alone with her now, but whatever it was, he wanted her with a need that was almost painful.

"Who's Jed?" she asked, breaking into his thoughts.

Having finished her chicken leg, Viola Mae tossed it back on the empty plate, whipped the napkin from Seth's shirt collar, and began to clean his face.

"How do you know about Jed?" he asked, trying to dodge her ministrations.

"When I came in earlier and found you asleep, you were calling his name." She continued to swab at his mouth. "Or was it a *her* whose name you called?"

"Not many women named Jed."

"How about Jedwina?"

Seth chuckled. "If my little brother heard that, I don't think he would be too pleased."

"Now if that don't beat all." Viola Mae's face lit up with amazement. "For some reason, I never pictured you having a brother. Somehow it doesn't suit you."

Seth laughed. "Suit me? I don't believe any of us have much control over having siblings. But I do have a brother, whether it suits me or not. Jed is ten years old. If everything goes as planned, he'll be joining me here in Pensacola in time to start school."

"Here? But what about your parents? I don't reckon they're none too happy that you're going to steal him away from them."

"Steal him away?" His expression held a touch of sadness. "I don't think that will be much of a problem. Since their deaths, I've been responsible for my brother. It's only Jed and me now."

Viola Mae wanted to yank out her tongue as soon as the words were out. She understood all too well how it felt to lose a loved one. She still missed her grannie. Some days the hurt was so big she felt hollow from her head clean down to her toes. She reckoned Seth must be feeling the same way if the sad expression on his face was any indication.

"I'm sorry," were the only words she could offer, although she knew apologies weren't much solace for someone's grief.

It was the first time since taking the Yankee prisoner that Viola Mae realized that the railroad boss had a life beyond his job, beyond the day when he first arrived in town.

As she thought about his other life, she decided that folks were basically the same no matter what part of the country they came from. Everyone had hurts, and like her old grannie used to say, pain was one of the many seasons of the heart. You had to learn to deal with it just like you dealt with the seasons of the earth.

She wanted to share this bit of wisdom with him, but somehow the words wouldn't form. She felt his gaze upon her, and as usual when he looked at her with his sea-green eyes, she went all ticklish inside.

"I appreciate your sympathies," he whispered, his words barely audible.

Smiling softly, she tilted her head back to look at him. She wanted to see him smile again as he had done earlier. Viola Mae had liked the sound of his laughter and had been enjoying their conversation. She wanted his good humor to return.

"I reckon it ain't none of my business, about your family, and all, but I just want to say I bet you make a mighty fine big brother."

Her words had the desired effect. He smiled at her again and said, "Now I'd be interested in hearing what makes you think that."

Now she'd really gone and done it. Picking up the food tray, she set it aside. She hadn't expected Seth to require a list of his attributes. There surely must be some, but she hadn't discovered too many of them thus far. But not wanting him to go all unhappy on her again, she plunged ahead, drawing from her little experience of him.

"Well, for one thing, you know about beavers."

"Yes, I do know about beavers," he confirmed.

After a moment of consternation, she added, "And you know how to rescue damsels in distress."

Using Viola Mae's stylistic speech, Seth said, "I reckon you're that damsel."

"Saved me twice, you did."

She laughed, recalling her first bicycle ride in the square when Seth had broken her fall. "Miss Snooty-Hooty Harriet looked as though she had eaten a lemon when she found us wallowing together on the ground."

Seth must have thought Harriet's expression was funny, too, because soon they were both laughing like children over a misdeed they had gotten away with.

Several moments passed before their merriment died. Viola Mae's ribs hurt from too much laughing, and she leaned forward over her knees to ease the pain.

Seth watched her. She was like a child in her merriment, the way she collapsed across her lap. With her head so close to his legs, he could feel the heat of her. Silver strands of her hair clung to the denim of his trousers and to the cotton of the sheet. It reminded him of a silken web spun by a spider.

He wanted to reach out and touch it, to entwine his fingers through the silvery threads, to become ensnared in its gauziness. Seth reached toward the silky mass. With shaky fingers, he gently caressed her tumbled mane. It felt as cool as satin to his touch.

She didn't move, but his heart beat so rapidly he shook from the impact. If Viola Mae was aware of the contact, she didn't let on that she knew. As he leaned forward, he could see the graceful line of her neck, the beginning of her fragile backbone that disappeared beneath her dress collar. Throwing all caution to the wind, Seth buried his face in the silvery pillow and breathed in the essence of her. Her scent carried him beyond the hot, close, sawdust-and-dung smell of his prison, to the cool, open woods of evergreens and wild violets.

He could have stayed that way forever, but the pulling motion beneath his face brought him back to reality. She was trying to sit up. Seth lifted his head several inches, freeing her hair, but captured her again when their gazes locked. They froze in that position, their faces mere inches apart.

Seth stared into the depths of her eyes before his gaze dropped to the inviting rosy pink of her lips. God, he wanted to kiss her. As though she read his mind, her face edged closer to his, and they met in between. She slanted her head to the left, he slanted his to the right, then their lips brushed ever so lightly before they pulled apart.

Viola Mae thought her heart would jump clean out of her chest, not only because her breasts felt like they might explode out of the constraining fabric of her dress, but because it was the headiest sensation she'd ever experienced.

Stunned by the impact of their lips brushing, Viola Mae jerked upright. Seth looked none too pleased when she jumped to her feet, distancing herself from him, but she didn't care.

What had her grannie always told her? *If you play with fire, you're gonna get burned.*

"Please," he whispered, his voice sounding husky, his eyes revealing a smoldering flame.

Smoldering flame. Maybe that was the fire her grannie had warned her about.

"Gotta go," she told him, grabbing up both the trays and whirling toward the door.

Viola Mae felt hot all over, like a stack of dried kindling ready to burst into flames. There was no doubt in her mind that the Yankee had stoked some kind of fire inside her.

She ran past the chickens, slammed the trays down on the porch, startling Soapwort, who lay beneath the stoop, and ran straight for the creek.

There was nothing like an ice cold bath to cure what ailed you. Whatever was causing the fever to rack her body, she intended to drown it in the stream.

Chapter Eleven

"Jedwin Rowe, now do be careful, you hear?"

"Yes, ma'am, I will."

Jed jumped down from the wooden platform that skirted the stage depot and kicked a pebble across the sand. He'd met Miss Finch on the train ride from Jacksonville. She was returning to her home in Milton, Florida. He knew from his map that the town sat across the bay from Pensacola.

Miss Finch forgotten, Jed paused several feet from the Concord coach that would carry him the rest of the way to Pensacola. He moved to stand beside the big back wheels that were more than five feet across. Stretching up on his toes, he tried to touch the wheel's rim with the top of his head.

"You got a few inches to grow, young fellow," the station attendant informed him, smiling. "But don't go rushing it. You'll get there soon enough."

Jed stood taller and crossed his arms against his chest. "Oh, I'm pretty big," he answered.

While the man worked his way around the coach, greasing the wheel axles, Jed accompanied him.

"This your first stage ride?" The attendant straightened and began checking the oil in the coach's side lamps.

"Yes, sir. But I've ridden in plenty of carriages."

"A carriage ride on a tame city street is a far cry from crossing wild country in a stagecoach. Makes me wonder what a whippersnapper like yourself is doing traveling alone."

Wild country! The man's statement captured Jed's attention, reminding him again of his brother's letters. He, too, had talked about the wilderness.

"Oh, I'm not so young, sir." He cleared his throat, then tried to make it sound deeper than it was. "I'm used to traveling alone."

This last declaration prompted the station master to study Jed more intently.

Jed swallowed hard before continuing. "I'm joining my brother in Pensacola. He's expecting me."

Sorta, Jed thought to himself.

The attendant appeared satisfied with Jed's answer because he no longer studied him speculatively. "Well, all I can say, sonny, is that you're in for the ride of your life. Almost eighteen hours' worth."

Together they stood back and watched the stock-tender hitch up the six-horse team that would pull the coach. After a moment, the man spoke again.

"Think you're up to eighteen hours of travel with no rest in between? You might get to stretch your legs when the coach stops for fresh horses, but don't count on it."

"Oh, my legs don't need much stretching, sir," Jed answered, "and eighteen hours isn't too long." The adventure he'd been waiting for was about to begin, and he wasn't about to let anyone tarnish his excitement.

"I bet you'll change your tune before this trip is over," the man told Jed, patting him on the head. "But you have a good trip, son. Do as the driver tells you, and I'm sure you'll be fine. Now if you'll excuse me, I need to ready the mail for the driver."

"Thank you, sir." Jed watched the attendant move back toward the station house, all the while thinking about his statement that the country was wild. Though it hinted of danger, the thought excited Jed.

Thus far, his trip south had been more mild than wild. After leaving Atlanta, the train had passed through mile after mile of pine forest, and Jed had quickly lost interest in looking out the window. It wasn't until they had approached the Florida border that the scenery had begun to change and Jed's interest had again been piqued.

Passing over marshes, he had spotted a snowy white bird with pencil-thin legs, standing among reedy grasses. Jed had seen feathers similar to the bird's on his aunt's Sunday hat. In Jed's mind, every floating log the train passed became an alligator—one of the leather-plated swamp dragons he'd read about in books.

When they arrived in Jacksonville, they'd had a short stopover. Jed, along with the other passengers, had left the train to roam up and down the wharf's length that was built over the water. The St. Johns River could be heard swishing against the pylons beneath the loading platform, and he could see the smooth expanse of blue water beyond the shore. From a vendor Jed had purchased fresh oranges, a loaf of bread, beef jerky, and several alligators' teeth. The latter were the favorite of his purchases, but certainly not sustenance for the remainder of his trip.

After the train left Jacksonville for Chattahoochee, the scenery had consisted of rolling hills and stately trees, much the same as that around Atlanta. Knowing he would soon be traveling by coach from Chattahoochee to Pensacola, Jed had looked forward to the last portion of the trip, hoping to see the wilderness that Seth had referred to in his letters.

Now having thoroughly inspected the vehicle, he stepped back onto the platform. Several other travelers were waiting to board the coach: three men and the lady, Miss Finch. Shortly after he'd made her acquaintance, she had appointed herself his keeper. Not that he needed a keeper, but Jed soon concluded that the fidgety little woman needed to have him to worry about, so he'd tolerated her hovering.

The door to the station house flew open, and the driver scurried out. Thrown over his shoulders were packs labeled "U.S. Mail." He slammed to a stop as though remembering his passengers for the first time. Turning to face them, he shouted, "Time to board. We leave in five minutes."

Jed took note of the driver's appearance. He was a wiry little man whose protruding front teeth reminded Jed of a beaver. Like a real cowboy, the driver wore a leather vest, a bandanna, and a big Stetson on his head that looked as though it had seen better days.

"Name's Booger Butts," he told the passengers. "If you've a weak stomach, don't like to be bitten by sand gnats and mosquitoes, require a bath and a decent night's sleep at the end of the day, then don't board my coach. But knowing these minor discomforts, and if you're still wanting to go, I'll take you to your destination. I guarantee you'll be there on time."

He looked over the anxious travelers. When no one spoke, he took their silence as consent and climbed aboard the driver's seat, dropping the mail sacks into a leather boot.

Jed clambered into the coach behind the others, taking a seat beside the window. Miss Finch took the seat next to him. The leather curtains covering the windows were rolled up, and he knew he would have a good view of the passing land.

"All aboard!" the driver shouted from his seat on the front of the coach.

The stage lurched forward at runaway speed. The impact caused Jed's head to slam back against the wooden panels while the passenger sitting opposite him nearly slid from his seat into Jed's lap. Miss Finch's bonnet flopped forward on her forehead. She righted it, causing the brown feathers to bob. Jed didn't mind the temporary pain caused by the bump to the back of his head. The pain dulled quickly as the station rushed from Jed's sight. For the first time since leaving Atlanta, he felt that his adventure had truly begun.

Groggily Viola Mae sat upright in the bed. The temperature inside the cabin was no longer hot, having turned cooler during the night when the wind had come up. She could feel the sudden, strong rush of air beneath the cabin's flooring that made the wooden boards creak and expand on their cypress pylons. Sporadic raindrops plopped against the tin roof.

She blinked several times, trying to focus in the dark. She looked beyond the mosquito netting covering the bed, and the interior of the house was pitch black. Outside the windows, the yard was cloaked in inky darkness with no sign of a moon.

Viola Mae pushed back the netting and rolled onto her feet. Could Mr. Whitehead's prediction about a storm brewing be true?

In tune with nature herself, Viola Mae believed in the physical signs that the earth provided humans. Yesterday's smothering heat, along with the heavy stillness that had hung in the air, was a definite sign of bad weather. Although it was too early in the season for storms, Viola Mae suspected they were in for a real blow.

She crossed the room to the window. A streak of yellow fur darted in front of her feet, nearly tripping her. "Stupid cat," she scolded, "you'll make me fall and break my dang neck."

As she approached the window, the netting swelled outward on the breeze, lifting gracefully before falling back into place like a kite losing its draft. Viola Mae anchored the curtain with her hand, bent forward, and peeked out at the night sky.

Clouds, dense and thick like a bubbling caldron, rolled across the moon's surface almost obliterating its light. Gusts of wind made the trees bordering the yard claw and stab at the sky.

She moved to the mantel clock to check the time. Daybreak was less than an hour away. She hoped by then the squall would have passed.

Instead of returning to bed, she made a small fire in the fireplace and put on a pot of coffee. Because of the change in the temperature, the blaze wouldn't heat up the cabin's interior and make it unbearably hot as it did most days in the summer.

Her task finished, Viola Mae lit a lamp, then dropped down on a stool by the kitchen table. By now Gracie would have delivered her note requesting a meeting with Mr. Archibald. She expected to be contacted by the railroad man sometime today. Viola Mae would allow him until this evening before she . . . did what?

What exactly did one do with kidnapped victims if the kidnapper's demands weren't met?

Not wanting to dwell on this aspect of her plan, Viola Mae jumped up and moved to the door to let the cat outside. She slid back the heavy wooden bolt that secured the door at night, and opened it several inches to allow Mustard to exit.

A strong gust hit the panel of wood, snatching it from Viola Mae's grasp. The door slammed back against the wall. A frightened Mustard shot from the stoop and hit the ground running.

Stepping outside, Viola Mae crossed the porch and looked toward the henhouse. A gray dawn lightened the sky, and the wind scuttled leaves across the yard.

What if Archibald didn't come for the Yankee today? If there was a storm brewing, she knew she couldn't leave Seth chained up in the henhouse.

Although her grandpa had built their cabin to withstand bad weather, the henhouse and barn weren't as sturdy. The chickens could fend for themselves, but the coop wouldn't be a safe place for a man to ride out a storm.

That meant she would have to bring Seth inside. And after last night's kiss, how in the name of heaven could she keep him in her house, chained a few feet away from her, and keep her sanity?

After her swim in the creek last night, she had returned to the cabin and crawled into bed. Surprisingly she had had no trouble falling asleep, but she knew it was because she had swum vigorously for almost an hour.

But her dreams had not allowed her such comfort. They had been filled with Seth and the memory of the kiss they had shared. As soon as her eyes had opened this morning, the memory had popped into her consciousness, tormenting her. But she had pushed it aside because she had a dozen chores to do and she didn't need to be thinking about a man.

The wind ruffled the hem of her nightgown, bringing her back to the moment. "It's not going to storm," she told herself, returning indoors.

Viola Mae dressed and poured herself a cup of coffee and grabbed a day-old biscuit. She had just sat down at the table when she thought she heard someone calling her name.

"That dang Yankee."

All she needed was for him to be calling her twenty-four hours a day. If it was him bellowing, his caterwauling would mess up her egg-laying hens. She lunged up from the chair, grabbed her shotgun, and stomped to the door she'd left open earlier.

Once outside, she heard the voice again. It came not from the coop, but from the front of the house.

"Viola Mae, its me, Earle Forbes."

Earle Forbes. What in tarnation was he doing coming to visit at such an ungodly hour? She never had visitors. With the railroad boss chained up like a bull in her henhouse, a visitor was the last thing she needed or wanted.

She tromped toward the front of the house. Beyond the fence she saw Earle perched on his wagon. At least he had the good sense not to barge into the yard unannounced. Country folks who lived away from town and civilization would just as soon shoot first and ask questions later. That was why it was best to stay afield until your presence was known. Old-timers knew the law of the woods.

"What brings you over this way so early?" she called, stepping down from the porch and walking toward him.

The wind whipped at her skirt, tangling it around her ankles before slapping it back in the other direction. Her unbound hair blew around her head.

Earle grabbed at his hat, which was about to be lifted from his head. "Doggone wind is about to scalp me."

Viola Mae chuckled to herself. His head was as bald as an egg, and there didn't appear to be much left to scalp, but she wasn't about to tell him so. She paused inside the fence.

"Sorry to be disturbing you at such an early hour," Earle said, "but I've just come from town. Had to deliver some feed yesterday and stayed the night with my sister."

"How is Miss Isabella?"

"She's fine, but her joints were aching when I left her. Blames it on this weather."

"Then we're in for a storm?"

"That's why I came by. They've got the storm warning flags up in town. Barometer dropped, and heavy swells are blowing in from the southeast. The port authority received a telegraph message from Tampa that says we're in for a nasty blow."

"That means we'll have to batten down the hatches," she said.

Viola Mae's grandfather had been the captain of his own ship, and her grannie had passed on a few lines of sailor lingo to Viola Mae. If what Earle said was true, she would be boarding up her windows and seeing to the safety of her animals the rest of the morning.

"You got enough boards to do you?" Earle asked. "We can expect the worst of this tempest by some time tonight. I've orders to ride by the railroad camp and tell them fellows out there to head for town till the storm passes."

His latest piece of information caught Viola Mae off guard. She gulped down her stomach, which had leapt to her throat at the mention of the railroad. "Who told you to do that?" she croaked.

"Mr. Archibald. He saw me as I was leaving town. Asked me to ride by the site and inform them about the storm's approach."

"Did he tell you anything else?" she asked, hoping Archibald had sent a reply to her message with Earle. With this new problem facing her, she wanted to be rid of the Yankee.

"Naw, it's jest like I told you. He said them workers will probably want to be heading home to their families. If they choose to stay, they'll be put up with folks in town."

Viola Mae knew one railroad man who wouldn't be heading anywhere. Dangnation. What else could go wrong with her plan?

"You gonna be all right?" Earle asked her, his question pulling her back from her thoughts. "If you've a mind to, you're welcome to bed down with me and the missus. You know we've got a heap of young'uns, but we always got room for one more. Especially in a time of need."

"Thanks, Earle. I appreciate your neighborliness, but I'd best stay here. I've got my animals to think about."

"Guess we're lucky we built on high ground, huh? We don't have to worry about flooding like them folks in town do."

"We are at that. My grandpappy built his house strong enough to weather any storm, or so my grannie always said.

I'll be as snug as a bug in a rug," she assured him.

"Yes'm, I expect you will be, Miss Viola." Earle placed his hat back upon his head, pulling it low over his ears to anchor it. "You take care now. When the worst is over, I'll be back by to check on you."

"Thanks." She waved good-bye and watched until Earle and his wagon disappeared into the woods.

A hurricane. Viola Mae pushed aside the memory of the last storm she'd witnessed. She had been ten years old at the time, and in her mind it had been worse than any nightmare she'd ever had. A recurrence of that dream was not something she cared to think about.

Besides, the last thing she needed was interference from Mother Nature. Especially when she already held a prisoner who wreaked havoc on her normal good sense. Now she would have two tempests to deal with when she brought the Yankee into her house—one outside threatening to destroy everything she held dear, and the other inside threatening to tear down her defenses with a heated look from his sea-green eyes.

Life just wasn't fair.

Seth thought he heard someone calling Viola Mae's name. He rolled over on his makeshift mattress and propped up on one elbow.

It was too early for callers, or so he reasoned as he glanced about his small prison. Gray daylight seeped through the only door and the narrow cracks of the shed's siding.

He could have been dreaming again. Or the sound could have been caused by the wind that had come up during the night.

Or was he the one who had called out Viola Mae's name from the depths of his troubled sleep? She had certainly been on his mind after she'd left last night, after he'd kissed her. Sweetest damn kiss he'd ever experienced, but it had set him on fire. Hours after her departure, Seth still ached with the desire her kiss had stoked.

Thwack. Thump. Something hit against the side of the shed. He jerked his head toward the striking sound. The chickens clucked and screeched at the loud assault before dropping from their nests and scattering like balls of white yarn. It had to have been the wind he had heard earlier, he reasoned.

He looked toward the empty dinner trays. Viola Mae had not snuck back in during the night to retrieve them. Not that he'd expected her to. Again he was reminded of the kiss they'd shared. He knew women and he suspected the impact of their kiss had affected her as much as it had him.

As though his thoughts had conjured up her image, she appeared in the doorway. Even in the soft light of dawn, her vision took his breath away.

Framed by the door's gray light, she looked tiny, her bone structure delicate. The wind tugged at the long silver mane of hair, whipping it about in disarray. She'd changed her clothes. Seth was so used to seeing her in faded calico that the black skirt and white blouse she wore today displayed her in a more feminine light. Her bosom was full and round, her waist narrow, and when the wind kicked up, practically blowing her skirt over her head before she anchored it with her hands, he was treated to a peek at her small ankles and shapely calves. And, of course, those tantalizing bare feet.

"You'll be having your breakfast late this morning," she told him, moving toward him to collect the trays.

"Oh, and why is that?"

His eyes feasted on her graceful curves and the pink toes that peeked from beneath the hem of her skirt as she paused in front of him.

"Storm's brewing."

This got Seth's attention. His gaze traced up her length before coming to rest on her face. "Storm?" he asked.

"Yep. I fear we're in for a good blow."

"And how do you know that?" Seth suspected from what he'd learned about Viola Mae since he'd met her that she probably predicted the weather like most farmers . . . by signs. "Did one of your hens crow?"

A smile tugged at her lips. "Hens don't crow, greenhorn, only roosters."

"Oh, but they do when a storm is approaching, or so I read in the *Farmer's Almanac*."

"Didn't fancy a city fella like yourself would enjoy such reading material."

His reply was husky, low. "You'd be surprised what a fancy city fella like me considers entertaining."

He caressed her with his eyes, and she blushed from the tips of her bare toes to the top of her silvery head.

"Just because you and me experimented in a little lip-brushing, don't be getting any ideas it will lead to anything more than that." She glared at him, her high color diminishing somewhat.

Seth chuckled. "I'll be satisfied with just *that*. You let me know when."

He'd meant only to tease her, but as soon as he said the words he knew they were true. He would like to kiss her again, although the way he felt right now, as if he was going to bust the front seam in his britches, he doubted if he'd ever be satisfied with that.

Realizing what she had said, or what Seth construed she had said, Viola Mae's color deepened once again. "I mean, there'll be no more of *that* or anything else you might have a mind to."

She bent over to pick up the trays. Once again, her scent came to him, reminding him of evergreens and wild violets. Of outside—freedom. If he was ever to be free again, he had to stop thinking with what was between his legs and use his head instead.

"So we're in for a northeaster?" he asked.

"No, in these parts we call them hurricanes."

Hurricane. A feeling of dread kicked at his gut. "This early in the season? I understood hurricanes struck much later in the summer."

Straightening, she faced him, positioning the trays on her hip. "It's early, but it does happen. But you don't need to worry none. We're on high ground."

"Now that's encouraging," he responded. "At least I know I won't drown. Although there is a good possibility that me and this chicken coop I'm chained to could blow into eternity. And who would be the wiser?"

Although Seth fought the desire to look at her, he couldn't

control his gaze. He was very much aware of the sensual curve of her hip beneath her well-worn skirt, the deep indention of her waist where the trays rested, and the way the material of her white blouse tightened across her breasts when she breathed.

"If something happened to you, I'd be the wiser," she answered, "and I ain't too excited about the prospect of losing my chickens' roost. But you, you're a different story altogether."

"In other words, you'd be glad to see me gone?" Maybe this storm would work to his advantage. "As I said last night, you could let me go. They'll be needing me at the site. I promise no one will know about this incident."

She pondered his suggestion before she answered. "Sorry, but I can't do it. In time, maybe, but for now I believe I'm stuck with you."

Concern for his men's safety made Seth's earlier desire fade. He jumped to his feet. "Look, I need to get back to the railroad camp. If we're due for a storm, someone needs to warn my men, tell them what they should do. They are my responsibility, you know."

She turned to leave, but stopped in mid-stride. "If it will set your worry to ease, that's taken care of already. Mr. Archibald sent word for the crew to come into town until the storm blows over. Folks there will put them up until the worst passes, or if they live within easy traveling distance, some might chose to join their families."

"Damn—I mean, darn—another delay."

Although this delay was beyond anyone's control, the idea of his railroad crew being scattered all over the outlying countryside didn't sit well with Seth. They might not ever come back. If that was the case, how would he complete the laying of the tracks?

"Delay!" Viola Mae's anger flared, igniting blue sparks in her eyes. "Is that all you care about? Another delay?"

"Yes, well, I mean, no. I care about my men. Remember, I told you they were my responsibility. But I also care about the railroad being completed on schedule." He continued bitingly, "Chained up like a dang bull, I'm not much use to anyone, now am I?"

She looked at him long and hard before she answered. "You're useful to me. And until I see fit to free you, I guess you'll have to get used to being chained up like a dang bull."

He watched her sashay toward the door. It no longer mattered that he be civil. He had tried that, and it had failed.

"Wait," he shouted. "You can't keep me here like this. If there is a storm coming, I refuse to be blown away with these stinking chickens."

Viola Mae jerked to a stop. "Oh, you don't need to worry none about that. My stinking chickens won't blow away. They've got wings and can fly." With this remark, she disappeared through the doorway.

"Come back," he yelled. "What about me? I don't have wings. You have to let me go."

Only the gusts beyond the flimsy walls heard his demands. They replied with an eerie wailing cry, reminding Seth how vulnerable his position was.

"How in Sam Hill am I going to survive a storm—in this?" He eyed the roughhewn walls skeptically. Not only was it demeaning to be held prisoner by a crazy woman who cared more for her chickens than a human life, but in addition he faced the possibility of being blown to hell and beyond in this worthless excuse for a building. If he disappeared, no one would ever know.

Seth turned and braced his hands on the wall. He jerked hard on the manacle that chained him, trying to break free. His effort caused a sharp pain when the bracelet encircling his ankle dug into his tender flesh. At that moment his feelings for Viola Mae were not romantic.

Chapter Twelve

It seemed as though hours had passed since Viola Mae had left him. Seth's stomach growled with hunger as he waited for the breakfast she'd promised. Maybe she'd decided to abandon him, concluding that the approaching storm would be an easy way to get rid of him with no questions asked. And who would be the wiser when they stumbled upon a nameless gnarled and twisted body?

This last thought didn't sit well with Seth. If he should meet such an end, then what would happen to Jed? No, he wouldn't dwell on his little brother. Instead he would have to come up with a plan to escape.

But what plan? Everything he'd tried so far, like trying to break the chain that held him prisoner, had been useless. Civility wasn't working either. In fact, he now believed he was playing into her hands by not putting up more of a fight. Maybe he shouldn't be so cooperative.

Sunlight glazed the interior of the shack, warming it to a muted gold. He glanced toward the door. Yes, sunshine. It did look brighter outside. Not quite so gray. With this discovery, his spirits lifted.

Maybe there wasn't to be a storm after all. Maybe it had veered away from Pensacola. Hopeful, Seth watched and listened. The wind still blew in strong gusts around his prison, but there were also calm periods in between. He blinked against the sunlight that gilded an oblique rectangle of light against the sawdust-covered floor. As he watched, the mirage of the opening faded from gold to a gunmetal gray, and his bout of optimism disappeared.

Disheartened, he rubbed his sweaty brow against his sleeve. He felt like the devil. His body itched from numerous mosquito bites, and his clothes and body were caked with sweat and grime. He no longer knew if the odor that plagued him constantly was his own or the stinking chickens he'd been sharing quarters with.

How long had he been here anyway? Had one or two days passed? It seemed like weeks. Originally he figured that if he hadn't returned to camp in two to three days Riley would come looking for him. But with a hurricane bearing down on the coast, Riley would probably decide Seth had chosen to remain in town. Especially if Archibald had sent word to the camp with orders for everyone to head into town until the storm had passed.

Bracing himself, he pulled with all his might, trying once again to dislodge the screw from the wood. It wouldn't budge. Maybe if he thrust his weight against the siding, it would eventually give way, and he could escape through the opening.

With no more than a couple of feet separating him from the wall, he couldn't build up much momentum. He would try anyway. Hunching his shoulders, he propelled his weight against the wood. After several attempts, he fell against the siding, his energy depleted, his breathing heavy, his shoulders aching from the impact.

If he still had on his work boots, he would kick the damn wall down. But without them, kicking would be impossible. Frustrated, Seth slid back to the floor and leaned against the planking.

A shadow crossed the shack's entrance. His breakfast had arrived at last, but Seth was finished with being cooperative. He was tired of taking Viola Mae's orders. She came toward him bearing no gifts of food. Instead she carried only her shotgun.

Stopping several feet away from where he sat, she ordered, "On your feet."

Seth didn't move. He sat where he was and glared up at her.

"You had a hearing loss since I left you?"

He could tell she wasn't prepared for his show of stubbornness. Up until now, he'd been the perfect prisoner, doing all of her bidding, but that was about to change. If she intended to treat him like her grannie's bull, chaining him like an animal, he'd show her how bullheaded he could be. He sat with detached obstinacy, and she reacted exactly the way he expected her to.

The barrel of the shotgun centered on his chest. She stirred uneasily at its opposite end. Seth curled the fingers of his hands around the gun's barrel and pushed it aside. She raised it again, this time pressing it into his chest.

"Go ahead. Shoot me," he told her. "The way I see it, if a storm is coming through here and I'm to ride it out in this shack, you might as well kill me and get it over with. If nothing else, it might save me a lot of suffering."

His ultimatum took her by surprise. He watched the play of emotions cross her face. She looked away, then moved her blue eyes back to his.

"Ain't you smart enough to figure I'd never shoot you inside my henhouse? At this close range, the noise would certainly make my hens quit laying. Can't afford that."

Seth figured he'd probably be dead if the look Viola Mae shot him was any indication of her strength. Maybe she was capable of killing him, and maybe he was pushing his luck. What did he really know about the woman, other than that she was as sensual as a kitten when she didn't have her claws out? Right now she looked as though she'd like to scratch his eyeballs out.

"On your feet," she ordered again. "If I'm going to have to blast you, I'd prefer doing it outside. Now get up."

Inside his head, Seth weighed his options. No matter how he hoped to play it, he knew the person holding the gun had the advantage. But if he made it outside, maybe he could overpower her and make a run for it.

He held his tied hands up above his head to show compliance. "You win, Viola Mae. I'll get up." But not to allow her to believe she had the upper hand, he added, "I still don't believe you could shoot me, but I'd feel a heck of a lot better getting to my feet if you'd aim that thing somewhere else."

"Does here suit you better?" She lowered the barrel to his personal parts. "Now get up like I told you."

Although the weapon was several inches away from his person, Seth felt it as though it rested against his flesh. Her look warned him against any funny business.

"All right. All right." Seth tottered to his feet using the wall for support. "What's gotten into you all of a sudden?"

"Let's just say between holding you and this storm that's breathing down my neck, I'm quickly running out of patience."

She squatted down, the gun still posed on the target below his belt, inserted the key into the bracelet that encircled his ankle, turned it, then slowly stood up again.

"Now listen to what I say because I'll only say it once. I'm taking you inside my house. If you take a notion to run, I promise, if you're lucky enough to still be breathing, you'll be picking buckshot out of your behind into the next decade." Her gaze didn't waver.

Seth still didn't believe she'd carry out her threat, but then again, maybe she would. His only consolation was that she was moving him out of this dung hole. That in itself was a step in a better direction.

"Now turn around," she ordered.

He did.

"Walk."

When he began to move forward, Seth could feel the cold steel of the shotgun digging into his flesh. A desire to survive told him this wasn't the best time to test her.

It had been so long since he'd moved more than several feet in either direction, his legs felt wobbly as he exited through the shed's door. Once outside, he breathed deeply of the fresh air.

Although a sporadic covering of clouds skittered across the sky, once his eyes adjusted to the outside light he could see patches of blue among the gray. A strong wind blasted him, plastering his shirt against his chest and flattening his hair against his head. As he walked, his bare feet found every buried pebble inside the chicken yard, and every piece of corn feed the chickens had missed. He felt as if he were walking on nails as they left the small confining space of the chicken pen.

Although the main yard contained grass, it was broken up by patches of gritty sand. As he high-stepped across the yard toward the house, he called over his shoulder, "All I can say is you must have hooves for feet if you can walk barefooted on this."

Her only reply was a forceful nudge in his backbone with the gun. When they reached the steps that led up to the porch, he hesitated. She prodded him again.

The hound dog Seth had seen beneath the stoop the first day he'd found Viola Mae's house looked up at him through the stair rungs with slothful eyes.

"Soapwort, stay," his mistress ordered. The dog obliged her by not moving, holding his pose of a crumpled mass of bones and stretched skin.

Once he was on the porch, the wooden flooring felt satiny smooth beneath Seth's feet. Upon closer inspection of Viola Mae's dwelling, he knew the house was sturdily built. His spirits lifted again. They had lifted and fallen since he'd been taken into captivity. Maybe he would survive the storm after all.

When they reached the entranceway, she held back the netting that covered it and nudged him inside. It was dim within the cabin, and several moments passed before the room came into clear focus.

His first impression was that he had stepped inside a wood-lined chest. Every wall was made of wood, warmed with the patina of age. The large one-room dwelling had a high cathedral ceiling with thick round beams running across its width. The fragrance of dried herbs and flowers, hanging from every available space on the rafters, made Seth feel as though he'd dived into a bowl of pomanders.

He didn't realize that he had come to a standstill until he felt the point of Viola Mae's gun dig into his spine again.

"Keep going," she ordered, urging him forward. "If you're going to be sleeping in my bed, you dang well need a bath."

"In your bed? Well, uh," Seth sputtered like a nervous schoolboy. "Are you sure—I mean—"

The idea of crawling into her bed was appealing; in fact, he'd thought about almost nothing else for the last two days, but he'd never dreamed Viola Mae would seriously entertain such a thought. Especially after she'd assured him that there would be no more lip-brushing.

"Yeah, I'm sure. Your stench would gag a maggot. Move," she ordered again.

Not believing his good fortune, Seth moved deeper into the room, smiling inwardly at the delights he believed awaited him. He felt amorous and cocksure, intent on making their little tumble pleasant for them both, and he decided to tell her so.

"I'll be more than happy to accommodate you. I assure you it will be an experience you won't soon . . ."

Seth's words trailed off. He halted in mid-stride. "Bath. Did you mean bathe?"

"What else would I have meant?" she asked. "And since you're so happy to accommodate me, it's a good thing the water is heated and waiting for you."

His cockiness vanished as he glanced across the room. In front of the clay-lined fireplace sat a long copper tub. From its depths, steam rose upward like fog over swamp water.

Certainly she doesn't expect me to strip while she watches me.

Seth swung around to face her. "You can't be serious." Her next movement convinced him that she was.

She stepped toward him and, withdrawing a knife from her pocket, snipped the rope that bound his hands. Her movements were swift and deliberate, and before he could protest, she had the shotgun aimed at his chest again. She nudged him toward the tub. "What's the matter, you opposed to bathing?"

"Hell, no, I'm not opposed to bathing." He ran his fingers through his hair. "But I am opposed to being ogled while I do it."

"Like I told you before." Her eyes never wavered from his. "The way I see it, folks ain't made no different than animals. One bull's hung pretty much like the next one.''

Not thrilled with the prospect that she would soon be seeing him in a different light, Seth responded angrily, ''When are you going to get it through your thick head that I'm not some prize stud you can order around at will?''

''Oh, you surely ain't no prize and you surely don't know nothing about bulls. Ain't met one of those critters yet that followed orders without a little prodding.'' She stepped closer. ''Now strip. Before I do it for you.''

Belligerently Seth folded his arms across his chest. ''I'm not stripping in front of you.''

''Yeah, you are.'' Her fingers inched toward the shotgun's trigger, and she centered the barrel on his private parts. ''A castrated bull ain't much use to anyone. You get my drift?''

When she didn't move or falter, but instead stared him down, Seth cursed the day she had ridden into his life. Disgusted, he grumbled, ''Okay. We'll do it your way.''

Seth yanked his shirt over his head and tossed it onto the nearest stool. Then his fingers moved to the buttons of his fly, working them loose. This done, he wrestled the denim trousers over his hips, past his knees, and stepped out of them and kicked them across the floor. Straightening, he watched a blush creep up Viola Mae's neck.

''Just what I expected,'' she answered, her gaze locked on his privates. ''Ain't no different from any other old bull I've seen.''

Seth tried to think of an appropriate response, but found himself at a loss for words. Instead he turned, presenting his backside to her scrutiny, and strode toward the steaming tub, hoping the water would give him a modicum of privacy. Never had he met a more infuriating woman.

Ignoring her, Seth lowered himself into the water. Soon his earlier discomfort at being put on display was forgotten. Not even the rotten-egg smell of the sulphur water could detract from the therapeutic effect of the long-overdue bath. Leaning against the tub's back, he closed his eyes. After spending two days in hell, he felt like he was in heaven. But too soon he learned that he wasn't to be allowed such an easy admittance.

His tormentor marched toward him. From beneath his lowered lashes, Seth watched her advance. A rag slapped against his half-submerged chest, and a heavy bar of soap exploded the calm when it hit the water.

"Wash," she ordered as she bent to pickup his discarded clothes. Holding them between her thumb and forefinger as if they were infested with bugs, she tromped to the door and tossed them outside.

Her actions made Seth almost shoot straight up from the tub, but recalling his nakedness, instead he stayed hidden behind the tub's walls, shouting demands. "Those are my clothes. You can't do that."

"I just did," Viola Mae responded, brushing her hands together to rid them of the excess grime, "and you ain't getting them back until I see fit to give them to you."

"Just what am I to wear in the meantime?"

"When I decide, you'll be the second one to know. Now wash."

Unable to do anything but her bidding, Seth picked up the bar of soap, lathered up the rag, and began to scrub away the two days of dirt that caked his body. The embarrassment he was suffering was worth it, since he knew that he wouldn't be spending another night in that stinking chicken coop.

While he bathed, he watched Viola Mae flitting around the cottage. She bent over an old trunk, then moved across the room to a large wardrobe.

She was a spunky little thing, he'd have to say that for her. In spite of his embarrassment at having been put on display, Seth couldn't help but admire her pluck. She'd stared at him as bold as gold. Her straightforwardness was one of the many things Seth admired about Viola Mae. If his nakedness had bothered her, she would have disguised those emotions with her usual insults.

Most women, or most of the ladies Seth knew, would have swooned on seeing a nude male for the first time. But not Viola Mae. He paused in his thinking. Maybe a nude man wasn't a novelty. Hadn't she suggested that he would be sleeping in her bed?

No! Seth wouldn't believe what his mind suggested. He recalled instead the way she'd colored on seeing him naked and the way she'd studied him as though he were some kind of rare insect viewed for the first time. Hers was not the look of an experienced harlot.

His thoughts somewhat settled, Seth relaxed against the tub as Viola Mae circled behind him. He tried to appear unbothered by her presence, but her explanation of why he needed a bath kept jumping into his mind. *You ain't sleeping in my bed without a bath.* Warmth spread through him. Maybe being held prisoner by such a desirable woman wouldn't turn out so badly after all.

While Viola Mae busied herself at the fireplace behind him, he pretended disinterest. He wasn't about to let her know that he was curious about what she could be doing. Instead he leaned forward and pretended concern over a particularly nasty mosquito bite on his knee.

It was at that precise moment that she chose to douse him with another bucket of water. Like a flood tide, the tepid water washed over the top of his head, temporarily blinding him, and practically drowning him as he sucked in a shocked breath.

"What the devil?" he asked, coughing and choking at the same time.

"I don't want no lice in my house," she told him. Viola Mae pulled a stool up beside the tub and began to massage a godawful-smelling salve into his scalp and hair.

Before Seth could protest, she warned him, "If this gets into your eyes it'll blind you, and if it gets into your mouth it'll burn your tongue out. So if you're as smart as you think you are, you'll keep both closed until I tell you to open them."

Like an obedient child, he obeyed, making Viola Mae feel very pleased with her little half-truth. The acetic solution she massaged into his hair wouldn't blind him or burn out his tongue, but her little fib would keep him silent.

As she washed his hair, sweat beaded above her upper lip, and her body felt as though it was on fire. Viola Mae blamed her current discomfort on the steamy bathwater and the hot coals that burned in the fireplace a few inches away from where she sat. She was unwilling to admit it was her body's reaction to Seth's nakedness that made her feel hot all over. He sat unmoving while she tried to scrub her present discomfort away on the top of his skull.

There was no doubt in Viola Mae's mind that the Yankee was the comeliest-looking fella she'd ever seen. He was the first and only naked man she'd ever set eyes upon, and his state of undress disturbed her greatly. She had thought him attractive with his clothes on, but with them off he took her breath away.

Her earlier remark about all bulls being hung the same was a gross misconception. There were no similarities between the parts of the man basking in her tub and those of an ornery old bull. Cattle had heavy bodies, long tails, and cloven hooves. Seth certainly didn't qualify for that description. In fact, in Viola Mae's estimation, he was beautifully put together.

Instead of heavy, his body was lean and sinewy, his shoulders powerful and broad. From working outside in the sun, he had developed a farmer's tan; his neck and arms were bronzed to a golden brown, while his chest appeared somewhat paler. Water droplets like crystal jewels clung to the burnished hair that sprinkled his wide chest. The glossy pelt trailed down his muscular stomach to the darker nest between his thighs.

Viola Mae jerked her eyes away from the fascinating object and scrubbed harder on Seth's head. She was glad his eyes were closed so he couldn't see her ogling him. Of its own volition, her gaze strayed again to that mysterious part of him and she felt heat explode inside her belly.

She recalled Seth's statement about his plumbing being different from hers. After seeing him in the raw, she knew what he meant.

Seeing him, all of him, made Viola Mae wonder about her grannie's teachings on procreation and how babies were made. "A sacred act between a man and woman," her grannie had told her, "that should involve commitment from both parties."

Up until this moment, Viola Mae had never considered

what went on between a man and a woman. But the Yankee railroad boss had changed all that. His nakedness had made her wonder about that sacred act and how it would feel to have his plumbing connected with hers. The thought made molten heat scald her innards, and she yanked hard on a hank of Seth's hair.

"Ouch!" he mumbled, jerking his head from her grasp, but still heeding her warning not to open his eyes or mouth.

Viola Mae released his hair and jumped up from the stool. Enough of this. Disgusted with her musings, she reached for the bucket of rinse water. Intent on drowning her thoughts, or perhaps the man responsible for them, Viola Mae dumped the bucket of icy water over Seth's head.

He yelped like a wounded puppy and sprang to his feet. He blinked against the deluge that slid down his face. "I've had just about enough of your abuse. And I don't give a damn if my tongue does fall out."

She slapped a towel against his chest. "Well, you better give a darn because it might just eliminate those other parts that you seem so dang intent on exposing to my view."

Shaken by her comment, he dropped his gaze, then the towel, using the cloth to cover his sex. On seeing the stricken look on his face, Viola Mae softened.

"Oh, you don't have nothing to worry about. It's diluted."

"Denuded?"

Rolling her eyes toward heaven, she explained her statement. "The rinse water diluted the salve. It's like I said, you don't have to worry about losing nothing."

"I believe I have plenty to worry about," he grumbled, drying himself and taking special care to keep a certain part of his anatomy hidden beneath the towel. "Maybe you would be kind enough to enlighten me as to what I'm supposed to wear since you tossed my clothes outside."

"That's all taken care of, too," she told him. She walked across the room to the trunk she'd been going through earlier. "It ain't much, but it'll have to do." Crossing the room to stand in front of him again, she held the garment up for his inspection.

Seth looked at it, then back at her. "Oh, no," he said,

shaking his head. "There's no way in hell I'm putting that thing on."

"Fine. Suit yourself." She tossed it down on the stool beside the tub. "If you'd prefer wearing that towel, or perhaps parading around this cabin in the raw, it's your choice. It won't bother me none, one way or the other."

Turning her back on him, she moved toward the cupboard on the kitchen wall. She heard him step from the tub, heard the towel swishing against his skin, and heard him mumbling. Busying herself, dishing up scoops of coffee, Viola Mae used the moment to gain control of her earlier thoughts while also allowing Seth some privacy.

"Viola Mae?" His call broke into her work, and she paused. "Couldn't you allow me to put my own clothes back on?"

She heard him fumbling with the garment she'd given him and sensed his frustration.

"I . . . I can't wear this. What if someone came by here and caught me dressed in this . . . this . . . frippery."

Without turning around, she answered, "Your clothes need to be washed, and I ain't got time to do laundry with this storm approaching. You don't need to worry about no visitors because people don't come calling during a hurricane."

The fire crackled to life in the fireplace as a draft of wind swooped down the chimney, reminding them both that reasons beyond their control had forced them into this situation.

After a moment, Seth mumbled disgustedly, "What the hell. Nobody but a damn crazy woman's going to see me anyway."

Viola Mae smiled to herself. Then, satisfied that he was dressed, she turned around to face him. "Now ain't you the—"

Seth glared at her, stopping her in mid-sentence. It took all her willpower not to laugh. After swallowing several aborted giggles, she told him, "My grannie was a tall woman."

"But not tall enough." He stretched his arms out in front of him as though he were visiting his tailor. "If your grannie could see me now, I'm sure she'd be real pleased to see me decked out in her lace-trimmed nightie."

"Aw, she wouldn't mind."

Viola Mae's lips twitched into a smile as Seth's scowl grew deeper.

"Maybe she wouldn't mind, but I sure as the devil do." He whirled away from her and began to pace, making the cotton gown swirl several inches above his hairy ankles.

Although her grandmother had been a tall woman, almost five foot ten, and very buxom, her size couldn't compare to Seth's. The feminine gown looked silly on his very male body.

He'd left the collar unbuttoned, and the Watteau pleated front zigzagged like a drunk across his broad chest. Instead of covering his wrists, the deep cuffs of the sleeves hit midway down the length of his arms. Although the gown was much too short for his height, at least it covered him.

He looked comical, and they both knew it. She didn't dare say so for fear that Seth would strip on the spot, so she lied.

"You look just fine, and besides, you'll only have to wear the gown until I can get your clothes washed."

"Only! There's nothing else in your magic trunk? What about your grandfather? Didn't he have any clothes?"

"Oh, the moths ate those years ago." She cocked one eyebrow playfully. "But there is a corset and a petticoat if they would be more to your liking."

A muscle clenched in Seth's jaw. It was evident he'd lost his humor along with the loss of his clothes. "Then give me my clothes, and I'll wash them myself."

"Can't do that. Besides, I don't want you sloshing water all over my floor. You'll just have to make do with those duds until I get my chores done. As soon as I feed you, I've got to get busy."

Strolling past him, she walked to the pie safe. After several moments, she returned with a glass of milk and some corn pone and placed it on the table.

"Sit and eat," she ordered.

Reluctantly Seth obeyed. As he flopped down on a chair beside the table, his legs tangled in the gown's fullness. While he wrestled them free, Viola Mae plunked a cup down in front of him, then put the coffeepot on to boil. Soon the room was filled with the coffee's rich aroma.

While Seth ate his breakfast of corn bread and milk, Viola Mae emptied out the tub, a bucket at a time, and pushed it to one side of the fireplace. After the coffee had boiled, she poured them each a cup and sat opposite him at the table.

A thick silence hung between them. Only the wind gusting against the house, the clicking of the mantel clock, and the shuffling of the low-burning embers in the fireplace broke the strained quiet.

Finally Seth asked her, "What can we expect from this storm?"

She took a swallow of coffee, then replaced the cup on the table, studying its contents before she answered. "Mostly a lot of wind and rain. It's hard to tell how strong a blow we'll be getting, but let's just hope it ain't a real bad one." Viola Mae took another sip of the strong brew. "I ain't been in no storm since my grannie died. She wasn't scared of nothing."

Her last statement made Seth wonder if *she* was afraid. "Are you frightened?" He found it hard to believe that Viola Mae would be frightened of anything.

"Heck, no, I ain't scared." She looked away hastily, then muttered, "Besides, my grandpappy built this house to withstand all kinds of weather. It's cool in the summer and warm in the winter."

Seth glanced around the room. "It's a fine house, too. Even a greenhorn like me can see that."

His comment made her smile. She liked talking to this man, especially when he worked at being congenial. "Much better than my chicken coop, huh?"

"Much better," he replied. "Present company included."

His answer and the way he looked at her made her grow hot all over. *Dangerous.* The thought returned unbidden. Viola Mae practically inhaled the last dregs of her coffee before she jumped up from the table. "I've wasted enough time. I've got to get busy."

"Let me help you," Seth volunteered.

"Don't need your help. Besides, you ain't exactly dressed for hard labor."

"No, I'm dressed for bed," he replied sarcastically. "Which is exactly where you're headed."

"Bed?" For the first time since his bath, Seth looked beyond the living area of the room.

There, standing catty-cornered from the wall, was Viola Mae's bed. It was a bed that dreams were made of. Seth had seen a similar one several years back pictured in a copy of his mother's *Godey's Lady's Book*. Cottage furniture, designed for simple country cottages; factory-made pieces painted with gay floral motifs or decorated with spool turnings. It was an apt piece for Viola Mae's cottage.

White mosquito netting hung from the ceiling and surrounded the bedstead in a gossamer web. *Her bed.* For a moment, Seth allowed himself to imagine lying beside Viola Mae inside the cocoon that looked like spun sugar. His fantasies made his body quicken with desire. Although she had said only that he was going to bed, surely when her chores were finished she'd be joining him there.

"Yes, bed. Now march," she told him.

Somewhere in between her announcement that he'd be going to bed and her command to march, she had retrieved the shotgun. It rested again in the familiar spot against his spine.

Seth walked toward the big bed, and when he stopped beside the canopied confection, his breath soughed between his teeth. He said a prayer of thanks for the gown he wore because its fullness hid his growing arousal brought on by his fantasies.

A prod from the gun's barrel to his backbone and the sound of Viola Mae's voice brought him back to the present.

"That way," she told him, "over there against the wall."

Wall? Seth looked in the direction she indicated, and he felt as if she had doused him with cold water.

An iron bedstead that looked no bigger than the cot he'd been sleeping on in the railroad camp stood against the cabin wall. The lumpy mattress was covered with a vividly colored quilt. But it wasn't the size or the condition of the mattress that made Seth's spirits plummet, but the rope lengths tied to the headboard and footboard that waited to receive their prisoner.

"Come on, Viola Mae. You're not going to tie me up again, are you?" He swung around to face her, ignoring the indentation the gun barrel made in his skin as he rotated.

To assure him that she was, she jabbed him hard in the stomach. "Gotta. It's like I told you earlier, I've got chores to do before this storm hits."

Seth held out his arms in disgusted adjuration. "Do you honestly believe that I would try to escape—in this?"

"Sorry, but I can't take no chances," she told him, backing him up against the bed. His knees buckled, and he landed in the center of the moss-filled mattress.

First she tied his ankles to the iron bed frame, then his wrists. Once she had him secured, she stepped back.

"Viola Mae, please," Seth pleaded. "Untie me and let me help you. I promise I won't try to escape. You can trust me."

If Seth thought she believed him, he had sorely misjudged her. She admitted there were moments when she sorta liked him, like last night when they'd practiced lip-brushing, or a few moments ago when they'd sat jawing over coffee. Although he looked ridiculous in her grannie's old nightgown, he still had the power to make her senses reel.

But trust him? Never.

As far as Viola Mae was concerned, trusting any man, especially one who worked for the railroad, was on her list of things that would never happen. Long ago she'd vowed never to fall victim to a man's charms. Never to end up like her mother. She might like a man, but trust him? Never, she reaffirmed. Not even one as natty-looking as Seth Thomas Rowe.

Chapter Thirteen

"Hellfire and damnation," Seth grumbled, trying to free his limbs from their new restraints. Just when he'd thought he was making progress with the woman, the tables had turned, and he'd found himself at odds with her again.

Hold on, brother, he told himself. *Just because you're so dang horny for the woman doesn't mean the feelings are reciprocated.*

What kind of fool was he anyway, believing because she'd referred to him sleeping in her bed that she'd meant it literally? Now that common sense had replaced his fantasies, he realized he probably *was* sleeping in her bed. The big bed must have belonged to her grandparents. And if he wanted to take it a step further, he was sleeping in *her* cabin as he had slept in *her* henhouse the previous two nights. Again he cautioned himself to think with his brain.

He dropped his head back against the mattress. This time she'd tied him spread-eagled on the small daybed. It was so short that he couldn't stretch out to his full length. He looked toward his feet. The bumps of his knees sticking up beneath the nightgown reminded him of how foolish he must look.

What in the devil did Viola Mae hope to gain by holding him? Seth searched his brain for an answer, but none was revealed, and she'd never told him outright. She had only implied that she needed him and would keep him until she saw fit to let him go. Why? The question kept taunting him.

He jerked the restraints. After several more failed attempts to free his limbs, Seth fell back on the mattress. He felt as helpless as a turtle on its back.

Although he was still her prisoner, his accommodations had certainly improved. No longer was he bunking with the chickens, and the smell was much more pleasant, his own odor included. The bath had made him feel human again, in spite of the less-than-private accommodations he'd been forced to endure.

Seth sighed. For want of anything better to do, he began to inventory the cabin's interior.

Viola Mae's house was nothing like he expected it to be, but he hadn't given much thought to how it would look until the day he'd happened upon it. The memory of that day reminded him of his stupidity. He should have heeded her signs. If he had, he wouldn't be in this strange predicament.

Not one to dwell on past mistakes, Seth glanced toward the cabin's only two windows. He strained to see beyond the netting that covered them. As far as he could tell, the day remained overcast. A breeze eddied through one of the windows, fevered with summer, bowing the mesh inward because it was weighted close to the floor. The curtains weren't adornment for the windows, but a necessity to keep the mosquitoes and other insects out. Each of the three doors had the same mesh curtains, but because the doors were closed, the filmy netting was pushed to one side.

Upon further inspection of Viola Mae's house, Seth noted that the furniture appeared to be of fine workmanship and design. Nothing like the antiques and works of art that Seth had grown up with, but well-made pieces that were both functional and handsome in a utilitarian way.

He looked toward the pine trestle table where he had eaten his breakfast of cold corn bread, to the food safe with the door panels of decorated tin. Although too far away to make out the tooled designs, he could still tell it was a quality-made piece.

Because the one-room cabin served many purposes, it looked as though it was divided into two areas. Where he lay was the bedroom, while across the room, in front of the fireplace and windows, was the keeping part of the room. Besides the kitchen furniture, there was a settee, a bookcase that looked to be filled with books, and a rocking chair beside a small lamp table.

For a moment, Seth allowed his thoughts to wander. He placed Viola Mae in that chair, reading by the lamp's soft glow. The picture gave him a warm, comfortable feeling.

Reading. Maybe she couldn't read. Until this moment, he hadn't considered that possibility. Several of the men who had taken jobs with the railroad had been unable to read or write. Recalling the carefully lettered warning signs he'd discovered on her property, Seth concluded that Viola Mae must be able to read and write, but he would ask her when she returned.

His gaze traveled over her grannie's bed, the huge wardrobe against the wall, and the old blanket chest before returning to the area of the room where he lay staked like a man left to die.

He chuckled at this absurd thought. Once he'd realized who his captor was, Seth had never really feared for his life. If he knew nothing else about Viola Mae, he knew she wasn't a killer. Anyone who would rally against a man like Booger Butts because of his mistreatment of horses couldn't take a human life. Although Viola Mae enjoyed being his personal tormentor, Seth knew beyond a doubt that his life was not in jeopardy.

Passing time, he continued to study the cabin's interior. The only really masculine touch was the style of furniture close to where he lay. The tiger maple desk and bookcase facing him, he thought, would have been more at home in a fine house than in the almost Spartan cabin. A miniature of a nineteenth-century sailing ship and several scrimshaw carvings sat upon the opened writing top. Like the other bookcase in the keeping area, the one above the maple desk, too, was filled with leather-bound books, their titles engraved in gold. Sitting beside this heavy piece was an oversized Spanish colonial armchair.

Also occupying the space was a black leather campeachy chair whose well-worn seat still contained the imprint of the user's large behind, and a maple stand whose surface was painted with a yellow and black checkerboard.

Although Viola Mae's speech and actions were less conventional than most of Seth's friends, Seth felt, after seeing the inside of her home, that he had stumbled upon a part of her that he never knew existed—perhaps she was more cultured than he had first believed. This realization made him want to get to know her better and made him anxious for her return.

A loud thump against the wall and several taps at one of the windows grabbed Seth's attention. At first he thought it was the wind until he saw a shadow move beyond the window's glass panes. Another audible blow hammered against the wall. Several moments passed before Seth realized that Viola Mae was boarding up the windows, preparing for the storm.

"Viola Mae, let me help you," he called.

Either she ignored him or couldn't hear him. He heard only the sound of more tapping. A feeling of total uselessness frustrated him. He watched until the gray light beyond the window dulled to near-darkness, then tracked her movements by the sounds he heard on the opposite side of the wall.

When she moved to the next window, he heard the *thump* the ladder made when it hit against the house and the pounding of the hammer. He heard no other sounds from outside, and inside daylight could no longer filter through the windows. The cabin's interior was submerged in near darkness.

A good hour passed after the sounds had stopped before Viola Mae returned. On a rush of damp air, the door flew open, and she hurried inside.

"Our first squall," she told him, turning to bolt the door.

Although it was almost dark indoors, Seth could tell she was dripping wet. Her hair hung in damp ringlets around her face, and her blouse and skirt were plastered to her body like a second skin. He smelled her dampness as she hurried past him.

Beyond his range of vision, she changed out of her wet clothes. They plopped heavily against the floor, and he heard the rustle of a towel against her skin before she moved across the room to light a lamp. Soon a globe of golden light reflected off the wooden walls, illuminating the flaxen-haired beauty who stood across from him in her white dressing gown.

She ran her fingers through her hair trying to smooth it. It was such a graceful, feminine gesture and such a natural one that she wasn't aware of how fetching it made her look. Few women would choose to entertain a man in her dressing gown and be so casually unconcerned about her state of near-undress. In fact, if she knew the feelings her image aroused, she would probably flee the cabin, or better yet, throw him out into the storm and hope he blew away like debris.

Moving toward him, she stopped several inches away from where he lay. "I guess since you and me are stuck together for the duration of this storm, we'll have to make the best of our situation."

She looked as though she had more to say, so Seth lay quietly, waiting for her to finish. He didn't have to wait long.

"So here's how I figure it. I'll give you freedom in my house, only because I ain't figuring you're stupid enough to try to escape as long as this tempest is beating down upon us."

She smiled, looking up and down his long length. "And I don't think you're none too anxious to run anywhere wearing my grannie's nightgown."

"That's right, but what about my clothes? You did say I'd only need these until mine were laundered."

"You don't need to worry none about your duds. You'll get them back, just like I promised you. For the meeting."

"Meeting? What meeting?" Seth asked.

This was the first mention of any meeting that Viola Mae had made, and from the look on her face, it was a slip she hadn't intended to make. Seth realized she could be holding him for ransom. But if she were, he was still to be kept in the dark.

Completely ignoring his questions, she continued. "For the time being, I'm using those duds as my insurance—to make sure you don't make a break for it.

"Another warning, and one you shouldn't be too quick to forget. I'll not hesitate to blast you with my shotgun if you take a fool notion to run." To prove her point, she lifted the gun from within the folds of her gown. "If I feel a need to tie you up again, I'll do it without hesitating. In the meantime, don't give me no cause to."

Seth looked up at her. "You have my word that I'll be a model prisoner."

"Don't need your word. It ain't worth nothing anyway. I've got my insurance—the storm, your clothes, and this." She tapped the gun against her leg. "More than enough, the way I see it."

She moved to untie him. As soon as the knots were released, Seth swung his feet to the floor and, sitting on the edge of the cot, massaged the circulation back into his fingers.

"Now what?" he asked.

"I'm gonna muscle us up some dinner, then we can settle in for a long night."

He rose from the bed and dogged her footsteps. "Let me help you."

"I don't need no help and I don't want you trailing behind me like a lost puppy." She moved into the kitchen area. "Find a seat or walk around, but don't forget I can see you from every corner of this room."

Like a lost puppy was exactly how Seth had felt ever since Viola Mae had taken him prisoner. Looking toward the three closed and bolted doors to the cabin, he wondered if she really would carry out her threat to shoot him. If he was lucky enough to escape, would the tempest outside be worse to deal with than the one inside? Deciding one was just as bad as the other, Seth chose to stay where he was and enjoy his temporary freedom.

Viola Mae walked to the fireplace. Stretching up on her toes, she placed the shotgun in a special rack above the mantel.

"In case you get any ideas about grabbing my shotgun, I'd advise you to forget them right quick." She pulled a small pistol from the pocket of her nightgown. "This is loaded, and I'm a dang good shot." Dropping it back into her pocket, she turned to the hearth and reached for the pot of coffee she'd brewed earlier that morning. "More coffee?" she asked. "It's still warm."

"Sure," Seth replied, looking around the room. "I like your home. It's very comfortable."

She ignored his compliment and nosed around a cupboard until she found the pot she was looking for.

Viola Mae appeared to be an excellent housekeeper. Everything was neat and in its place.

Taking his coffee, Seth walked to the pie safe that he had noticed during his earlier inventory of the cabin's furnishings. The tin panels were pierced with renderings of sailing ships, and each of the safe's four legs sat in a tin cup filled with water.

When she saw him study the liquid-filled cups, Viola Mae told him, "This climate's a booger for household pests. To keep the pissants out of my vittles, I have to drown them before they can crawl up the legs."

Seth nearly choked on the coffee he'd just swallowed. Viola Mae never ceased to amaze him with her plain speaking. He chuckled as she whopped him on the back. Soon he was breathing normally again, and Viola Mae returned to the business of preparing their dinner.

There were other food-storage pieces around the kitchen, including a jam and jelly cupboard. He scanned the jars of canned compotes, then stopped midway. Several jars of blackberries filled one shelf. They were not unlike the ones that had caused the plague of dysentery on the railroad camp. Seth's heart raced. Could Viola Mae have been responsible for the mysterious appearance of the preserves? Impossible, he told himself, merely coincidental. He imagined that most of the women in these parts canned their own preserves.

Upon further study of the kitchen, he decided he liked it. Four ladder-back chairs with rush bottoms sat around the kitchen's well-worn table. What looked like a carpenter's toolbox sat in the table's middle. But instead of tools, it was filled to overflowing with fresh vegetables and fruit: cabbage, cauliflower, squash, tomatoes. Viola Mae lifted several of the items from the box and began cutting them up and placing them inside the big iron pot.

"It'll be a good night for soup," she told him, as though he had requested the menu.

"Did you grow all those vegetables yourself?"

"Most of them. But some I buy from Gracie's General Store in town." With the back of her wrist, she pushed several strands of hair away from her eyes. "How much I buy depends on the time of year or how good a crop I grew. Because Pensacola is a seaport, a lot of ships bring in fresh vegetables and fruit from farther south. There ain't no need for me to have a big garden since I've only one mouth to feed. When I do have a bumper crop, me and the neighbors share."

"How about the preserves, did you make those, too?"

"I certainly did. Every spring I gather blackberries from the bushes that grow wild in the woods. Best dang blackberries you'll ever eat."

"Not me. I'm allergic to the fruit."

"Or they used to be the best, before the railroad came and dug up all them vines. You wouldn't believe the passel of berries I used to pick."

He watched her grab a big potato and begin to pare it.

"Yep, like everything else, those no-good scoundrels went in and knocked the vines down when they decided to clear the roadbed. Paid no mind to the destruction they caused to the land."

"Like the cattails you told me about?"

"Exactly. But don't get me started on the rail—" Her mouth snapped shut. She looked at him, then at the blackberry preserves. A look of guilt crossed her face before she spun and moved toward the dry sink.

Seeing Viola Mae's reaction confirmed his earlier suspicion. There could easily be a connection between her preserves and the ones found outside of the railroad camp. Not wanting her to believe that he'd noticed her response, Seth moved across the room to where the settee was located, along with the glass-doored bookcase filled with books.

Unwilling to believe his suspicions, he perused the leather-bound titles: works by James Fenimore Cooper, Charles Dickens, Charlotte Bronte, Henry David Thoreau, Harriet Beecher Stowe. All in all, it was a fine collection of literary works, and Seth was even more curious about the woman who owned them.

A book entitled *New American Practical Navigator* and several other books on ships made Seth wonder who in her family was interested in the sea. Pensacola was a seaport, and the other objects he'd noted earlier made him think that perhaps there was a sailor in her family. "Who's interested in the sea?"

While he had looked over the books, Viola Mae had returned to the table, where she now cut up several large squash. She paused in her chopping and answered, "My grandpappy was. He owned his own sailing ship. He sailed all over the world."

Seth thumbed through the latest copy of the *Farmer's Almanac* before placing it back upon the stack of earlier issues and walked toward her. "Tell me about him. He was obviously an educated man. You have an extensive library, and I'm surprised—"

"Surprised? Why? You think us backwoods folks don't know how to read?"

"I never said that."

"But you implied it." She glared darts at him.

"I never implied anything. I'll admit I was surprised because not many people have such a wonderful collection of books."

"Not dumb farmers anyway." Viola Mae dared him to challenge her. When he didn't, she continued, "Oh, it don't really matter what you think anyway. It's been my experience that most folks believe what they want to. Or they invent what they want to believe and really ain't interested in the truth."

As always, Viola Mae's little insights into the workings of the human mind never ceased to amaze Seth. More curious than ever about the woman, he concentrated on her tale.

"My grandpappy loved his books, and most of the ones you see belonged to him. The others belonged to my grannie. She brought them with her from her childhood home.

"My grandpappy's parents owned a shipbuilding business in Charleston. My old grannie said he didn't want no part of shipbuilding. Instead he wanted to captain his own ship. And he did just that. Met my grannie on one of those seaporting trips to Virginia. Stole her away from her pappy's plantation and brought her here. Of course, she went willingly."

Seth watched her as she told the story of her grandparents. Her blue eyes took on a dreamy look as she related the proud history of her family.

"Grandpap wanted to build my grannie a big fancy house in town, but she wanted no part of a house in town. She wanted land like her pa before her. So instead my grandfather purchased fifty acres of fine timber land, built her this house, and planned to replace it with a mansion. But she liked it just like it was. Here's where she stayed until she died."

Her voice grew raspy, and she quickly looked away until she had her emotions under control again. Seth wanted to go to her and comfort her. He, too, knew the pain of losing someone he loved. Or he guessed he did. Seth had loved his parents, but now, after their deaths, he realized that he'd never really known them.

Their relationship had not been a close one. He and Jed had both been raised by nannies, then sent to boarding school when they turned six. Seth loved his parents perhaps because he was supposed to; Viola Mae, on the other hand, adored her grannie. This realization left him longing for that special closeness he'd missed.

Viola Mae's voice broke into his reverie. "You know, I loved her so much that even though she's been dead for two years, I still ache inside when I think about her."

Wanting to comfort her, and to have something in common with her, he decided to tell her about Jed.

"Yes, I know how that feels. I feel the same way about my younger brother. We never were really close until this last year, but he's become very special to me."

"I see." Her eyes danced with excitement. "Tell me about him, Seth."

He smiled. "You mean Jedwina?"

Viola Mae reciprocated his smile when she heard him use the feminine name she'd given his little brother earlier. He was glad she realized he was teasing her.

"There's not a whole lot to tell about Jed, but that he is a typical ten-year-old boy. He has mahogany-colored hair and eyes with dozens of mahogany-colored freckles on his face.

He drives my poor Aunt Cloe and her housekeeper Tilly crazy with his boyish shenanigans.''

While he talked, Viola Mae threw the last of the chopped vegetables into the pot. After pouring water over them, and sprinkling them with various spices, she picked up the heavy iron pan and carried it to the fireplace, where she hung it on the chain and hook put there for that purpose.

Turning back to face him, she asked, ''Where is Jed now?''

''He's staying with Aunt Cloe in Atlanta until I can find us a place to live in town. Then I'll send for him. We'll make our home in Pensacola until the railroad's finished.''

Viola Mae sighed audibly when he finished telling her about his brother.

''It must be nice to have a brother. I always wanted a big family with lots of brothers and sisters. Heck, I'd even be satisfied with just one other sibling.''

Curious, Seth asked her, ''Why don't you have any brothers or sisters?'' Once the question was out, he wanted to recall it. Viola Mae's earlier light mood disappeared, and he realized she wasn't about to tell him anything else about her family. He wondered about Viola Mae's parents—she talked of her grandparents, mostly her grannie, but she never mentioned her mother or father.

''I'll make us some biscuits,'' she told him on a more serious note, cutting short the conversation they'd been having.

''We had best get the lamps filled. I've got spare kerosene and I'm sure we'll be needing them throughout the night. You think you could fill them for me?'' Not waiting for him to answer, she retrieved four lamps from various parts of the room and placed them on the table.

Disappointed that the earlier Viola Mae had disappeared, Seth moved toward the table to do her bidding.

Chapter Fourteen

Dang. She'd nearly done it again. Twice this afternoon Viola Mae had almost let her position against the railroad be known to her captive. First when she'd slipped and mentioned the hoped-for meeting with Archibald, and second with her condemnation of the railroad for its abuse of the land. She could almost see Seth putting the pieces together inside his handsome head, especially when he'd eyed her blackberry preserves as though they might contain poison.

She found the spare kerosene she had brought inside this morning, and placed it with a funnel on the table beside the lamps. Eventually he would have to know that he was a pawn she planned to use in order to get the railroad to pay attention to her complaints. But now that she had determined that he was almost human, in spite of his connection to the railroad, she felt twice as guilty for holding him hostage.

Was she supposed to consider her hostage as being human? *How was I to know he could be compassionate and was responsible for his ten-year-old brother?*

Seth took up his position at the table, and Viola Mae moved to the desk in the bedroom area where she kept a record of her farm stock. She'd taken Rosemary the cow, her horse Ginger, and Seth's horse to the fenced-in pasture in case the barn was crushed during the storm. The animals' reflexes would be to turn their backs to the wind and hunker down, and they would probably survive the bad weather.

But her chickens were another matter. Viola Mae had secured them in the wired pen and then blocked the entrance to the henhouse. She hoped the wind wouldn't blow them away or that they wouldn't be killed by flying debris. There was nothing else to do but say a silent prayer for their survival. Locating her journal, she made a note of today's date and beside it the number of farm animals in her keeping.

When she'd finished, Viola Mae sat quietly, contemplating her circumstances. She almost wished she hadn't given Gracie the ransom note to deliver to Archibald, especially with this hurricane breathing down their necks. If she hadn't demanded that Gracie deliver the message, she could have freed Seth before the storm hit, allowing him to walk away. But the note, coupled with the approaching storm, made Viola Mae aware that nothing could be changed. As usual, she had gotten herself into a real pickle, and she saw no way out.

And what about Gracie and everyone in town? How safe would they be so close to the bay, especially if this storm turned out to be a bad one? A shiver of apprehension snaked up her spine on this last thought.

Seth had asked her if she was afraid. *Hang, yes, I'm scared.* The only other storm of any magnitude she'd been in had been when she was ten years old. She'd felt safe because she was with her grannie, but her memory of the wind and destruction wasn't something she liked to remember. Yes, she was frightened, but she'd never allow Seth to know it.

Viola Mae stood and walked to the blanket chest to check again on the number of blankets. The chest also had strips of sheeting she could use for bandages if the need arose.

She was as prepared as anyone could be. Earlier she'd filled a number of jugs with water and left them on the porch to bring in later. Crossing to the door, she stole a look at Seth. He still sat at the table, his brow furrowed as he carefully filled the lamps.

Giving Seth a chore to do had kept him from asking her more personal questions about her life. For one who never shared herself with anyone but Gracie, Viola Mae couldn't understand her desire to tell the handsome devil all about her past. What was even worse, she wanted to know about his as well.

Because Viola Mae had heard country legends about approaching storms and how the pressure building up with them could have adverse effects on people and animals alike, she blamed the tumultuous state of her emotions on the weather instead of on her attraction to Seth. The allure was still there. More so now than when they had first met.

She recalled that day in town when he had saved her and Ginger from crashing into the coach. Then she'd blamed her attraction to him on the gratitude she had felt. But it was like her grannie had always told her. "You have to take responsibility for your actions." Even now she was trying to blame her feelings on the weather, when in truth she knew she was still suffering from that dang love bug's bite.

As a reminder of why the two of them were closed up tight in the house, the wind blasted against the side of the dwelling, making it tremble on its foundation. Seth's gaze settled on hers, and his lips lifted in an encouraging smile. Viola Mae ignored it and told him instead, "I better bring in the water I pumped earlier." She headed for one of the side doors.

He was beside her in an instant, helping her lift the heavy wooden bolt. He braced the door panel with his hand to keep the wind from sending it flying backwards when they opened it.

Viola Mae started to protest his following her outside, but the sight of the approaching storm silenced her. On leaden feet, she moved toward the porch's edge. Seth came to a stop beside her.

It alarmed her to see how the sky had changed in such a short length of time. Above the trees the sky was hung with a dark sagging roof of yellowish clouds, while a menacing, soundless glow of heat lightning charged the sky. The woods surrounding the yard dipped and swayed in the wind, and the air was thick with a heavy mist.

"Those jugs." Viola Mae pointed to the water at the end of the porch. "We need to take them inside." Together they moved toward them, their white gowns whipping in the wind. After the task was finished, they returned to the porch and stood transfixed by the approaching storm.

A ball of yellow fur jumped up on the porch and streaked past Viola Mae's feet. She watched as Mustard ran for the safety of the house.

"Maybe I should bring Soapwort in also," she told Seth, walking to the front of the house and the stoop where the old hound made his home.

Bending over, she called, "Here, boy, come on." She clapped her hands together and called again. "Here, boy, here, boy." The ancient dog refused to budge from his favorite spot.

"Leave him," Seth told her. "He'll be fine beneath the house."

She was about to ask him when he'd become such an expert on the weather, but she stopped. They both turned and faced the trees, listening.

The sound made her believe all the birds of the forest had gathered in the branches to warn them of the approaching danger. She caught glimpses of blackbirds, warblers, cardinals, and blue jays. The clatter they made did not sound like the usual bird calls she was used to hearing. All of the birds were calling at the same time, wailing. It reminded Viola Mae of a panicked human voice.

Above them the sky turned more jaundiced, then a tarnished brass color. The grass and trees picked up the sky's reflection, mirroring the eerie glow. Soon the discordant bird sounds ceased, and everything grew very quiet and still.

While Viola Mae stood mesmerized by the sudden silence, Seth leapt to the ground. "I'll get the dog," he said.

Before Viola Mae knew what he was about, he'd retrieved the old hound from beneath the stoop and returned to the porch, carrying him across his arms. "We had best get inside," he said.

She stared at him, puzzled. His concern for Soapwort surprised her. She would not have expected this of a man being held captive. In that brief moment, their roles had switched. Seth had become the protector and she the protected. The idea was unsettling to say the least. The wall of defense she'd built around herself was being breached inch by inch, and Viola Mae wondered if she would ever be the same again.

Continuing with his role as protector, Seth stood by the door and motioned for her to precede him. He followed her and placed the bony dog down on the floor. As Viola Mae shot the door bolt back into place, the wind started blowing again. The gusts came now at short intervals, each one seeming a little stronger than the last one.

They moved back toward the kitchen with the hound traipsing behind them. Pausing in front of the fireplace, she ordered the animal to sit. The dog moved to the end of the hearth and completed several revolutions before he plunked down on the floor.

"Good, Soapwort, good dog."

Viola Mae bent over the soup pot, picked up the lid, and gave it a quick stir. She put the biscuits in the brick oven and straightened.

Seth stood several inches away from her, his elbow propped on the wooden mantel, his sea-green eyes reflecting the fire's flames as he followed her every move.

She eyed him speculatively. He was too dang handsome for his own good, and she found his nearness stifling. The cavalier pose he struck, even wearing her grannie's nightgown, made her stomach feel as though she'd swallowed a dozen jumping frogs. Taking a calming breath, she stepped away from him.

"Where did you come up with the name Soapwort?" he asked.

Happy to have something else to think about, Viola Mae answered, "It was my grannie's practice. We named all our animals after herbs. Soapwort, also known as bouncing bet, seemed a right proper name for a full-of-life pup." She looked toward where the old dog lay. "He don't bounce much these days, though—he's getting too old."

"From what I've seen, he doesn't bounce at all." Seth looked toward the sleeping yellow cat in the rocking chair. "Let me guess. Mustard must have gotten his name because of his coloring."

"He sure did. I named him and also Rosemary, the cow. Her milk is the essence of our very existence. Just like the herb rosemary is held in high affections by all us homemakers."

His brows raised inquiringly, then admiringly. "How about Ginger?"

It surprised Viola Mae that Seth had remembered her horse's name. Her wall of resistance crumbled another inch.

"My grannie named her. Ginger's also getting up there in years. My grannie got her as a yearling. At that time her coat was the color of ground ginger. Now that she's old, she's turned more silvery gray."

"And of course," he said, "we can't forget Joe Pye."

"Joe Pye was just Joe Pye. It seemed a fitting name for a rooster."

Seth smiled, warming Viola Mae all the way down to her toes.

"There are the sows," she said. "You never met them."

A flicker of amusement stirred in his sea-colored eyes. She began to tell him about her two pigs. "Their names were Frankincense and Myrrh. Old Frankincense, she's been gone a long time, but parts of Myrrh are still hanging in the smokehouse."

Looking decidedly uncomfortable, Seth swallowed. "Praise the Lord, we're not having pork chops."

"And then there are the hens. I named them mostly after herbs with lady-sounding names—Angelica, Sweet Cicely, Myrtle, Tansy—"

Seth held up his hand to stop her. "Please, you don't have to tell me the names of all of them. Anyway, I won't remember what name belongs to whom. One chicken looks like the next one. White."

"Since you ain't exactly fond of my chickens, I don't expect you'll be calling them anything but stinking."

He chuckled. "That's right. I'm not exactly missing their company."

The rain began to pelt against the roof, almost drowning out the sound of their voices.

"Maybe we should eat," Viola Mae said. "The soup is cooked, and I'm sure the biscuits are done."

Not waiting for his response, she ladled the pungent concoction into big crockery bowls. Then she placed the pan of biscuits on the table along with a jar of honey. She and Seth sat down opposite each other and began to eat. Above their heads, the rain began in earnest.

Seth eyed the roof skeptically.

"It's pretty strong," she said. "If the wind does rip off the tin, there are wood shingles beneath. I added the tin last fall because I like the sound of the rain hitting it. Also, metal isn't as apt to catch fire if lightning strikes it. Lightning is one of the perils you have to be prepared to suffer if you live in the piney woods."

"Now that's encouraging, especially if that earlier lightning we saw is any indication of what's to come."

Who knew what was to come? Viola Mae surely didn't want to dwell on the possibilities. She jumped up from the table and carried the empty biscuit pan to the dry sink while Seth carried their bowls over. Viola Mae placed soap and water into a dish pan and began to wash the dishes.

"Need my help?" Seth asked.

"Naw, ain't much to do. I'll just tidy up a bit. You go read a book or something."

When his gaze landed on the bookshelf above her sink, Viola Mae wished that she could retract the last part of her statement. This particular shelf contained her private sketchbooks. She had drawn pictures of all the plants and herbs she grew, as well as the ones she found in the woods. To her they were as priceless as the other books in her library, but she feared an outsider would believe them to be worthless.

"Ah, you wouldn't be interested in seeing those," she said.

Her response didn't deter Seth. He reached for them. "May I?" he asked.

For a moment she hesitated, not wishing him to see her drawings or to be standing so close. She could feel the heat of his body through her gown. His nearness made her as edgy as the approaching storm did.

"Go on, take them," she said, deciding it was the best way to get him away from her.

Anything to keep you from breathing down my neck.

Seth obeyed. A few moments later she heard him thumbing through the pages.

"Who's the artist? Your grandmother?" He looked admiringly at several pages. "These drawings are very good. She was a very talented lady."

Viola Mae was surprised by the unexpected praise, which brought a blush of pleasure to her cheeks. She'd had one teacher when she attended school who had lauded her drawing ability, but that teacher had not stayed in Pensacola very long. She had married a sea captain and had sailed away to see the world, taking a piece of Viola Mae with her.

Most of her other teachers were interested only in teaching the basics: reading, writing, and arithmetic. They had no patience for the rather odd child who preferred the company of the flowers and wildlife she sketched over that of the other children.

Viola Mae turned from the dry sink and moved to stand beside the table. She watched him thumb through the pages. His approval was evident as his gaze slid over her ink drawings. His recognition of her abilities caressed her very soul.

After a moment she said, "They're mine. I drew them."

He looked up at her, and amazement and admiration sparked his expression. "You drew these?"

"Yes," she responded breathlessly.

"They're wonderful, Viola Mae. *You* are a very talented lady."

She blushed to the roots of her hair. Flustered, she said the first thing that came to her mind. "Oh, I ain't no lady." Then realizing how silly her statement must have sounded to Seth, she corrected herself. "I ain't talented."

For a long moment, he stared at her as though he were unsure how to respond. Then his long fingers curled around her hand where it rested on the table.

"You're both, Viola Mae. A lady, and very talented."

His hand felt as hot as smoldering wood. After a moment she broke the contact by jerking her hand away. But Seth continued to commend her art and acted unconcerned by her reaction.

"These drawings are good enough to be published," he told her. "Your attention to detail, the color washes. I think they're excellent."

Seth read the penned description next to each drawing that outlined the plants' usefulness for both medicinal and culinary purposes.

"They're charming," he said, skimming back through the pages.

"You . . . you really think so?"

"Yes, I really think so."

Viola Mae's gaze locked with Seth's. She cupped the hand that he had so recently touched, pressing it to her heart. Her fist still burned from the contact as though she'd been branded.

Above their heads, the rain beat down upon the roof with a vengeance. It no longer pattered evenly against the tin, but lashed with fierce curls and streaks, hissing like some prehistoric monster. The overhead fury made her wrench her gaze away from his to look at the ceiling.

"It's finally begun." She shifted uneasily as nervous flutterings pricked her chest.

The wind blew savagely, rising and falling with such force that the house shuddered on its foundation. With the storm's arrival, Viola Mae was haunted by her past. Her childhood fear had returned, and this time she didn't have her grannie to comfort her.

Seth watched her. Sensing her terror, he moved around the table to stand beside her. When a heavy object careened into the side of the house, the loud thump propelled her straight into his arms. He welcomed her, hugging her close. She felt almost childlike, her tiny, delicate body trembling against him.

Seth leaned his head toward her ear and whispered. "Viola Mae, don't be frightened. We're safe inside." He wasn't certain he believed the truth of his own words. "I promise I won't let anything happen to you."

She pressed her face against his chest and Seth stroked the silvery mop of curls. She clung to him as though he was her only lifeline in a raging, terrifying sea. When more flying debris slammed against the house, her arms tightened impulsively around his waist.

It was hard for Seth to imagine that this was his Viola Mae, the spirited girl who until now had appeared to fear nothing. As he had done with Soapwort earlier, he picked her up and carried her to the rocking chair. Using his foot, he sent Mustard bounding to the floor by tipping the rockers. Seth sat down, cradling Viola Mae on his lap, and began to rock.

She shivered against him, and Seth understood why. The sound beyond the walls was a noise like none he had ever heard before. The wind yowled at a runaway speed, sounding like a fast-moving train bearing down on the cabin. It was enough to make a grown man quake as the low moaning cry changed to a high-pitched scream.

Since conversation was impossible above the roar, Seth rocked them gently in the chair. Beside the hearth, oblivious to the noise, Soapwort lay in a knobby half-moon shape, while Mustard cowered beneath the table, his yellow eyes reminiscent of amber as he stared daggers through Seth for usurping his place in the rocker.

More wind-driven debris clawed at the walls before being jerked away by a strong blast of air that felt as though it might take the house with it. As the foundation trembled and shook beneath his feet, Seth prayed that the house wouldn't go.

After a moment, the structure appeared to shudder loose from the wind's treacherous hold. Seth rocked, waiting for the next blast of fury from the wind. He felt responsible for the small, warm package on his lap. Only Viola Mae's fear of the storm kept his at bay. The inhuman sounds beyond the cabin's walls brought home to Seth how insignificant man was in the overall scheme of things.

After what seemed like hours, the wind stopped as quickly as it had begun. An eerie quiet settled over the now-still world. Viola Mae stirred on his lap, but her arms remained around his chest. He touched them; they were cold.

"You are freezing," he told her, sitting her away from him. His voice echoed throughout the room, sounding almost uncanny in the silence.

He looked at Viola Mae. She was still frightened. Her blue eyes were as large as saucers in her china-doll face, and signs of weariness tinted her skin purple above her high cheekbones. The fear he saw in her eyes reminded Seth of a cornered animal.

"It ain't over yet," she told him. "There's more to come."

Ignoring her warning, Seth helped her to stand. Holding her close with one arm, he guided her toward the kitchen. "Let me get you a drink of water. Then maybe if you could get some sleep, you would feel better."

She drank the water he offered, her gaze darting to the walls. "It ain't over," she warned him again.

Seth didn't know whether to believe her or not. She had lived in this area of the country all her life and had said she'd been through a storm with her grandmother. If Viola Mae believed it wasn't over, then maybe it wasn't, though the wind had certainly stopped. But at the moment, he was more concerned about her than if the storm had blown itself out.

Not only was she scared half to death, but she appeared near exhaustion as well. It was as though the wind had blown the starch right out of her spine.

"If it's not over, it doesn't matter," he told her. "We've made it this far, and I'm sure we'll survive whatever else is to come. What does matter to me is you. You are cold and must be exhausted after working outside today, getting ready for this storm." He took her by the hand. "Come, let me put you to bed."

Appearing reassured by his words, Viola Mae allowed Seth to lead her toward her bed. He stopped beside the big frame and the shower of mosquito netting that lavished it. With his free hand, he lifted the filmy curtain to allow her entrance.

She refused to budge or release his hand. Instead she insisted, "You come with me."

Seth swallowed convulsively. "I don't know if that's a good idea."

A few hours earlier he would have been more than happy to accept such an invitation, but now he wasn't so sure that sharing a bed or lying beside her was such a good idea. He knew her invitation was not wanton, but Seth also knew he wanted her physically, so much so that her nearness caused him to ache all over with desire.

But Seth certainly didn't wish to take advantage of Viola Mae's fear. She clearly wasn't herself, at least not the self that Seth knew.

Besides, Viola Mae affected him differently than any

woman he'd ever known. In the last two hours, seeing her so helpless had made him feel responsible for her welfare. How in hell could he be responsible for anyone, much less the woman who before the storm had insisted on keeping him her prisoner?

For all he knew, he might no longer have a job with the railroad—not after his prolonged absence. If he was lucky enough to still have a position, he'd be concentrating all his efforts on finishing the project so he could bring Jed here to live with him.

No. He had no time for a woman in his life. Even one as alluring as Viola Mae.

"Please," she begged. "I know this storm ain't over yet. Please, won't you just hold me until it is?"

She sounded so trusting and sincere that Seth had trouble resisting. His earlier arguments against not crawling between the sheets with her seemed insignificant pitted against her small request for comfort. Seth's logical self told him that the storm wouldn't last forever and that he could control any base need he might have until it ended. But his illogical self warned him that he was playing with fire as he crawled into the large bed where Viola Mae waited.

The minute he settled his long frame on the softer-than-cloud mattress, he knew his earlier thoughts about Viola Mae's bed had been true. It was indeed a place where dreams were made.

With the gossamer web surrounding them, he felt as though they had been transported to some celestial region beyond the earth. Viola Mae, who sat cross-legged only inches away from where Seth lay on his side facing her, looked like a silver-haired angel in her pure white gown, minus wings and halo.

"Nice bed," he told her, rubbing his hand over the downy softness, but wanting more to reach out and caress her satin-smooth skin.

"It was my grannie's. My grandpappy had this mattress made special for her."

"Your grandfather must have loved your grandmother very much."

"He did, but rightly so. She was the fairest lady in the county when he stole her away."

Not unlike yourself.

Pushing this disturbing thought aside, he concentrated on the spark that ignited once again in Viola Mae's conversation. He wasn't sure if it was because the wind had ceased its howling, or because she was ensconced in her grannie's bed. But whatever it was, it had brought color back into her face, and he wanted to keep it there.

"It must be wonderful to experience the kind of love your grandmother and grandfather shared," he said, wanting to encourage her to talk about her past.

Seth wondered, fleetingly, if he would ever experience that kind of feeling for another person, but decided he wouldn't.

Where he'd come from marriages were usually arranged; monied families married into other monied families—not unlike his own parents' marriage. Seth knew firsthand that the arranged ones more often than not turned into failures, and because of the loss of his family's fortune, even that kind of financial alliance was no longer available to him.

But he didn't have time for such fanciful thoughts. To Seth, a wife was a luxury he could no longer afford, one luxury he could definitely live without.

It was still quiet inside the room, and for the first time since the storm had begun, Seth heard the ticking of the mantel clock. He listened to all the accepted sounds that had been blotted out by the wind—Soapwort's snoring, Mustard's purring, and the bed's creaking when they moved. This cabin had become their refuge, their haven. In that moment, Seth doubted he would ever forget this experience or the woman across from him.

"Why don't you lie down and try to get some sleep?" he asked.

After a moment, she stretched out beside him. With her eyes searching his face, she said, "I'm glad you're here. Until that wind began howling, I'd forgotten how awful a storm could be. If I'd been alone, I don't think I could have stood it."

"Oh, I'm sure you would have done just fine. From what

I've seen, I'd say you're pretty tough.'' He stroked the silver curls back from her face. ''You want to tell me why you're so frightened? Was the other storm so terrible?''

Viola Mae hesitated a moment before she said, ''I was ten years old at the time. To this day, I'll never forget how frightened I was. I'm sure it's that memory that has made me look like a yellow-bellied coward.''

''A feeling you *ain't* too happy about,'' he teased her, cupping her under the chin.

''That's right, mister.'' She smiled at him, then looked away. ''This storm seems as bad as the other one. The wind's stronger, or maybe my memory's dimmed. All I know is, I'll be dang glad when it blows itself out.''

''Viola Mae, you shouldn't worry about being frightened. We all have something we fear. It makes us realize we're human, don't you think?''

''Oh, yeah! And what makes you so smart all of a sudden? And if everyone fears something, what do you fear?'' Her expression challenged him.

After several moments of pretended deep thought, he answered, ''A silver-haired wench who totes a shotgun.''

His answer made her blush. ''About that—''

She didn't have time to finish because the calm inside the cabin was shattered again by the building wind. It was as though the storm was repeating itself. But this time, the gusts loahed at the opposite side of the house. The windows rattled against the keening wail, and Viola Mae squinched her eyes shut, covered her ears, and rolled toward him.

Seth accepted her into his embrace and pulled the sheet up to cover them. Viola Mae was wedged so close against his length that he could feel every soft and womanly inch of her. As he fought to keep his desire in check, Seth wasn't certain which of the two tempests was the most perilous. The one outside, or the one he wanted to be inside in the worst way.

Chapter Fifteen

Automatically Seth's hand caressed her back. With each stroke, his body became more and more aware of the woman lying beside him. In spite of the storm raging outside, in spite of his resolve to keep his hands off her, he was having a hell of a time doing it.

She fit perfectly against him. She seemed no bigger than a marsh mosquito, and he feared he might crush her if he rolled on top of her. But Seth had more to worry about.

When he tried to break body contact and roll onto his back to give himself a little breathing room, Viola Mae stuck to him like a sandbur. Her proximity caused him as much pain as one of those grassy little spikelets.

Her round firm breasts pressing into his ribs felt as hot against his skin as two branding irons. He desperately needed to think about something besides her breasts' scalding heat.

Iron, he recalled from his college chemistry classes, was a silvery-white, lustrous, malleable, ductile, magnetic, metallic, element used in many important structural materials.

The incongruity of picking such a topic to compare to Viola Mae with was almost funny. Especially when he examined the properties.

The silvery-haired temptress who lay beside him, whose skin took on a lustrous glow in the soft lamplight, at the moment seemed very malleable and readily controllable. Her magnetic qualities were such that they had him wanting to attach himself to her and never let go. As for her character, she had more mettle than any woman he'd ever known. Her structural possibilities were too damned fine for a man of his momentary weakness to overcome. Seth wanted her with every inch of his hard male body.

He groaned, believing the sound wouldn't be heard above the roaring of the wind. His eyes automatically slipped to the face of the woman who was causing him so much discomfort. He realized now his first mistake had been crawling into her bed, and the second was finding her eyes wide open, staring at him, her expression mirroring his own needs. So his next move seemed to be the natural thing to do. He covered those rosy lips with his own, responding as her soft mouth demanded.

She kissed him with a hunger that matched his own. Shivers of desire shot through his body as she somehow wound up on top of him, their legs and limbs entwined. After a near-breathless kiss that left them both trembling and wanting more, he pulled his mouth from hers and gazed into her eyes.

They both knew they were being pulled toward a vortex that would leave them spinning out of control, but neither seemed concerned with the consequences.

Seth mouthed the words that couldn't be heard above the wind's roar. "Are you sure?"

Her response was smothered against his lips; then she gave her consent when she buried her face in his neck and breathed several hot kisses there.

For Seth, there was no turning back. He would make Viola Mae his for this one night and he would make their joining as beautiful for her as he knew it would be for him.

He urged her to sit. Reluctantly she released him and sat back on her haunches. With nervous fingers Seth fumbled with the small pearl buttons at the neck of her nightgown.

She smiled radiantly and offered him her assistance, causing Seth's heart to accelerate to the wind speed outside the house. When together they had worked the buttons free of their loops, Viola Mae helped him to remove her gown.

Her body was beautifully formed with firm breasts, narrow waist, curving hips, and slender thighs and calves. And of course, those tantalizing feet that had driven him mad since their first meeting. Her beauty took Seth's breath away, but Viola Mae wasn't about to allow him the sole pleasure of her nakedness. She was determined that he should be as bare as she was.

He read her lips. "Your turn," she told him.

Knowing that his nakedness wasn't something she hadn't seen before—this very morning, to be exact—he was more than happy to oblige her. Seth ripped off the ridiculous gown and tossed it to the foot of the bed. In childlike abandonment, they were soon lost in the beauty of discovery.

Viola Mae's first thought on feeling Seth's naked length against her own was that she was lying on a sun-warmed rock with the blinding Florida sun beating down on her bare skin. The warmth of his body seared her, penetrating to her very bones, which suddenly felt as though they were made out of clay.

He kissed her deeply, his tongue plundering her mouth. His kiss caused a pressing urgency to build in her lower stomach and move outward from its center, until her toes, fingers, and nipples tingled with the unexplained sensation.

Viola Mae returned Seth's kiss with a matched hunger. Her tongue probed the silken regions of his mouth, making her want to sink into his skin and disappear into the warmth of his body.

"Please," she murmured, wanting more, but not certain exactly what she wanted. Her fingers gliding against the smoothness of his skin, the weight and fullness of his sex pressing against her thighs, made her dizzy with want. "Please."

"Are you sure this is what we should do, Viola Mae?" he asked in a husky voice.

She almost laughed at his question. If they didn't do whatever it was her body was crying out for, she might explode at any moment and be blown away with the treacherous wind.

Writhing beneath him, she allowed him full control of her body. He trailed kisses over her breasts, her stomach, and back up her body again. When Seth moved above her, spreading her thighs with his own, she knew that he was all she had ever wanted, that this joining of bodies and souls was what she'd dreamed of. Maybe not consciously, but in her heart, she felt it had been written in her destiny from the first day their paths had crossed.

With gentle fingers, he guided his sex to the entrance of her womb. With one quick thrust, he entered her, her warm and moist flesh accepting him.

She felt his fullness buried inside her, and the emptiness that she had felt most of her life drifted away as her body drew him in deeper. She quivered beneath him, urging them both to a crescendo of new sensations.

Soon they moved together in perfect rhythm, each giving and taking in turn. In her mind's eye, she was a dewdrop, a jewel on a velvety green leaf. The smell of the forest was all around her. As the sun reached its zenith, its heat warmed the tiny droplet to near boiling. A thousand prisms of light danced in the crystal droplet before it slid slowly back to earth and she became one with the man still poised above her.

Locked in his embrace, she felt him shudder before he collapsed against her. He crushed her to him, his mouth finding hers as he gasped for air. Viola Mae delighted in his nakedness, his dewy slickness that mingled with her own. In the Biblical sense, they were one. From this day forward, Seth belonged to her.

Fingers entwined, they lay on their backs basking in the afterglow of their joining. Although the wind still rattled the cabin, rain still pelted the roof, and occasional airborne flotsam still slammed against the house, the two lovers, safely ensconced in their bed, were oblivious to the turmoil outside.

Seth had made love to numerous women in his past, but none before Viola Mae had made coupling as enjoyable or seem so right. She now lay in sated repose, her voluptuous body innocently inviting as he studied her appreciatively.

In the dim light, she looked ethereal. The luster of her silvery hair spread over the pillow would put the finest silk to shame. Her eyes were closed, and her thick sooty lashes shadowed her creamy complexion that was blushed with the glow of their lovemaking. A relaxed smile turned up the corners of her perfectly shaped lips. From all accounts, his little forest nymph appeared to be a lady clearly satisfied, but only for the moment, Seth hoped.

He turned on his side and propped on one elbow to better see into her face. Lifting a strand of her flaxen hair, he tickled her beneath her nose. Her blue eyes popped open, revealing their clear depths. A man could drown in those eyes, Seth thought. Viola Mae smiled up at him and stretched like a contented cat.

"My lady," he asked teasingly, "now that you've milked me of my manhood, am I to assume that I am to be abandoned and discarded like an empty milk pail?"

Viola Mae regarded him with amusement. "It's been my experience that a milk pail will give you many good years of service."

To prove her statement, she launched herself against him, joining her satin smooth skin to his. The friction of that contact brought Seth to full arousal.

Barely able to breathe, he whispered, "Only if you treat that pail with the greatest of care."

Her mouth twitched with humor as her warm fingers closed around his sex. "You mean like this?" She caressed him with expert finesse.

"Mmmm, you're learning." He buried his face in her neck and nibbled at her ear.

"Like a good wife," she said.

"You'll make an excellent wife," he willingly agreed, all conscious reasoning abandoning him. His heart felt as though it might cease to beat while her fingers continued to stroke him.

She snuggled closer, her body pressing into his. " 'And they shall cleave to one another until death shall part them.' "

"Honey, if this is cleaving, then I don't want it ever to stop." Seth traced the pulse point in her neck with his tongue, then lowered his lips to kiss her breasts.

Feeling that he was about to lose control, he rolled Viola Mae to her back and positioned himself between her open thighs.

She squirmed beneath him, giving him full access to her body. Breathlessly, between nibbling kisses, she told him, "When we're married we can do this all day long."

She shivered and moaned aloud as Seth slipped inside her. "All day long," he murmured, nuzzling her breasts as she accepted his length.

Viola Mae began to move her hips against his, matching his even thrusts. The pressure building inside his loins made him feel as though he were about to explode. When he felt her muscles tighten around him, he knew instinctively that she, too, was hovering on the brink of fulfillment.

"When we're married . . ." Her speech trailed away on a sigh.

He thrust faster and with more determination. A moment later, Seth felt her give herself over to sensation.

"When we're—" But his own words were forgotten when he followed Viola Mae's lead and shuddered to an explosive climax.

Hours later, Viola Mae opened her eyes. It was unbearably warm, and although she was naked, her body felt hot and sticky. The wind no longer howled beyond the walls, and the room was so thick with humidity you could stir it with a spoon. The storm had passed, and she and Seth had survived. Because of the storm and the man who slept several inches away from her, her life had changed irrevocably.

Before she left the confines of the bed, Viola Mae allowed herself the pleasure of studying Seth's body. As she did she recalled all the delights of the flesh that they had shared throughout the long night. Even now the memory made her blush. Last night she had discovered a part of herself she never knew existed. The womanly part she had always denied.

Throughout her life, she had compared her mother's circumstances to those of her grandmother's. While her grannie had chosen wisely in love, her mother had done the opposite. The result of her ill-chosen decision had been a child born out of wedlock; a child she later abandoned. Because of her unfortunate birth, Viola Mae was snubbed by some children, cruelly taunted by others. When she was grown-up enough to understand the reasons for the ridicule, she had made a vow never to follow in her mother's footsteps.

If a child had been created from her and Seth's joining, then Viola Mae was determined it would not suffer the cruel ostracism that she had growing up without a mother and father.

She and Seth would be married. From this day forward their lives would be patterned after that of her grandparents. They would be united as one, as her grannie had said the Good Book intended for a man and woman—especially after they had enjoyed the pleasures of the flesh.

She looked at Seth. She found him powerless to resist, and she loved him. The realization that they would be spending the rest of their lives together filled her with an eagerness to sample more of the delights she'd experienced in his arms. But Mustard and Soapwort's position by the door pushed the thought from her mind. Besides, she told herself, there would be plenty of time for lovemaking after they'd visited the parson in town.

Right now, first things first. She found the nightgown that she'd so shamelessly tossed aside and slipped it on. Most of her day would be spent checking on the damage caused to her farm by the storm. She would need to round up the animals and bring them back to the barn, providing the barn was still standing. Heaven only knows what might await her when she opened the cabin door.

Viola Mae was about to slip from the bed when Seth's hand restrained her. She turned to face him. Still half asleep, he smiled at her before pulling her close.

"No good-morning kiss for your prisoner?" he asked sleepily.

More than willing to comply with his request, she leaned toward him and brushed his lips with hers. When he tightened his arm around her, she snuggled closer. Crossing her arms on his chest, she propped her chin on her wrists and studied him.

"I reckon you'll be needing my grandpappy's straight razor," she said, "or someone will be mistaking you for a wild grizzly."

"Is that so?" Seth fingered the collar of her nightgown with disfavor. "Well, I reckon you ought to take this thing off, then, and allow this old grizzly his breakfast.'' He peeked at her breasts beneath the collar's opening. "Besides, I like you better naked."

His words thrilled her. Viola Mae liked him naked, too, but she had too many chores to do before the day was over, and no time for dallying.

"If you're expecting me to lie with you all day, well, it ain't gonna be." She sat up, but tweaked the golden hair on his chest playfully, making him twitch. "Now that the storm is over, I've got work to do."

With this announcement, Seth sat upright. He tilted his head, listening for the sound of the wind that had haunted them throughout the night. After a moment, he smiled. "By golly, it *is* over. See, I told you we would come through it fine."

As far as Viola Mae was concerned, they had come through it better than fine. Because of the storm, she and Seth would build a new life together. They would marry and have a family. Her hand slipped over her stomach protectively. For all she knew, she could have a part of him growing inside her belly right now. Hadn't her grannie told her that dallying made babies? And she and Seth had definitely dallied the night away.

Contentment filled her. Smiling, she told him, "We lived through it, but heaven only knows what's waiting outside." She moved to the edge of the bed and pushed back the mosquito netting. "Mustard and Soapwort must be fair to bursting to go outside. If I don't oblige them soon, they just might explode."

Her feet slapped against the floor, and she padded to where the animals waited beside the door. Seth followed her and helped her lift the heavy wooden bolt. Noting he was still as bare as the day he was born, she only opened the door enough to allow the pets an exit. She slammed it shut, scolding, "Get your clothes on. What if someone should come by and see you?"

He grabbed her around the waist, picked her up, and swung her around. Nibbling on her neck, he slid her down his length.

"Could this be the same lady who only a few hours ago liked me naked?"

"I still like you that way, but my neighbor Earle Forbes probably wouldn't." She shoved away from him and headed toward the big wardrobe. "I need to get dressed and check on the farm."

Seth moved to the bed, fished the offensive nightgown from beneath the covers, and slipped it on. "I'm coming with you."

When she was dressed, Viola Mae opened the door again, and they stepped outside.

After the darkness of the house's interior, the light was almost blinding. Beneath the withering sun the air fairly boiled, clinging like a steaming blanket beneath the eaves. The once-clean porch was now littered with leaves and branches, and they were obliged to step carefully over the acorns, nuts, and berries scattered among the wind-blown debris.

"Snakes," she said. "We have to be on the lookout for the poisonous fellas. When their homes are destroyed by the wind and rain, they do what all critters do—they move into whatever is left."

"Snakes?" Seth quickly looked at the greenery surrounding his bare feet. "I'll need my boots, don't you think?"

Instead of answering him, Viola Mae looked beyond the porch to the yard.

Because the cabin sat on high ground, most of the area was dry. But in low places puddles remained. As still and slick as a looking glass, they bore witness to the heavy downpour of the night before, while reflecting the cobalt blue of today's sky.

Beyond the yard trees stood stripped bare of their leaves. Several of the weaker ones had been ripped from the ground, roots and all, and looked like giant broccoli.

"It's a crying shame," Viola Mae remarked, upset by all the destruction.

"It is a shame," Seth agreed, appearing as upset as she was by the havoc.

"Dangnation!" she said, hurrying to the side porch. "Look

at my chicken coop.'' Although it was still intact, the wind had tumbled it over on its side. ''I just hope my chickens survived.''

Seth slapped at the mosquitoes swarming around his head. ''Looks like the barn made it, however. I'd hate to have seen that monstrosity lying on its side.'' Scratching a bite on his face, he complained, ''Damn, these nasty little vampires. They're thirstier than usual this morning.''

''Unfortunately for us humans, mosquitoes and their eggs aren't blown away by the wind. The biters will be out in force, with more hatching daily.''

Already she could see the welts appearing on Seth's neck. ''We'd best get inside before you're completely devoured. Those little pests surely seem to like the way you taste.''

''It's my Yankee blood,'' he told her, following her back into the house.

''If that's true, why ain't those pests laying legs up?'' She giggled at the look he shot her.

The minute they were indoors, Viola Mae dropped the mosquito netting over the door. It felt hotter inside now than it had earlier, so she opened the other two doors and windows, securing the netting over the openings.

''I had best get us some breakfast,'' she told him, walking toward the fireplace. ''It's too hot to cook, but I could sure use a cup of coffee!''

While she coaxed a flame into the embers, Seth stood beside her, his restlessness evident in his stance.

Viola Mae could feel the tension building, and worried how she should handle the kidnapping now that they had coupled. Their lovemaking had shed a new light on their circumstances, changing things. Surely a person didn't hold her future husband hostage even if they did have opposing views on the railroad.

There was still that dang note she'd left with Gracie to be delivered to Archibald. Viola Mae wasn't certain what to do about that. Maybe she could convince Seth to go to his boss to announce their upcoming marriage, and then ask Archibald to disregard the note. Harriet would probably croak when she learned that Viola Mae had snaked her man from beneath her turned-up nose.

Seth's voice broke into her reverie. "Viola Mae, I think it's time we talked."

He removed the lid on the large crockery jar where she stored corn bread and lifted out a slice, eating several bites before he spoke again. "Don't you believe it's time you told me the reason you're keeping me here?"

"Uh, well, uh . . ." She raked her brain for an answer. Anything but the real reason. After a moment she told him, "I reckon it's because I fancy you."

"Fancy me?" Seth laughed. "I'm flattered. But what about a few days back when you knocked me on the head? That's a strange way to show your affections, wouldn't you say?"

"Yeah . . . well . . . that's all changed now. I mean, after last night."

Humor lit up his face, and he made his brows dance devilishly above his eyes. "Now I understand. You kept me here because you wanted me in your bed?"

She felt the backs of her ears burn, and looked down at the floor.

"Instead of kidnapping me, why didn't you issue an invitation? It would have saved us both a lot of trouble. Besides, I've thought of nothing else but taking you to bed since the first day I met you."

"Really?" His answer made her pulse race.

Viola Mae understood that some folks married for convenience, hoping that love would follow. But Seth's admission that he had thought of nothing else but bedding her since their first meeting told her he cared as much for her as she did him. Their marriage had to be a match that was made in heaven.

Viola Mae also figured that if her grannie did know and see all things from her heavenly seat, and if she had frowned upon her granddaughter's unladylike behavior last night, this morning the old dame must be sitting on a cloud, grinning. This assurance made Viola Mae decide to tell him the truth.

"You better sit," she told him. "I got something important

to say, and I ain't got but a few moments before I have to
see to my animals.''

Seth did as she asked, pulling a chair away from the table
and sitting down. She sat across from him, unsure of where
to begin. Viola Mae suspected that he already knew she was
responsible for the tainted preserves left in the railroad camp,
but was he also aware that it was she who had doctored up
the privies?

Before this conversation was finished, she reckoned he'd
know it all.

''It started months ago,'' she began, cupping her hands on
the table. ''Long before your arrival in town.''

''What started?''

''When the railroad building began, so did destruction of
the land . . . birds losing their nests in the downed trees, the
fire I told you about, erosion to the land.''

Seth leaned forward, listening intently.

''I wrote Mr. Archibald several letters, voicing my concerns, but he didn't even pay me the courtesy of a reply.''

From beneath her lowered lashes, she peeked at Seth. He
seemed to be concentrating on what she was saying, but he
didn't seem worked up by her concerns. At least not the way
she thought he should be.

Deciding she needed to strengthen her stance, and hoping
to rally him to her cause, she blurted out, ''We don't need
no railroad from Jacksonville to Pensacola anyway!''

Although he said nothing, Seth shifted restlessly on the
chair, his expression suggesting he wasn't buying everything
she said. She presented her next argument.

''The way I figure it, we've done just fine without a railroad so far. My grandpappy used to say that the railroad
would ruin the shipping business. Once it went through, spi-
derwebbing across the United States, then no one would be
shipping goods by water anymore. Stevedores and sailors
would be put out of work, and the port of Pensacola would
dry up.''

Seth's chair scraped across the floor, and he stood.

''Viola Mae, you don't know what you're talking about! Not
if you say there is no need.'' He began to pace. ''The railroad

will create more jobs, especially for those people who live in dire poverty along the stage route. The conditions are deplorable.''

This was not the reaction Viola Mae expected, or the one she wanted to hear. She jumped to her feet.

''You calling my grandpappy a liar? He knew what he was saying because he was a sea captain. And I sure as heck know what I'm saying.''

It bothered her that Seth wasn't taking her side. She had thought after what they had shared that his earlier determination to finish the tracklaying would have disappeared. Wasn't your intended supposed to support you in all things? The notion that he didn't got her dander up.

''You're just a Yankee. You don't know what folks need or don't need in this part of the country. You've been here only a few weeks and already you believe you're an expert.''

''I'm not claiming to be an expert, but I know what I've seen and what I have learned in the past year.''

''Oh, yeah? And what all-fired more have you seen than I have? It appears you ain't learned too much if you can't see what the railroad is doing to the land.''

He ignored her argument. ''I know poverty when I see it, and I saw lots of it on my trip here by coach. I know how it feels to want a job and not be able to get one because there aren't any to be had. I also know how it feels to have a family depend on me to put food on the table, and how useless a man can feel when he can't do it.''

Viola Mae was so angry she allowed his words to roll off her like water off a duck's back. She propped her hands on the table and faced him down. ''You don't know squat, Mr. Know-It-All Dandy. You think because you've traveled all over the world, and because you can call people like Harriet Archibald your friend, that it makes you an authority on what folks need.'' She seethed with anger. ''The rich ones always want to tell the poor what's best for them.''

Seth stopped his pacing. ''I'm not claiming to be an authority, but you're a fine one to talk about what folks need. The first day I met you, you were bucking authority by telling Booger Butts how he should treat his animals. First you badgered him, and later you kidnapped me. Who knows what other laws you've broken.''

"Laws I've broken?'' she sputtered.

He sure had his nerve accusing her of breaking laws. His own behavior hadn't been of the gentlemanly kind when he'd coaxed his way into her bed. She shoved aside the memory of how he'd held her and comforted her when she'd been scared senseless by the storm. Besides, it wasn't her fault that he was so dang handsome that he could coax a girl out of her drawers, or that once he'd done so he'd been unable to control his *itch*.

With a sudden flash of defensive spirit, she turned on him, "Kidnapped? You don't look like no kid to me,'' she retorted, "even though you act like one. And a spoiled-rich one to boot.''

Seth's eyes flashed with anger. "You certainly didn't seem to think I was a kid when you took me into your bed. Or, then again, maybe that's the only way you can get a man to sleep with you—by kidnapping him.''

His words hurt, but Viola Mae drew on her anger. She wasn't about to allow his words to have the power to wound. "I should have left you chained inside my chicken coop and prayed that the storm would blow you away. Instead I took pity on your Yankee hide and brought you inside.''

"That's right. You brought me inside, forced me to strip while you watched, then took me to your bed. You might have forced yourself on me, but I'll not be forced to agree with your lunatic ideas.''

"I forced myself on you?''

"Yes, that's the way I see it.'' Their gazes locked in open warfare. "Just give me my damn clothes and let me get out of here. Unlike you, I have a responsibility to someone other than chickens, cows, or whatever else it is you feel responsible for.''

"Leave? Ha! You're dumber than dirt. There ain't no way you'll be leaving here without me.''

"Oh, yeah—just watch me. I've suffered enough humiliation at your hands; one more little embarrassment doesn't matter. If I have to go to town wearing this stupid nightgown, then so be it. I'll tell everyone who sees me that the wind blew my clothes away. But at least I'll be rid of you.''

Seth strode toward the door.

While he tangled with the netting covering the opening, Viola Mae grabbed her shotgun from the rack above the fireplace and joined him at the entrance.

Jamming the gun's barrel hard against his spine, she warned, ''Hold it right there, mister. I don't expect you'll be going anywhere without me.''

He might be thinking he was gonna walk away free as a bird, but Viola Mae knew different. Her old grannie always said a person was responsible for his actions. She was holding Mr. Seth Rowe responsible for his.

''The way I see it,'' she said, ''we've got a date with the preacher.''

''Preacher?''

''Yeah—preacher. According to the Good Book, you and I are as good as married. But now we're gonna make it legal.''

Seth's mouth fell open. ''What?''

''You heard me. You and me are gonna get hitched.''

Chapter Sixteen

"Hitched! Like in married?" Seth blurted out.

The precariousness of his position slammed into his gut as if Viola Mae had hit him with her gun instead of just poked him with it.

"There's only two kinds of hitching, and since we ain't no mule team to be hitched to a wagon, that just leaves getting married."

"Married," Seth croaked. "Surely you don't believe that you and I can get married. Hell, I can't support myself, much less a wife."

"You should have thought of that before you took a notion to scratch your itch."

Seth felt as though he had fallen into a bottomless pit and was trying to claw his way out. While he tried to think of a way to reason with her, Viola Mae shifted on her feet and glowered at him.

"We'll be jumping the broom together right soon. And the way I see it, the sooner the better."

"The way you see it?" Uneasiness clawed at Seth's insides. "How about the way I see it?"

"Your way don't count. I'm the person who's been compromised, and you're the one who's going to make an honest woman out of me."

"Is there to be no mutual concessions?"

"You mean like give-and-take?"

"Exactly."

"It appears to me we did enough of that last night when I was being compromised. I gave, and you took."

With heavy sarcasm, he replied, "Don't play coy with me, Viola Mae. You knew what you were doing as much as I did—you wanted me, and I wanted you."

She lifted her chin and met his accusing stare. "I still want you. And I plan to have you."

It appeared that he had gotten more than his itch scratched when he'd bedded Viola Mae. Unless he could do some fast talking, he would soon become her bridegroom. Even though he knew that a match between them was impossible, she still had the power to stir his blood. The memory of all they had shared during the night was still too fresh in his mind to just dismiss it. He would have to work harder at overcoming her overwhelming appeal.

"I don't understand," he said. "Why force someone to marry you who doesn't wish to be married? It's like I told you the other day when you asked me about Harriet. I can't marry anyone."

"I reckon you should have thought of that before you crawled between my sheets."

"If you'd made your position clear, I would have."

"You made yours clear enough. When we were stroking away at one another, you told me that I would make an excellent wife."

"Me—I never said that."

Seth paused, trying to recall which particular stroking she'd been referring to. In his mind, they all fused together into one big satisfying sensation. He shook his head in denial. "An excellent wife—are you sure I said that?"

"You sure did. And that ain't all you said. When I quoted from the Good Book about cleaving to each other, you distinctly said, 'If this is cleaving, then I don't want it to ever stop.' And when I told you that when we were married we could do this all day long, your reply was, 'All day long.' "

Seth couldn't recall saying such things, but he did recall his fevered state. It was possible he could have uttered such nonsense. But surely Viola Mae didn't believe that words spoken in the heat of passion were to be taken as a proposal.

One look at her expression convinced him that she did.

"Sometimes when a man is aroused, he says things. . . ."

"The way I see it, it don't matter one way or the other about the words. What does matter is that in the Biblical sense you and I are as good as married. I'm going to see that Preacher Hunt hitches us up legal-like."

Seth took a calming breath. "What about my obligations to Jed? I can't even take care of him properly. How am I to take care of a wife?"

"You don't need to worry about me. Been taking care of myself most of my life. It's our offspring who'll be needing a father."

"Offspring! Surely you aren't thinking that you're in the family—" Seth almost stopped breathing. "Surely . . ."

He eyed her suspiciously, his gaze sliding over her nubile curves. Was there a chance that Viola Mae had been with another man before him, and now she needed a father for her unborn child? Instead of anger, jealousy impaled his gut like a railroad spike. *I would have known,* he assured himself. No. Viola Mae had been a virgin when he'd taken her. Besides, he'd seen the proof on the sheets this morning.

Interrupting his thoughts, she said, "Babies ain't left under leaves, you know. They don't just happen. It's like my old grannie always told me, a person has to take responsibility for his actions."

"But . . . couldn't we wait . . . until you're sure?"

"Wait for what? I'm already sure. I don't propose to bring a babe into this world without a father."

Seth knew she was guessing about her condition because they had only made love throughout the night. But as he watched her, he sensed she was wrangling with another problem besides the immediate one. Something flickered deep in her eyes as if she wanted to reveal a painful secret. She shifted uneasily, swallowed, and looked everywhere but at him. After several moments, she squared her shoulders and began.

"You once asked me about my parents—why I didn't have any brothers or sisters." She licked her lips nervously, her weariness seeming to grow. After another tense silence, she blurted out, "I'm a briar-patch child."

"A briar-patch child?" Seth waited a full minute for an

explanation; when none came, he demanded, "What the hell is a briar-patch child?"

A briar-patch child. To Seth, briars were plants with woody, prickly stems—a patch meaning a mass of them. What could she mean? Maybe she was born under a leaf after all.

He watched her curiously, still waiting for an explanation. She looked troubled, and beneath her long-lashed lids, her eyes were shiny with unshed tears.

Tears. Suddenly her meaning hit Seth like a hammer to his gut. He could have kicked himself for his stupidity. Where he'd come from, if Viola Mae had made such a confession, she probably would have said she'd been born on the wrong side of the blanket. But no matter where you came from, the expressions meant the same thing—a child born out of wedlock.

Slowly the pieces fell into place, and his earlier anger disappeared. It was as natural as breathing for him to open his arms and accept Viola Mae into his embrace. After she threw herself against him, Seth was conscious only of the tortured whimpers that racked her small frame. She wept aloud, deep soul-wrenching sobs that tore at his heart. He rocked them back and forth, ill equipped for this vulnerable side of Viola Mae, who always appeared so tough.

Wanting to ease her hurt, he stroked her hair as he would a kitten's back, crooning words of comfort in her ear. After a time, when she had quieted, she lifted her eyes to his, the pain still alive in those blue depths. With the pads of his fingers, he brushed away her remaining tears.

His words sounded choked to his own ears. "Viola Mae, surely you don't believe that you are to blame for the circumstances of your birth." He sat her away from him. "Look at you. You're a very capable and beautiful woman, and you can be proud of yourself. Nobody could ever hold your illegitimacy against you."

"Oh, yeah?" She buried her face against his chest again. "Only the Harriet Archibalds of this world and a few others like her."

Now he understood the evident dislike between Viola Mae

and Harriet. Maybe in a small community like Pensacola, where everyone knew everyone else, Harriet and her circle of friends would ostracize a child of Viola Mae's background. Most likely mimicking their parents' attitudes.

But as adults, couldn't they put aside their pettiness and recognize Viola Mae's goodness and accept her as an equal? Or had they allowed the old wounds to fester and cloud their judgment? In his limited experience with the two women, Harriet had always seemed to treat Viola Mae as a source of irritation. If his own circumstances had not been altered, would he, too, be as unforgiving of one less fortunate than himself?

Probably not. His answer didn't please him.

"So you see," Viola Mae interrupted, "that's why you and me have to get wedded up. I made a vow to myself that I would never end up like my mother. That I would never bring a babe into this world to have it become a victim of the cruelty of others."

With her admission, the cutting edge of her sorrow had seemed to dull. Some of her earlier mettle had returned, and her expression went from softness to hardness as she related more facts to him.

"It nearly broke my grannie's heart when her only daughter bore a child out of wedlock. My mother refused to give the man's name, and to this day no one knows my father's identity. When I was two years old, my mother struck out on her own, leaving me with my grandparents. My grandpappy searched high and low for her, but he never found her. I believe it was his heartbreak that sent him to an early grave."

As Seth listened to Viola Mae's past, his own problems paled significantly. When his father had lost their fortune, leaving their family penniless, and then had killed himself, Seth's life had changed dramatically. He had been forced to give up his cushioned style of life, and was thrust into a world he knew nothing about—one of responsibility. He had his distraught mother's and nine-year-old brother's livelihood to consider, and no experience that would get him a proper job. But his misfortunes couldn't compare with those Viola Mae had suffered. Her suffering had endured all her life.

So when she looked at him and asked, "Don't you understand?" his only response was to draw her into his arms, and hope that his nearness would somehow alleviate the pain she had suffered.

He does care for me, Viola Mae thought as Seth held her in his arms. All along, he'd meant to marry her. He'd just needed to get used to the idea.

Wiping away the last of her tears, she stood away from him. "I reckon you'll be needing your clothes if you're to help me clean up this place. After we've put things in order, we'll be needing to make a trip to town. I'm sure Preacher Hunt will be more than happy to wed us."

With her last remark, Seth's wariness seemed to grow. Avoiding her gaze, he told her, "I'll need my clothes. I can't work in this." She watched him dispassionately finger the gown he wore. She had thoroughly expected one of his playful retorts.

Seth's indifference bothered her. Although Viola Mae didn't know a lot about people, she did know about animals, and right now his manner reminded her of a horse with a broken spirit. This wasn't the same stubborn man she had fallen in love with, and she wanted to see the old fire return to his eyes.

"I'll get your clothes," she said, moving toward the trunk and pulling out an aged and worn box. "And here's the straight razor I promised you earlier." Turning, she handed it to Seth.

"Inside, you'll find a shaving brush and mirror. While I get your clothes, you can shave in the kitchen. There is soap on the dry sink. In the future, when we get the porch cleaned, you can use the mirror and stand outside. That's where my grandpappy always shaved."

Appearing in deep thought, Seth made no motion to move or to acknowledge her. Viola Mae moved beside him and nudged him toward the kitchen. "Get on with you," she told him. "I'll fetch your duds and be right back."

Once she was outside, all thoughts of Seth vanished. It saddened her to see the destruction caused by the storm. Debris was everywhere, and it would take weeks to return the farm to its former condition. When she made her way across the yard toward the smokehouse, she noted that several pieces of roofing had blown off the barn and would have to be replaced.

In the pasture, a big oak limb had crushed the length of the fence on the far side of the field. Ginger, Rosemary, and Clyde were apparently oblivious to the damage and the easy route to escape. The animals seemed content to chomp the succulent grass made juicier by the rain.

She knew Rosemary would need to be milked soon. After she delivered Seth's clothes, she would return the cow to the barn not only to relieve her of her milk, but also to get her away from the moist grass that sometimes caused bloat in cattle.

With all the work she had to do, how would she fit in a wedding?

Besides, what damage had the town of Pensacola suffered? If it was bad, Preacher Hunt might not be too anxious to perform a marriage ceremony. Could be he'd have more pressing problems to attend to, serious problems like burying folks and attending the bereaved.

Death. She pushed aside the disturbing thought. She hoped her friend Gracie, as well as everyone else in town, had come through the storm unharmed.

Passing the barn, she entered the smokehouse. After retrieving Seth's clothes, she returned to the house. He stood in front of the dry sink with the mirror propped against the wall, shaving. His chest was bared to the waist, her grannie's nightgown hanging around his hips like a skirt. The sight of him performing such a manly task made Viola Mae's heart sing. In the future, she would see him perform this task daily, and for that reason she hoped he wouldn't grow a beard.

"Here they are," she said, walking toward him and plopping his garments down on the table. "Ain't got no time to iron these, but they're clean. Your boots are in the wardrobe."

Scraping the last line of lathery soap from his jaw, Seth turned to face her. His determined look had returned, but his words weren't exactly what she wanted to hear.

"Viola Mae, I need to go to town. Although it's not important to you, and I know you're not particularly fond of my employer, I'm still responsible to the railroad until it is finished. Or until it's finished with me, which may be the case, considering my lengthy absence."

The mere mention of the railroad made her angry, but she wasn't so pigheaded that she couldn't see that she and Seth needed to be receptive to each other's needs. He had already exhibited his selflessness when he'd comforted her earlier. Now it was her turn to try to be a little flexible.

In all her life she couldn't recall a time when she'd allowed her heart to rule her mind. Except with her grandmother. But maybe love did that to a person. It was an unsettling thought, and one that would take some getting used to.

She said, "We'll both be going to town soon. I want to check on my friend Gracie. You and I will be needing to meet with the preacher."

She felt him studying her. His look was so intense it lifted the hairs on her arms. At last he said, "Viola Mae, I need to go alone. How do you think it will look to the townspeople if you and I show up together, announcing that we plan to marry? Especially after my prolonged disappearance. They'll wonder about my whereabouts during the storm. Questions will be asked. We don't want to draw undue attention to our predicament."

Viola Mae wasn't certain she understood what he meant by their predicament. As far as she was concerned, they'd already solved it. But she wasn't in any mood to argue and she certainly didn't have the time. Perhaps there was some validity to Seth's suggestion. She knew how gossip traveled in the small community, and she wanted their relationship to be untainted and as respectable as any.

"Let me think about it," she said.

Seth seemed placated by her answer. He picked up the folded shirt and slipped his arms into the sleeves. He buried his nose against the material's folds and inhaled. "Smoked ham!"

"You remember Myrrh, don't you?"

"You mean Myrrh whose parts are hanging in your smoke-house?"

"Yep, that's the one. After I washed your clothes, I hung them in the smokehouse to dry. Figured during the storm that would be the best place to hang them since I couldn't bring them inside."

"You dried my clothes in the smokehouse?" He picked up his trousers, sniffed them, and eyed his socks skeptically. "Viola Mae, I don't believe this. First I smelled like your chickens, and now I'm to smell like your hogs."

"Ain't nothing wrong with smelling like chitlins and crack-lin's. Me, I kind of like the smell. Besides, where do you think soap comes from?"

"The store."

His answer made her roll her eyes heavenward. "No, city boy. From the white fat of a hog."

"Please," he begged, stepping into his trousers and jerking them up beneath the gown that clung to his hips, "spare me the details. Just bring me my boots and let me get busy."

Seth sat down and pulled his socks on. His nostrils flared as he inhaled the strong scent of pork emanating from the cotton. "You reminded me earlier that there are chores to be done, and I'm more than happy to help you. But come to-morrow, I intend to return to town."

As she retrieved his boots from the wardrobe, she heard him mutter. "Chitlins and cracklin's. What next?"

He sure was in a testy mood all of a sudden. Maybe the idea of getting married was making him edgy. It wasn't every day a fella jumped the broom.

"Before you go outside, you'll need this," she told him, thrusting a bottle into his hands. "Rub this all over your ex-posed skin, and the mosquitoes will stay away."

He took the bottle, pulled out the cork, and sniffed. "What is it?"

"Oil of thyme. I made it myself."

When Seth inhaled the oil's fragrance, his eyes took on a faraway look. "Oh, yes. I've smelled thyme growing on the Mediterranean hillsides."

Viola Mae wasn't sure she liked the dreamy look he had

in his eyes. His musings reminded her of how different they were. He had traveled all over the world, and she'd traveled back and forth to town. Their backgrounds weren't exactly compatible, but Viola Mae didn't have the time or inclination to dwell on such trivial matters.

"I've only smelled thyme growing in my herb garden," she said. "Since our mosquitoes ain't never been to the Mediterranean, they don't fancy it like you do. Trust me. Put it on."

"Damn, it's hot out here," Seth grumbled, leaning against the toppled henhouse and wiping his forehead on his sleeve. Sweat ran in rivulets over his body. There wasn't a hint of a breeze, and the ball of fire in the sky beat down on him mercilessly. His body's salty excretions burned his eyes, and he blinked against the sting.

After Viola Mae returned the animals to the barn, she had remained to milk Rosemary. He worked alone on the toppled henhouse, cursing the heat and the woman who'd turned his world upside down.

Earlier he and Viola Mae had checked on the hens and found that although they looked a little skittish, all of them had survived the storm. Their house hadn't been as lucky. Seth had set himself the task of returning the shed to its upright position.

Now he was busy anchoring ropes to the roof just below the eaves. Once that was accomplished, Viola Mae would bring Ginger to help lift the frame upright, and together they would guide it back on its rocky foundation.

Seth held no tender sentiments for the chicken coop, or anything else that had to do with farming. As far as he was concerned, he'd had enough chickens and hogs to last him a lifetime. After being a guest in Viola Mae's chicken coop, he'd sworn to himself that he would never eat another bite of the domestic bird. Every time he got a whiff of his clothing, the smell pushed him closer to giving up pork as well.

Maybe he would become a vegetarian, but one thing he wouldn't become was a farmer. This last thought brought him back to his problem—what to do about Viola Mae.

Marriage. A wife was the last thing Seth wanted. And if he was forced to marry Viola Mae, what chance would an alliance between two such different people have? The farm and the land were her life. He couldn't imagine Viola Mae living anywhere else. She loved the area and, like her grannie, she expected to live and die right there. He liked the woods well enough, but if he married Viola Mae he would probably be forced to live out the rest of his days in wooded isolation. That didn't fit in with his plans for himself and Jed.

Jed's welfare was foremost in Seth's mind. In order to find work, Seth needed to live close to a town, possibly a big city. After establishing himself as a capable engineer there, he would have all kinds of job opportunities opening up for him. Maybe even back in New York City.

He'd also toyed with the idea of him and Jed heading west. He'd never been to California, and the chance to see San Francisco intrigued him. Seth enjoyed the amenities a city offered: restaurants, hotels, theaters. The only culture Jed would encounter on this farm would be raising plants and animals. The way Seth saw it, the only improvement would be to the stock, not Jed.

And then there was Viola Mae.

Her image brought a smile to Seth's lips. What would his little brother think of her? Would he like her? Hell, yes, he'd like her. He didn't think anyone could help but like Viola Mae. As he thought of the two of them together, he decided they were a lot alike—childlike and accepting. He imagined them together, exploring the woods and tending the farm animals. It wasn't a bad picture, but it was one he wasn't certain he could accept.

Jerking hard on the rope he had just strung through a beam, Seth knotted it. What to do about Viola Mae? The thought annoyed him like the sting of nettle. After learning about her past, he wouldn't be able to live with himself if he didn't marry her as she expected him to. The way Viola Mae saw it, he didn't have a choice; he must marry her.

He threaded another rope through the cross beams. Of course, she couldn't know she was carrying his seed. It was too soon to tell. But that wasn't the only problem. Because she'd given herself to him, and he'd taken freely of that gift, in her hard little head the giving and taking made them as good as married.

He slammed his fist against the roof. "Damnation. What a fine kettle of fish." They hardly knew each other. Viola Mae was an intelligent woman. She must realize one night was nothing to build a marriage upon.

He would marry her tomorrow if he thought she was pregnant with his child, but that didn't mean he had to like the idea. She *could* be pregnant. All it took was one time, he reminded himself, and they had made love several times during the long night. But there wouldn't be a repeat performance. Not tonight, not ever.

The lady who had been tormenting his thoughts for the last half hour interrupted his musings. "I've brought Ginger," Viola Mae said.

Seth slid a sideways glance at her. She sat astride the giant horse. Even now, knowing all he knew, he was still dazzled by her beauty. She wore the same faded calico dress she'd worn the first day he'd seen her. Again her shapely knees were revealed above her boots and below her rucked-up skirt. Seth gazed at the exposed flesh. He remembered kissing the rose-petal softness of that skin, and the memory incited other thoughts he had no business thinking.

Angry with himself, he spoke sharply. "Put her over there," he said, indicating the opposite side of the shed. *Instead of Ginger wearing blinders, I should be wearing them.*

"I see shaving ain't changed you overmuch. You may not look like an old grizzly, but you're sure grumpier than any old bear I ever met."

Instead of responding, he scowled as he tied more knots in the rope.

She tilted her pert nose in the air and ignored him, moving Ginger to the other side of the shed. She stopped where the opposite ends of the ropes lay on the ground.

Calling over her shoulder, she asked, "Does this suit Your Highness?"

"Suits me just fine, thank you."

Viola Mae dismounted and held the reins. "Since you're

the fancy engineer, you'll have to tell me what to do next.''

Wiping the sweat from his eyes, he told her, ''We'll tie those ropes to Ginger's harness. Once I get these planks in position, I'm hoping I can get enough leverage to pry the downed side off the ground. When I tell you to, you move Ginger forward slowly. If the frame lifts as it is supposed to, I'll be able to steady it and steer it back up on its foundation. I piled a retaining barrier of firewood on that side, so you won't end up dragging the coop too far. Maybe the obstruction will keep it from slipping away from us. Just be sure that when I yell stop, you do.''

''Ginger is a good draft horse. We'll do just fine.''

''One other thing. If I yell run, don't ask questions, just do it. I'm in no mood to see the two of you flattened by this structure if it decides to fall that way.''

''Oh, it don't weigh much,'' Viola Mae responded.

''It weighs a hell of a lot more than you. Now let's get going.''

All in all, it was surprisingly simple to right the small building. Ginger did prove to be a good draft horse, and of course her driver proved to be exceptional, too. It still amazed Seth that Viola Mae, as delicate as she looked, could do the work of two men and thrive while doing it.

But who needed a woman who could work like two men? Not him. Seth liked his women soft and alluring. Even as he thought it, a picture popped into his head. It was an image of Viola Mae's body, soft and alluring, lying naked beside him. He realized that she'd been all those things and more. But no matter, he still didn't want a woman who worked like two men. In fact, he didn't want a woman at all.

They worked together, side by side, for the rest of the afternoon, stopping only for a lunch of cold biscuits. As the Earth rolled over on its belly and the sun began to set in the west, Viola Mae and Seth decided to call it a day.

The sun and the humidity had pulled every ounce of energy out of their bodies, and when they finally went inside the cabin, they felt completely wrung out. Each of them had bright pink, sunburned faces, and every other part that was exposed to the sun's violent rays was bright pink as well.

With the approach of darkness, the air cooled. Earlier in the day Seth had removed the wood from the windows, and both were propped open, as were the cabin's three doors. Inside, the house felt cool and comfortable. Outdoors, a symphony of frogs and crickets had begun their nightly serenade, and the familiar hoot of an owl soon joined in the song.

"What shall we eat?" Viola Mae asked him.

"Please, no corn bread." He held up his hand to ward off such a thought. "I've eaten so much of that stuff, my skin feels as coarse as meal." Weary, Seth dropped down on a stool and began to pull off his boots. "Now, what I'd really like to have is a stiff shot of whiskey. Besides, I've no appetite. It's too bloody hot to eat."

Viola Mae moved to a cupboard on the wall and returned a few moments later. She placed a glass and a bottle of whiskey on the table beside him.

"Whiskey? In your house?" He raised one brow. He had never expected anyone who believed in the Holy Scriptures the way Viola Mae did to keep the devil's brew beneath her roof.

"It's for medicinal purposes only," she said.

"Of course. And since I'm feeling a bit poorly . . ." He uncorked the bottle and filled the glass to the brim.

Viola Mae eyed the amount dubiously.

"It's a small glass," he said, holding it up so she could see it. "I'll even chase it down with that horrible-tasting water."

Leaving him, Viola Mae busied herself lighting the lamps around the cabin. Seth quickly downed the glass of whiskey and poured himself another drink. The way his muscles ached, as if he'd driven fifty miles of railroad spikes, he deserved two glasses. The whiskey's curative powers would take the edge off his pain.

Although he felt close to dead on his feet, he also felt alive. There was something about physical labor that put a person in tune with the world. He sighed contentedly. Just as Seth had enjoyed working beside his men laying tracks, he'd also enjoyed working beside Viola Mae today. She would make some man—one who truly loved her—a good helpmate.

It was quiet in the cabin. From the other side of the room, he heard Viola Mae's boots clunk to the floor, then the whisper of her footsteps as she moved around the room. The mantel clock ticked out a contented rhythm while the moths outside, drawn from the darkness to the light, hit against the windows. Their attempts to reach the flames were thwarted by the mosquito netting, but Seth could hear their smudgy brown wings beating against the material.

Coming up behind him, Viola Mae asked, "Would you like a bath? If you would, I'll be happy to build a fire and heat you some water."

"Thank you, ma'am, no. I've had enough of your baths to last me a lifetime, and my weary body couldn't withstand the abuse. Besides, I probably smell enough like a roast, between the ham and the thyme, that my true smell is disguised."

She responded with that bell-like laughter of hers that sent shivers up and down Seth's spine.

"Come to think of it," she said, "you do smell good enough to eat."

True to its purpose, the liquor had blunted his aches, but it was having the opposite effect on his libido. Or so he told himself, trying to blame his body's response on the whiskey instead of attributing it to the woman standing beside him.

With her face kissed by the sun, she looked even more beautiful tonight than she had last night. And last night her beauty had damn near taken his breath away.

As tired as Seth felt, he still wanted her. Wanted to bury himself inside her woman's body and be concealed within a sensual world that for a brief time would hide reality.

But Seth refused to give in to his desire. Instead he distanced himself from her, moving from the stool to a chair, and pretended to study the room's interior. His gaze settled on the leather bible that he had missed the night before when previewing her books. Its presence was a cold reminder of the responsibility of his actions.

Viola Mae had moved to the dry sink, where she poured water into a bowl, took up a rag, soaped it, and began scrubbing the grime from her face and arms. He watched her. She stood with her back to him, performing her ablutions as though she were alone in the room.

Wanting to think of something other than his need, he asked her, "Have you thought about our conversation this morning—about my going into town ahead of you?"

She lifted her silver hair with one hand, and with the other, she slid the rag over her neck and across the delicate bump at the top of her spine. When she cleansed the skin hidden beneath her shirtwaist, her fingers rippled the fabric like the wind on a still pond. The wavelike movement sent pulsations of desire throbbing though Seth's body.

"Well?" he asked, wanting to think of other things.

When she'd finished her toilet, she turned to face him. Her expression was unreadable. "I reckon you had best go ahead without me. It ain't what I'd prefer, but I guess it will have to do. Lord knows I've got plenty to do around this farm, and a day or two delay won't matter much one way or the other. The way I see it, Preacher Hunt will be so busy he probably couldn't hitch us real proper for at least a week."

Seth couldn't believe his good fortune. She was going to allow him to go. Alone. Her next words cooled his brief light mood.

"I'll be expecting you to make the necessary arrangements with the preacher. I'll also be sending a note with you to deliver first off, before you do anything else, to my friend Gracie."

She came to stand beside him. "Can I trust you to do it?"

"I'll do it. I promise," he answered, fully intending to deliver Gracie's note as Viola Mae requested. Making the necessary arrangements was another matter.

When she made an effort to sit on his lap, he allowed her, feeling guilty as hell about his half promise.

"I expect you'll be leaving early in the morning, so don't you think we ought to go to bed?" She draped her arms around his neck and kissed him lightly on the forehead.

It took all of Seth's efforts to remove her arms from around his neck. He held them with shaky fingers against her lap. She smelled of soap, sunshine, and pure woman, and Seth couldn't think of anything he would rather do than grant her her request and crawl into bed with her. But he'd sworn this morning that there would be no repeat performance of the night before, and he meant to keep that promise. No matter what the cost.

"Viola Mae, I'd like nothing better than to bed you, but I'm not going to do it."

Disappointment showed on her face. "Why ain't you?"

"Because you and I aren't married."

"Yet," she reminded him.

"But still, under the circumstances, I think it would be best if we slept in separate beds."

"But we already did it once, more than once, so what would one more little time matter?"

"Trust me on this, Viola Mae. It's best we sleep apart until—"

"We're married."

Until this is resolved, Seth had meant to say, but seeing her expectant gaze, he didn't have the heart.

"I can abide by your decision if you can," she said. "I'd still rather be sleeping next to you, instead of sleeping away from you. But because you're going to be my husband, I have to respect your wishes and trust you."

It was some time later, when the lights were out and they lay in their separate beds with only the moonlight glazing the cottage's interior, that Seth wished he'd reneged on his promise to himself. On the too-short, lumpy cot, he lay on his side curled into an S, and ached in the worst way a man could ache for a woman. He stared across the distance at the big bed where Viola Mae's womanly curves, draped in white, stood out in relief against the darker shadows.

"You asleep yet?" she asked him after several quiet moments had passed.

"Almost," he lied. He would never fall asleep in his present condition, but she didn't need to know it.

"I've been thinking," she said, "about what my grannie used to say."

Seth faked a bored yawn. "What was that?"

"She always said, 'If you love something let it go. If it comes back to you, it's yours. If it doesn't, it was never yours to begin with.'"

Chapter Seventeen

Seth clopped along, enjoying the old horse's easy pace. Old Clyde might be slower than a slug, but at least he was carrying him back to civilization. For the last few days, Seth had felt lost in an alien world, so when he recognized the sandy road as the one he'd been taking to town the day he'd detoured, he knew he was back on course.

Before he'd left the farm, Viola Mae had told him the quickest and easiest route to town. He'd started out not long after daybreak with a note in his pocket and explicit orders for delivering it. Viola Mae had told him that the moment he arrived in town he was to give the letter to Gracie at the General Store. He had promised Viola Mae that the missive would be delivered and had tried to put it out of his mind. But the mystery of its contents had worried him like a bad toothache for most of the ride, and he decided he'd be happy to be rid of it.

Already the day felt steamy and promised to be another scorcher. Everywhere he looked he saw evidence of the storm's fury. Downed trees and moss-laden branches were strewn across the earth like poker chips over green felt.

Having come upon a tree that blocked the road, Seth detoured into the woods. Birds and squirrels that weren't as lucky as Viola Mae's chickens lay dead and twisted on the forest floor.

"Golly damn." Seth jerked Clyde to a standstill. Several feet away from where he had stopped, a raccoon was tangled in the stringy roots of a downed tree. The animal's head hung at an unnatural angle on his body, his masked eyes staring at the terror he must have known before he died.

A nervous uneasiness clawed at Seth's stomach. The death and destruction he'd seen thus far made him question what might possibly await him when he arrived in town. He prodded Clyde forward, locking his eyes on the distant horizon as he passed the raccoon's gnarled and broken body, glad that Viola Mae hadn't been witness to so many random deaths of her forest friends.

As the woods opened to a broader expanse of land, evidence of how strong the wind had been was brought home to Seth. If he hadn't heard and felt the storm's power firsthand, he wouldn't have believed what he saw now. In the middle of a field a skiff rested, its flat bottom moored to the grassy sea. The boat looked as though it had been rowed there, then abandoned by its owner.

After a while the road meandered by a cemetery. He read ''St. Michael's'' on the white columns standing like sentinels on each side of its entrance. Beneath the huge oaks and Spanish moss that canopied the hallowed ground, the air felt cooler. Seth paused, drawn to the quiet place. Except for streamers of moss that hung haphazardly over several tombstones, the area appeared untouched by the storm's savage wind, as though some divine power had deigned to leave it unscathed.

Instinctively Seth felt that this was the burial place of Viola Mae's grandparents. For reasons unknown to him, seeing their graves was important. He checked his fob watch. It was still early enough to visit the wizened old woman whom Viola Mae held in such high regard.

It was damp beneath the century-old trees, and the earth smelled of years of mulch. Seth dismounted and picked his way around the family plots until he found the name Smith. Removing his hat, he stopped at the foot of the wide marble headstone and read the engraved epitaph:

HENRY AND BEATRICE
*Two consorts in heaven are not two,
but one angel.*

It was a fitting inscription, he thought, judging from the way Viola Mae had described her grandparents' love. His eyes strayed to the deep lavender flowers that entwined the lovers together in their eternal sleep. The open blossoms lifted toward the sky, groping for the sun's slanting rays through the leafy branches and the threadlike tangled moss.

"Passion flowers," he said aloud.

Seth squatted down beside the two graves, fingering the delicate blossoms. Their satin smoothness and violet color reminded him of the woman he'd left behind.

Disturbed by his thoughts, he stood. Was it possible that he missed the lady who had tormented him, both physically and mentally, for the last few days? Denying the possibility, Seth turned and retraced his steps to where Clyde waited.

He was about to mount up when he felt the breeze flutter the paper tucked inside his shirt pocket. Viola Mae's note. He settled the folded message deeper into its stronghold, but his fingers remained poised on the paper's edge. Although he wasn't in the habit of reading other people's mail, he wanted to read this one. Because Viola Mae's instructions about its delivery had been so important to her, Seth suspected the letter's contents had something to do with him—something to do with her reasons for taking him prisoner. Lifting the paper from his pocket, Seth began to read:

Gracie, If you're reading this note, I take it you survived the storm. I prayed to God for your safety and everyone else in town, even those I ain't too fond of. You'll recognize the man who delivers this to you and you'll be pleased to know I released him. Like you told me, he ain't such a bad lot, and I guess that old love bug knew what he was doing when he first bit me, because the Yankee and I are gonna get hitched. This change in events has put me in a real pickle, though, since I expect you delivered the note about my meeting with Archibald. I never heard from the rascal, but I reckon it wasn't because he didn't want his railroad boss back, but because of the storm. When I see you I'll tell you about what I did to the railroad that I didn't tell you about before because I didn't think you would be too pleased with my mischief, especially since you weren't too keen on me kidnapping the Yank in the first place. Put on your wedding shoes 'cause next time you see me, I'll be near to jumping the broom. And I'll also be needing your advice about what to do about that dang fool note I sent. Until then, I'm still your friend, Viola Mae.

One reading wasn't enough. Seth reread the note several more times before he folded it up and put it back inside his pocket.

"Of all the foolish, harebrained schemes," he mumbled. "Didn't she understand the seriousness of her actions?"

Viola Mae had been responsible for the tainted fruit, which he'd already suspected when he saw the preserves in her cabin. Now that he'd read the note, he believed she'd also been responsible for the privies. And the burned railroad ties! If Archibald had received the note from Gracie, then Viola Mae could indeed be in a real pickle.

Like pieces of a puzzle, suddenly everything fell in place. Now he understood what Viola Mae had meant when she'd hinted at holding him until the meeting. He had been her hostage, her trump card that she believed would make Archibald listen to her complaints about the railroad and the destruction of her woods.

"Damn fool woman."

Tainted fruit and filled privies were nothing more than pranks, but arson and kidnapping were crimes. Instead of being on her way to the altar, she might find herself headed to jail.

Seth threw his leg over Clyde's back and nudged the horse into motion. He'd tarried way too long. Leaving St. Michael's behind, he rode toward town and headed straight for Gracie's store. Together maybe the two of them could figure out how to save Viola Mae from her own folly.

Although he wasn't too excited about the prospect of marriage, Seth sure as the devil didn't want her rotting away in some jail.

Jedwin Rowe stood at the base of the rickety barn. With his hand shielding the sun from his gaze, the ten-year-old stared up at the silver-haired young woman sitting astride the roof's peak. After several moments went by without an acknowledgment of his presence, he called to her.

"I never saw a lady ride a house before."

Jerked from her concentration by the call, Viola Mae eyed the young stranger standing on the ground below her. Slowly she removed the nails she held clamped between her teeth, taking her time to size up her unexpected visitor.

It wasn't often that Viola Mae received callers, especially young kids traveling alone. Children usually were accompanied by their parents, unless, of course, they were locals who happened by. But this lone one didn't look like any of the children she knew from town or like any of her neighbor Forbes's litter.

She looked at the surrounding woods, searching to see if the boy had an accomplice. After a disaster struck it was not unusual for rampant looting to occur. Although her farm was a good distance from town, she couldn't be too cautious. Pillagers, like buzzards, preyed on the defenseless.

Still uncertain if he was friend or foe, she glanced toward the house for signs of a companion. The doors were propped open against the oppressing heat, and right now someone could be inside pilfering her things. Viola Mae cursed her negligence for not having her shotgun at her side. She hoped the boy would turn out to be exactly what he appeared to be—a lone kid who posed no threat to anyone but himself.

From the top of the barn, he didn't look much like a menace. But neither did a rattler when you first came upon it sunning itself on a rock. And the kid had the advantage with her open position on top of the barn.

Until she figured out what his intent was, she intended to keep his attention focused on her. Trying for cordiality, she said, "If you ain't never seen a lady ride a house before, it must mean you ain't from these parts. If you were, you'd know you ride a barn to break it, just like you gotta ride a wild horse."

She felt his eyes on her. Their color was indistinguishable, like his purpose, but she could see that he had a shock of mahogany-colored hair and a face full of matching freckles.

He scanned the barn and the discarded wood at his feet. After several contemplative moments, the boy spoke. "Looks to me like you already broke it."

The lad's quick wit made the corners of Viola Mae's mouth lift into a smile. Already she liked him, but she still didn't trust him.

The boy toed the wood by his feet while Viola Mae eyed the traveling bag that sat on the ground several spaces away from where he stood.

"Where do you hail from?" she asked him when he didn't offer the information willingly.

"Milton," he replied.

"Across the bay, huh? How did y'all fare the storm?"

"It passed west of us. Mostly rain and a little wind."

When he offered no other information, Viola Mae tried again. "Your folks got a name?"

The youth looked at her as if she was dumber than a stump.

"Course my folks have a name. Do yours?"

His response made her chuckle. The boy was as frisky as a young fox, but nowhere near as dangerous. Confident now that he was no longer a threat, Viola Mae finished hammering in the nail she'd started on when he first appeared.

She wiped her face on her sleeve. "I was just getting ready to get me a drink of lemonade. Being it's so hot, I thought you might like to share a glass."

"No, thanks, ma'am. I'm not too keen about drinking after strangers."

This time Viola Mae laughed heartily. "I ain't too keen on drinking after them neither, but I feel sure I could muster us up two glasses, if you'd be interested."

He licked his lips, wondering whether or not he should accept her offer. As she waited for an answer, she couldn't help but think that something about his appearance seemed familiar. The valise at his feet was an indication that he was on the run. Boys ran away from home all the time, and the thought saddened her. Afraid that he might be a runaway, and afraid that he might bolt before she could find out, Viola Mae called to him as she neared the ladder where it stood propped against the roof.

"Would you be so kind as to steady this here ladder while I climb down?"

Instead of moving to assist her, he stood rooted to his spot.

"I ain't exactly excited about being thrown from this here barn. You know they can do that, if you ain't careful."

With the manner of a boy twice his age, he crossed his arms against his chest. "Barns can't throw people," he told her. "They are inanimate objects."

Inanimate? A big word for such a little kid. "Barns may not throw people," she repeated, "but ladders are a different animal altogether, especially if they don't have a man like yourself to steady them."

"Where's your husband?"

"I ain't got one of those. Not yet, anyway."

He shrugged his shoulders and trudged to the ladder's base. "Then I guess I'll have to help you."

With arms that looked no bigger around than a rooty carrot, and were almost the same color because of the freckles, he steadied the ladder while she climbed down. When she neared the last few rungs, he stepped back, allowing her to drop to the ground.

"I appreciate your help," Viola Mae told him, turning to face him, "and since you helped me, I'll get us each our own glass of lemonade, and we'll sit a spell. It ain't often I get company."

Viola Mae led Jed to the shady side of the porch, motioned for him to have a seat, and told him she'd bring out their drinks. When she returned, she found the boy sitting on the edge of the porch, his feet dangling. Mustard had taken over the duties of hostess and was rubbing her furry sides against the boy's back and shoulders, weaving first to one side, then the other. The boy's pleasure bubbled into laughter.

"She likes you," Viola Mae told him, coming to sit beside him on the porch's edge. Together they sat, dangling their legs and enjoying their lemonade.

"I like her, too," he told her between great sugary sips. "I never had a pet."

"Her name's Mustard, and she was wondering what yours is."

''Cats can't wonder,'' he replied, ''but tell her it's Jedwin.'' His stubby fingers scratched the cat behind one ear, and Mustard rolled on her back for a tummy rub.

''Jedwin what?''

''Rowe,'' he replied.

His announcement made Viola Mae almost choke on her last swallow. *Jedwin Rowe. It couldn't be.* She looked closer at the boy beside her. Seth had said his little brother had mahogany-colored hair, freckles, and eyes. Leaning around to get a better look at the child's face, she felt her heartbeat speed up.

No wonder he'd looked familiar to her earlier. Upon closer inspection, she could see that he had the same-shaped face and jaw that Seth had. But instead of sea-green eyes, Jed's were the color of tarnished pennies.

Wiping her hand on her skirt, she extended it in his direction. He accepted her hand, allowing her to pump his up and down.

''Howdy, I'm Viola Mae. I know your brother, Seth.''

''You know Seth?'' Excitement lit up his child's face. ''You aren't Harriet Archibald, are you?''

''Thank heavens, no.''

Viola Mae wasn't pleased that the brother of her intended husband seemed so familiar with her lifelong enemy. She put her negative feelings aside, however, happy to discover that Jed was Seth's brother and was sitting beside her on her porch.

''This isn't the railroad camp, is it?'' the boy asked, looking around the yard.

''I'm afraid it ain't, but then your brother ain't at the camp noway. When the storm came, the railroaders headed to town.''

''You mean Seth's in town?''

''I saw him heading that way this morning.''

She wanted to tell him about their upcoming nuptials, but the moment didn't seem right. Before she said anything, she wanted to find out what Jed was doing in Pensacola. ''I thought you were supposed to be in Atlanta, staying with your aunt.''

Guilt showed beneath his abundance of freckles. "I was . . . but now I'm here."

"But your aunt, and the other lady you were staying with, do they know where you are?"

"By now they do, because I left them a note."

"A note?"

Oh, lawsy, Seth was going to explode with anger when he found out his brother was in Pensacola. And those poor old ladies back in Georgia must be worried sick about his whereabouts. "How long you been gone from Atlanta?"

"Around a week. The storm kept me in Milton for a while."

"Milton? How did it keep you in Milton?"

"This lady, a Mrs. Finch, I met her on the train. She was visiting her sister in Jacksonville. She appointed herself my guardian when she found out I was traveling alone."

"That was mighty nice of her," Viola Mae said.

"Not really. I don't need a guardian."

Jed swung his legs back and forth while stroking Mustard, who'd staked a claim on the boy's lap.

"Took the stagecoach after the railroad tracks ended. Wow! What a ride. When we got to Milton, they made us stay there because of the approaching storm. Mrs. Finch took me home with her."

Thank goodness for Mrs. Finch, Viola Mae thought. She couldn't imagine a ten-year-old boy traveling all the way from Atlanta alone. Here she was twenty-two years old and had never traveled anywhere.

"I assume the ferry is running again," Viola Mae said. "Let me guess, she put you on it and sent you on your way."

"Well, not exactly." Jed shifted nervously. "Every time I told her I wanted to leave, she kept insisting that I wait another day. Her husband was supposed to find out how Pensacola had fared, but I don't think they wanted me to leave. Finally, this morning at daybreak, I sneaked out of the house and caught a ride across the bay with a fisherman."

"You didn't tell them you were leaving?"

Jed shook his head and stole a sideways glance at her before answering. "But I did leave them a note, thanking them for their hospitality."

Another note. The folly of notes, Viola Mae thought. Hers to Archibald had worried her ever since Seth's departure.

"Notes," she finally told him, "can get you in a passel of trouble."

"Not me. I know Seth will be glad to see me, or I think he will." Taking this as a cue to leave, he jumped up from the porch. "I had best be heading to town if that's where my brother is."

Viola Mae jumped up when he did and stood facing him. He wasn't much shorter than she was, and she imagined that one day he would be as tall as his brother.

"You know, me and Seth are pretty good friends. He told me all about you, and I sorta feel responsible for you even though I know a man like yourself don't need no lady frettin' over him. But in a few days, after I make a few more repairs around the farm, I planned to go to town. I was hoping that maybe you'd consider staying the night, and since I don't like riding alone, you and me could head that way together."

"Well, ma'am, I don't know if I can spare the time." He brushed Mustard's hair from his travel-worn shirt. "You see, I'm getting kind of anxious to see my brother again."

"Me, too," she told him, missing Seth something awful since he left the farm. "But it's a good ways to town, especially traveling on foot. Now, I got me a real fine horse that loves to pull my old wagon. He'd be happy to carry us both."

"A horse? Wow! You should have seen the team that pulled the stagecoach."

"You like to ride?" she asked him.

"Never had much chance in New York, but I know I can."

"I know you can, too. In that barn over there is one of the finest horses in all of Pensacola. Her name is Ginger, and I bet a young squirt like yourself would like to ride her. For exercise, you know. Right now I'm too busy to do it myself with all the cleaning up I'm doing around here."

Jed's brown eyes were as big as half-dollars. "A horse. You'd let me ride her?"

"I surely would. It would be a big help to me. That is, if you decide to stay a spell."

After a moment of indecision, Jed answered, "I guess since you haven't got a husband to help you, I could stay a day or two. But no more."

"Let's shake on that, partner." Viola Mae thrust out her hand, and Jed slammed his into it. "We got us a deal," she said.

A friendship began to blossom between the two with that handshake. Viola Mae rested her hand on Jed's shoulder and steered him toward his valise.

"Let's get your bag and take it inside the cabin, and in the meantime I'll tell you about the finest horse you'll ever ride in this lifetime. She's a Percheron. My grannie said her lineage dated back to the fifteenth century, and that her ancestors carried many a knight into battle. . . ."

Chapter Eighteen

As Seth rode up Palafox Street toward the center of the business district, Pensacola was alive with activity. The sound of hammers and saws filled the air. Voices mingled as the townspeople went about the business of making repairs. Relieved to see that the town had not been flattened by the storm, he pulled Clyde to a stop in front of the General Store and dismounted. After throwing the reins over the hitching post, Seth sprinted toward the building's entrance.

Because of the boarded-up windows, the store's interior was dark except for the light that spilled through the open doors on each end of the building. The plate-glass windows were still intact, but the wood flooring was covered with a heavy dusting of powdery sand and dried mud. Along with the mixed scents of soaps and spices, molasses, and barrels of kerosene, the salty smell of the sea assaulted Seth's nostrils. A quick glance around the store's interior told him the owner had battled rising water because the floors had been cleared of the usual stock. Tables and chairs were stacked haphazardly with the extra goods.

No one was at the front counter. After looking around, Seth walked toward the back of the building where he heard furniture scraping across the floor. Several moments later, an out-of-tune voice broke out in song. He could hear the distinct swish of a broom against the floor accompanying the singer.

"Cindy went to preaching;
She shouted all around.

She got so full of glory,
She rolled her stockings down."

He approached the female from behind and watched unde-
tected as the vocalist became caught up in her music. As she
warmed up to the chorus, she pounded the floor with her
broom and beat out the rhythm.

"Get a-long home, Cindy, Cindy,
Get a-long home,—
Get a-long home, Cindy, Cindy,
I'll marry you some day. . . ."

Her last note was held in a wobbly finale. Seth couldn't help
but smile at the enthusiasm with which the woman sung. This
rather broad-beamed, spirited woman had to be Viola Mae's
friend, Gracie. The girl he'd seen her in church with that
Sunday a lifetime ago. Her tune finished, the woman straightened. She rested her free hand on her ample waist and
stretched her back.

Interjecting speech into the sudden quiet, Seth said, "Excuse me, ma'am."

The startled singer nearly jumped out of her skin before
she swung around to face him.

"I'm sorry, ma'am. I didn't mean to frighten you."

Her plump cheeks turned as pink as ripe apples. "No matter," she told him, shrugging. She inspected him from his
head to his toes, then allowed her gaze to settle again on his
face. Smiling, she extended her hand. "I'm Gracie Marle.
How can I help you?" Not waiting for his answer, she continued. "You're Mr. Rowe, the railroad boss."

Seth nodded. "Are you surprised?"

She dismissed his question with her own. "How's Viola
Mae? Did she make it through the storm safely?"

"Viola Mae is fine." Seth reached for the note inside his
pocket and handed it to her. "I'm to deliver this."

Her eyes left his temporarily to read the message. Several
moments later, she looked up, elation lighting up her features.

"Am I to understand congratulations are in order?"

Having read the note, Seth knew she referred to their impending marriage. But at the moment he had more pressing things to discuss. "You're to understand that your friend is in deep sh—I mean trouble, especially if you delivered her ransom note to Mr. Archibald."

Cocking one brow, she studied him. "And if I didn't?"

"She's still in deep trouble. Possibly for arson."

"Arson?" Gracie moved toward the front of the store with Seth following her. "Certainly, Mr. Rowe, you don't believe that Viola Mae would set a fire that would endanger those woods she adores?"

"Truthfully, I don't know what to think. Of Viola Mae or any other lamebrained scheme she might be a party to. But Miss Marle, it doesn't matter what I believe. Sheriff Breen knows about the fire and is conducting an investigation to see who started it."

"Does he suspect Viola Mae?"

"Your guess is as good as mine. But I fear if Archibald received that ransom note and took it to the sheriff, he probably has put the two together along with the other mischief the camp has been plagued with lately."

"Other mischief—like what?"

"Like tainted fruit that caused dysentery among the men, the camp's water supply being dammed up, and the privies being filled with sand and decorated with poison ivy."

The woman's hand flew to her mouth as though smothering a laugh. "Now, they sound like things our Viola Mae *would* do."

After a moment, Gracie walked behind the counter. Several moments passed before she opened a drawer and pulled out a piece of paper. She thrust it toward him.

"You know, I never approved of her kidnapping you and I told her so. When she asked me to deliver that note to Archibald, I told her I wouldn't do it. But as usual, Viola Mae assumed I'd do her bidding and left it at that."

A smile lit up the woman's face as she shook her head in amazement. "She told me she was only borrowing you and planned to give you back."

Seth couldn't help but smile. He could hear Viola Mae saying something like that and not seeing anything wrong with it. Glancing down at the note in his palm, he felt relief wash over him. "You can't believe how glad I am that you didn't deliver this."

"Even if the storm had not come, I wouldn't have delivered it. I planned to make a trip out to the farm to try to talk some sense into that girl. But once I learned the storm was heading this way, I couldn't chance it. I had to stay here and make preparations."

"It appears the storm did minimal damage." Seth tore the note into pieces and handed the shreds back to Gracie. "No fatalities, I hope."

She took the pieces and deposited them in the trash. "None, thank the Good Lord. Several boats in the harbor washed ashore, and there was about a foot or more of water on Palafox Street. Most folks suffered broken windows and lost roofing and siding. But amazingly, considering the ferocity of the wind, we came through it with flying colors."

"I'm glad to hear it. Viola Mae and I were both concerned about the town's fate."

"Everyone here has joined forces to rebuild and repair. It's a cooperative effort on all our parts, and already we've succeeded far beyond our expectations."

"I hope to be of some help, but first, I need to check in with Archibald." Seth turned to leave, but Gracie stopped him.

"Are you going to marry that girl, Mr. Rowe?" Her look clearly indicated that she knew what had gone on between them.

"At this point, Miss Marle, I'm more concerned with keeping her out of Sheriff Breen's jail. As for marriage, I'm in no position to support a wife. For all I know, I may no longer have a job."

"With your money, Mr. Rowe, I find it hard to believe that you would even take employment."

"My money?"

Her assumptions angered Seth. He put his hands in his pants pockets and jerked them out to show their emptiness.

"I'm penniless, Miss Marle. I don't know what you've heard about my background, but my father's fortune is gone. Every black cent of it—thanks to his gambling debts and bad investments.

"Now I'm the sole support for my ten-year-old brother, who's staying with my aunt in Atlanta until I earn enough money to pay for a place for us to live here. That was my intent when I took this position with the railroad. As you can see"—he shook his upturned pockets—"I can't support myself, much less a wife."

His economic problems didn't seem to bother her overmuch. After several seconds of silence, she said, "If you've compromised my girl, Mr. Rowe, it's only proper that you should marry her. I take it she believes you intend to make an honest woman out of her."

She leaned forward across the counter. "I presume you know Viola Mae's history. If that child gave herself to you, she didn't do it lightly. Her heart is the most guarded treasure in the state of Florida. Believe me, if she gave you her body, her love was included in the gift—and you've been given a lasting treasure."

"Love, my dear Miss Marle, will not put food on the table."

"I see," she said, pulling back as though he'd suddenly sprouted horns and a tail. "If you break my friend's heart, I'll come after you and pull yours out with my bare hands."

Taken aback by her vehemence, Seth turned and left without another word.

Outside he stood beside Clyde, feeling lower than dung on someone's boot. He stroked the old horse's hide, checked his cinch, and was about to mount up when he heard someone call out to him.

"There ye be, lad; I've been wondering where ye be hiding."

Seth turned to see Riley, his foreman, strolling across the street toward him. When he reached Seth's side, Riley slapped him on the back so hard it nearly knocked the breath from his lungs.

"I thought the storm had blown ye clean to me homeland

when I didn't find you in town." Riley bent toward him, his nose wrinkling. He took several quick sniffs of Seth's clothing and drew away from him. His ruddy face was lit with mischief when he focused on Seth. "Ye don't smell like corned beef, but ye do smell good enough to eat."

The Irishman laughed, and Seth found his humor contagious.

"Ham," he told him, realizing how much he'd missed his newfound friend. Their laugher mingled and rose on the warm summer breeze.

"Ye been hiding out in someone's smokehouse, have ye?" Riley's brows raised in question.

"You might say that," Seth answered, not about to tell him that his clothes had done exactly that.

"Well, lad, I'm not caring to be nosy, but where have ye been?"

"It's a long story, Riley, and one I don't wish to go into right now. I need to see Archibald. I know I shouldn't be asking my foreman this question, but do I still have a job with the railroad?"

He looked at Seth questioningly. "Lad, have ye been out of yer mind? Of course, ye still have a job. Archibald told me to put the word out to you and to any of the other men who showed up in town. The bosses postponed the tracklaying until the town can be put back in order. We'll be paid for our efforts here. Most of the lads are here, working our jewels off. Plenty for us all to do with roofing and everything else that needs fixing."

Seth nearly smiled. He'd been working his own jewels off, but not in the same fashion as his men. He was sure that he'd enjoyed his work more.

Damn Viola Mae, anyway. After what Gracie had said, he couldn't stop thinking about her. Recalling his and Viola Mae's time together, the things she had said, Seth more or less suspected that she did love him. But he sure as the devil didn't know what to do about that love. It was something he hadn't planned on.

Riley interrupted his thoughts. "Miss Archibald, she's been inquiring about ye, lad."

The Irishman's words hit him like cold water. Harriet Archibald was the last person Seth wanted to see, or to think about for that matter.

Riley elbowed him in the ribs. "I believe the lass fancies ye. A beauty she is, but in my Irishman's eyes, she can't hold a tallow to the bonnie lass Viola Mae. Now there is a beauty who makes this old Irish heart flutter."

His friend Riley stood with his hand over his heart, his eyes closed as though calling her image to mind. Jealousy as green as the sea streaked through Seth. While he fought to control the green-eyed monster, he saw one of Riley's eyes wink open. Did Riley suspect where Seth had been for the last few days? Seth suspected he did. The crusty old Irishman was baiting him, but Seth was unwilling to take the nibble.

Instead he asked, "Where are you staying in town?"

"Me and some of the other lads are bunking down in an empty warehouse near the wharf. There's always a spare cot, and ye are welcome to join us if ye have no other place to stay."

Again the Irishman seemed to be digging for clues. When none were forthcoming, he continued. "The fine ladies of Pensacola are preparing meals for the workers and anyone else who needs food." He winked at Seth. "Don't tell Tater I said so, but they put on a spread much better than his."

"I promise I'll be the last to tell our ornery cook anything." Looking his foreman in the eye, he asked, "By the way, Riley, is it possible to send a telegram? I need to wire my brother and my aunt in Atlanta. If news of this storm has traveled north, I'm sure they will be worried sick."

"Sorry, laddie. Wires are down, and it's expected to be days before they're mended. Same's true with the town's two telephones. Getting word out or in is damn near impossible."

"Damnation. I guess there is not much that can be done except get to work. I'll take Clyde to the livery, then I'll join you. Where do you think you'll be?"

"By the time you get old Clyde boarded, it will be time for the fair ladies of our town to serve us lunch."

"And where might the fair ladies of the town be doing that?"

"Ye know the marine terminus on the wharf? That's where I'll be, along with every other hungry man in Pensacola. See ye there, lad."

The men parted. Riley went one way, and Seth mounted Clyde and urged him in the direction of the livery. Just as he tapped the horse's sides with his heels, Gracie appeared on the threshold of her store. Seth doffed his hat in parting, but she did no more than stare bullets through him.

On his way to the livery, Seth saw evidence that the town had suffered damage, but most of what he saw appeared more superficial than disabling. Dead and rotting fish were scattered throughout the streets, the stench overpowering as the unrelenting sun beat down on the decomposing remains. The same powdery sand and mud that had covered the floor in Gracie's store clung to the boardwalks and storefronts.

But all in all, it looked as though the town had come through the storm with only minor wounds. There were no black ribbons hanging on doorways he passed, which in itself was a miracle. No one had lost their loved ones. There would be no new graves in St. Michael's.

The thought of St. Michael's Cemetery made Seth think about Viola Mae's grandparents, and then Viola Mae. He wondered how she was faring on the farm without him. His body tightened as he thought about their night of lovemaking; his heart swelled when he thought about the love he'd recognized in Viola Mae's eyes when he rode away. Now that she'd set him free, he missed being snared in her net. He even missed *her*, and that was the craziest thing of all.

A half hour later, Seth stood outside the warehouse on the wharf. Inside, he heard men laughing, chairs scraping against the floor, the hustle and bustle of life going on in spite of the odds.

He inhaled the clean fresh air deeply and looked around. Where the land stopped and the water began, small waves slapped against the bulkhead and the bellies of ships that were anchored on the blue water. Beyond Pensacola Bay was the open sea. Today the water looked sparkled with prisms of light reflecting off its surface. It was one of those days when it was nearly impossible to tell where the sea ended and the sky began. A flock of brown pelicans flying in a V formation flew across the boundlessness, fragmenting it into pieces when they dove into the water with a foamy splash.

Gulls screeched overhead. The sun heated Seth's skin and his clothes. Sweat beaded his face, and he wiped it on his sleeve. When he did so, the smell of roasting pork grew stronger.

He let loose with a good solid laugh. "Oh, Viola Mae. What's a man to do with you?"

Suddenly feeling better than he had in days, Seth pushed open the door and went in search of the redheaded Irishman.

True to Riley's words, the ladies of Pensacola had outdone themselves with the repast they'd prepared for the workers. Seth hadn't realized how hungry he was until he pulled up a chair beside Riley and began feasting on the food he'd piled on his plate. He had avoided the corn bread and the fried chicken, but had helped himself to generous portions of fresh vegetables, mashed potatoes, cheese grits, salads, and roast beef. Even the water he washed his food down with no longer bothered his taste buds.

Tater, the cook, and several other men from the camp arrived. They shook his hand and greeted him like a long-lost friend. No questions were asked about his whereabouts the last few days. For those who had lived through the disaster that had struck the port, the past no longer mattered. It was the present they were all concerned with, and they were happy to be alive and looking to the future.

As he listened to the conversation buzzing around him, Seth realized that the residents who were close to the water had experienced a terror that he and Viola Mae had not. Rising ocean water. The water had risen as the storm progressed toward land, washing inland with a depth of several feet. That explained the sand, mud, and the dead fish Seth had seen scattered throughout the downtown streets.

"We've got to get them boats back in the water," a man at the end of the table told them. "The harbormaster has called for volunteers to work with the tugboats this afternoon. Tide will be in, and they figure if we men can push from the beach side, tugboats will be able to pull from the water side.''

Seth didn't recognize the man who'd spoken as one of the railroad's crew. But then, the bulk of the men present in the dining room were unfamiliar to him. He supposed they were either sailors, longshoremen, or residents of Pensacola. But they all had one purpose—to put their town back in order.

''A little swim would feel good in this heat,'' he heard Riley say. ''Ye can tell the harbormaster he can count on me. What about you, Seth, you in for a dunking?''

''Sounds good to me.''

''Maybe ye can wash the stench of ham from those clothes. Phewee! You smell country-cured.''

The man on Seth's right leaned toward him and sniffed.

''Well, I'll be blasted. It was you I've been smelling all this time. I thought this here beef was ham. Couldn't figure out why it smelled like it but didn't taste like it.''

Seth chuckled good-naturedly. ''I guess these garments could use a good saltwater soak.''

''Hear tell that's how they cure pork. Maybe we ought to call you Porky.'' Everyone agreed on Seth's new name.

Lefty, the man from the railroad camp, chimed in. ''Hope no fishes think you're a hunk of bait and carry you out to sea.''

''I'll keep the lad anchored,'' Riley said, chuckling.

Seth sat surrounded by the men he knew from his camp and men he'd never seen before today. He enjoyed their easy laughter, their easy acceptance. Some of the gathered men knew him as their boss, while others didn't know him at all. But they all accepted him as an equal, and the realization made Seth feel as though he belonged with these men.

A feeling of euphoria settled over him. Belonging anywhere was something Seth hadn't experienced since his father's death, when he'd been thrust into an environment he knew nothing about—that of a working man. Now, as he sat among his new friends, enjoying the easy camaraderie, he wondered when the person he'd been had slipped into his past, becoming less important as he stepped forward into his future.

The outside door opened, and the men in the hall fell silent.

"Seth, there you are," Harriet Archibald called.

The woman's fashionable slippers beat a delicate tattoo across the wooden floor. All eyes followed her as she moved among the diners to Seth's table.

"I've been worried sick about you," she announced to all of Pensacola.

She was dressed in a yellow poplin frock with a yellow-and-black-striped sateen underskirt, and looked as though she were dressed for a garden party instead of a work party like the other ladies stationed about the room. On top of her perfectly coiled brunette hair, a straw skimmer, trimmed with a yellow and black band that matched her dress, sat at a jaunty angle. Her hands were gloved in white lace, and a yellow parasol hung from her wrist. Every man in the room appreciated her presence. Everyone but Seth.

Rising to his feet, he said, "Miss Archibald, it's nice to see you again."

She smiled at him, her cheeks dimpling. Her gaze floated across the worshiping faces of the other men, dismissing them as though they were faceless statues. "Walk with me," she demanded.

Seth didn't want to walk with her; he preferred to stay where he was. But manners dictated that he obey her summons. Excusing himself, he fell into step beside her, and they walked toward the exit. Once outside, away from the others, she stopped and faced him.

"Daddy and I were so worried about you. I just knew you were crushed under one of those nasty old pines. Anyway, Mr. Riley assured me that you were fine. He said you'd stayed in the railroad camp to look after the equipment. It must have been dreadful out in those woods in that storage shack all alone."

It looked as though he owed Riley another round of thanks. These last few weeks he'd come to depend on his foreman not only as an experienced railroad man, but also as a friend.

Harriet looked across the pier to where the boats were blown against the shore. "This whole storm has been dreadfully boring. Because of it, all entertainments were canceled, and my friends and I, the ones you met at the beach party, have been beside ourselves with inactivity. Can you believe that we had to cancel our musicale?''

Pretending concern when all he felt was indifference, Seth said, "I'm sorry you were disappointed."

"Well, we were. Regrettably so. Now who knows how long it will be before we can plan another." She smiled prettily. "And the noise . . . I've been bothered with the most awful headache. The continuous hammering and sawing will be my death. I just don't know how I'll make it through these next few days.''

Seth wanted to tell her she could volunteer to help as the other ladies in the community had done, but he realized the suggestion would be lost inside her pretty head.

"Gosh! What is that dreadful smell?" She pinched the end of her nose. "Do you smell it? It reminds me of smoked ham." She coughed and cleared her throat. "The whole town reeks of dead fish and seaweed. You can be sure I won't eat fish again." Glancing around them, she searched for something she couldn't see. "But ham, and on the wharf of all places.''

It was all he could do to keep from laughing. He wondered what Harriet would say if she realized the odor that was making her gag emanated from his clothes.

"Oh, never mind the disgusting ham," she told him. "What matters is that you're back. This evening I'm having a few of my friends in for a little get-together. To break up the monotony." She batted her velvety lashes. "Daddy and I will expect you to be there.''

Seth shook his head. "Sorry, but I've no clothes to wear to your social. Besides, I'm sure I'll be working. I'm supposed to help the other men move those boats back into the water.''

"Silly old boats." She looked disapprovingly at the beached craft. "Surely that shouldn't take long.''

"It will take longer than you think. We have to wait until the tide comes in and then goes out again. I'm not certain when that will be," he lied.

"Well, pooh! Tides go in and out all the time. It's settled, then—I'll just tell my friends you'll be arriving late because of the moon.''

"You haven't heard one thing I've said. I have no other clothes with me but these. Everything else I own is stored in a trunk at the railroad camp.''

"Well, pooh! Then you'll just have to buy some." She pulled a hankie from beneath her lace-sleeved cuff. "That ham smell is about to choke me." She waved the lacy square to clear the air. "Remember, I'll see you at seven. Now I must run before I swoon.''

Like a yellow and black tornado, she whirled around and darted away, leaving Seth to stare after her in amazement before shaking his head and returning to the building.

It mattered no longer that she was the boss's daughter. He had more important things to do than attend her social with her shallow little friends.

Chapter Nineteen

Viola Mae and Jed lay on their stomachs on a flat rock that hung over the edge of the translucent pool. Water belched upward from a deep spring in the belly of the earth, surfaced, then smoothed out to magnify and distort the depths of its algae-covered sides.

Dragonflies skipped across the water's glassy surface as the reflection of two faces—one with skin as creamy as sweet milk and crowned by a mop of silvery hair, the other with skin as speckled as a lake trout and with hair the color of rust—stared at their reflections in the natural mirror.

"My old grannie used to say that freckles were angel kisses. It ain't everybody who can claim that many heavenly bodies loving them."

"I ain't never been one for kissing," Jed replied. In the last few days, his speech had started sounding like Viola Mae's. "I've got so dang many freckles, I'm almost brown."

"Ain't nothing wrong with that color neither. What's important is being able to accept the way God made you."

"Yeah, well, it would be a heck of a lot easier if he'd made me a mite prettier."

"Jedwin Rowe. Since when did a man want to be pretty?"

"Shucks, I don't know. Maybe because you're always telling me how pretty my brother Seth is."

"I reckon what I meant to say is he's about the handsomest fella that I ever laid eyes on."

Jed's reflection turned somber. Wanting to replace it with a cheerier one, she said, "And you, my young friend, are the second." Their gazes locked in the glassy pool. "First day I laid eyes on you, I knew you were going to nuzzle yourself a spot inside my heart.''

Viola Mae reached over and ruffled Jed's damp hair. ''You look like your brother, you know?''

''Naw, I could never be as handsome as Seth.'' He studied his likeness, straining to see some resemblance.

''You look just like him. Same chin and same-shaped noggin.''

''But he doesn't have these dang freckles splattered all over his face.''

''So—maybe that means you're more special than he is. It's my guess he ain't as favored among the angels as you are.''

''You really think so?'' Jed asked, his voice filled with hope.

''I really think so.''

Viola Mae rolled to her back, and Jed copied her, rolling onto his. The two lay side by side, their eyes squinting at the fiery-white sun overhead. Refreshed from their swim, they allowed the sun's warmth to chase away the gooseflesh from swimming in the icy spring.

After Earle Forbes's visit last evening, Viola Mae had decided it was time for the two of them to seek out Seth in town. Earle had told them that repairs had been made in record time to the damaged buildings in town because of the joint effort made by all the townspeople. This afternoon there was to be a celebration with street dancing, games, food, and later fireworks over the bay. Viola Mae and Jed had washed their hair in the spring, and were planning to join in the festivities later.

A swallowtail butterfly darted across the rock where they lay. Their eyes followed its bobbing flight, watched it pause among the clusters of bird's-foot violets that grew around the spring before becoming airborne again and continuing on its wiggly course. Above their heads a silky breeze whispered through the pine needles, while a woodpecker thumped a hollow tree in search of dinner. They listened to the *chip, chip, chip* of a pine warbler, its chipping rattle echoing through the trees.

After a moment of quiet and wonder, Jed broke the silence. "I love it here, Viola Mae. If Seth doesn't want to marry you, then I will."

"Land beholding! I'm almost speechless." She slapped her hand to her heart. "Two such fine-looking fellas vying for my hand." Viola Mae turned on her side, propped her head on her hand, and smiled at Jed, who lay several feet away. "I can't think of a more flattering offer. I'll tell you a secret. If you were a few years older, you'd be my first choice. I have a weakness for fellas with freckles."

Jed blushed. "Naw, you don't, but I'm growing fast and someday I'll catch up with you."

"And if I ain't already a married lady, I'll take you up on your proposal."

They shook hands, sealing their bargain.

After several moments of companionable silence, Viola Mae said, "Jed, I've been thinking about what you told me about all them poor folks you saw on your trip here. Makes me wonder if maybe I've been selfish in not wanting that railroad built. I so love these here woods, and all the critters who live in them, but I ain't too happy about folks so poor they can't feed their young'uns."

Jed rolled over on his stomach and broke off a tall blade of grass that grew beside the rock. He stuck the end in his mouth before he spoke. "Once we boarded the stage in Chattahoochee, the poverty got worse. Mrs. Finch told me that most of the river towns couldn't ship their cotton until it rained and the rivers rose. People in those towns lived in dilapidated shacks and did without food because the stores ran out of goods when the boats and wagons weren't running. She said them poor folks needed a railroad, for no other reason than to get rid of the fleas in their houses."

"Poor as church mice, sounds to me like."

"Yeah, maybe poorer. That's what my father said about us after he lost all his money. He said we were poorer than church mice."

Jed's voice broke, and Viola Mae reached to squeeze his arm. She wanted to erase the bad memories about his past that he'd related to her after they had become friends. First his father's death, then his mother's soon after. How they'd been forced to move out of their home and how Seth hadn't been able to find work. How they'd moved in with Aunt Cloe in Atlanta and how Harriet Archibald's father had given Seth the job that had brought him to Pensacola.

This last part brought her back to thoughts about the railroad. If it hadn't been for the railroad that she'd tried to keep from being built, Viola Mae never would have met Jed or Seth. Now the two Rowe men had become the most important things in her life. It was strange to think that her two worst enemies in all the world, Harriet Archibald and the railroad, had brought her new friends. As her grannie always said, "The Lord works in mysterious ways."

"I think, young fella, you and me better get in that house and get ourselves dressed. If that brother of yours did as he was supposed to, you and me got us a wedding to attend."

"Yeah!" Jed hollered, jumping to his feet. "I guess if I can't wed you, I'll settle on you being my sister."

"Sister," Viola Mae said, taking his extended hand in hers. "I always wanted a brother or sister, but I wasn't lucky enough to get one. Now I'll have me a brother. Shake on it, partner."

She squeezed Jed's hand to seal their bargain.

Later that afternoon, the two rode into town. Jed drove the wagon, and Viola Mae sat on the seat beside him. The closer they got to Pensacola, the more fidgety she became.

It seemed as if months had passed since she'd last seen Seth, when in truth it had only been a few days. Sometimes she wondered if she'd dreamed the whole episode with him, the times they had made love with their bodies, thus pledging themselves to each other forever. But at night when she lay alone in her bed and became flustered and warm with desire as her mind recalled the memory of their lovemaking, she knew it hadn't been a dream. Two people couldn't have shared such bliss if they were not destined to be together.

"You sure I look all right?" Viola Mae asked as she directed Jed to park the wagon in front of Gracie's store.

"You're the prettiest sister I ever had," was Jed's response.

"I'm the only sister you've ever had, or will have," she reminded him warmly.

Jed pulled the wagon to a stop. While Viola Mae sat on the wagon seat worrying about how she looked, he jumped down, took the ribbons, and tethered Ginger to the hitching post the way Viola Mae had taught him back on the farm.

Before Seth had come into her life, Viola Mae hadn't cared two scraps about her appearance. Now all that had changed. Since Seth had already seen her in her blue dress, she'd chosen to wear the only other Sunday-go-to-meeting dress she owned, the brown one.

Knowing that today might also be her wedding day, she'd rummaged through her grannie's trunk, trying to find something pretty to gussy up the garment's plainness. Her efforts were rewarded when she found an ivory and beaded lace pelerine that had belonged to her grandmother. Viola Mae didn't recall ever seeing her grannie wear the short cape, but unlike Viola Mae, her grannie fancied pretty things. She never wore most of them, but kept them hidden away inside her trunk, taking them out on occasion to enjoy their touch and feel. Those were the times when she would tell her granddaughter of the days when she was a young belle on her daddy's plantation.

Standing before her looking glass before she'd left home, Viola Mae had agreed that the cape definitely improved the appearance of her brown twill gown. She had coiled her hair into the style she wore when she attended church, and had decided immediately that her old bonnet wouldn't do.

Among her grannie's hat boxes, stored in the large wardrobe, Viola Mae had found an English straw bonnet with ivory roses and an ecru ostrich plume attached to its brim. Ignoring her aversion to feathers being worn on hats instead of remaining on the birds they belonged to, she'd fastened the straw-and-feather creation to her head. It wasn't every day, she'd reasoned, that a girl got hitched to the man she loved.

"Hey, Viola Mae," Jed called, "there's a note on the door addressed to you."

She looked toward Jed, who stood in front of the closed-up store. "Read it to me, then."

Jed did so. " 'Viola Mae. Figured you'd come by here first, so I left this message for you. I've been called upon to set up tables so I couldn't wait. About your note to A., don't worry. I took care of it. See you in the square. We need to talk. Love, Gracie.'

"See," Jed said, "I ain't the only one who leaves notes."

"No, you surely aren't the only one, but I've come to the conclusion that maybe note-writing ain't always the best way to get our thoughts across."

She jumped down from the wagon and headed for the wooden walk. "I reckon it's time you and me go and find that brother of yours. I'm sure he'll be surprised when he sees you escorting me."

They fell into step and walked toward Plaza Ferdinand, where Viola Mae always stopped to savor Gracie's cinnamon rolls.

The festivities were to take place around the fountain in the plaza. Beneath several trees that grew around the square, tables were being set in place for food, and Palafox Street, which ran in front of the park, had been swept clean for dancing. Already the music had begun. A group of local musicians had gathered, puffing out the lively *oom-pa-pa* beat of a polka. Several of those in attendance had grabbed a partner and begun to hop-step-close-step in a circle in the closed street.

Seth stood with Riley in front of the dry goods store, one of his recently purchased shoes tapping to the beat of the music. "You mean the man confessed?" he asked, expressing disbelief.

"He did that, laddie. Walked right into Sheriff Breen's office and said he'd been the one that set the railroad ties on fire."

"The same man I fired?"

"The same bully."

"But I don't understand. What made him confess after all this time?"

"It's my understanding he woke up drunk and disoriented during the storm. He was on the wharf, where the rising water and wind were the worst. He had enough mind about him to cling to an outhouse that floated past."

Riley shook his head. "It's amazing to me that the man survived, considering the mixture of booze, rain, and water. Next morning a ship coming into port found him adrift about a mile or two out. When they picked him up, they say he was almost delirious. Kept raving that he'd found God during that storm. Made a promise to God that if He let him live, he would change his life. The minute he got on land, he went straight to Sheriff Breen's office and confessed."

"Well, I'll be damned. All this time I thought—" Seth caught himself before he said what he thought.

It looked as though Viola Mae had not set the fire as he'd first suspected after reading her message to Gracie. Viola Mae was guilty of nothing more than mischief. No one could send her to jail for that.

Riley's announcement relieved the anxiety that had nagged at Seth for days. One part of him had urged him to go to the sheriff and tell him what he knew about Viola Mae's involvement, but another part of him had urged him to hold off a day or two longer. Now he was glad that he had. The weight he'd been carrying around for days lifted from his shoulders. Just as his spirits had lifted on hearing this latest piece of news. His light mood soared on the warm current of air with the gulls above their heads.

"Well, I'll be damned," he said again.

"Well, you better quit damning, because here comes ye admirer, lad. I best be leaving ye to her clutches. I'll be scooting over to the band to see if I can talk the lads into playing an Irish jig. Then I'll be looking for a young lass to join me in a turn around the floor."

"Riley, wait," Seth insisted, but his foreman was already

halfway across the street. With no time to escape, he turned to greet his admirer.

"Miss Archibald, how are you on this fine afternoon?"

Beneath the confection of pink roses and satin ribbons of her white straw bonnet, she smiled prettily at him. "I'm fine, Mr. Rowe, even though you did stand me up." Her eyes raked over him admiringly. "I see you took my advice and purchased new clothes, although they didn't bring you to my little social the night before last."

Seth crooked his arm, allowing her to hook her pink gloved fingers in its bend. "I apologize profusely for not being able to attend, but moving those boats took longer than we anticipated. You did receive my note, begging your pardon for my absence?"

Seth had spent that same evening in the company of the men he'd been working with throughout the day. A team of horses couldn't have pulled him away from his new friends—especially not Harriet and her dilettantes. He'd never been one to pass judgment on others, but Seth had discovered that since his circumstances had changed, he'd begun to see people like Harriet as boring and shallow. The way he supposed *he* used to be.

"I did get your note," Harriet said, bringing Seth back to the present. "I have to say I was terribly disappointed that you couldn't make it. But I'll be happy to forgive you, especially if you promise to dance with no other lady but me."

Elation over the news that cleared Viola Mae of guilt had made him feel gracious. He supposed if Riley had asked him to dance he would have agreed. When the musicians struck up the chords of a waltz, he bowed to Harriet to grant her at least one dance, if for no other reason than to show her his gratitude for all that she'd done for him.

"My lady, may I have this dance?"

Harriet curtsied prettily and allowed him to lead her onto the makeshift dance floor.

Every pair of male eyes in attendance were upon the belle of Pensacola, Harriet Archibald, as she twirled around the street. Every pair of feminine eyes feasted on the tall, handsome gentleman dressed in gray trousers and a snowy white shirt with a burgundy silk vest.

But another person looked bewildered and outrageously furious as she gazed on her betrothed.

Viola Mae had just found Gracie, who had immediately borrowed Jed to help her fetch something she needed from her store. Viola Mae had chosen to stay at the plaza hoping she would spy Seth among the revelers, but she hadn't been prepared to see him dancing with Harriet Archibald.

Anger impeded her breathing. She wanted to run to him and shout, to tell Harriet that she had no right to be dancing with her man; instead, her feet stayed rooted to the ground, her anger simmering inside her like boiling liquid.

Along the edge of the picnic grounds where the food was being set out for the meal, she watched the handsome couple swirl around the floor. The ham she and Jed had brought from the smokehouse sat among the many dishes already on the table.

Red, white, and blue streamers ruffled above her head, and lanterns with citronella oil were filled and ready to be lit to brighten up the dining area and ward off the mosquitoes when evening approached.

Viola Mae paid no mind to the pretty colors. She had eyes only for the couple who danced before her.

As she watched Seth and Harriet together, her anger faded to a dull ache. He bent toward his partner and whispered something in her ear. Harriet threw back her pink-crowned head and laughed up into his face, and for the first time since meeting Seth, Viola Mae felt lacking.

"My, my, Viola Mae, aren't you spiffied up this afternoon. I daresay, child, I hardly recognized you."

Viola Mae turned to acknowledge Miss Sophie, who'd walked up to stand beside her. "You do look lovely, child. I'm sure all the local swains will be asking you for a dance when they discover you hiding beneath this tree."

"Thank you, Miss Sophie, but I ain't in the mood for dancing." Her gaze lingered on the couple still swirling to the waltz tune. "Besides, I don't know how to dance."

"Well, you should learn, child, or you won't ever catch yourself a man."

"Yes, ma'am."

Miss Sophie's gaze followed Viola's. "Ah, yes," she said, her eyes locking on the dancers, "they do make a handsome couple, don't they? You remember me mentioning Harriet's beau when I saw you in Gracie's store before the storm?"

Numbly, Viola Mae nodded. "Yes, Miss Sophie."

"Rumor has it those two will be announcing their engagement soon." She leaned toward Viola Mae and whispered, "I understand her papa isn't too thrilled with the match, but he always gives in to Harriet's wishes. Sooner or later he'll come around.

"After all, the man may be low in pocket change, but he surely isn't low in breeding. I hear tell his family rubbed shoulders with the Rockefellers and the Vanderbilts. Not a bad catch now, wouldn't you say? Besides, Harriet's father has enough money to share with a son-in-law. My Herman always said, 'If you buy a good stud, you get a good brood.' "

When Viola Mae made no response, the older woman looked at her. "Where's your head, child? You aren't coming down with the fever? Heaven to Betsy, we certainly don't need a yellow fever epidemic after this storm."

"No, Miss Sophie. I reckon I'm just feeling a little peaked. It's probably the heat."

Viola Mae's eyes stayed glued on the dancers. Even though she wasn't the one being swirled around the street, she felt as lightheaded as though she were.

She didn't know who the heck the Rockers and the Vanders were, but from the way Miss Sophie was going on about them, they must be royalty. And if Seth had rubbed shoulders with royalty, he sure shouldn't have been rubbing the rest of himself against *her*. She wasn't exactly the equal of monarchs.

But then, hadn't he tried to tell her that? All along he'd said he didn't want a wife. He hadn't wanted *her* as a wife was what he'd really meant.

"Viola Mae, have you seen him yet?" Jed ran up to her

and pulled on her hand. She smiled down at the boy, blinking back tears.

She and Jed would never be brother and sister now. He would belong to Harriet just as Seth would. This thought hurt almost as much as the realization that she would never be Seth's wife. They were too different, she realized now. Marriage between her and Seth would be like trying to cross a redbird with a blue jay, and God would never allow that to happen.

Gracie came up and stood beside her, her hands squeezing Jed's shoulders. "I expect we'll be seeing him real soon though, don't you, Viola Mae?"

Viola Mae had to be strong for Jed. It was up to her not to spoil Jed's reunion with his brother. Seth would be angry enough at the boy when he learned that he'd run away from his aunt's house in Atlanta. Once Seth got over the surprise of Jed being here, she would sneak away.

"There he is!" Jed shouted. "But who's the lady he's dancing with? I thought you and Seth were supposed to be getting—"

"He sees you," Gracie told Jed, silencing him by pushing him toward the street where the musicians had ended the last strains. Seth looked their way just as the words were out of Gracie's mouth. He started toward them with Harriet dogging his footsteps.

Seth moved toward Viola Mae. He never remembered seeing her look as beautiful as she did at the moment when their eyes met. Those eyes that had reminded him of crystal marbles the first time he'd ever gazed into them. The marbles he'd coveted as a lad. The ivory lace cape that draped her small shoulders was almost the same color as her hair. Several pieces of the silken flax had popped loose from her combs and now curled around her face. Until that instant, Seth hadn't realized how much he had missed her these last few days. He missed her plain way of speaking, her humor, and her loving.

True, he'd thought about her constantly, especially when he sniffed the smell of ham in his clothes. But instead of washing out the smell, which would have certainly been

cheaper than buying new garments, he couldn't bring himself
to have the old garments laundered. They were too much a
part of the woman he'd grown to love, and he couldn't wash
away the memory of what they'd shared. If she had one of
her damn chickens with her, he felt so foolish about her he
would probably even kiss it.

Seth was jerked out of his musings when a mahogany-
colored head slammed into his chest. Two bony arms encircled his waist. When he looked down and discovered that the
bundle of warm flesh plowing into his stomach belonged to
his brother, he was beside himself with joy. "Jed, what are
you doing here?"

He picked up the lad and swung him around. "Oh, squirt,
you don't know how I've missed you."

He put the boy back on his feet and squatted down beside
him. "Aunt Cloe and Tilly, where are they?" Seth looked
around the crowd that had gathered, searching for the two
older women.

"They ain't here."

"What do you mean, they aren't here? I can't believe they
would allow you to travel this way alone."

His gaze sought Viola Mae's. She shook her head as
though to caution him to go slow and be patient with his
questions.

The boy hung his head in shame. "They didn't let me
come. I left them a note."

"You mean you left them a note, and then you just left.
Jedwin Rowe, those old ladies must be worried sick."

Seth stood up and looked to Viola Mae for support. She
was nowhere in sight. Searching the crowd and not finding
her made him feel as though the sun had burned out. Just like
a woman to disappear when you needed her.

He looked back at his brother. "You know, I haven't been
able to send a wire because of the damages done by the
storm."

"Seth!" someone in the crowd called out. "I hear tell they
have the telegraph working again. You might want to check."

"Yes, thank you, Lefty, I think we better do that. You,

young man, better come with me. You have a lot of explaining to do."

"Seth," Harriet called, "wait!" She stepped toward him as the circle of onlookers broke apart to allow the boy and man to pass. "Who is that child?" she asked.

"This child is my ten-year-old brother, Jed, who was supposed to be staying with our aunt until I could send for him. Don't you remember, Harriet? I told you about Jed when you were visiting in Atlanta."

"Send for him? Why in heaven's name would you send for him? Certainly a boarding school, or some other appropriate place, would be better for the boy than here with us."

"It was my intention all along to bring Jed here. As far as boarding school, I wouldn't send him to one if I had the money. He and I are going to stay together."

"The two of you? But I thought you wanted to travel to Europe, see the world."

"I've seen it, Harriet. Now, if you'll excuse me, I need to wire my aunt." He grabbed Jed by the shoulder and marched him to the telegraph office.

The sun was dropping lower in the sky when Viola Mae pulled to a stop by St. Michael's Cemetery. Leaving Ginger to munch on the grass, she made her way to the plot of ground where her grandparents were buried.

Ever since she'd left the plaza she'd done nothing to stop the flow of tears, allowing them to flow freely. Heck, what difference did it make? There would be no one looking at her for the rest of day, or for that matter, for the rest of her life. Standing between the graves, she dropped to her knees between them.

"Well, Grannie, it looks like I really messed up this time." She removed the bonnet from her hair, dropped it on her lap, and fingered the ostrich feather as she spoke.

"I always swore I'd never end up like my mother, that I'd never fall for a man and never cause you and grandpappy the kind of pain that she did."

Her tears came in earnest now, slipping from her eyes and dropping like dewdrops on the rose petals on the hat. "I guess it's good y'all aren't here to see another fallen angel because it might break your hearts in two. It's breaking mine, I know that.''

She gulped back her sobs. "Oh, Grannie, I loved that man with all my heart. And if I do have his seed growing inside my belly and I'm to bear his babe, I'll be proud to do it.'' Viola Mae dropped her head in her hands. "But I surely don't want it to have to suffer ridicule the way I did because it ain't got no father.''

Above her head, a dove cooed. Its mournful sound matched her mood. "It's like you always said, though. It ain't the babe's fault it ain't got a daddy. But I promise you, it will have a mama. I won't never desert my baby. I'll keep it and raise it and give it all my love just like you did me, Grannie. I'll raise it in a house filled with love and understanding.''

"And with his father beside him.''

Viola Mae jerked around to face the intruder. Seth stood several feet away from her. She rose to her feet, wiped away her tears, lifted her chin, and squared her shoulders.

"How'd you know I'd be here?''

"It was a good guess, don't you think? Besides, I stopped here the other day on my way to town.''

"Here? Now why would you go and do that?'' The idea that he would intrude in her private moment angered her. Hadn't he done enough already? "You ain't got no business here.''

"I didn't think you would mind if I visited your grannie. After all, we're to be family, aren't we?''

Her heart pounded in her chest. Surely he wasn't suggesting they still could be together. No, she told herself, her wanting him, and even daring to believe that he might want her, was only her heart wishing.

"I want to marry you, Viola Mae.'' He stepped toward her.

"No, it's impossible. You and me, we're two different kinds of birds, I know that now. We can never make a life together.''

"Will you let me have my say before you push me away?''

"I'll listen, but I ain't gonna change my mind. You and Harriet are the same kind of birds—you come from similar backgrounds. She'll make you a better wife.''

He placed his finger against her lips. ''Listen. Harriet means nothing to me. The only thing I ever felt for her was gratitude because she helped me get this job. My life as it was is over, and it is no longer important. What is important is here and now. I like working for a living, doing something that I was trained to do. For the first time in my life I have a purpose.''

''But you rubbed shoulders with the Rockers and the Vanders?''

''Rubbed shoulders with whom?''

''Oh, I don't know, you're confusing me. Miss Sophie named some people I never heard of. Sounded like they were mighty important whatever their blasted names were.''

''I love you, Viola Mae. I want to spend the rest of my life proving to you just how much. Jed and I both love you.''

Unable to comprehend his sudden revelations, she concentrated on his last remark.

''Where is Jed?''

''I left him in town with Gracie. But I didn't come here to talk about Jed.''

''You didn't?'' she said softly.

''No,'' he said, smiling gently. ''I just told you I love you, and for the time since I met you, you've got nothing to say.''

She thought a minute, then asked, ''Are you sure?''

''More sure of this than anything in my life.''

He pulled her against him, and his body pressing hard against hers made her feel lightheaded, dizzy.

''I ain't rich or cultured, and I don't know if I'll ever like the railroad.''

''We'll work on the latter part. But as far as being rich, your friend Gracie told me your love was the greatest treasure of all, and I think I believe her.''

''You really think so?'' Her arms encircled his neck, and she pulled his face down to hers and kissed him passionately on the lips.

He wrapped his arms around her waist and smiled down at her. ''I don't just think so, I know so.''

They stood together, their bodies nestled as close as possible while fireflies blinked like shooting stars in the approaching twilight. Above the trees the sun dipped lower, gilding the swaying moss with gold. A few feet away, Ginger chomped grass, oblivious to the lovers. But the two consorts, resting in the twin graves beneath the entwined violet flowers, turned to each other and smiled their approval.

Author's Note

My heroine, Viola Mae, was born on my first visit to the charming bayside town of Pensacola, Florida, when I wandered into a shop near the historical square called The Herb Cottage. It was such a delightful place; a room that conjured up the past with the beautiful scents of roses and lavender. The proprietress, like her shop, was a delight. She was so helpful with her knowledge of the growing of herbs, showing me her own living garden, recommending invaluable research books, and filling my head with tales of her resident ghost. On my next visit to Pensacola I was disappointed to learn the shop was no longer there, but to this day I still recall the charm of that tiny little cottage.

When planning this book, I decided to make Viola Mae an eccentric character, the town's oddity, an Earth Child who revered the woods and her grannie's teachings above all else. So when the railroad began its path across the panhandle, it became the perfect catalyst to bring the hero, Seth, into Viola Mae's life.

At the time of my story, Pensacola, a busy seaport for foreign vessels, was experiencing the growth of its timber and lumber trade. With the development of the railroad across the panhandle it was believed that Pensacola's emerging timber-export harbor would make it the main Gulf port.

The P&A Railroad was chartered, surveys completed, and full construction began in 1881 under the direction of Colonel Chipley and other officials. These men were confident that Pensacola trains would be crossing North Florida to Jacksonville by 1883. The completion of the Escambia Bay Bridge on August 15, 1882, allowed the first train ever to cross the Escambia Bay and travel to the town of Milton. The first through train of P&A cars arrived from Pensacola in Jacksonville on April 26, 1883.

In fiction, characters once born begin to take on their own personalities and direct their stories in the way they want them told. And so it was with Viola Mae and Seth. As the memory of The Herb Cottage lingers with me, I hope their love story, too, will stay with you. "What we learn with pleasure we never forget." (Alfred Mercier, *New Dictionary of Thoughts*.)

I'd love to hear from my readers. You can write to me at 5361 Redfield Circle, Dunwoody, GA 30338.

Our Town

...where love is always right around the corner!

__*Harbor Lights* by Linda Kreisel__
0-515-11899-0/$5.99
On Maryland's Silchester Island...the perfect summer holiday sparks a perfect summer fling.

__*Humble Pie* by Deborah Lawrence__
0-515-11900-8/$5.99
In Moose Gulch, Montana...a waitress with a secret meets a stranger with a heart.

__*Candy Kiss* by Ginny Aiken__
0-515-11941-5/$5.99
In Everleigh, Pennsylvania...a sweet country girl finds the love of a city lawyer with kisses sweeter than candy.

__*Cedar Creek* by Willa Hix__
0-515-11958-X/$5.99
In Cedarburg, Wisconsin...a young widow falls in love with the local saloon owner, but she has promised her hand to a family friend—and she has to keep her word.

__*Sugar and Spice* by DeWanna Pace__
0-515-11970-9/$5.99
In Valiant, Texas...an eligible bachelor pines for his first love.

__*Cross Roads* by Carol Card Otten__
0-515-11985-7/$5.99
In Pensacola, Florida...Viola Mae Smith meets her match in the infuriating Yankee crew boss, Seth Rowe. Once her heart takes a fancy to a man, there's no turning back...